Dear Target Reader,

I was searching online for new story ideas when I clicked on an article about women who served in the American Civil War disguised as men and found myself engrossed by their information and stories. One woman, who went by the name Albert D. J. Cashier, not only served her entire three-year enlistment with the 95th Illinois Infantry (fighting in approximately forty battles and skirmishes), but she was never discovered to be a woman while in the military and went on to live her entire adult life as a man. She was only discovered by a surgeon two years before her death at age seventy-one. Another woman, Frances Clayton, enlisted with her husband in a Missouri regiment. When her husband was killed in battle, she reportedly stepped over his body and continued the fight.

The more I learned about these women (there were hundreds of them!), the more I wanted to understand: Why don't we know this history? Why are we taught that women during the Civil War were subordinate, passive, and uninvolved with much beyond their families? Why do we believe that those who did serve only did so as nurses or, in a few cases, spies?

About this same time, I started paying more attention to news and articles about women serving in today's military and learned that women served in the most dangerous battle zones long before they were officially allowed to be there. Even though most of those archaic rules are gone now, the career advancement of thousands of women was hindered, and they are still feeling those effects.

I have two older brothers whom I watched go to the post office when they turned eighteen to register with the Selective

Service, and I assumed that when I turned eighteen, I would go as well. It came as a shock to me, then, to learn that females do not register. I remember feeling relief that I would never be drafted and sent to war (this was just after the Gulf War, so war felt like a very real threat), yet I also felt like I was being told I wasn't good enough, strong enough, smart enough.

All of this inspired me to learn more about women in today's military and the violence, discrimination, and misogyny they deal with on a daily basis. I read memoirs of veterans of both genders who are struggling with the emotional, physical, and social effects of their service. That's when I noticed, again, that women were being overlooked. Their stories weren't being taken as seriously as those of men. These women who volunteer to serve and who risk their lives in service to our country are being ignored or outright dismissed as unimportant, and that makes me angry. We need their stories.

The book you hold in your hands, *Today We Go Home*, is my love letter to these women, to all women who have ever served in the military (whether we know about them or not). You might find it interesting to learn that I don't typically enjoy books about wars or the military, yet I wrote one. I felt the subject was that important. Even if you aren't a person who would typically read a book about the Civil War or about veterans, I hope you'll give this one a chance. If you need more convincing, it's also a story about bravery, family, and hope.

I am thrilled that *Today We Go Home* was chosen for the Target Book Club. I hope you enjoy it.

Happy reading!

Kelli Estes

Praise for *Today We Go Home*

"*Today We Go Home* shines an illuminating light on history and the female soldiers who have served this country from the Civil War to Afghanistan today. Kelli Estes passionately brings the past to life, interweaving the story of two women from different centuries whose journey toward hope is timeless."

—Gwendolyn Womack, *USA Today* bestselling author of *The Fortune Teller* and *The Time Collector*

"Illuminating, sympathetic, and deeply human, *Today We Go Home* shines a much-needed light on the brave, bold women of all eras whose military service puts even more than their lives on the line."

—Greer Macallister, *USA Today* bestselling author of *Woman 99* and *The Magician's Lie*

Praise for *The Girl Who Wrote in Silk*

"Vibrant and tragic, *The Girl Who Wrote in Silk* explores a horrific, little-known era in our nation's history. Estes sensitively alternates between Mei Lien, a young Chinese American girl who lived in the late 1800s, and Inara, a modern recent college grad who sets Mei Lien's story free."

—Margaret Dilloway, author of *How to Be an American Housewife* and *Sisters of Heart and Snow*

"*The Girl Who Wrote in Silk* is a beautiful story that brought me to tears more than once and was a testament to the endurance of the human spirit and the human heart. A powerful debut that proves the threads that interweave our lives can withstand time and any tide and bind our hearts forever."

—Susanna Kearsley, *New York Times* bestselling author of *A Desperate Fortune* and *The Firebird*

"*The Girl Who Wrote in Silk* is a beautiful, elegiac novel, as finely and delicately woven as the title suggests. Kelli Estes spins a spellbinding tale that illuminates the past in all its brutality and beauty, and the humanity that binds us all together."

—Susan Wiggs, *New York Times* bestselling author of *The Beekeeper's Ball*

"A touching and tender story about discovering the past to bring peace to the present."

—Duncan Jepson, author of *All the Flowers in Shanghai*

"It was one of the best books I have read in a long time. I can't stop gushing over it...such a beautiful and engaging story."

—Samantha Scott, Auburn University Bookstore (Auburn, AL)

"I was completely blown away! What a beautifully written story by Kelli Estes, but it is Mei Lein who has stitched her story on my heart."

—Joan Krzykowski, Sunshine Booksellers (Marco Island, FL)

"I loved it... Mei Lein's story is moving and a page-turner."

—Mary Ferris, Penguin Bookshop (Sewickley, PA)

Also by Kelli Estes

The Girl Who Wrote in Silk

today
we go
home

today
we go
home

a novel

KELLI ESTES

Published by Sourcebooks Landmark, an imprint of Sourcebooks
P.O. Box 4410, Naperville, Illinois 60567-4410
(630) 961-3900
sourcebooks.com

Library of Congress Cataloging-in-Publication Data

Names: Estes, Kelli, author.
Title: Today we go home / Kelli Estes.
Description: Naperville, Illinois : Sourcebooks Landmark, [2019]
Identifiers: LCCN 2018052437 | (trade pbk. : alk. paper)
Subjects: LCSH: United States--Armed Forces--Women--Fiction. | United
    States--History--Civil War, 1861-1865--Participation, Female--Fiction. |
    Women soldiers--United States--History--19th century--Fiction. |
    Post-traumatic stress disorder--Fiction. | GSAFD: Historical fiction.
Classification: LCC PS3605.S7355 T63 2019 | DDC 813/.6--dc23 LC record avail-
able at https://lccn.loc.gov/2018052437

Printed and bound in the United States of America.
WOZ 10 9 8 7 6 5 4 3 2 1

Dedicated to all women, past or present,
who have served in the military.

Thank you.

"Home isn't where our house is,
But wherever we are understood."

—Christian Morgenstern in *Stages: A Development
in Aphorisms and Diary Notes*

Prologue

April 16, 1861: Wilson Family Farm, Stampers Creek, Indiana

The sounds of gunshots echoed across the field, each one making Emily clench her teeth tighter together until her jaw ached. For an hour, she'd listened as her menfolk shot at whatever they were shooting at, and she'd told herself to stay out of it. She knew they were doing more than hunting by the way they'd whispered among themselves when David arrived home from town and then grabbed their muskets and headed to the creek. With each shot, her imagination conjured an explanation that was worse than the one before. A rabid dog. A pack of wolves. Brutal Shawnee here to reclaim their land.

She moved the soup pot off the stove and yanked on her warm coat. She was through waiting. If no one saw fit to inform her of the danger, she'd discover what it was herself and help dispel it. She'd been shooting all her life alongside her brothers and often bagged game for dinner. Whatever was out there, she could handle it. Women weren't supposed to be the strong ones, but she did not always have to pretend to be weak.

She reached for a musket behind the door but found the men

had taken them all. Looking around, her gaze landed on the kitchen knife. Any weapon was better than none. Gripping it firmly in her fist, she set out across the fallow cornfield toward the creek. She couldn't see anyone, but the gunshots directed her to the wooded area where she and her brothers had spent countless hours playing as children, back before Mama died and Emily had become the woman of the house.

As she reached the trees, the sound of three shots firing almost simultaneously made her jump, and she realized she'd best announce her presence before one of them shot in her direction. "Pa, I'm coming your way. Don't shoot!"

Holding her knife firmly, ready to attack anything that might run toward her, she followed the path into the clearing, her heart pounding in her ears as loudly as the gunshots. But she was ready. She'd defend herself and her family against whatever threat awaited her.

What she saw made her stop short.

There was no danger.

Her brothers lay on the ground with muskets in hand, calmly listening to whatever Pa was telling them. Uncle Samuel stood behind them, puffing on his pipe and watching, his own musket resting in the crook of his elbow.

"No, not like that," Pa said to Ben. "You want to lie flat on your belly and only raise up as much as you must to fire. Make yourself into the smallest you can be so you're harder to hit."

Emily released her pent-up breath and watched as Ben straightened his legs so he was lying flat on his belly. Propping himself on his elbows, he sighted the shot.

"Now imagine there's a secesh hiding in those bushes," Pa coached. "Take a breath as you aim, and as you exhale, pull the trigger."

As the musket fired, a puff of smoke rose from the barrel. David, lying beside Ben, fired his weapon. Both of her brothers rolled to their backs to reload without sitting up.

Emily crossed the clearing and stopped next to Uncle Samuel. "What's a secesh?"

He glanced at her before returning his gaze to her brothers. "It's what they're calling people from the seceding states." He grunted. "Short for secessioner."

"Why are we shooting at them?" She watched as her brothers fired again.

"Keep going," Pa said to the boys. "Try to make your shots hit that beech tree there by the water." He stepped over Ben's legs and came to her with a sheepish smile. "Did we miss supper? Sorry, Em."

Emily shrugged. "Why are you pretending to shoot at secesh?"

Pa sent a look to Uncle Samuel, who lifted one eyebrow and kept puffing on his pipe, and then he turned to her. "I don't want to worry you, but word has come that we're at war against the Southern states who have seceded from the Union. President Lincoln called for volunteers yesterday, and Governor Morton says we're to gather in Indianapolis for training."

She stared at him. "Who is to gather?"

Pa shuffled his feet and looked away. "The Indiana volunteers, of course."

He didn't need to say it for Emily to understand he would be one of them. She watched her brothers fire on the beech tree. Both missed. Calmly, she reached for the musket Uncle Samuel held, trading it for her knife. "Is it loaded?"

Samuel left the pipe clamped between his teeth and wordlessly handed her a paper cartridge from the pouch at his waist.

As the men watched, Emily expertly ripped the cartridge open with her teeth, poured the powder into the barrel and shoved the ball inside, pulled out the rammer, pushed down the shot, and replaced the rammer. Then, shoving her skirts out of the way, she settled onto her stomach on the ground between her brothers.

Without saying a word, she cocked the weapon, aimed, and

fired. A chunk of gray bark flew off the beech, right where she'd aimed.

Satisfied, she got back to her feet, handed the musket to her uncle, and faced her pa. "I'm coming with you."

Chapter One

Present day: Lakewood, Washington State

*L*arkin Bennett grabbed hold of the cold, steel handle and noticed her hands were shaking. She felt as vulnerable as if there were armed insurgents on the other side of the gray metal door, but it was only her best friend's storage unit. She blew out a breath and shoved the rolling door up so hard it rattled and banged. When the light flickered on, she saw only stacked cardboard boxes, a couple of lamps, and bulging black garbage bags. The innocuous objects might as well have been insurgents firing on her for the pain that swept through her entire body.

For several long moments, she could do nothing more than stare at Sarah's belongings. Mentally, she went through all the reasons why she had to do this now rather than run far, far away.

It was December. The rental contract on the unit would end at the close of the month, and there was no reason for Larkin to waste money renewing it.

The storage unit was an hour away from her hometown, two with traffic, and she had no plans to come back to this area anytime soon. She needed to deal with it while she was here.

There was no one else to take care of this, and besides, Sarah had wanted her to have these things.

The last one was the kicker.

Nausea rolled through Larkin as she reached for the nearest box and stacked it on the rolling cart she'd brought up in the elevator. She intended to load everything into her car and take it all to her grandmother's house, where she'd be living until she figured out what to do next. Once she got Sarah's stuff there, she could go through it another day, when it wouldn't hurt so badly.

Moving robotically, she stacked another box on the cart and reached for a third, trying her hardest not to think about Sarah or why she wasn't here to clean out her own storage unit.

This third box was heavier than the last two, and Larkin grunted as she lifted it. Pain shot through her legs and back, and she welcomed it.

Larkin's cell phone rang from where she'd stuck it in her back jeans pocket. "Damn it," she muttered as she lurched to the cart and bent her knees to set the box down. She misjudged the placement, though, and it tilted sideways and crashed onto the floor, the top seam bursting open and scattering Sarah's things.

Her damn phone was still ringing. Larkin yanked it from her pocket without looking to see who was calling. "What?"

"Larkin, is that you?"

Guilt shot through her, and she took a moment to draw a breath in through her nose to calm down, her eyes squeezed shut. Her grandmother didn't deserve her temper. When she trusted her voice to come out evenly, she opened her eyes and answered, "Yes, Grams, it's me. Sorry, I just dropped something."

"Where are you? I thought you'd be here by now."

Larkin eased herself down onto the edge of the flatbed cart and dropped her head into her free hand. "I'm sorry, Grams. I decided at the last minute to take care of something. I'm in Lakewood, down by Joint Base Lewis-McChord. Cleaning out Sarah's storage unit."

Silence greeted this announcement, and then Grams's voice

came softly through the line. "Lark, are you sure that's a good idea? If you wait, one of us could drive down there to be with you."

Larkin looked at the spilled contents of the box in front of her. A silver tube of lipstick, an old MP3 player, a silver bracelet, a brown leather book. "I was passing through and didn't want to have to drive back down here, you know? It has to be cleaned out this month, and I know you are all going to be busy with the holidays."

"If you're sure." Grams didn't sound convinced, but she went on with the reason for her call. "How long will it take? Tomorrow is Sunday, and I was hoping to invite everyone over so we could welcome you home properly. Will you be here?"

By "everyone," Larkin knew her grandma meant her entire extended family of parents, cousins, aunts, and uncles. Grams kept the family connected, and it was at her house where everyone gathered. All fourteen of them.

Even though Larkin had planned to load her car and finish her drive to Grams's tonight, the idea of a family gathering sucked the energy from her. "I'm so sorry, Grams," she lied. "I don't think I'm going to make it tonight. Probably not even until late tomorrow night. Sarah has some furniture here that I need to get someone to pick up and too much stuff to fit into my car, which means I need to sort through it and donate what I don't want to keep. It'll take some time."

The tiny closet of possessions stared back at her, mocking her lies. Larkin turned her back on it.

"I guess we can celebrate your return in a few weeks when everyone is here for Christmas anyway." The disappointment in Grams's voice made Larkin's already raw heart ache even more. "But you'd better call your mom and tell her. They were excited to see you tomorrow."

"Okay, I will." Larkin pushed stiffly to her feet. "I'll see you tomorrow night, Grams. Love you."

"I love you, too, soldier girl," Grams replied, using the nickname

7

Larkin's grandfather had given her years ago. Hearing it made tears come to her eyes. "I'm so happy you're finally coming home."

Larkin swallowed. "Me too." She hung up, wondering if that was a lie. She really had no idea.

She dialed her mother, then righted the box and started putting the spilled items back in as she waited for her to pick up. When she did, Larkin got straight to the point. "Hi, Mom, it's me. Grams told me to call you since I won't be home tonight after all. I won't be there in time for a party tomorrow either."

"Why not?"

Larkin explained about the storage unit and that she would rent a hotel room tonight. Her mother, already angry Larkin was moving in with Grams and not back into the house where she'd grown up, did not hold back from laying on the guilt. "Oh, Larkin, I am so disappointed. Your father will be, too. Can't you at least stop and see us on your way through town? It's been a year, and after all that's happened, we need to see you."

"I know, Mom. I'm sorry." Larkin was about to explain, yet again, how she needed the peace and quiet at Grams's house, and also that Grams didn't work and both of her parents did, which meant she'd have someone around to help her adjust to civilian life again. But she didn't say any of this because her mother already knew all of it, and really, Larkin just wanted to get off the phone. "I'll stop by on my way through Seattle tomorrow, okay? What time should I be there?"

"Oh, good. Your father will be happy. How about six?" Kathryn Bennett sounded smug. "We'll order some dinner."

Resigned, Larkin agreed and ended the call, feeling the last of her energy drain away. She stuffed the phone back in her pocket and picked up the book that had fallen out of the box, intending to toss it back.

It looked well used with a stiff, brown, extra-thick leather cover sporting an embossed floral design. A leather thong wrapped around the book and tied it closed.

Curious, for she'd never seen Sarah with the book, Larkin undid the thong and opened the first page. In an old-fashioned hand, someone had written *The diary of...* followed by something that had been scratched out, and written below that was the name *Jesse Wilson*. She looked closer at the scratched-out part and thought it looked like... Was it *Emily*?

Something nudged at the back of Larkin's brain, and she turned the page to the first diary entry, dated 1861. Flipping quickly through the rest of the book, she found it full of the same old-fashioned and difficult-to-read handwriting. Every now and then a word jumped out at her. *Union. Army. Battle. Musket.* The memory that had been poking at her burst forth.

It was the day she and Sarah had graduated from Norwich University and were commissioned as second lieutenants into the U.S. Army. Sarah's family hadn't been there, of course, and so Larkin had made her an honorary member of her own since her parents, grandparents, and two of her cousins had flown in for the ceremonies. After everyone had gone back to their hotels and Larkin and Sarah had returned to their dorm room for their last night as roommates, they'd gotten to talking about why they'd wanted to join the Army in the first place.

For Larkin, it had been because of her grandpa, who had fought in the Korean War, and because of the trip she'd taken with him to Washington, DC, in junior high when she'd learned that women were in the military, too. It wasn't only for boys. Sarah had an even better story, though. She'd told Larkin that night about an ancestor of hers who had disguised herself as a man and fought in the Civil War. The news that women had fought in the Civil War had blown Larkin's mind. Sarah's grandmother had given her the diary when she was a little girl, and Sarah had wanted to be like Emily Wilson ever since.

This had to be that diary.

Larkin's hands shook. When she'd learned that Sarah had left all of her possessions to her, she hadn't expected to find anything so valuable. Surely there was someone in Sarah's family who should have this instead?

But Sarah hadn't been close to her family. They'd done nothing but hurt her, and ever since they were freshman rooks at Norwich, Sarah had said Larkin was her only family. Larkin had never had a sister, but she grew up with two cousins close to her age who were like sisters. She'd missed them terribly when she'd moved across the country for college, and Sarah had filled that hole. Now, there was a Sarah-shaped hole in her life that would never be filled.

Maybe Sarah really had meant for her to inherit this diary.

Larkin would much rather have Sarah back.

A splotch of water fell onto the open diary page, and Larkin realized she was crying. *Damn it.* She never cried.

She wiped away the tears and moved to shove the diary back into the box. But then she stopped. No. She wouldn't leave it crammed in some box. The diary would stay with her.

With her new plan to stay at a hotel overnight, she didn't want her car full of boxes that might tempt someone to break in. She returned the boxes to the storage unit, rolled the door back down, and fastened the lock. She had all day tomorrow to face this. For now, she'd get something to eat and a good night's rest.

Back in her car, she carefully placed the diary on the passenger seat, next to the urn that she had buckled in with the seat belt. Sarah's final requests had specified that she was to be cremated and her ashes placed into a biodegradable urn made out of pink Himalayan salt. Larkin was to scatter her ashes on the beaches of Sarah's home state of California, and when they were all gone, she was to throw the urn itself into the ocean where it would dissolve, leaving nothing behind for anyone to have to deal with in the years to come.

Larkin had driven from Fort Leonard Wood, Missouri, where she'd processed out of the Army, to San Diego, where she'd had every intention of following Sarah's instructions. But once she got there, it was too soon to say goodbye. So, she'd driven north up the coast toward her final destination of Woodinville, Washington, intending to stop at another beach to scatter the ashes once she was stronger.

She'd stopped at ten different beaches, and each time, she hadn't been able to part with Sarah. She couldn't let her go yet.

"Look what I found," she said to her friend as she latched her seat belt and started the engine. "It's that diary you told me about. I'll start reading it tonight, as soon as I eat something." She hadn't eaten since Eugene, Oregon, over five hours ago.

As she pulled out of the storage facility, she saw a hotel next door and a Mexican restaurant across the street. Perfect.

She thought about taking her dinner to go, but a beer sounded too good to pass up. She drank a Corona with lime while she waited on her food and asked for another as a huge plate of cheese enchiladas was placed before her.

She didn't realize how hungry she was until her first bite made her salivate. Heaven on a plate, that's what this was, she decided, savoring another bite. She hadn't had good Mexican food for over a year. No surprise, of course, that she couldn't find any in Afghanistan, but even when she'd returned to the States, she hadn't found enchiladas like this in Memphis or Missouri.

She was so caught up in her food that it took a moment for the conversation at the table behind her to sink into her consciousness. But when it did, she found she could focus on nothing else.

"Yeah, she's hot," said a young male voice. "Just be warned. They say women in the military are either bitches, sluts, or dykes. I vote for the middle category."

The two men laughed and went on boasting about what they would do to the women in question, each claim filthier than the last. Larkin looked around to see who they might be talking about and found two women in Army combat uniforms paying for a take-out order at the bar. They had no idea the two perverts were talking about them and, from the fatigue clearly weighing them down, had likely just ended a long day and wanted to go home and eat their meal in peace.

Larkin had dealt with men like them her whole military career—from JROTC in high school through her last deployment to Afghanistan. From civilians and military members alike. She'd learned to ignore the comments and to make sure her behavior was always above reproach.

But she wasn't in the military anymore, she realized. She no longer had to worry about jeopardizing her career.

Before she knew what she was doing, she picked up her full glass of beer and pushed to her feet to go stand beside the men's table. As she'd thought, they were college kids, full of their own importance and the erroneous belief that women existed only for their pleasure.

"Hey, boys." She greeted them with a smile. "I heard you talking about those women." She motioned to the two soldiers with her beer and then took a sip, acting like she wasn't pissed. "They are real pretty, aren't they?"

The blond kid, who had the look of a star athlete, smiled at her, his perfect teeth so white they had to have been bleached. He looked like he was going to agree with her, but his buddy, a more studious-looking guy with glasses, shot him a look and asked Larkin, "Can we help you?"

Larkin stopped pretending to be nice. She slammed her beer on the table and leaned on both palms so she was hovering over them. "Yes, you can help me. First, by apologizing to those women and paying for their meals. Second, you can thank them for volunteering to put their lives in danger for your freedom. And third, you can never let such sexist and shitheaded words leave your mouths again."

The blond sports star scowled, arrogance making his perfect face turn ugly. "Why would we do any of that?"

"Because," she told him, allowing the disgust she felt for them to deepen her voice. "You disrespected members of the military who work hard every day so that shits like you have the freedom to jack off in your daddy's basement and congratulate yourselves on being men."

A clapping sound made her look over, and when she saw the two women watching her with huge grins on their faces, Larkin realized she'd been speaking louder than she thought.

She looked around and saw the entire restaurant watching her. Many of the customers were in uniform, as they were only a couple of miles from Joint Base Lewis–McChord, also known as JBLM. Most smiled and nodded at her. Some had already turned back to their meals.

Larkin looked back at the two men in the booth. "So? Are you going to apologize to these women, or do I need to teach you some manners?"

Sports Star laughed. "What are you gonna do? Pour your beer over us? I'm so scared."

Larkin deliberately lifted her beer to her lips and downed the final few gulps. When her glass was empty, she gripped it tightly in her palm and raised her arm to smash it against the asshole's head. As she began to swing, though, someone grabbed her wrist and the glass slipped out of her hand, crashing to the floor.

Furious, she looked to see who had stopped her and was surprised to see a familiar face.

"Don't do this, Captain."

She had to look at his name tape before she remembered who he was. Cohan. Tim Cohan. They'd been in training together at JBLM a couple of years ago, though they'd never really been friends. She was surprised he remembered her. "I'm not a captain anymore."

He nodded curtly. "I'd heard. I'm sorry. But still, you don't want to do this." Before Larkin could say another word, he dropped her hand and turned to the men at the table. "I suggest you pay for your meals and get the hell out of here."

13

Anger made her whole body feel like it was buzzing, but she held herself completely still as the two jerks dropped money on the table and slid from the booth, their faces smug as they brushed past her and disappeared out the door.

Larkin turned on Cohan. "I had it under control."

He stepped back with his hands held out to his sides. "I was only trying to help."

All the anger she'd felt when she'd heard the men's sexist comments earlier still boiled in her belly. It called forth the rage she'd always had to push aside over her years in the Army as she put up with such comments or men like Cohan, who thought every woman needed a man to save the day. Gritting her teeth, she stepped forward until she was right in his face. "Men like you need to back the hell off. You got that? We can't even have a fucking meal without being degraded, and then you step in and tell me I'm not allowed to demand a little common decency?"

"You were about to smash his head in, Bennett."

"Maybe he needed his head smashed in."

Cohan swallowed, his Adam's apple bobbing. "I see your PTSD treatment didn't work."

Larkin reared back. How the hell did he know? What had he heard? She opened her mouth to demand the answers but realized it didn't matter. He didn't matter. None of this mattered.

Deliberately, she turned away from him and reached for the rucksack that served as her purse, which she'd left on the bench seat at her table. Without another glance Cohan's way, she drew out enough money to pay for her meal, dropped it next to her plate, and walked out.

For several long moments, she sat in her car in the dark and battled back the sting behind her eyes.

"I wish you were here, Sarah," she said when she finally calmed down enough to speak. "You would've kicked their asses and been done with it. I looked like an out-of-control loser in there."

She imagined she heard Sarah laughing, and it made her smile. "I did manage to scare those shitheads at least a little, didn't I? Maybe they'll think twice before saying crap like that again."

She started her engine and drove across the street to the U-shaped, one-level motel where she planned to spend the night.

Her room was a total dive. A bed was crammed into a corner with a piece of orange Naugahyde-wrapped plywood attached to the wall as a fake headboard. An old brown towel was thumb-tacked over the window where a curtain should be, and in the bathroom, a round toilet seat barely covered an oblong-shaped toilet bowl. Water dripped into the stained bathtub.

It was just one night. The door locked, and the bed looked clean enough.

She carefully placed Sarah's urn on the middle of the tiny, scarred table and dropped her travel bag on the chair next to it. The floor looked too questionable to set anything on.

Soon, Larkin had her teeth brushed and her pajamas on, and she settled into bed with the diary.

She had no idea what to expect from the story other than what Sarah had told her, but all she really wanted was to feel close to Sarah.

And so, she unwrapped the leather thong and opened to the first entry.

April 18, 1861: Today, Pa and David answered Lincoln's call for volunteers for the United States Army, where they will fight against the secessioners and make our country whole again. Pa says they'll be home in three months, but I hope the Southern rebellion ends much sooner. Pa gave me this diary so I can write down and remember everything to tell him about the farm and Stampers Creek when he returns. I wish he had let me go with him instead. I can shoot a musket as well as, if not better than, David!

We got the beanpoles constructed and vegetables planted.

Ben plowed the north field. Uncle Samuel kept us busy until nearly dark, what with being shorthanded now. Being busy did not keep me from missing Pa and David. Three months is going to be a very long time.

Chapter Two

April 18, 1861: Wilson Family Farm, Stampers Creek, Indiana

Y ou know I can shoot better than David," Emily Wilson said to her father, not for the first time. She squeezed her hands into fists. Outside the kitchen window, birds filled the morning with song, but she ignored them. Her heart was too heavy. "I can do my duty as well as any man. Why can't I go with you?"

"And me too," chimed in her younger brother, Ben, as he handed Pa his satchel of extra clothing and food. "I'm almost eighteen. I can fight."

Two days had passed since they'd learned of President Lincoln's call for 75,000 volunteers, and both Emily and Ben had spent all of those days begging their father to let them go with him and David. They'd each expressed their loyalty to their country, but Emily had kept her true motivation—a deep, aching need for adventure—to herself. Pa wouldn't understand why she would want anything more in life than a home and family.

Pa's lips pressed together, and he seemed to be considering their arguments. He had taught all three of them a strong sense of patriotism. Pa had been proud to serve the United States of America in the Mexican War, and he often told them stories of his own father who had served during the War of Independence. "Our family will always stand for what's right," he said now. "And the side of right in this uprising is to preserve our great Union. I'm proud you want to be part of that."

He took a step closer and placed his bear paw of a hand on Ben's shoulder. "Each of you would be an asset to our great nation's cause, but soldiers must already be eighteen." His eyes shifted to Emily. "And a battlefield is no place for a woman."

"Besides," he continued as he turned toward the rolltop desk in the adjoining sitting room where he kept the farm's accounts, "I'm sure we'll put this rebellion to rest in no time. David and I will be home before you know it."

When he turned back to them, he held a book in his hands. Shyly, he held it out to Emily. "I, uh, I got this for you. It's a diary. Keep record of all the goings-on around here so you can tell me all about them when I return."

Emily took the book and inspected the leather thong wrapped around the stiff, thick book. The cover was carved with a floral design that reminded her of the flowers in Aunt Harriet's garden. "Thank you, Pa." She had to bite her tongue to stop herself from begging him yet again to take her with him.

As Ben went to help David fill his satchel with the leftover breakfast biscuits, Pa stepped closer and gently took the book from her. In a low voice so only she heard, he said, "It has a secret compartment built in right here." With his pocketknife in hand, he pried the leather cover open to reveal a depression hidden inside, only about a quarter-inch deep and the size of Pa's hand. "Look, there's even a place to store a pen inside. Keep your treasures in here, and no one will find them."

Emily knew Pa was referring to Uncle Samuel, who would be looking after them while Pa and David were gone. He was a miserly and sometimes mean old man who was never happy about anything. She pressed the lid back into place and carefully set the book on the kitchen table. "Thank you, Pa. I'll write in here every day. Just promise you'll hurry home so you can read it."

"I will." He kissed Emily's forehead before reaching for something behind the kitchen door. "Benjamin, I want you to have my Springfield rifle. You're the man of the house now, and I'm counting on you to protect your sister."

Ben solemnly took the weapon. "Don't you need it for fightin' the secesh?"

Pa shook his head. "The government will provide me with a weapon. This one is for you."

Too soon, it was time for them all to make their way across the potato field to Aunt Harriet and Uncle Samuel's house, where Pa bid farewell to his sister and brother-in-law and their two children.

Aunt Harriet was weeping, making it more difficult for Emily to keep her own tears in check. She swallowed hard, and as Pa turned back to her with another hug, she breathed him in, trying to imprint his scent of soap and leather onto her heart to carry her through the coming days. "You take good care of your brother now," Pa murmured into her ear, "and be helpful to Aunt Harriet and Uncle Samuel. They need you if they're to keep the farm going until we return."

"What if you don't?" Emily had heard his stories from the Mexican War. She knew that even short battles took lives. "What if you don't return?" She bit hard on her bottom lip to stop it from trembling.

Pa pulled back and held her at arm's length. His gray-blue eyes softened and his mustache twitched. "If I should die fighting to preserve our great Union, I'll consider my life well spent. I'll expect each of you to do your part, too." He released her and looked at Ben. "If it comes to that, you'll enlist, but not before your birthday, you hear?"

Ben nodded. His eyes shone with excitement at the prospect.

"And you, dear girl," Pa went on, giving Emily a stern look, "are to sew socks and flags and roll bandages and help provide anything else our soldiers might need. Women's work at home is equally as important as the men's on the battlefield."

Emily secretly believed she could do more good on the battlefield. "Come home to us, Pa. You too, David."

"We'll do our best." Pa rested his palm on her cheek before turning again to Ben. He pulled him into his arms and pounded his back. "I'll miss you. Both of you."

As he stepped back, David took his place and gave them each a hug. "If you've a mind to, I'd be obliged if you called on Nancy from time to time. Tell her I'll be home soon."

David had confided to Emily just last evening after supper that he wanted to marry Nancy Polson, but he did not think it would be kind of him to propose until after he returned from the fighting. Emily reassured him, saying, "I'll be sure she does not forget you, Brother."

"We'd best be going," Pa said. He tipped his hat to his sister and brother-in-law and turned toward the road, David at his side.

Emily followed them to Aunt Harriet's garden gate but stayed on the inside when Pa and David stepped onto the road heading north. She dug her fingers into the top rail to stop herself from running after them. Pa didn't look back at her. He turned his boots north toward Indianapolis where the Indiana regiments were to be formed and mustered into service, and he didn't look back once. Every few yards, David cast a regretful grin back to her. Emily squeezed harder on the gate and silently willed Pa to turn back and call for her to join them.

But he didn't. Nor did he turn to wave before he disappeared around the copse of trees marking the edge of their farm. Emily remained at the gate, barely breathing, waiting to see if they'd come back. Every muscle in her body strained to run after her father and older brother because they were her family and they all needed to be together. Even in war.

She had been irrational about losing one of them, or so Pa

told her, ever since Mama died along with the baby she was trying to bring into the world. That was eleven years ago, and to this day, Emily could remember every horrible cry and scream, and the even more horrible silence that followed. She had been seven at the time, and it had been her job to keep Ben, only a year younger, occupied and out of the house. He had gone off fishing with David so she'd crept back into the kitchen to be the first person to hold their new sibling.

Instead of a new sibling, she'd gotten a fear so strong and deep that it still controlled her in most decisions regarding her family. She worked hard every day to keep them healthy and together, and now two of them were walking away and she might never see them again.

"Emily!" Uncle Samuel's demanding voice ripped her from her thoughts. "Stop wasting daylight and do your chores. Your aunt is waiting for you to construct the beanpoles."

She looked toward her uncle and found that everyone, even Ben, had drifted away. Uncle Samuel pointed toward the garden and then, knowing she'd obey, turned and limped into the barn. Samuel had served in the Army during the Mexican War, where he'd met Pa. The story went that Pa had saved Samuel's life when an enemy musket ripped off a chunk of his leg and Pa pulled him to safety before Santa Anna's man could finish the job. After the war Samuel had accompanied Pa home, and that's where he met Harriet and decided to stay.

Samuel walked with a limp now and had to stop and rest often, which is why he wasn't marching off with Pa to join up. Emily secretly wondered which side of this war Samuel would join up with if he were able. He'd been raised in Virginia and still had kinfolk down there. Emily and her brothers knew not to talk to him about states' rights or abolition, and not to even mention the name Lincoln because that would set Samuel off on a tirade none of them wanted to hear.

Emily searched the road one last time for any sign of Pa coming back for her, but the only thing moving was a cottontail hopping across to nibble young grass on the other side. She finally turned away and saw Ben leading the mule out of the barn to begin the day's plowing. He was as upset as she about being left behind, she knew, but he hid his emotions better than she did.

"Come on, Emily," a little voice said, interrupting her train of thought. "I'll help you."

Emily looked down at her six-year-old cousin just as Ada slipped her tiny hand into hers. Big blue eyes full of sympathy looked up at her. The little girl was the best thing about being left on the farm, Emily decided. She was like a little sister, and Emily had always felt protective of her, what with an angry father and a mother who worked herself to the bone. "Thank you, Ada. I'd like that."

Hand in hand, she and Ada walked to the vegetable garden and set to work constructing beanpoles and sowing seeds in the rows Aunt Harriet dug with her hoe. By the end of the day, they'd have spinach, peas, carrots, cabbage, beans, and onions tucked snug in the ground and covered with a thick layer of straw to ward off frost.

It was one of the longest days of Emily's life. Despite her aunt's and uncle's efforts, she could not stay focused on the tasks at hand, and she found herself constantly shifting her gaze between the close-up work of gardening and the long-distance work of watching the road for Pa and David.

With each passing hour, she grew more despondent. They were gone.

Later that night, after she'd helped Aunt Harriet wash the supper dishes, she and Ben walked the path through the potato field to their own house in the light of the quarter moon. "Do you really think the war will take the entire three months of their enlistment?" Emily asked her brother as she clenched her fingers into fists inside her pockets to make them warmer. The temperature had dropped with the sun, and she wore her father's old work coat buttoned tight to her chin. Her back ached from stooping to plant seeds, but she dared not complain because Ben had struggled all day with the mule and plow. They'd both appreciate their beds this night.

"Nah. Folks say the secesh aren't serious. Once their men start dying on the battlefield, they'll rejoin the Union like that." He snapped his fingers.

"Do you think there will be a lot of battles?"

"There will be some, yes. But don't you worry. They'll keep each other safe."

They continued walking in silence until they reached their yard, where the house stood completely dark. It was a stark reminder that no one else was inside with a warm fire and welcoming drink. It was just the two of them now.

In unspoken agreement, they delayed going into the empty house and sat on the porch steps together. "Do you think you'll settle here when you find a wife someday?" Emily finally asked, more to break the silence than because she wanted to know.

"Oh, unquestionably," Ben answered, warming to the subject. "David and I talked about this. Pa says we'll inherit his half of the farm, and we can split it between us unless one of us moves away. David says he'll stay, and I want to as well." Ben snatched a long blade of grass from beside the porch steps and set to work shredding it with his thumbnail.

Emily sighed and looked out across their fields. "I can't imagine leaving here, yet it's all I think about some days."

"I don't know why you turned down Teddy Hobson when he asked you to marry him. You could have your own farm on the other side of town right now and a baby on the way."

Emily's face grew hot at the embarrassing reminder. She hadn't even known Teddy was interested in her that way until he started coming around last summer, offering her pa help with the chores and lingering until she was forced to invite him to supper. After two weeks of this, he'd asked her one night to walk him to the road, and she'd obliged. It was there that he'd asked her to be his bride. She had been so surprised that she'd failed to take his feelings into account and blurted out, "No!"

Poor Teddy. He'd started stammering and shuffling his feet, and she'd realized her mistake. "I'm sorry," she'd tried to explain. "It isn't that I don't want to marry you. I can't right now. My family needs me." When he still refused to look at anything but his worn boots, she tried again. "I'm all they have as far as cooking and cleaning and mending. They need me. Maybe once David brings a bride home, I can think about it. But not right now."

After that, Teddy had not returned to their farm, and whenever she saw him in town, he turned his back to her. Lately, he had Betsy Clayton hanging on his arm.

Emily tucked her skirts tighter under her legs to avoid the cold seeping from the steps. "I don't want to marry someone just so I can have my own farm," she finally said to Ben. "When I marry, it will be because I love him and he loves me."

"It sounds to me like you're going to be hanging around here for a good spell," Ben teased her. "That's fine by me. You can be a doting aunt to my children someday and teach them how to climb trees while their mother and I pretend not to see."

Emily burst out laughing, remembering when she'd taught Ben to climb and they'd taken turns dropping from the highest branch of the chestnut tree into the swimming hole. Mama had been furious with her, but that didn't keep them from repeating the adventure often.

Across the fields, down by the creek, a lone prairie wolf let out a howl. They fell silent as they waited to see if his pack would respond. Only the sound of a bullfrog answered. A feeling of intense loneliness came over Emily, so strong she had to move to keep it from overwhelming her.

She pushed to her feet. "Come on, little brother. I'm sure Uncle Samuel has a long list of chores for us tomorrow. We need our rest."

"You go on in. I'll just be a moment."

Emily knew Ben was as bothered as she was by being left at home. Maybe even more so, being a man and all. She laid her hand on his shoulder. "Thanks for watching out for me," she told him. "I don't know what I'd do without you."

"I'll always watch out for you." Ben put his hand over hers and gave it a tender squeeze. "Good night, Sister. See you in the morning."

"Good night, Ben." With one last look up the darkened road for any signs of Pa, she finally turned and went into the empty house. In the distance, the prairie wolf howled again. Almost immediately it was joined by several others, all yapping together and setting Uncle Samuel's coonhound to barking.

Emily changed into her nightgown and settled at Pa's desk to write in the diary he had given her, relieved that the prairie wolf wasn't all alone.

Chapter Three

*L*arkin read several entries in the diary, until fatigue forced her to set it aside. The handwriting was difficult to decipher at times, and it forced her to go slowly. Plus, there was only so much a person could find interesting in the daily reports of a nineteenth-century farm woman. Sarah had said the diary had inspired her to join the military, but so far, the woman hadn't stepped foot off her farm.

The next morning, Larkin woke late to an overcast, drizzly day, which suited her mood perfectly. The storage unit awaited her, as did a dinner with her parents and the final drive to Grams's house. The only appealing part of any of that would be the very end, when she would see Grams and she would be home.

She didn't have to move in with anybody. She had enough savings stashed away to rent an apartment and support herself for a year or so before she had to worry about an income. With her disability rating, it might take that long to find a suitable job. But she wasn't ready to even think about a job yet, and she wasn't ready to live alone yet either. She needed safety, love, and, most of all, peace. She needed Grams.

Like a carrot at the end of a stick, the promised reward of

home pulled her through the emotional chore of loading her car with all of Sarah's belongings. All of Larkin's stuff had already been shipped to Grams's, so all she had with her was an overnight bag. There was plenty of room for Sarah's boxes and bags. When the car was full, Larkin stood beside it with the two lamps in her arms, trying to figure out where they might fit.

The only available space was on the passenger seat with the urn, but that felt wrong. Disrespectful. As though the urn were just another object and not holding the remnants of her best friend.

There simply wasn't room, she decided. The lamps most likely had held no sentimental value for Sarah anyway. And Larkin couldn't possibly hold on to everything, could she?

She left them next to the dumpster by the front office. If someone wanted them, they could help themselves.

With the sun already setting, Larkin steered out of the storage facility's gates and turned north on Interstate 5. She welcomed all the childhood memories that came to mind as she drove through Tacoma and into Seattle because they kept her from thinking about Sarah and Afghanistan.

As she drove past Boeing Field, she watched a small jet land in front of the Museum of Flight, where she'd gone on a field trip in fifth grade. All the other girls had been bored, but Larkin had been fascinated. She'd studied every inch of every fighter jet, military helicopter, and bomber there and was the last to board the bus back to the school. In one of her own storage boxes somewhere was a picture of her ten-year-old self smiling from the pilot seat of a McDonnell Douglas F/A-18A Hornet.

She'd spent eight years in the Army and the four years before that at college in Vermont, which meant she hadn't spent much time in Seattle in over a dozen years. As she drove through downtown, it seemed like a new city with all the new skyscrapers and dozens of lit-up cranes constructing even more.

By the time she pulled into her parents' driveway, she was tired of reminiscing and wanted only to eat and go to bed.

Unfortunately, she still had to spend a couple of hours talking and making her parents believe she was fine.

"Here I go," she said to Sarah, even though she still had her hands wrapped around her steering wheel. "Wish me luck."

She moved to open her door but paused as guilt nagged at her. Sarah had died estranged from her family. Maybe Larkin should try harder with her own mother. The curtains on the front window twitched, and she knew she'd been spotted. No backing out now. No doubt Mom was winding up for a scolding about Larkin taking too long. "She really brings out the worst in me. Always has," Larkin muttered aloud, reaching again for her door handle.

The front door opened, spilling light onto the wet flagstone steps winding through the professionally landscaped yard. Larkin's mom stood in the doorway, wearing slacks and a blue sweater, looking as if she'd spent the day at her office rather than at home like everyone else on a Sunday. Sighing, Larkin pushed open her car door and got out. A blast of cold air hit her, carrying raindrops that pelted her skin. She should have put on her coat, but figuring she was already wet and cold, she decided to run to the front door, ignoring the pain in her bad knee.

"Hi, Mom," she said, reaching for a hug.

Kat Bennett took a step back. "You're all wet! Come in. I'll get you a towel."

Larkin's arms dropped to her sides, and she followed her mom into the grand entry hall where a curving staircase led to the bedrooms upstairs. Larkin remembered feeling like a princess floating down those stairs on prom night as her date gaped from where she stood now.

"Here." Her mom shoved a fluffy bath towel into her hands. "You can leave your shoes on the tile in the powder room. I don't want water staining the hardwoods."

Larkin did as she was told, taking a moment to rub the towel over her wet hair and arms before leaving it folded on the powder-room sink. When she emerged, she followed the sound of instrumental music into the kitchen, where her mother poured a glass of wine and her father sat at the granite island in front of his laptop. When he saw her, he closed it, slid off his barstool, and came to her with open arms that he wrapped around her in a hug that took her back to her childhood and all the nights when he'd gotten home from work at his brokerage office. "How's my girl?" he asked, giving her a squeeze.

Larkin smiled as the hug ended and she got a good look at her father. His hair had turned whiter over the last year. She hadn't noticed during their Skype video chats. "I'm good," she answered. "How are you? Work keeping you busy?"

"You know it." He motioned toward the couches in the adjoining great room. "Here, come sit. Want a glass of wine? Dinner should arrive any minute."

Larkin took the glass and settled cross-legged into the corner of the couch where she'd always sat as a teenager. This spot on the leather sectional had the best view of the TV, and she'd spent countless hours stretched out here with her friends and cousins. On the side wall hung an unfamiliar painting with demure splashes of pale color. "Is that new?" she asked, searching for something to talk about.

"It is," Mom answered as she took the armchair by the fireplace and primly crossed her legs. She was still wearing heels. She went on to tell Larkin everything she knew about the artist and the gallery where she'd bought the painting. It was all Larkin could do to feign interest.

The doorbell rang, and Kat gracefully got to her feet to answer it. She returned carrying a huge paper shopping bag full of boxes emitting a delicious aroma. "I hope you like dumplings. This place makes the best outside of Taiwan."

Larkin didn't care what she ate, so she agreed that she did, even though she doubted she'd ever eaten dumplings. The three of them sat at the dining room table, where candles had already been lit and linen napkins waited at each place setting, making Larkin mentally roll her eyes. Would it kill her mother to eat straight from a cardboard box for once?

"Try this one first," her dad said, pointing with his chopsticks to a white pocket of dough on her plate that was artfully crimped along one side. "It's pork and vegetable. My favorite." He expertly picked the dumpling up and placed it on a spoon he held in his left hand and then poked it open with his chopstick so the juices spilled out onto the spoon. After carefully blowing on it, he popped the dumpling and juice into his mouth and moaned in delight.

Larkin copied him, realizing as she did that if she'd stuck the dumpling straight into her mouth, the hot juices inside would have burned her. She, too, moaned in appreciation. Dad had not been exaggerating. It was delicious.

"I'm glad you were able to stop by today, Larkin," her mother said as she used a knife to cut her dumpling in half on her plate rather than follow the messy process her husband had performed. "I know you wanted to go straight to Grams's house, but what would people think if they knew my daughter drove right past without stopping to see us after all she's been through this year? It's bad enough that you don't want to live here." She placed a bite in her mouth and chewed.

Larkin had to force her own bite down her throat, which had threatened to close up at her mother's words. *What would people think?* That was the problem. That was always the problem with her mother. What would people think of her? Larkin knew her mother didn't really care about Larkin herself. She only cared about how *she* looked to anyone who might be watching and judging, and a daughter who came home from war and didn't stop to do the whole my-daughter-is-finally-home routine was asking for criticism.

Maybe that was a side effect of her mother's profession. Kat McKinnon Bennett had founded and ran a successful skin-care and cosmetics business. Her entire identity was wrapped up in how she looked.

Kat had always hated that her only daughter didn't care one tiny bit about wearing makeup or painting her nails or wearing the latest fashions. Except for on prom night and a few other times in her life, Larkin had never been interested in that stuff. She clipped her nails short, kept her boring brown hair in a style requiring the least amount of upkeep and satisfying Army regulation, and usually wore nothing more on her face than lip balm. A fancy night out might warrant a swipe of mascara and lipstick, but that was it.

And to make matters even worse, she'd chosen a dirty, smelly, and dangerous career. To her mother, she might as well be an alien.

Her dad tried to change the subject. "We've been so worried about you, Lark."

Larkin swallowed a retort and plastered on a smile. "I'm still in one piece, despite what they might have told you."

Her mother let out an unladylike snort of disgust. "They told us you nearly died in the blast and that at Landstuhl you tried to kill yourself. We were all set to fly over to see you, but they said you refused."

A stab of regret shot through Larkin as she saw the hurt in her mother's eyes. She looked away and sipped her wine, trying to come up with a response that wouldn't ignite more pain nor reveal too much. Outside the wall of windows, she could see the lights of Kirkland shining across Lake Washington, as they always had. The view calmed her, and she was able to turn back toward her mom. "I knew they were sending me stateside. There was no reason for you to go all the way to Germany. And then, when I got back, I went straight into inpatient treatment for six months. There wasn't time."

Mom leaned over and laid a hand on top of Larkin's. Kat's hand was pale and unlined, her nails gently rounded and lacquered in the red color she'd always favored. Larkin's hand, though thirty-one years younger, was marred with scars, sunspots, and the beginnings of wrinkles from all her time in the sun. She slowly pulled her hand away and hid it under the table on her lap.

Dad tried to say something, but his voice failed him and he covered it with a cough. He averted his eyes from Larkin and stared out the windows.

Mom waited a beat. "Why did you try to kill yourself?"

A sudden, familiar rage engulfed Larkin, and she wanted nothing more than to leave. Every muscle in her body strained to stand and walk out of this house, far away from this conversation and every reminder of what had happened. Far away from her mother's questions and judgments.

But the look on her mother's face told her that if she did, her mother would march after her and harass her until she got some answers.

Larkin shot a look at her dad, hoping he might help, but he looked like he was about to cry. His watery eyes were a punch to her gut.

She studied the crown molding as she searched her brain for words to explain the one thing she didn't want to talk about at all.

Her dad prompted, "Maybe you could tell us about the day of the bombing?"

Larkin snapped her gaze to meet her father's. "No. I won't discuss that."

Surprise flashed across his face. He nodded. "Okay. What can you talk about?"

"For heaven's sake, Christian. She's not a baby." Mom set aside her fork and leaned toward Larkin, staring her down. "We know they sent you to Landstuhl, Germany, for surgery and that you were supposed to return to your unit in Kandahar once you healed, but that something happened and they instead put you on psych watch and eventually gave you a medical discharge. What did you do?"

The question—*what did you do?*—echoed in Larkin's brain. Her parents knew she'd tried to kill herself. They knew how she'd tried to do it. So the only thing her mother could be asking, she figured, was what had she messed up so badly that it led her to take such drastic action. Mom didn't ask what happened to her; she asked what Larkin had done, as though there were no other explanations. The only possible reason, in Mom's mind, for Larkin trying to kill herself was because she'd messed up in a big way.

And, of course, her mother was right.

They deserved the truth. As much as she could voice.

For several moments, Larkin concentrated on drawing air into her lungs and releasing it along with the tension in her body, as her therapist had taught her to do. When her heartbeat had slowed to a pace that no longer made her feel like throwing up, she started talking, directing her words to the food on her plate to avoid the emotions she knew she'd see in her parents' eyes. "Like I said, I won't talk about the…the bombing. But like you said, I was injured, and I was flown to Germany where I was patched up. They said I could return to my company once I'd healed enough, but then they told me about Sarah and the others, and I started having nightmares and things."

"Things? What sorts of things?"

Another deep breath. "Visions. Hallucinations. Outbursts."

Mom must have heard the anger in Larkin's voice because she didn't ask anything else. The silence stretched over them.

"Go on, Lark," Dad urged. "You're safe."

Unexpected tears surged up her throat, and she looked down at her lap to hide them. The only sound in the room was the music on the sound system. She cleared her throat. "I managed to get my hands on some drugs. I don't even know what they were, but I figured if I took the whole bottle, they'd do the job."

Mom gasped. Dad made an anguished sound.

"The nurse found me right away, and they pumped my stomach. A few days later, I was informed that I would not be returning to Afghanistan and would instead be flying to Memphis for PTSD treatment." Relieved she was finally near the end of the story, Larkin lifted her chin. "After the six-month inpatient program, I returned to Fort Leonard Wood where I was outprocessed and officially given a medical discharge."

"Did they give you a pension or any benefits for all your years of service?"

Larkin's mouth dropped open. "Seriously, Mom? That's your question?"

Mom sputtered an explanation, but Larkin cut her off. "Don't worry about me. I'll be fine." She started eating again to signal the end of their conversation, though she no longer tasted the food.

"Are you in counseling?"

Larkin avoided looking at her mother. "Yes, I have a therapist I call once a week until I find someone local." They didn't need to know she hadn't called her therapist in two weeks and she had no plans to look for a local doctor. She was tired of talking about her problems and ready to be normal for a change. Ready for a fresh start.

"Do we need to worry you're going to commit suicide? Because that would kill Grams to find you, you know."

Larkin gritted her teeth. Was her mother really more worried about Grams finding Larkin's body than about Larkin herself? "No, Mom. I'm not going to kill myself." She folded her napkin and placed it on the table next to her plate, no longer hungry.

"What about—"

Larkin held up her hand to cut off her mother's next asinine question. "I should have let you guys come see me, or at the very least called you more often. I'm sorry I didn't, and I thank you for worrying about me. I needed time. I still need time to figure out what to do with the rest of my life. I thought I was going to be in the Army forever. I loved my job. It gave me purpose. Now I don't have any purpose, and all I seem to be good at is disappointing people. But I'm trying, okay? I'm trying."

She refused to break down. Already, she'd opened herself up more than was comfortable. Without giving them a chance to respond, she pushed back from the table and carried her plate to the kitchen where she dumped the food in the trash and stood over the sink taking several deep breaths. Her chest still felt hot, so she grabbed a glass from the cupboard, filled it from the tap, and drank the whole thing without pause.

"We have sparkling water in the fridge if you'd prefer."

Larkin carefully placed her glass and plate in the dishwasher. "No, I'm fine." Forcing a wide smile, she looked at her mother, who had propped one hip against the kitchen island, wineglass in hand. "Thank you for dinner, Mom. I really appreciate it. I'd better get going, though. It's been a long trip, and I'm tired."

"Already?" Mom left her half-full wineglass on the counter. "I have something for you. You'll be looking for a job, and I found a website that has all kinds of ideas for people with psychology degrees—"

"No." Larkin cut her off and put a hand on her arm. "I'm not ready. Please. I just need time."

Mom's face filled with such confusion that it would have been comical had Larkin not been so emotional already. She was in a place where most mornings it took all of her energy to get out of bed. Someone like her mother—who had been driven toward success her whole life and for whom everything had fallen into place—could not comprehend what this was like.

Her father came into the kitchen, and Larkin went to him. "I'm heading out, Dad." She stepped into his embrace. "I'll see you later," she said, not willing to commit to anything more concrete.

When she stepped away from her dad, her mom was there, and this time, she opened her arms to Larkin. Larkin hugged her and felt like the little girl she'd been who'd wanted so badly for her mother to love her, but who could never figure out how to make that happen. "Bye, Mom. Thanks again."

In the car, she backed out of the driveway and murmured sarcastically to Sarah, "That was fun." As she turned onto the main road, she added, "Grams's house will be different."

A sense of peace filled the car, and Larkin knew Sarah understood. Anytime they'd talked of home while on deployment, Larkin had always talked about her grandparents' house in Woodinville. Finally, she was going home.

Chapter Four

*T*he first letter Emily and Ben received from Pa had come a week after his and David's departure with the proud announcement that they were both mustered into service in the 9th Indiana Infantry regiment. They were to spend a month training at what had been the old state fairgrounds, now given the official-sounding name of Fort Morton, before shipping out to the front lines.

The second letter came from David nearly a month later, telling them to be proud of Pa, for he had been elected first lieutenant of their company. David went on to describe how their regiment had been chosen to march in review for Governor Oliver P. Morton and General George McClellan before boarding a train bound for Grafton, Virginia. They were the first regiment to leave Indiana. On the way, residents throughout Ohio waved and cheered for them as their train passed.

The last letter Emily and Ben received had been written by Pa. In it, he described their first battle at a place called Philippi in western Virginia and made it sound like a grand adventure. Emily could tell Pa was not telling them everything so they would not worry, but she worried anyway. She missed her father and older brother, and every day with them gone felt more difficult than the last.

And then the letters stopped coming. The more time that passed without word, the more Emily worried and fretted. One Sunday in mid-July, as the sun blazed hot from the moment it rose above the horizon, they'd all gone into town for church, as was their custom. Before his sermon, Reverend Daniels read from a newspaper clipping given to him by Mrs. Chambers, who had received it from her sister in Terre Haute. The *Terre Haute Star*, dated July 11, reported that Union forces, among them their own Indiana boys in the 9th Regiment, battled against Confederate forces led by Brigadier General Robert S. Garnett in a place called Laurel Hill in western Virginia. Emily found herself shaking. As Reverend Daniels bowed his head to pray for their boys at war, Emily quietly slipped from the pew and went outside.

Even standing in full sun in the middle of the churchyard, she could not get warm. Pa and David had been in battle. Was that why she had not heard from them in so long? Were they injured? Were they dead?

After the service, it was all she could do to put on a brave act for David's sweetheart, Nancy, who fretted about his safety. Emily, remembering her promise to David, reassured Nancy that he would return to her and that he asked about her in every letter home.

The following week was a long one. Emily startled every time the dog barked, and her gaze flew to the road to see if a messenger or neighbor was bringing word from the Army. The days passed, but Emily felt as if her life would not move forward until she received word from Pa and David telling her they were alive.

On Monday, Emily woke knowing she could not wait one day more. She was supposed to help with the laundry, as was their routine, but she thought that dull task might make her lose her senses.

"Aunt Harriet, may we delay the laundry until I've returned from Paoli?" The sun was peeking over the horizon, and Emily had caught her aunt returning from the outhouse before breakfast.

Harriet jerked to a stop when she heard Emily's voice, her hand flying to her chest. "Goodness, girl! You gave me a startle."

Emily dropped her chin. "I'm sorry, Aunt. I did not mean to. It's just that I want to stop by the post office and see if there is any word from Pa or David, or, lacking that, I plan to ask around to see if anyone has heard news." Stampers Creek had a post office but the postmaster had enlisted, so until a replacement could be found, residents would need to go into Paoli for their mail. Paoli was five miles to the west, and a much larger town than Stampers Creek. Chances were good that someone there knew something.

Aunt Harriet's brows knit together. "I'm worried about them, too. Go on. I'll get started without you."

Moving quickly, Emily saddled her father's mare and climbed on. Now that she was doing something other than waiting, she couldn't seem to move fast enough.

The roads were quiet this early in the morning. She waved to neighbors in their yards feeding farm animals or heading to their fields early to beat the heat of the day. The nearer she came to town, the more activity increased until she arrived at Courthouse Square and found herself in the middle of a flurry of horses, wagons, and people, all either hurrying to their destination or completely unmindful of those needing to pass as they blocked the sidewalks and dusty street to share pleasantries with one another. The imposing building with Greek columns, from which the square had gotten its name, towered over everything from its perch in the middle, the rising sun blinding off the white paint.

The post office was located on the far street facing the

courthouse, and Emily made a beeline there, arriving just as the postmaster unlocked the door for the day.

"Good morning, sir!" she greeted him, trying to hide the urgency she felt.

"Good morning, Miss…"

"Wilson," she supplied as she followed him inside. "Emily Wilson from Stampers Creek." They exchanged polite well-wishes for the Stampers Creek postman who had gone off to fight. Emily clenched her hands tightly together and forced herself to be patient.

"Wilson, you said." He finally pushed through the swinging half door and took his place behind the service counter. "I do believe I have some mail for your family, if you would give me a moment."

"I'll also take anything you have for my uncle, Samuel Hutchinson." Emily held her breath as she waited for him to disappear into the back room where mail was sorted. He emerged carrying two letters. Two letters! He handed them to her.

"Oh, thank you!" She recognized David's handwriting on the first envelope and hugged it to her chest. The second was addressed to both her and Ben, but it was not written in Pa's handwriting. She hurried through a few more pleasantries with the postmaster before escaping outside to tear open the mystery letter.

To the family of First Lieutenant Calvin Wilson, 9th Indiana Infantry, she read. *It is with my deepest condolences that I write to inform you of First Lieutenant Wilson's death in battle at Laurel Hill, Virginia, on the morning of the seventh of July. He was shot by enemy musket and died instantly. He did not suffer. Our forces, under Major General George B. McClellan, defeated the Confederates, and so it is my honor to tell you that your loved one did not die in vain. I, and our great country of the United States, thank you for First Lieutenant Wilson's service.*

Emily felt herself falling and could do nothing to catch herself. She landed hard on the ground in a pool of gingham skirts, causing her mare to skitter away from her. She sat there, her arms limp in her lap, the letter glaring up at her, mocking her with its simplicity.

Nothing was simple any more. Pa wouldn't be coming home. Tears dropped unchecked onto the letter, but she could not bring herself to move to wipe them away, or to pick herself off the ground.

Pa was gone.

How could this be? Pa was stronger than anyone she knew. He could shoot better than anyone she knew. He was supposed to read the diary she'd been dutifully writing in every night for him. He was supposed to stay safe. He was supposed to serve their country and then come home.

"Miss, are you all right? Can I get someone for you?"

She looked up to find a man and woman on the sidewalk staring at her. The man bent down to hook his hand under her elbow. "Here, let me help you. You don't want to soil your pretty dress by sitting in the dirt, do you?"

Emily let him pull her to her feet, and she thought she mumbled words of thanks, but she couldn't be sure. Her mind was full of Pa—the way he smelled of saddle leather and rain-washed soil, the touch of his calloused hand on her cheek, the way his eyes squinted in the sun. The way his fingers picked out Mama's favorite tune on his guitar late at night when he thought everyone was asleep.

The couple was still hovering over her, asking questions and offering help. She needed to be alone. Thanking them again, she stuffed the letters in a saddlebag, untied her horse's reins from the hitching rail, and quickly mounted. Without a care for propriety, she galloped toward home.

At the copse of trees marking the boundary of their farm, she peeled off the road and led the mare down to the creek. It was the place where she went when she needed to be alone, and she'd never needed solitude more than she did now. She couldn't face her aunt and uncle and tell them the news. She couldn't even tell Ben yet. What would she say?

With her back against the trunk of a willow tree, she read the captain's letter again, and this time she let the deep, tearing sobs inside her come out. She held her head in her hands and cried. As the pain turned to anger—at the secessioners for causing this war, at Pa for dying, at the Army for not protecting him—she opened her mouth and screamed.

"Emily?" Ben appeared, scrambling onto the ground beside her and pulling her into his arms. "What happened? Are you hurt?"

She buried her face in his shoulder and cried some more, knowing that she would have to tell him and then he, too, would feel his life shatter.

After several long moments, she finally found the breath to speak. "Ben, I'm so sorry." She looked into his terrified brown eyes and watched them fill with horror at her next words. "Pa has been killed."

She let him read the letter from the captain, and they cried together, lost in their shared pain. When she remembered the letter from David, she rubbed her sleeve over her eyes and jumped up to snatch it out of the saddlebag. "I haven't read this yet. I forgot about it."

She ripped open the envelope and spread the dirt-stained paper across her knee. Aloud, she read her brother's words: "'My dearest sister and brother. It is with great sorrow that I write this letter. It is one I never thought I would write, and it wounds me deeply to know that it will cause you pain. Pa has been killed in battle. He led a charge against Confederate cowards who were hiding in the bushes on Laurel Hill. He was shot in the head, and as he fell beside me, I knew there was nothing I could do to save him. I am so sorry. I tried.'"

Emily could not keep reading. She shoved the letter into Ben's hands.

He cleared his throat and had to take several breaths before he began. "'I must also apologize, dear siblings, for something else about which you will be upset. I must break my promise to return home at the end of my three-month enlistment. We have been offered a reenlistment bounty to extend our service and sign on to a three-year term. As the head of our family now, I feel the money, which is more than we'd make in a year from the farm, is the best way for me to do my duty to you. I have signed the contract already and will not be allowed time to come home to see you before I must report for my next duty. I will send that bounty to you as soon as I receive it, and I will continue to send you my pay when I can so that you may be independent from Uncle Samuel and Aunt Harriet in some ways. Please don't be angry with me. Love, David.'"

They both sat in silence as his words sank in. Only the sounds of the creek gurgling in front of them and the bumblebees looking for nectar filled the air. Emily imagined that this morning had not happened, that the letters had not arrived, that she and Ben were here doing nothing more than enjoying a summer day at the creek as they'd done so many times before. But she couldn't fool herself. The sun looked dimmer now, the flowers less vibrant. Even the water did not beckon with its promise of cool refreshment. She already felt cold. And heavy. And so very tired.

"I wish he was coming home." Ben's voice sounded as worn down as she felt.

"Me too." The anger she'd felt earlier coalesced into a darkness she'd never experienced before. She understood that David felt he was supporting them by extending his enlistment, but she knew he would best support them by being here with them. The three of them should be together to mourn Pa and give him a proper burial. Just as the family pulled together after Mama died, they should pull together now and help each other through. But David wasn't coming home. Maybe not ever.

After a long time together under the willow tree, Ben finally nudged her with his elbow. "We'd better get back. Aunt Harriet saw you turn off the road and come down here, and that's why she sent me to you. They've got to be wondering where we are."

Emily nodded in agreement and allowed Ben to pull her to her feet, her body sore and stiff from sitting for so long. Together, they walked home, the horse trailing behind them.

As they entered the yard, Uncle Samuel rounded the corner of the house and met them by the barn. "Who do you two think you are, disappearing all day while we're left to do your chores? I didn't agree to look after you so you could run off and shirk your duties!" His face grew redder with each word until a vein appeared on his temple.

"We have some news, Uncle," Ben told him.

"I don't want to hear your excuses. Get back to work!" Samuel turned toward the barn, his dog beside him.

"Pa is dead," Emily told him, hoping the words might snap him out of his meanness.

Samuel did stop, but he kept his stiffened back to them.

"No!"

The cry made them all look toward the house where Aunt Harriet had appeared on the porch in time to hear the announcement. Her face had gone pale, and she held a rag to her mouth. For the first time, Emily remembered that Pa was Harriet's brother. They should have been more careful in telling her the news.

Emily shoved the mare's reins into Ben's hand and rushed across the yard to pull her aunt into her embrace. Harriet's whole body shook with her sobs, and Emily felt her own tears spill again.

Uncle Samuel finally turned around to face them. Emily expected him to give words of comfort to them, or at least to his wife, but instead, he snarled, "I guess I'm stuck with you now."

Emily gasped. Ben's hands curled into fists.

"When David returns, we'll have to sit down and come up with a plan for running this farm short one man."

"David isn't coming home." Ben said the words calmly, his eyes boring into his uncle. "He reenlisted for three years."

"What?" Aunt Harriet pulled back to look at Emily for confirmation. She nodded, and Harriet's eyes filled with tears again. She covered her mouth with her cloth and shook her head in silence.

Samuel and Ben were still staring hard at each other. Finally, Samuel gave a jerk of his head and pivoted on his heel with the words, "Get back to work." He disappeared into the barn with Ben staring holes into his back.

Aunt Harriet pulled Emily into another hug. "I'm so sorry about your pa, sweetie. What can I do?"

Emily forced her lips to form a smile for her aunt's sake. "I don't think there is anything any of us can do but get back to work."

Solemnly, they did just that.

Chapter Five

Present day: Woodinville, Washington

*T*he moment Larkin climbed out of her car at Grams's house, she was met with a wall of sensation. The rain had let up, and the forest was alive with scent unlike anything she'd smelled in Afghanistan or in Memphis. Even though she was eager to get inside and see Grams, she paused and breathed deeply of the moss, molding leaves, rich soil, and the mix of pine, cedar, and fir. With each inhalation, she felt energy course through her.

Home. She was home.

A sudden crashing sounded from the dense undergrowth separating Grams's house from the neighbor's. Instinctively, Larkin reached for the weapon strapped to her thigh. But her Beretta M9 wasn't there.

They'd taken her weapons away from her. She was defenseless.

A black-and-brown dog burst from the bushes and crossed the driveway to her, tail wagging.

"Here, Bowie," came a call from the direction of the covered porch.

Larkin looked over and found Grams coming down the steps, one hand grabbing the dog's collar and the other reaching for her. Larkin went to her, meeting her halfway, and pulled her grandmother into a desperate hug.

"It was hard for your grandpa when he got home from war, too," Grams said into her ear in a voice that indicated she noticed everything. "He reached for his absent weapon for months."

Larkin didn't respond. She was doing everything she could to maintain control.

"It will get easier, Lark. I promise."

Her heartbeat finally eased, and Larkin thought she might be able to talk without shattering. She pulled back to look at Grams. "I'm sorry I wasn't here for the funeral, Grams. I wanted to be."

Grandpa McKinnon had been her biggest supporter and Larkin his biggest fan. When Larkin first became interested in being a soldier, a boy at school had laughed at her and told her that only men were soldiers. It was Gramps who told her women could be in the Army, too, and then proved it by taking her to the Smithsonian in Washington, DC, and showing her pictures of women in uniform. He never told her women weren't allowed in combat, but when she'd found out on her own, he'd encouraged her to not let that stop her. She'd chosen military police as her occupational specialty because, at the time, it was one of the few jobs in the armed services that put women into situations where they would see combat, regardless of the official rules. Gramps had encouraged her every step of the way.

"Oh, honey, don't you worry about that," Grams told her with a pat on her back. "You were on the other side of the world doing important work. I understood, and I know Gramps would have, too."

Larkin felt so lucky to have this woman in her life. "Thanks, Grams."

"I know you're hurting, Larkin," Grams said, holding Larkin's shoulders, her eyes serious. "I know you don't want to talk about it yet, but I think you'll feel better if you do, and I'm here whenever that time comes. I love you, soldier girl. Remember you aren't alone, okay? I'd walk through fire for you."

About to shatter, Larkin nodded and took a step back. She looked at the love shining on Grams's face and tried to say something, anything, in response. But nothing would come.

"Larkin! You're home!" Her cousin Jenna stepped onto the porch, a huge smile on her face, her tall, slim figure encased in jeans and a burgundy raincoat. Jenna ran down the steps and launched herself at Larkin, bringing the scents of coconut lotion and coffee with her.

Larkin laughed. "Yep, you're stuck with me now."

Jenna squeezed. "That makes me so happy." When she pulled back, she looked at Larkin as if she'd never seen her before, even though they talked on Skype or FaceTime on a regular basis. "Come in. Kaia is here, too, and dying to see you."

"What about Evan?" Larkin asked, referring to Jenna's husband.

Jenna shoved her mahogany hair out of her face. "No, he had something else going on."

"I can't complain about having you all to myself," Larkin told her, though she was certain she'd seen a shadow cross her cousin's face at the mention of her husband.

Larkin collected her rucksack, overnight bag, and Sarah's urn from the car, and they went inside. Bowie came trotting in with them, which surprised Larkin since Grams had never allowed pets in the house before.

Grams shrugged and grabbed an old towel from a hook next to the door, wiping Bowie's wet fur. "I got her after Gramps died, to keep me company."

Larkin dropped her bags on the floor and kicked off her shoes. She kept the urn cradled in one arm.

"Larkin!" a familiar voice called.

Larkin looked up and found her younger cousin, Kaia. It wasn't until that moment, when she stood in the cramped entry hallway with her three favorite people, that Larkin realized how deeply she'd missed them. To the very marrow of her bones. "Kaia, come here."

Kaia's blond ponytail swung as she left the kitchen doorway, skirted around Bowie, and finally stepped into Larkin's one-armed hug. Kaia felt small and fragile, but her grip was strong. "Oh, I've missed you."

"I missed you, too. All of you." Larkin breathed in her cousin's fresh laundry scent.

"Come on in, and we'll fix you a plate," Grams offered. "You must be starving."

"I ate at Mom and Dad's." Larkin pulled away from Kaia. "Thanks, though." Together they padded into the combination kitchen and family room, which was already decorated for Christmas with a lit tree in the corner, evergreen boughs on the fireplace mantel, and lights strung up the stair railings. Seeing the lights squeezed Larkin's heart in an unexpected way. Sarah had always strung her bunk—wherever she was in the world—with Christmas lights. She'd said they made her feel happy.

"You girls sit," Grams directed. "I'll make us some tea."

Larkin chose the same chair she'd always sat in since she was a kid spending summers here with Grams and Gramps and her cousins. She set Sarah on the table in front of her, next to the red candle centerpiece. Although she noticed Jenna and Kaia both looking at the urn and then at each other, Larkin didn't feel up to an explanation.

As Kaia slid into the chair next to her, Larkin saw her eyeing the scars on her arms. Larkin tucked her hands under her thighs and wished she had a sweatshirt to hide under.

Jenna sat with her back to the sliding door that led to the back deck and yard. It was dark outside, but soft landscape lighting kept the blackness from feeling oppressive. "It's so good to have you home and safe," Jenna told Larkin as she cupped her hands around the mug of tea Grams set in front of her. "What was it like over there, really?"

Larkin's first reaction was to hide behind jokes. After her first deployment three years earlier, she'd answered questions like this honestly. She'd talked about her job as a military police officer in Kandahar, where she'd patrolled streets and manned checkpoints alongside their Afghan National Police counterparts; of conducting route security or supporting special forces on raids in search of weapons caches; of training Afghan policemen who openly sneered back at her because she was a woman; and of training Afghan policewomen who took their jobs seriously and were making a difference in their communities.

But then she'd started seeing how civilians here at home simply didn't care. Afghanistan was far away and had little to do with their everyday lives, so why should they think about peace in Kabul or Herat? Most Americans asked about the war just so they could launch into their own opinions about the president or why they thought the war was stupid. In fact, most civilians she met believed the war had ended. Far from it. The ongoing conflict might no longer be labeled a war, but men and women were over there putting their lives on the line every day, with some of them losing. Like Sarah.

"It was hot and dusty." Larkin sipped her tea and hoped Jenna would drop the subject.

Jenna's cell phone rang, and she answered without moving away from the table. *Saved by the bell.*

"I'm still at Grams's," Jenna murmured into her phone as her whole body slumped. "Larkin just got here."

The room was quiet enough that Larkin could hear Evan's voice, though she couldn't make out the words. His angry tone, however, came through clearly.

"Do we have to do this now?" Jenna hissed as she got to her feet and shot them a look of apology. She turned to go into the front living room. "I'll leave pretty soon..."

Larkin spoke in a low voice. "Is everything okay with them?"

Grams rubbed at an imaginary spot on the table. "He's been real busy with work is all, I guess."

Jenna walked back into the room, her phone clenched tightly in her hand. "Sorry to cut this short, guys, but I need to head home. Thanks, Grams, as always." She gave Grams a hug and turned to Larkin. "I'm so happy you're home. I'll call you tomorrow, and we'll plan something fun so we can catch up."

After finishing her round of hugs with Kaia, Jenna headed for the door. Both Grams and Bowie walked her out.

Larkin shot her younger cousin a look. "Do you know if everything's okay with her?"

Kaia shrugged and got up to finish loading their dinner dishes into the dishwasher. "She hasn't said otherwise. Hand me Jenna's mug, will you?"

Larkin grabbed the mug and carried it to the sink, where she started to hand it to Kaia. Instead of taking it from her, though, Kaia paused. "Are those from the blast when you lost your friend?"

Larkin looked down at the scars left from the shrapnel that had shredded her arms. For a moment, she wasn't standing in Grams's kitchen. Instead, she was back on that Kandahar street, horror exploding all around her.

She couldn't do this. Not yet. Maybe not ever.

She carefully set the mug on the countertop. "You know, I'm feeling pretty tired. Does Grams have me in the same room as always?"

"I'm sorry, Lark," Kaia rushed to say. "We don't have to talk about it."

Larkin forced a smile. "It's okay, Kai. Really. I'm just tired."

Grams came back into the kitchen, Bowie at her heels. "Come on, soldier girl. I'll walk you up."

Larkin collected her rucksack and duffel bag from the entry hall and hoisted Sarah into her arms. Grams's gaze flickered over the urn, and her lips pressed together sorrowfully. To her credit, though, she didn't say a word. "I put you in the green bedroom. I know how much you love looking out into the forest. Kaia has the yellow bedroom."

"Oh, she's staying the night?"

"Kaia has been living with me." Grams led the way up the stairs. "She's saving money for a down payment on a house, which we all know will take a while in this market, and I love having her company. It's a win-win situation, and now I get you, too."

Grams flicked on the overhead bedroom light and crossed to the adjoining bathroom to turn that light on as well. "Towels are under the sink where they always are, but if you need more, you can find them in the laundry room. I put new shampoo, conditioner, and body wash in there for you, but if you want something different, we can go to the store tomorrow. Is there anything else you need tonight?"

Larkin looked around the small corner room and let the peace envelop her. Grams had decorated this room in soft moss and cream tones with splashes of pink, Larkin's favorite color. The queen-size bed butted against one wall with a window over each of the nightstands. The other wall was filled with floor-to-ceiling windows that looked out on the strip of forest separating Grams from the neighbors. Larkin wouldn't need to close the blinds for privacy if she didn't want to. "It's perfect, Grams. Thank you for letting me stay here." She dropped her bags on the floor but kept the urn in her arms.

Grams laid a warm hand on her arm. Her intense gaze made Larkin want to look away. "You girls have always had a home here."

The pesky ball of emotion that had plagued Larkin since she left Missouri was back, stronger than ever and filling her throat until she felt like she was choking. All she could do was nod and hug her grandma when she was pulled into her arms. The urn felt awkward between them, a reminder that she would never hug Sarah again and that Larkin didn't deserve all the love Grams heaped on her. Tears started spilling from her tightly clenched eyes. Unwilling to let them show, Larkin turned away from Grams. "I'll see you in the morning, Grams. Good night."

She hurried into the bathroom, shutting the door behind her, and held her breath until she heard Grams leave. Then she slid to the floor, still hugging the urn. With a bath towel pressed to her face, she sobbed.

Larkin lay in bed for what felt like hours, but sleep would not come. Her mind was alert, her body ached, her heart felt like a raw wound. Coming home was the best thing—the only thing—she could do right now, but it was also difficult. Out in the world, she could pretend to be strong and unwounded. Here, they knew her. Knew her innermost self and all the not-so-pretty things that hid there.

But they didn't know it all. They didn't know what she'd done.

Before her thoughts could go further down that road, Larkin clicked on the bedside lamp next to Sarah's urn and got out of bed to dig through her rucksack, looking for the diary she'd found in the storage unit. It had put her to sleep last night. Maybe it would do the trick again.

With the book in hand, she settled back in bed and opened the diary to where she'd left off.

July 22, 1861: My heart aches so that I fear it will never be healed. My worst fear has happened. Pa has been killed. The captain of the 9th Indiana Infantry wrote in his letter to us that the skirmish at Laurel Hill, Virginia, had been a Union victory, so Pa's death was not in vain. I feel such anger when I think about that, as though his life meant nothing more than his usefulness to the Federal cause. His usefulness to us, his family, was much, much greater, and now he has been taken from us. He will never read these words. He will never stand beside me at my wedding. He will never hold a grandchild. He will never again look across his fields with his eyes crinkling in the corners the way they always did and say, "We are blessed." No one is blessed now. Not so long as there is war.

Also received a letter from David today with more terrible news: he is reenlisting after his term is up in a few weeks. Now that he is the head of the family, he feels the enlistment bounty will be of more use to us than his return right now. They've both gone and left us here alone.

Larkin closed the diary and shut it away in her nightstand drawer, regretting that she'd read it at all. Emily's list of all that her father would miss echoed through her mind and turned into a list of all that Sarah would miss. Falling in love, getting married, having kids, growing old.

She was so stupid. People got killed in war all the time. Why had she thought reading this Civil War diary would be a good idea? She could only imagine what her therapist would say if she knew. *This is a sensitive subject for you. Maybe you should read something different, something life-affirming.*

Or nothing at all. That's what she'd do. She'd avoid all books. She'd avoid everything, in fact. And since her doctors did not trust her with prescription anti-anxiety meds, she'd use the next best thing.

Larkin cracked open her bedroom door and listened. Silence. Grams and Kaia must be asleep by now.

In the dark, she tiptoed down the stairs to the corner cabinet in the family room where Gramps used to store his booze. It was too dark to see what was there, but she didn't care. Anything would do. Grabbing the first bottle she saw, Larkin unscrewed the cap and took a slug, ignoring the sting as it went down her throat.

Vodka.

Pausing to breathe, she felt tears leaking from her eyes and used her sleeve to wipe them away.

With the bottle in hand, she settled on Gramps's old recliner, sitting sideways so she could see through the windows to the dark backyard and know if anything was out there. Too bad she didn't have her night-vision goggles. Then she could really protect her family.

Protect her family. Yes. That's what she must do.

Gulping more vodka, she got to her feet and started to clear the room—search it for threats—when she remembered she didn't have a weapon.

Gramps had guns, but they were locked away, and besides, Grams probably took all weapons out of the house before Larkin arrived. They couldn't let a suicide risk be near weapons, now could they?

Larkin laughed at the image of herself as a crazed person searching for a gun so she could blow her brains out. That's not how she'd do it. It's not how she'd tried it. She'd used pills. Guns were too messy. With pills she could go to sleep and never wake again.

She took another drink and stumbled into the kitchen in search of something to use as a weapon. A knife? No. Grams would kill her if a perp got blood on the carpet. The metal meat mallet? Yes. Perfect.

With her new weapon in one hand and the vodka in the other, Larkin set about clearing the house of threats. Methodically, she went room to room on the ground floor, searching all dark corners and potential hiding spots for invaders, insurgents…bad guys. She giggled at that one and then hushed herself. This was serious work. She checked every window and door lock twice, tugging on them to make sure they were tightly latched.

When she was satisfied the first floor was secure, she moved up the stairs to repeat the process there. Four bedrooms, four bathrooms, one linen closet. Larkin started with the empty guest bedroom and bathroom, then she moved to Kaia's room.

Easing the door open, Larkin peered inside and could just make out the shape of her cousin lying on the bed. The only noise was Kaia's deep, even breathing. Still, that didn't mean there wasn't someone else in here, waiting to attack. Moving quickly, Larkin checked behind the door. Clear. She went to the windows and made sure each was closed and locked. The deep shadow between the wall and the dresser could hide a person, so she swung the mallet into the space, hitting nothing. Getting on her hands and knees, she peered under the bed and wished she'd brought a flashlight with her. Awkwardly, she shifted onto her stomach and swung the mallet into the dark. When the mallet hit something, she hit it again, harder, before realizing she was hammering on a plastic storage box.

She pushed up to standing and realized with dismay that the vodka bottle had spilled onto the carpet. Damn. She left the empty bottle on the dresser. Kaia's room was secure. Now for her bathroom.

Out of habit, Larkin switched on the overhead lights as she crept into the bathroom, and then cursed as they seared into her brain. "Damn it!"

Still cursing, she threw back the shower curtain to make sure no one was hiding behind it.

"Larkin?" She froze. Kaia's voice. *Uh-oh.* "Larkin, is something wrong?"

Larkin forced a laugh. "No, no, nothing's wrong. Go back to sleep." She turned off the light and hurried to the door.

"Want me to make you some tea or something?" Kaia was standing next to her, but she didn't look right. Larkin squeezed her eyes shut and opened them again. Where her blond hair should be, Kaia had a dark cloth over her head. Instead of her kind blue eyes, Kaia looked at her with angry black eyes.

Larkin swung the mallet.

"Larkin, stop!" Kaia caught her arm in her surprisingly strong grip. "What are you doing?"

Kaia's bedroom flooded with light. Larkin blinked and saw that it was only Kaia standing there, not the insurgent she thought she'd seen. She didn't know what she'd thought she'd seen, now that she considered it. The room had been too dark to see much of anything at all.

"What's going on in here?" Grams stood in the bedroom doorway, her hair a mess and her knee-length pink nightgown making her look like a little girl.

Larkin dropped her arm to her side and tried to make sense of what was happening.

"I think Larkin was having a flashback or something," Kaia answered. "And she's drunk."

Larkin tried to think of something to say to apologize to Kaia for attacking her, to apologize to Grams for waking her, but nothing came.

"Come on, Lark." Grams gently took the mallet away from her, handed it to Kaia, and wrapped her arm around Larkin's shoulders. "Let's get you to bed. You must be exhausted."

Larkin let Grams escort her back to her room where she tucked her into bed as though she were five. Just before switching off the light, Grams sent her a look that was something between sadness and fear. "Try to get some rest."

She clicked off the lights and Larkin was left in the dark, wondering what the hell had happened.

Nightmares plagued her the rest of the night, and it wasn't until sunrise that she finally fell into a restful sleep.

Chapter Six

October 2, 1861: Washington, DC

*F*or nearly two months Emily did her best to be helpful on the farm, but her mind was always elsewhere. If she wasn't thinking about Pa and wondering if he could have been saved, had she or Ben been with him, she was thinking about David and wondering if today would be the day she would learn of his death.

She felt their absence in her body, as though a piece of her own flesh had been ripped away and discarded. The remaining wound stung and festered.

A surprising idea sprang to life one hot afternoon when they were threshing the wheat. Emily normally loved when she was allowed to do farmwork rather than women's work at the house, but her uncle was in a bad mood all day. From the way he yelled, one would think they had completely neglected to separate any grain from the seed heads, but when Emily looked at the pile of discarded straw, she could find few missed grains. Samuel's anger put them all on edge and turned Ben's ears red.

Emily had wanted nothing more than to step between her uncle and brother and yell back, but she knew better than to embarrass Ben and anger her uncle even more. Instead, she had kept silent and continued her own threshing work, all the while dreaming about a day when she and Ben wouldn't have to live under Samuel's rage.

She didn't know how it happened, but that dream had shifted into plans. They could escape Samuel, she knew, simply by walking off the farm.

They could go to David and stop worrying once and for all that he had been cut down by a rebel bullet.

They could follow his regiment and see that he got enough food and rest. She could wash his laundry, and Ben could hunt for squirrels to supplement David's rations.

It would be an adventure, and they would be a family again. What was left of it, anyway.

Without knowing she'd made a decision, Emily started preparing to set her plan into motion. She secreted food from Harriet's larder little by little until she had enough to sustain her and Ben during their travels to western Virginia, where David's last letter had come from. She collected clothing and some personal things she could not leave behind, like their family Bible, the diary Pa had given her, two steel nib pens, a bottle of ink, soap, and the money David had sent.

Convincing Ben to join her proved a bit more difficult.

"What would Harriet and Samuel and the kids do without us? They need us to keep the farm running."

Guilt nagged at Emily, but she pushed it away. "Andrew is old enough to do more work than they ask of him," she'd answered. "And you know they can always ask neighbors to help with the harvesting and canning and trading. Besides, nothing we do is ever up to Uncle Samuel's standards. He would be happy to be rid of us."

Ben had reluctantly agreed to think about the idea.

Emily knew she'd miss Harriet and Ada. She loved them as though they were her own mother and sister, but Harriet had never once defended Emily or Ben against her husband, and

Emily knew Harriet would always put them last. It was time for Emily to follow her aunt's example and put her own family first.

She'd finally convinced Ben to leave by reminding him that his eighteenth birthday was only a few weeks away. If he still wanted to, he could enlist and fight the secesh alongside David. She did not want to see him in danger, but she would be there with him, following the camp and taking care of her brothers. She'd keep them safe.

All that was left to do was to choose their day of departure, and that's when another letter arrived. This one was sent by a Private Thompson who informed them that David had taken ill and was being cared for at a hospital in Washington, DC.

Without knowing the nature of David's illness, Emily was beside herself with worry. She informed Ben that they would leave in two days.

They snuck away late on Saturday night after Emily told her aunt that Ben was sick and unable to attend church the following morning and that she, Emily, would stay home to care for him. She hoped their absence wouldn't be discovered until Sunday afternoon, or even Monday morning when they didn't show up for chores, giving them a large-enough head start that no one would come after them.

Traveling to the capital turned out to be much more difficult than they'd anticipated. With the help of strangers and railroad employees, they found their way, but it was more indirect than expected. They had to take five different trains—each with its own ticket—plus sleep a night in each town where they transferred.

Emily had never traveled beyond Orange County. She found that she loved watching the landscape pass by from her window seat on the trains, and she loved imagining what people's lives were like on the farms or in the cities they passed through. Emily could have managed on her own, and it rankled when fellow travelers looked to Ben as though he, being a man, was her caretaker.

By the time they finally arrived in Washington a week later, they were exhausted and down to half their cash.

Emily had never seen so many people and animals in one place, and the sights, sounds, and scents were overwhelming. She was grateful for the protection of her brother's strong arm as they crossed through traffic on a busy street, picking their way past wagons groaning under the weight of their loads, high-stepping horses with riders who did not seem to see pedestrians, and both open and closed carriages of every size. The number of people and horses on that street alone had to be more than the entire population of Stampers Creek.

Men had an advantage in a city such as this, Emily quickly learned. The trousers and boots they wore made stepping through mud and horse refuse much less of an ordeal. Emily did her best, but she could not move as fast as Ben as they made their way from the railroad depot to the hospital. He hid his frustration at having to slow for her, but she was equally frustrated. Now that they were this close to reaching David, they could not get there fast enough.

The partial dome of the Capitol Building under construction served as a landmark, and they headed that direction until it was time to veer down a side street to the private home turned into a hospital where David had been delivered two weeks prior.

They rushed up the steps and through the doors, where they were met by a stench that had Emily reaching for the handkerchief she carried in her sleeve. She gagged as the smell of rotting flesh and putrid wounds worked through the thin cotton she pressed to her nose. Through watery eyes, she watched a confusion of commotion as people bustled in all directions. Nurses in their starched aprons and caps carried armfuls of linens or trays of food. One passed them carrying a basket full of bloodied bandages. Soldiers, still muddy from the battlefields, leaned against the walls in various states of misery, awaiting attention. From a back room somewhere, she heard a man calling out for his mother and another yelling at him to shut his trap.

It all made Emily's feet want to turn right around and head out the door. But David needed her. She gripped Ben's arm tighter.

"Excuse me," Ben said to a nurse in a starched uniform rushing past with a brown bottle in one hand and a leather strap in the other. "We're here to see our brother. Can you tell us where we can find Private David Wilson?"

She did not break her stride as she shook her head and called back over her shoulder, "Ask the nun at the desk."

Seeing no desk, they pushed their way farther into the wide entry hall and finally found a reception desk near the back, although no one was working there. Emily looked around and spotted a soldier coming toward them from a side room. "Excuse me," she called to him.

The man had short, curly brown hair cut close to his head, and his rounded cheeks reminded Emily of Teddy back home. Although his arms were full of what looked to be bandages and bottles of medicine and he clearly had someplace he needed to be, he politely stopped for them. "I only have a moment. What do you need?"

Emily didn't waste any time. "Do you know where we can find our brother, Private David Wilson of the 9th Indiana Infantry? We were told he was brought to this hospital."

"Oh, yes, I know David. I'm Private Thompson, the one who wrote to you. I'm so relieved you came." Wasting no time, he pointed with his chin to the stairs at the back of the hall. "Upstairs, second room on the right. Bed in the corner."

Emily and Ben didn't need to be told twice. They pushed their way to the stairs and headed up. At the top, they found a hallway that ran the length of the building with open doors leading off both sides. In the second room, they found twenty beds holding what looked to be gravely ill men. Some had bandages covering various wounds, but judging by their pale complexions and the delirium in their eyes, all were ill with some malady or another. Emily's gaze landed on a boy who could not have been older than ten. He stared at Emily as though she were not there.

She tore her gaze away from the boy. David lay in the last bed, under an open window, and she hurried to his side. "David, we're here."

His skin looked waxy and sweaty. Two pink circles darkened his cheeks with fever. "Emily?" His voice shook as though he hadn't spoken in days, and he crumbled into a fit of phlegmy coughing.

"Hush, don't fatigue yourself." Emily smoothed his hair off his sweaty forehead and sent a concerned look to Ben, who sat on the opposite edge of the bed, his hand on David's leg.

"We're here now," Ben told him. "We'll take care of you."

David closed his eyes. A wheezing sound emerged from his cracked lips with every breath. Sweat darkened his shirt. Though only five months had passed since they'd last seen him, he looked different. He'd lost weight, and his cheekbones jutted sharply out of his face above a full beard. At home, David kept himself clean and groomed, and he shaved every morning. The man lying before her was undoubtedly her brother, yet changed in ways she couldn't have imagined.

And he was very ill, Emily realized as he flinched in pain in his sleep and let out a moan. She and Ben had come all this way so their family could be together again. They couldn't lose David now. A wave of fear overcame her, and before she could stop it, a whimper escaped her mouth.

She pressed her lips together and looked around the room for a way to ease David's discomfort. "Wait here, I'll be right back," she said to Ben, intent on finding help.

In the hallway, she searched for someone to tend to her brother, but every person she saw already had their hands full helping other patients. It was up to her and Ben to help David. At the top of the stairs, she found a table laden with clean cloths. She grabbed several and went in search of a basin and water. Although she had to go down to the kitchen in the basement for the basin and out to the pump in the backyard for the water, she soon had what she needed. Moving as quickly as she could without spilling, she hurried back upstairs to her brother, resolutely ignoring all the other soldiers who begged for her help along the way, her heart breaking a little more with each one that she passed.

Back with David, she set the basin on the bed between his legs and dragged a chair over from the bedside of another unconscious man. Moving quickly, she dunked a cloth in the cool water, wrung it out, and set about cooling David's fever with cold, wet cloths laid on his arms and chest. She gently ran another across his forehead and down his face. She'd nursed him through illness before, she reminded herself. And he'd always recovered. This time would be no different.

Emily and Ben talked to David and continued to cool him with the cloths all through the night. David did not stir again beyond an occasional moan or the seldom but welcomed sigh of contentment at the feel of the cool cloth on his skin.

It was a long, long night.

"Where did you come from?"

Emily jerked her head from David's bed. The sun had risen, and the window behind her was flooded with autumn light. Ben was nowhere to be seen, and David was glaring at her from his pillow. "What?"

He raised his voice. "I said, where did you come from?" A fit of coughing, so intense it shook the entire bed, overcame him.

Emily hurried across the room to pour him a cup of water from the jug she'd left on the table inside the door. He was still coughing when she returned to his bedside and forced the cup into his hand. "Drink."

He did, and the coughing subsided. Emily took the cup, and

David settled back against the pillow again with his eyes closed. She placed a hand on his forehead and found his fever still burning hot.

"Why are you here?"

Emily thought he'd fallen back asleep, and the question startled her. "To care for you. We're going to stay with you. And when you return to camp, I'll be there to care for you."

David's eyes flew open and he tried to sit up, but weakness and pain forced him to collapse back to the bed. "No, you are not. I forbid it."

"Don't you see, David? With Pa gone, we're all we have left. I'm not going to spend another day not knowing where you are. We are staying with you."

"We?" David's gaze searched the room, then returned to her. "Ben's here, too?"

She nodded. "Yes. So, you see, there's no use fighting us on this."

David shook his head, unconvinced. "But, Emily, your place is at home."

Emily shook her head. "No. My place is with my family."

"But, Em." She could see the argument was draining what little energy he had, but he kept on. "The women who follow the camps aren't like you. You would besmirch your own honor by taking this course of action." He struggled for breath. "If people discovered what you are doing, you would never find a respectable man to marry you."

His words ignited an ember inside Emily that she hadn't even known was glowing. She snapped back at him, "Since it's only men who have any agency, maybe I should become one. Instead of following the camp, which you find so shameful, I'll become a man and enlist! What do you think of that?"

His eyes bulged and his stomach contracted as though he was trying to sit up. "You will do no such thing!"

She hadn't meant it when she'd said it, but suddenly the idea didn't sound so absurd. "Why not? If all I do is sit at home and darn socks and sew flags, I will go mad with worry for you and Ben, who we both know is going to join you." She realized she was clenching her fists and forced herself to relax them. "You know I can shoot as well as you. You also know I can hold my own in a footrace. I am as fit as you or Ben to be a soldier, and if that means trading my future chance at marriage, that is a risk I am willing to take to keep my family together. You're all I have left."

David closed his eyes and was silent for several moments. All Emily heard was the wheezing of his breathing at a pace so rapid she knew he had not fallen asleep but was thinking. When he spoke, his voice was devoid of strength and she had to lean forward to hear him. "There are ways of men you do not know, little sister."

"If Joan of Arc could manage over four hundred years ago, I can do so now. Besides, I'll be careful." Sensing he was giving in, she tried to lighten the mood. "I'll have you and Ben to protect me, right?"

Her remark seemed to upset David even more. "They burned Joan of Arc at the stake." His Adam's apple bobbed as he swallowed several times. He didn't open his eyes, but his hand moved as though in search of hers. She took it between her own, flinching at the clamminess she found there. His voice was almost a whisper as he said, "Em, people die in battle. Believe me when I tell you it is not a place you want to be."

The heavy reminder of Pa's death fell over her. Emily dropped her chin to her chest and wondered when it would get any easier to think of him. "Why didn't you send his body home to us?"

He shook his head. "I couldn't. They said there was no way to preserve his body for the journey, and they didn't have time for that anyway. I buried him in a meadow under a pine tree."

Emily nodded, overcome by the realization that she might never be able to visit her father's grave site to pay her respects.

"Hey, you're awake." Ben's voice, bright with energy, interrupted the pall that had overcome them. He sat on the end of David's bed. "How do you feel?"

"I feel like I've been trampled by a team of six, but that's nothing compared to what you'll feel when I'm done with you." He gave Ben the sternest look he could muster. "What were you thinking, letting her come here?"

Ben flushed. "You know how stubborn she can be. Besides, I wanted to come, too. I'm of age now." He had turned eighteen two weeks ago, just before they left the farm.

David did not argue, but gave them a look of disappointment that reminded Emily of Pa. When he didn't say anything more, she knew he was too weak to keep up the argument. She tried to raise his spirits. "Nancy is well. She sends her regards." A small lie.

Rather than cheering him, the reminder of his sweetheart back home seemed to make him sad. His eyes closed, and his throat convulsed as he swallowed.

"What can we do for you?" Ben asked. "I can get you some breakfast."

David weakly shook his head. "Not hungry."

"Want to get up and walk around? I bet you'd feel much better with a little exercise."

The suggestion alone seemed to drain David's energy. He sank into the bed a little more. "No, actually, I could use a little rest right now. You two go on and find something to eat."

Emily, still holding his hand, squeezed it tighter. "No, we don't want to leave you alone."

He squeezed back. "Go eat and find some rest of your own. I'll be right here when you get back."

"You better be."

David's lips curved in a slight smile, even as his eyes closed. With one last squeeze of her hand, he released her. "Go on now."

Reluctantly, Emily followed Ben out of David's room and

down the stairs of the hospital. Her body felt stiff from her cramped position all night, but as she walked past soldier after soldier with missing legs and arms, she was reminded to be grateful she had a whole body.

"Excuse me, you are Private Wilson's siblings, right?"

Emily stopped and turned toward the voice. It was the doctor who had briefly checked on David in the middle of the night. "Yes. I am Emily, and this is my brother Benjamin."

"Dr. Chisolm," he reminded them and drew them to the side of the room, out of the bustle of the entry landing. Despite the fatigue around his eyes and mouth, he was a handsome man, his dark hair only slightly mussed from working through the night.

"We were just stepping out for breakfast," Emily told him. "Will David be all right while we are gone?"

The doctor didn't waste any time. "Your brother is very sick. He has typhoid with the added complication of pneumonia. There isn't much we can do now but wait and see."

Emily felt the floor tilting. She'd heard of typhoid and the misery it brought those it afflicted. Few survived. She reached out to Ben to steady herself. Ben's face paled, and the muscle in his jaw bulged.

"What can we do to help him?" Emily asked.

"Try to get him to eat and drink. Keep cool compresses on his forehead, face, neck, and arms to bring down the fever. Prop him on pillows to ease his breathing. I'm sorry we don't have more staff here to care for him, but it's a blessing you have arrived."

"Yes," Emily agreed, her mind reeling.

"I know this must be difficult for you, Miss Wilson." The doctor's voice held a note of condescension that caught Emily by surprise. "I can give you a draft to help you sleep if you would like."

Emily raised her eyebrows, shocked that even a man of learning such as this could be so belittling. Or maybe it wasn't shock she felt but frustration. The thought clearly had never entered the man's head that Ben might find their brother's illness too difficult to cope with. No, only she, a woman, was that weak. She forced a smile, as was expected of her, and politely demurred. "That will not be necessary, Doctor."

He nodded, already turning away. "If you will excuse me, I must return to my duties. Send someone, should you have need of me."

"Thank you," Ben said for both of them. Before Dr. Chisolm could leave, he asked, "Are we in danger of contracting the same illness?"

The doctor paused as though considering, his eyes clouded. "We don't really know what causes it. Some say it is miasma in the air; others say it is from contact with an ill person's excrement. It's good that your brother is next to the window. Try to keep fresh air coming in. And keep him clean."

As Dr. Chisolm walked away, Ben turned to Emily with shadows in his eyes. "You go back to David. I'll find us something to eat."

Emily nodded and numbly climbed back up the stairs to David's room. He lay as they'd left him several minutes earlier, though now that she understood his affliction, she saw how weak he actually was. His body looked shrunken. Every breath was a struggle.

She could not lose him.

Knowing what she needed to do, she gathered more clean cloths and fresh water and set herself to the task of wiping David's forehead. After only one swipe, the cloth felt hot. She rinsed it, wrung it out, and continued cooling his exposed skin, all the while willing him to get better.

Ben returned with biscuits and ham, which she ate ravenously before returning to her ministrations. When her arms ached, Ben took over and Emily rested, never taking her eyes or her hand from her older brother.

Time ceased to have meaning as Ben and Emily took turns

nursing their brother through the days and nights. Despite their constant efforts, David sank deeper into his illness. Occasionally, Dr. Chisolm or another doctor checked on him and administered quinine, but mostly the doctors and nurses who tended to the other patients left David's care to Emily and Ben, nodding in approval at their efforts to keep him clean and hydrated. Emily only left his bedside when she needed to visit the privy in the yard or purchase food from the cook in the basement kitchen for her and Ben. They did not bother to rent a room, for neither wanted to leave David long enough to make it worthwhile. When they needed a break, they went for a walk around the yard. When they needed sleep, they simply crossed their arms on the foot of David's bed and laid their heads down.

They may not have been soldiers, but Emily and Ben fought a war just the same.

Chapter Seven

*T*hat first night at Grams's house set Larkin's routine for the rest of the week. During the day when Kaia was at work and Grams was out meeting friends for lunch or at one of her many charity meetings and functions, Larkin either slept or sat around the house watching movies on her laptop and raiding the kitchen cupboards, Bowie at her side. At night, Larkin spent hours tossing and turning, and after Grams and Kaia were asleep, she'd tiptoe downstairs to get something to take the edge off from the liquor cabinet.

She became adept at clearing the house every night without waking anyone else, and she felt as though she couldn't return to her room until she'd made sure every entry point was secure and no threats hid in the shadows. Bowie slept in Grams's room, so Larkin was on her own for her rounds.

Once the alcohol had worked its magic on her mind and body, and her security routine was complete, Larkin would return to her bedroom where she would finally fall asleep.

But that's when the nightmares came.

Men, their faces covered with black cloth, riding in the back of green pickup trucks. Angry shouts in Dari and Pashto, their meaning clear even without translation. The flash of sun bouncing off the barrel of a weapon on a rooftop. Explosions.

There was always an explosion. And the cotton-in-her-ears aftermath where she was disoriented and terrified.

Body parts. Blood. Fire. Pain.

She jerked awake and felt the sticky dampness of sweat. It was still dark. Still night.

Kicking off the covers, Larkin reached blindly for the bottle on her nightstand and drank until it was empty. Exhausted but afraid to close her eyes, she laid her cheek on a cold spot at the edge of her pillow and stared at the sliver of moonlight that edged along the side of the window blinds. She just had to hold on until morning. Her nightmares weren't quite as bad when she slept during the daytime.

She was still awake when she heard Kaia pass her closed bedroom door and leave for work and a little bit later when Grams went downstairs and brewed coffee, the scent wafting up the stairs and under Larkin's bedroom door.

Even though winter darkness still hovered over the house, the gray light of coming morning had replaced the silver moonlight. Daytime was here.

With a sigh of relief, Larkin let sleep claim her.

Hours later, something bumped into the bed and Larkin woke with a start.

"I thought Grams was exaggerating when she told me you sleep all day, but I guess she was right." Jenna sat on the bed at Larkin's feet. "What should we do? I took the afternoon off—a perk of being married to the boss's son—and I'm all yours."

Jenna managed accounts receivable at the plastic tubing company her husband's family owned. Even though she sounded like blowing off work was no big deal, Larkin knew Jenna took her job seriously. She could even be called a workaholic. It was a big deal that she'd left work to see Larkin.

Larkin rolled over and squinted at the clock. Thirteen

hundred hours. Groaning, she rested her arm over her eyes to block out the light, as dim as it was, that was making her head hurt. "Where's Grams?"

"Working at the holiday bazaar at the Hollywood Schoolhouse. She said she'll bring pizza home for dinner."

Larkin moved her arm enough to allow one eye to see her cousin. "Are you babysitting me?"

Jenna didn't even bother trying to pretend otherwise. "Yep. And that means I'm in charge." She bounced off the bed and crossed over to open the blinds. Sunlight filled the room. "My first order is for you to get in the shower and get dressed. Then we're leaving the house."

Larkin slid her arm back over her eyes. "I don't want to leave the house. I like it here."

"We can figure that out later, once you're up and you've eaten something." She paused and Larkin hoped she'd gone away. That hope was dashed a moment later when Jenna said, "I'm not leaving until I see you go into the bathroom. Once you're in there, I'll go downstairs and heat some of the spaghetti Grams left in the fridge for you."

Larkin's stomach growled in response, her traitorous body siding with her cousin. "Fine, I'll get up. But close the blinds first."

Three hours later, Larkin had to admit she felt better than she had in days. After her shower and lunch, Jenna had compromised on her plan to get Larkin out of the house by agreeing to help her carry in all of Sarah's boxes and bags that had sat in Larkin's car for the past five days.

Sarah's possessions were now stacked along the wall in Larkin's bedroom, except for one box in the middle of the floor that they were sorting through. Bowie snored in the doorway.

"What about this?" Jenna asked, pulling off the cap of a silver lipstick tube and twisting it to reveal an inch of dark pink. "Garbage?"

Larkin took the lipstick from her and carefully twisted it back down before replacing the cap. "I was with her when she found this shade and fell in love with it," she told Jenna, her memories as real as if the images were being projected on the bedroom wall. "She'd convinced me to go to the mall with her so we could find dresses for the Regimental Ball our senior year at Norwich. She talked me into makeovers at the Clinique counter, and of course, she left looking beautiful. I looked like a tramp."

She carefully placed the lipstick in the "keep" pile next to the Ziploc bag of bracelets and earrings and the old T-shirts already there. So far, nothing was in the piles designated "give away" or "garbage."

Jenna pulled a stack of photographs out of the box. "She sure was pretty, wasn't she?" She handed the top one to Larkin.

In the photo, Sarah was wearing her service uniform, her curly black hair slicked back into a tight bun under her maroon beret. Sarah's smile lit her whole face, and her dark-brown eyes gleamed like she was laughing at something the person taking the picture had said. From the trees in the background, Larkin figured it had been taken when Sarah was stationed at JBLM before she'd deployed the last time.

"Do you know who these kids are?" Jenna handed over another photo.

Larkin looked at the two smiling kids, their arms wrapped around each other and their heads bent together. The girl in the picture was clearly Sarah. Her hair and her smile gave her away, even though she couldn't have been more than five or six. The boy with her was much older, a teenager. "I think it's Sarah and her brother, Zach."

"I didn't know she had a brother." Jenna took the photo back to look at it again, closer. "You never mentioned him."

Larkin shrugged. "She didn't have any contact with him. That's why she left all her stuff to me instead of him, I guess." She looked at several more photographs as Jenna handed them to her. "I think she said he was ten years older than her. When their parents divorced when she was six, Zach must have been around sixteen. He went to live with their dad, and she stayed with their mom. From the way she told it, her dad and brother abandoned her, and her mother became an abusive alcoholic. Sarah invited all of them to her Norwich graduation, but none of them showed. I felt so bad for her that day."

"That's so sad."

"Yeah. She wrote them off after that." Larkin fingered a picture of her and Sarah, taken one weekend when they'd both been on leave during their deployment so they'd flown to Paris, a dream for both of them. In the photo, they sat together at a café in Montmartre, both wearing cheesy Eiffel Tower sweatshirts they'd purchased the day before, toasting the camera with full glasses of red wine. "God, I miss her."

"Want to take a break?"

Larkin looked at her cousin and nodded. "Yeah. Let's find a bottle of wine to open. Kaia should be home soon, too."

As Jenna scooped everything back into the box and placed it on the pile along the wall, Larkin carefully propped the Paris picture against Sarah's urn on her nightstand where she'd see it every morning and night.

Downstairs, they found a bottle of Malbec with a label from the winery Jenna's dad ran in eastern Washington. As Jenna poured two glasses, Kaia arrived home.

"How was work?" Larkin asked Kaia as she kicked off her shoes.

"Great," Kaia answered and looked pointedly at the wine in Larkin's hand. "I'm putting together an exhibit for the Nordic Museum in Ballard on hygge and lagom that opens next month. It's been a lot of fun."

Kaia had carved a profession out of part-time curator positions at various museums around Puget Sound, as well as the occasional research job for companies and nonprofits. She also wrote a popular blog on food history and how people have prepared and used food throughout the ages, which was her true passion.

Larkin ignored Kaia's obvious judgment of her drinking and asked, "What are 'hueguh' and 'lawgom'?"

"'Hygge' is a Danish word that acknowledges a moment that feels especially cozy or charming. 'Lagom' is a Swedish concept that embraces just the right amount, or restraint." With a sly look toward Jenna, Kaia asked, "What did you two do today?"

They told her about Sarah's boxes.

"You know," Jenna said as she carried her wine to the table and sat, her feet propped on the chair next to her, "I've been thinking about Sarah's brother." She explained the photo and the siblings' lack of a relationship to Kaia and turned back to Larkin. "I think you should track him down. He'd probably want that picture, and maybe some of Sarah's other things. Whatever you don't keep yourself."

Larkin admitted the idea had crossed her mind. "But from the way Sarah made it sound, he'd made no effort to contact her over the years. Ever. Why should he want any of her stuff now that she's gone?"

"Maybe he wanted to get in touch but thought he'd have plenty of time later," Kaia mused.

Bowie stood and trotted out to the entry hall, signaling Grams's arrival. Larkin reached into the cabinet to get another wineglass. The subject of Sarah and Zach was forgotten as Grams breezed in wearing a Christmas sweater and carrying two large pizzas.

As soon as they'd all loaded their plates with food and refilled their wine, they gathered around the table.

"You're spending the night, right, Jenna?" Grams asked.

Jenna nodded as she picked up a slice of Margherita. "Yep. Evan is meeting some friends after work for drinks, and I thought it would be the perfect opportunity for us to have a girls' night."

Grams set her slice down and wiped her hands on her paper

napkin. "When are you going to tell us what's going on with you two?"

Jenna's eyes widened, but she quickly recovered and waved her hand in the air dismissively. "Oh, we're fine. Really. Nothing's going on."

Larkin could tell by the expressions on Grams's and Kaia's faces that they didn't believe her. For that matter, Larkin didn't either. Still, if anyone understood the desire to keep private matters private, it was her. Taking pity on Jenna, she asked, "Anyone up for a game of gin rummy for old times' sake?"

Soon, with cards in hand, Larkin looked at the faces gathered around her and felt a mixture of emotions. For her entire adult life, Larkin's tribe had been her fellow soldiers. Sarah and all the others she'd served with had been her family. She would have happily given her life for them, and she unquestioningly trusted them with her own.

For the last few months, after being told she'd have to take medical retirement from the Army, she'd believed that feeling of belonging was gone. She'd believed that she would never again feel so close to another group of people, and the loneliness of that had gnawed at her.

But she'd forgotten about her original tribe. The women who had been there since she was a kid, who had believed in her and celebrated with her as she achieved her goals. Tonight, sitting at the table with them as she'd done too many times to count, she remembered, and as she did, she felt a tiny chunk of the wall she kept between herself and the rest of the world break off and crumble away.

As they played, Grams met Larkin's gaze across the table. "Besides old photographs, have you come across anything else interesting?"

The diary sprang to mind, even though she hadn't looked at it in days. "I did find an old diary written by one of Sarah's ancestors. I haven't gotten far, but Sarah once told me she was a woman who disguised herself as a man and fought in the Civil War."

"What?" Kaia dropped her cards, placed both palms flat on the table, and looked at Larkin as though she'd lost her mind. "You have a primary source from the Civil War, and you didn't tell me?"

Larkin ducked her head. "Yeah, I guess I forgot." Kaia had been a fanatic about history from a young age. How Larkin hadn't thought to show her the diary already was beyond her.

Kaia was practically bouncing in her chair. "I've read there were hundreds of women who fought in that war, most of them disguising themselves as men, although it is impossible to know exact numbers since those known were either women who were discovered or outed themselves in newspaper articles or memoirs written after the war. The rest kept their secret hidden or were killed in battle without being discovered. Some bodies have been exhumed and found to be women." She leaned close to Larkin. "Will you let me read it? Please?"

Larkin agreed. "When I'm done with it, sure."

"Why don't you go get it right now and read a bit to us? I'd love to hear it," Grams said.

Larkin shook her head. "I'm taking a break from it right now."

"Oh, Larkin, please?" Kaia had clearly forgotten all about the card game. "I'm dying to know what it says!"

Maybe it wouldn't be so bad reading the diary if she wasn't alone. "Okay, fine. I'll go get it." Larkin went upstairs to her bedroom, hobbling a little from her knee acting up. When she got back to the kitchen, the deck of cards had been put away and someone had started a pot of coffee.

She gave them a summary of what she'd read so far, and then she opened the diary to the next entry and began to read it aloud.

September 25, 1861: I dared not write about our plans until after we'd gone, in case someone discovered this diary and interfered. Ben and I have left home. We are joining David. We will follow his camp and support him in whatever means possible. As long as we are together, I care not that I give up the comforts of home. We've lost Pa. We need to be together.

When we received a letter informing us that David has fallen ill and was sent to a hospital in our nation's capital, we made our plans and we left. I am finding train travel to be an exciting, although tiring adventure. I've shared train cars with soldiers, families, widows, and politicians. I was surprised to see that free black folk have a train car of their own at the back. I don't understand why they aren't allowed to ride with us.

I do hope we arrive in Washington soon and that we find David recuperating. I will be happy when the three of us are together again.

"I bet he has cholera," Kaia told them almost gleefully. "Or it could even be something like syphilis. STDs were rampant among the troops."

Larkin shrugged and kept reading. The next few entries were about Emily and Ben's travels, and then they arrived at the hospital.

October 3, 1861: David is engaged in a battle none of us foresaw when he left home. This one is not against secesh, but fever. We are nursing him the best we can. I cannot lose him. Not so soon after losing Pa.

October 6, 1861: Today I made a decision and while I can't risk putting it into writing, it will change the course of my life. Of that I am certain. I started this diary for Pa so he might know all that had happened at home during his absence. I found the writing of it helped me sort through my thoughts and emotions, and so I continue to write even though Pa will never read these words. Because I am about to embark on what could prove to be dangerous, I must write of my activities obtusely in case this diary should fall into the wrong hands. For now, all I will admit is that I will soon have more in common with my brothers. I must go now. A kindly soldier by the name of Private Franklin Thompson who works here as a nurse is calling for me. David must need something.

"No way!" Kaia jumped up. "Wait here. Don't read another word. I'll be right back." She dashed upstairs.

Larkin exchanged amused glances with Jenna and Grams as Kaia hurried out of the kitchen. Grams got up to pour them each a cup of coffee.

Kaia came back carrying her laptop. "Here it is, just like I thought." Her smile was smug. "Sarah Emma Edmonds, alias Private Franklin Thompson, was one of the known women who disguised herself as a man and served in the Army during the Civil War. She was in the Second Michigan Infantry and served the first six months or so of her enlistment in DC-area hospitals. She later served as a courier and orderly for General Poe. Later, she volunteered to be a spy." She nodded toward the diary. "This woman is legit."

"And Emily didn't even notice she was a woman?" Larkin had her doubts. "How could women possibly fool people into thinking they were men simply by cutting their hair and donning a uniform?"

Jenna nodded. "I was wondering the same thing."

Obviously happy to put on her historian hat, Kaia launched into an explanation. "You're making the mistake of judging the situation from contemporary eyes. Society was very different in the nineteenth century. Women never wore pants, only dresses with corsets to make their waists tiny and several skirts that completely hid the shape of their lower bodies. But it was more than clothing. Society's unwritten rules specified that women were to be demure and sweet, and they were to gracefully allow the men in their lives to manage all aspects of business and war. To people of the era, a woman did not put on pants and go to war any more than a man would've put on a hoop skirt or birthed a baby. So, if it looked like a man, it was a man. Simple as that."

Thinking of her experiences in Afghanistan, Larkin laughed. "Times sure have changed. Twice I discovered a man trying to smuggle weapons past security checkpoints by wearing a burqa."

Jenna leaned forward. "Remind me. Is a burqa the black one that covers all but a woman's eyes?"

Larkin shook her head. "No, you're thinking of an Arabian niqab. A burqa is the usually blue covering worn by women, mostly in Afghanistan, that completely obscures her from view. Even her eyes are covered by a screen." A memory of one particular burqa-wearing woman came into her mind, but she pushed it, and the accompanying pain, away.

"How did you know the weapons smuggler was a man?"

Jenna, Grams, and Larkin all gave Kaia a look of disbelief. "Believe me, you can tell during a pat down," Larkin told her, laughing.

"Yeah, Kaia wouldn't know about that," Jenna teased. "She hasn't had a boyfriend in so long, she probably forgot what a man's body feels like."

Kaia shot her a look, then ruined it by smiling. "Do all women wear burqas in Afghanistan?"

Larkin shook her head. "No, not at all. Sure, the more religiously conservative ones in places like Kandahar do, but many women dress in suits and business attire to go to their jobs in Kabul as elected government officials, attorneys, or business owners."

Jenna cocked her head to the side. "Are the women in burqas as oppressed as media would have us believe?"

"That's difficult to answer." Bowie bumped against Larkin's leg, and she reached down to rub the dog's head, realizing she felt agitated talking about all this, and Bowie was likely picking up on her discomfort. "By western standards, yes, many are oppressed. But, conversely, there are women who choose to wear the burqa for the freedom anonymity brings them. You see, Pashtun people believe that a woman should not show her face in public, and if she were to converse with a man who is not her relative, she would bring dishonor upon herself and her entire family. In a burqa, she does not bring scrutiny upon herself and, like some of the women I met, can even meet with her boyfriend in a public park with no bystanders able to identify her."

"How did you talk with them?" Grams patted her own leg, and Bowie eagerly went to her for more attention. Grams rubbed both hands on the sides of Bowie's neck as she listened to Larkin's answer.

"We had a female terp." At their looks of confusion, Larkin explained. "Interpreter. We arranged to have at least one female terp accompany every unit that might need to engage with local females. I made certain every unit had female soldiers as well."

"Did you say you lived at the police station in Kandahar?" Grams propped her slippered feet on the chair next to her, engrossed in what Larkin was telling them. Bowie lay on the floor next to her and went to sleep.

"As company commander, I made my rounds checking in with my platoons, which meant that I was usually on one FOB—forward operating base—or another, although sometimes my team and I stayed with my officers at the various Afghan police stations. Sarah was waiting for her paperwork to go through, promoting her to captain, so she volunteered to be attached to my company as platoon leader. This meant that she went back and forth between the FOB and the Kandahar police station in district one."

Larkin could see that her cousins and grandmother were

enjoying hearing more about her work. She was surprised she felt like sharing it with them. She went on, "As military police, we were tasked with support and training of the Afghan National Police in all matters of the job including patrols, security, detention, community relations, law and order, gathering intelligence from the population, searching suspects, protection of evidence, and raids on suspected Taliban strongholds. We also performed route security for any military operations in the city."

Grams shook her head. "I'm glad I didn't know any details of your job when you were over there. I was worried as it was."

Larkin smiled at Grams, grateful that she cared.

Kaia got up to refill her coffee mug. "So, interacting with the locals was part of your daily routine? Did any of them cook for you?"

Larkin smiled. Her cousin was so predictable. "Yes, a few times I was invited to share a meal with them and often with the Afghan police. There was a group of boys who played soccer in the street outside Sarah's police station, and it was only boys. Girls aren't allowed the freedom to run, laugh, and play in public. But anyway, I visited there periodically and befriended the leader of the group, a boy named Nahid. He started bringing naan from his mother's kitchen to me whenever he knew I would be there."

"Oh, that's so sweet," said Kaia, ever the tender-heart. "Tell us more about Nahid."

Larkin felt everything inside her freeze. Why had she said his name? The one topic, the one person, she could not discuss.

She jumped up to refill her coffee, cringing as she moved too quickly and the scar tissue in her knee and back pulled painfully. "I, uh…" She hid her face by turning her back to the others. "I think I'd rather get back to playing cards." Plastering on a smile, she faced them. "Shall we switch to Uno?"

They played and talked for several hours until Grams took herself off to bed with Bowie trotting up the stairs alongside her.

The cousins lingered at the table. None of them were ready to call it a night, so Larkin suggested, "There's an unopened bottle of Jameson in Gramps's liquor cabinet. What do you say we take it out and go for a walk? I've been wondering if our old fort is still there."

They found the Jameson and flashlights, then tugged on boots and raincoats and headed out the sliding back door to the deck. With the door closed firmly behind them, they felt like teenagers again, sneaking out of Grams's house. Larkin twisted off the bottle cap and took a slug. She handed it to Kaia, who did the same. "Hoo, that burns!"

That set Jenna and Kaia to giggling, but, to Larkin, it triggered echoes of her Army days. *Hoo-ah!* Her heart felt like lead in her chest. She took the bottle back and drank an extra-long gulp.

"Give me some." Jenna took the bottle from her and clicked on her flashlight before drinking. Her slug was followed by a moan of appreciation. Then, twining her arm through Larkin's, she said, "Let's go."

They made their way, arm in arm, across the darkened yard and into the forest that edged Grams's property.

Larkin led the way past dripping wet ferns, salal, and Oregon grape bushes, being careful to avoid blackberry thorns. They nearly missed the fort because a thick layer of debris and moss had covered the roof and walls. From behind, it looked like a large boulder tucked between the trees.

As they rounded to the front, their flashlight beams playing over the forest around them, Larkin was battered by competing memories. First, there was the summer when Gramps had let them take whatever they wanted from a pile of scrap wood he had in the garage and they'd constructed the three-walled shelter. They'd wanted a tree house, but the tall trunks of the evergreens would not support one, and no hardwoods on the property were strong enough. So, a lean-to in the forest it was.

But then her next memory shoved that one out of her

head. It was of a night raid on a compound on the outskirts of Kandahar. The night had been dark and cold, like this one except there was no rain, and they'd thought the compound was abandoned until a rocket-propelled grenade blasted out of the darkened mud building and nearly took out the vehicle she was riding in.

She shook her head and took another long swig of the whiskey. Their fort looked nothing like that compound. Why did Afghanistan have to intrude on everything in her life?

"Wow, that was close," Kaia said, her words slurring slightly, referring to a toppled cedar lying only a couple of feet in front of the fort.

"It got the firepit," Jenna added, shining her light on the massive tree lying where their ring of rocks used to be.

Larkin shined her flashlight into the fort and saw that years of dead leaves had collected inside. "I'm not going in there," she announced and climbed onto the fallen tree. It was so big that her feet didn't touch the ground. She drank again and tilted over until she was lying on her back, staring at the black sky. Her cousins settled beside her.

The whiskey had left a burning sensation in her chest, and she welcomed it. Maybe it would burn away the emotions there that kept bubbling up into memories she'd rather forget.

She knew her family had probably looked up PTSD on the internet and felt they now knew all about what she was going through, but they didn't know shit. Not even Grams and Kaia, who had witnessed her flashback that first night.

The fact was, her trauma was controlling her, and it felt like it always would.

She closed her eyes and tried to think about something else. Anything else.

The forest was silent. No birds sang. Birds should be here singing and calling to each other. This quiet felt like death. Was this what it felt like to be dead? Nothing else around but silence and decay. Molding leaves, decaying logs, shriveled-up ferns. Nothing sprouting from the soil. Nothing warming the leaves. Only death and dying.

And cold. She was cold. Too bad they didn't have matches, or she'd rebuild their fire ring and start a fire. She could stay out here all night. Maybe out here her ghosts wouldn't find her.

Larkin opened her eyes and stared at the patch of sky encircled by treetops. It was so dark that she couldn't tell if there were clouds or not. She couldn't see stars, but that might be because she couldn't quite focus. The night was too quiet. The trees needed music. The birds were gone, and the trees needed music. She could sing for them, she decided, and opened her mouth to belt out the first lines that came to mind, which ended up being from David Bowie's "Starman."

She fell quiet, wondering if her mind would be blown if a space person appeared.

Kaia sang the next line, before Larkin was ready to sing it herself, and Jenna joined in. She'd forgotten her cousins were there.

They fell silent again. The song had been one Gramps used to play on his CD player in the family room, and the girls had taken up singing it together. They would often sing together out here in their fort, but that was a long time ago.

To break the silence, Larkin said what had been weighing on her mind all night. "I'm sorry I'm not good company lately. I'm kind of messed up right now."

"That's okay, Lark." Kaia patted her forehead. "We still love you." For some reason, that made her start giggling, and soon Larkin and Jenna were laughing with her.

Suddenly, an important thought came to Larkin's mind and she sat up, swinging her legs toward the fort. "Do you guys know it was only the two of you and Grams who ever sent me care packages and regular emails when I was deployed? My mother couldn't be bothered, of course, and the idea probably never entered my dad's head. But you guys... Did you work out a schedule between you or something? I got something every couple of weeks from one of you. I really appreciated it."

"It was Kaia's idea." Jenna shifted so she was sitting cross-legged facing Larkin. "And sometimes we'd go shopping together for things to send to you."

Larkin shot Kaia a smile of gratitude. "Thank you. It meant a lot to me to know you were thinking of me."

Fat drops of rain started landing all around them. The forest filled with the tinkling sound of drops hitting leaves and bare branches. "Um." Kaia held her hands out to catch the drops. "Maybe we should go inside?"

Larkin and Jenna pointed their flashlights at her and laughed at the hair being plastered to her face, even as the rain did the same to them. In unison, they shook their heads. "Nah."

Larkin rolled over, even before she'd opened her eyes, and bumped into another body. Her first thought was that she'd done it again. She'd drunk so much she'd ended up sleeping with a stranger.

Afraid to look, but knowing she didn't have a choice, she peeled open one eye and was swamped with relief. Jenna lay beside her, still asleep, with drool darkening the pillow under her cheek. They were on the pullout couch in the family room where they'd fallen asleep after stumbling back to the house, drunk and soaking wet.

Larkin rolled onto her back and stared at the ceiling, thinking through the night before. She'd actually talked to them about Afghanistan. And it hadn't sent her into a fit of rage or despair like it usually did when her therapist forced her to talk about it. But still, she hoped no one asked her follow-up questions today. She'd opened up a lot, and that left her feeling exposed and raw, as though her skin had been flayed open.

But she had slept like a normal person. That was something.

"Oh good, you're awake."

Larkin rolled onto her stomach and peered over the back of the couch. The eastern sky was starting to lighten. Kaia sat at the end of the table with a steaming mug of coffee and a laptop, her hair piled on top of her head in a messy bun. "Morning."

Kaia nodded, distracted by what she was reading on the screen. "I had an idea last night when you were talking about Afghanistan, so I got up and started doing some research." She turned and looked at Larkin. "Did you ever eat mantoo?"

Larkin thought. "Is that a rice dish?"

"No, it's a sort of meat dumpling served with split pea sauce and garlic yogurt."

"Yeah, it sounds familiar." Larkin sat up and rubbed her hands over her face to wake up.

"What about a lamb and rice dish called Kabuli pilau?"

Larkin's stomach dropped, remembering the last day she had eaten that dish. She answered vaguely, "Yes, I ate it. It's good."

Kaia's head bobbed. "It's decided. I'll make you an Afghan meal soon."

"You don't have to go to all the trouble," Larkin said, racking her brain for a way to get out of it without hurting Kaia's feelings or revealing too much. "I'm sure it's a lot of work, and the food was just okay." A lie, of course.

Kaia had already dived deep back into research. She waved a hand toward Larkin. "No, no trouble. I'll make it into a blog post, too. It looks fascinating."

Once she'd settled on a food project, there was no talking Kaia out of it. She'd always been interested in the stories associated with foods. What parts of the world they came from, who discovered the ingredient or brought it to the attention of the rest of the world. Who got rich off of it, and who was exploited in its production.

Accepting defeat, Larkin untangled herself from the blankets and went upstairs to take a shower. The emotional walls that usually protected her were badly in need of repair, and solitude was the only way she knew to accomplish that.

Chapter Eight

October 6, 1861: Washington, DC

D avid!" Emily yelled. She grabbed his shoulders and shook him. "Wake up, David!"

His head flopped with the force of her shakes, and the sight unnerved her. She laid him back against the pillow and grabbed his hand in hers, squeezing tightly. "Come on, David. We need you. Wake up."

But he did not respond. His eyes did not open, and his chest did not rise. As Emily watched, the fever-bright spots on his cheeks drained away and his face was left a repugnant gray color. "Come back," she sobbed.

"Emily!" Ben's voice held a note of warning. He had a grim look on his face, and when she met his gaze, he nodded toward the other patients in the room.

She looked around and saw that her grief was upsetting the other sick men, and she knew her tears were reminding them of their own fragility. Worse, her tears probably reminded them that, should they die, no loved ones would be at their bedsides. They would die alone.

The young man in the next bed had his eyes closed, and tears ran down his cheeks. Emily felt ashamed that in the four days she'd been here, she'd never asked his name.

She looked one last time at David, who wasn't David anymore. As she pushed to her feet and forced her spine to stiffen, she said, "Please excuse me."

With her chin lifted and her teeth clenched together, she made her way down the stairs, through the ever-present throng of people, out the back door, and into the stables. She would have locked herself in a privy where no one could bother her, but the smell was too horrible. In the stable she hoped she could have a few minutes by herself. The first stall was empty, and the hay smelled fresh. Grateful for that small blessing, she sank to her knees.

Finally, with no one there to witness it, she let herself cry.

This wasn't supposed to happen. Pa and David were supposed to have come home to them after three months. When that changed with Pa's death—the thought sent another wave of agony through Emily, and she doubled over—the three siblings were supposed to be together. That's why she and Ben had traveled all this way. Now David had been taken from them, too.

This rebellion was supposed to be over by now. The Southern states were supposed to have given up their ridiculous demand for autonomy and rejoined the Union. Not only had that not happened, but they seemed to be more determined than ever. Evidence lay in all the newspapers reporting on skirmishes and battles and troop movements, but Emily had enough evidence right in front of her. The secesh took Pa from her, and now they'd taken David. If not for this war the secesh had started, David would not have been in that military camp where he'd contracted his illness.

Anger burned through her.

Part of her wished she had stayed home where she and Ben were far away from all this death and disease. But even there they would not have been safe from sorrow. Sorrow would have found them either way. She was not sorry they had come because they had been with David when he died. That was a small blessing, at least.

"Emily, are you in there?"

Quickly, she wiped her tears with her sleeves. "I'm here."

Ben appeared in the open stall door. Sorrow dragged on his face. "They want to take David's body, but I told them to wait. I thought you might want to say goodbye."

The words felt like a stake being rammed through her heart. She rubbed at her chest with the heel of one hand. "No, that's all right. I've said my goodbyes."

Ben was silent for a long moment. "Are you sure?"

She was crying again and could only nod in answer.

She could hear Ben's feet crunching over dead leaves as he walked away from her. A terrible thought came to her, and she jumped to her feet to run after him. "Ben, wait!"

He turned around, and raw pain flashed across his face. He'd lost his only brother, and she'd been too wrapped up in her own pain to help him. She opened her arms to him. "Come here."

Ben stepped into her embrace, and his body shuddered with silent sobs. The pain in her own chest grew even larger, and she tightened her jaw to keep from crying out.

"All that matters now is that we have each other," she said to Ben when she felt his body stop trembling. "I'll never leave you. I love you, little brother."

"Yeah, me too," he mumbled against her shoulder.

She knew that was the best she'd get from him, and she smiled, grateful that something was constant.

She took a deep breath and asked the question that had loomed over them these last few days, though she made sure to ask while Ben was still against her so he couldn't see her face. "What now, Ben? Do we go home?"

She felt him stiffen before he abruptly stepped back, his face a careful mask that showed no emotion. "I can't go home, Em. Don't you see?" His eyes slid away from her, and he kicked at a stone with his boot. "Pa wanted me to enlist. You heard him. And even seeing all the horror that this war inflicts on a man, I still want to go. I want to fight so that Pa and David did not lose their lives for nothing. Surely you understand?"

Emily studied her little brother and saw the man that he had become. "I do understand," she told him and, just in time, managed to hold back her next words. She understood, and she would be going with him. There was no way she would allow him to leave her. Too many had left already.

"So, uh." Ben glanced toward the hospital. "We'll talk more later. Right now, I need to get back. Do you want to be there when they prepare the...um...the body?"

She definitely did not. "No. Do you?"

Raw pain flittered across his face, but his nod was confident. "Yes. I think I need to be there."

Emily's heart thumped painfully. She swallowed. "I'm proud of you."

Ben dipped his head.

"I'm going to go find us a room to rent for tonight. Somewhere with a bath." Emily looked at the sky and saw the sun was low on the horizon. It must already be time for supper. "I'll send word so you can meet me there when you finish here."

Ben went back into the hospital, and Emily skirted the building to the street in front. She didn't want to think about what Ben would witness this evening as their brother's body was prepared for burial. Nor did she want to think about David's death, or Pa's death, or the fact that home would never be home again without them. She planned to distract herself from all this by taking the necessary steps toward her new identity. If everything worked out right, she would look very different to Ben when he walked into their rented room later.

But first, she had some shopping to do.

Shopping for a set of men's clothes proved more difficult than Emily had imagined. At home, she or Aunt Harriet had sewn all of the family's clothing, and what they couldn't make themselves, Pa purchased in Paoli. The difficulty wasn't in finding the items, for several shops sold men's clothes. The difficulty wasn't even in making the transaction, for she was well versed on how to choose quality products and to negotiate a good deal.

The difficulty in obtaining men's clothes for herself was the realization that doing so would strip her of the last of their cash and they would be left with nothing.

A thought occurred to her as she was crossing the street, and she stopped so abruptly she was nearly run over by a horse and wagon. Moving quickly to the sidewalk, she turned back the way she'd come. Losing David had upset her so much that she'd left all of their money and belongings at the hospital. She'd kicked the satchels containing everything they'd carried with them from Stampers Creek under David's bed and forgotten about them. If they were still there, she could wear the extra set of clothes Ben had brought.

She hurried back to the hospital and did not stop to talk to anyone on her way up the stairs to the room where they had tended to David. In the doorway she paused. In the bed where David had died now lay another man. A stranger. Deep in the throes of his own illness by the looks of things.

Emily felt sobs boiling up inside her again. The knowledge that David was gone forever kept hitting her mind anew, and each time felt as shocking and painful as the last.

Steeling herself, she crossed the room and, ignoring the sleeping man on the bed, looked under it for their belongings.

There they were, shoved against the wall, her satchel and

Ben's and an Army knapsack that must have been David's. She pulled all three to her and peered inside the knapsack.

David's meager possessions were there, including a pack of letters written in her own hand.

The knowledge that he would never use these things again nearly crushed her, but she shoved the emotions down and looped all three bags over her shoulder as she headed back to the busy street. She had work to do.

Night was falling, and the gas lamps had been lit. She would need to hurry. Respectable women would not dare to be caught out alone at night like this.

Luck was with her as she spied a sign for Mrs. O'Byrne's Boarding House only a block away. But when she asked the rotund woman who answered the door for a room, the woman crossed her arms.

"You've got to pay up front," Mrs. O'Byrne announced.

"How much?" Emily asked, refusing to be cowed.

Mrs. O'Byrne named an exorbitant price, and her jaw fell open when Emily drew a wad of bills from her satchel. "Where's your husband, dearie?"

Emily clenched her teeth as she finished counting out the payment. "I'm not married."

Mrs. O'Byrne eyed the cash. "I don't allow for any immoralities here."

Emily found herself explaining to the woman about her brother's death and her other brother's impending arrival, finishing with, "We need a safe place to sleep and a meal. Can you help us?"

Mrs. O'Byrne finally relented and showed Emily to a room. For a few dollars more, she agreed to send up a warm bath and to send a servant to the hospital with a note for Ben so he'd know where to find her. Once she was left alone, Emily dropped onto the simple double bed, exhausted.

The room held little to recommend it besides the bed, a spindle chair, and a bureau with an oval mirror tacked to the wall above it. An empty washbasin and pitcher sat on the scarred bureau top, and a chamber pot waited in the corner. A quick rap on the door announced the arrival of her bath, and Emily opened the door to the servants, who carried in a large washtub and buckets of water.

As soon as they left, Emily locked the door and dumped the contents of David's knapsack on the yellow bedspread. With two fingers, she picked up a pair of dirt-encrusted socks and dropped them onto the floor. She slipped the packet of letters into her own satchel. She'd decide what to do with those later, when simply looking at them didn't hurt so much. She found a shaving kit rolled into a piece of leather, which she set aside. David had left no extra clothing that would be of use to her, but she did find a small pouch at the bottom of his sack and, inside, a handful of silver dollars, three quarter eagles, and two half eagles. There was also a stack of papers that looked like paper money issued by a sutler for the 9th Indiana Infantry.

"Bless you, David," she said aloud as she stashed it all in her own satchel. The money would be needed. Even the sutler scrip. She was sure of it.

Turning her attention to Ben's satchel, she pulled out his extra clothing and laid it out on the bed. Then, remembering the rapidly cooling bathwater, she quickly stripped off her clothing and sank into the welcoming warm water. Closing her eyes, she leaned back against the cool metal and thought over the day.

She let her tears fall unchecked, even as she admonished herself. Ben would arrive soon and be in need of his own bath. Now was not the time to linger.

She tried to hurry her movements but allowed herself the luxury of washing her long hair as a goodbye ritual to the tresses Pa had always said were so pretty. She soaped her skin and let her hands run over her curves, saying goodbye to them, for after today, she would have to ignore her femininity and suppress all that made her a woman.

When she was clean, she rose to her feet and stepped onto the threadbare rug to dry off. Knowing Ben could arrive at any moment, she quickly donned his extra set of clothing, using a strip of cloth cut from her petticoat as a belt and rolling the cuffs of the trouser legs.

As soon as she looked at herself in the mirror, she realized she'd forgotten one important step. Taking up her discarded petticoat once again, along with the straight razor from David's shaving kit, Emily cut the fabric into wide strips. She slipped out of Ben's shirt and tightly bound her breasts.

With that done, she again put on the shirt, tucked it into the trousers, and faced herself in the mirror.

Not bad.

Now, her hair. Without stopping to think about it for fear she would lose her nerve, she grabbed a damp lock and, using David's straight razor, lopped it off above her ear, dropping it into the empty washbasin on the bureau. She knew if she looked in the mirror, she might stop, so she averted her eyes and kept cutting. The basin quickly filled with blond hair. As she cut off more and more, her head felt lighter. She had never thought about how much her hair weighed, but the lightness felt welcome.

A knock on the door made her freeze.

"Emily, are you in there?"

Ben was here. It was time to show him what she'd done and face whatever he had to say about it.

With a deep breath, Emily dropped the razor onto the bureau and crossed to open the door.

"Oh, excuse me," Ben said, stepping away from the door. He paused, searching her face, and his eyes narrowed. "Emily?"

She grabbed his arm and pulled him into the room, shutting the door firmly behind him and locking it again. "I've decided my name is Jesse. Call me that from now on. I'm your brother, and together we will enlist and finish the duty Pa and David were prevented from finishing."

Ben's mouth opened and closed several times as he backed slowly away from her. When the backs of his legs touched the bed, he sat, still staring at her in shock.

"Say something," she urged, wringing her hands. "Tell me what you think and get it over with. Just know you aren't going to change my mind."

"Em, surely you can't think you'll fool anyone into believing you're a man." He shook his head. "Women are too different. They can't fit into a man's world, and certainly not in the Army."

"They can," she assured him. "Remember Fanny Campbell?" Fanny Campbell was her favorite book heroine who dressed as a man to go to sea in order to rescue her fiancé from the British who'd taken him prisoner. Not only did she rescue her fiancé, but she became a pirate captain and was never discovered to be a woman.

Ben's face twisted. "Fanny Campbell was made up."

"What about..." She stopped to think and came up empty. "I'm sure there were others; I just can't think of them right now. But that's beside the point. I know I can do this, Ben."

Ben's mouth opened and closed again.

"Please?" she begged. She dropped onto the bed next to him and took his hand in her own. "This way I can stay with you. We're the last each other has."

Ben abruptly got to his feet to pace the small room. When he saw the basin full of hair, he paused. "I don't care if Fanny Campbell or anyone else can do it. I don't like the idea of you going to war. Pa would be furious with you. And me for allowing it."

"Pa isn't here." She spat the words at him and then sucked in her breath, wishing she could pull them back inside.

Ben froze, then pivoted away from her to lean both palms on the bureau, his head hanging low.

She went to him and laid her hand on his back. "I'm sorry. That was careless of me." When he didn't move or respond, she dropped her hand to her side but didn't move away. "I know you're trying to protect me, but this is something I have to do. I can fire a musket, I can march, I can sleep on the ground. I can do all of the things a man can do, and I want to do them right by your side."

"Why?"

Emily did not move. "I can't leave you. You're all I have left." Realizing that she needed another reason, something convincing, she added, "Remember when we were little, before Mama died? How I'd run free with you and David, and all three of us would run, jump, yell, and explore the farm?"

Ben looked at her quizzically. "I remember."

"Did you know that on the day Mama died, Pa sat me down and explained to me that I couldn't do those things anymore? That I was the woman of the house now, and I needed to spend my days cooking and cleaning and mending and canning and everything that meant I was locked up at home. I don't want to be locked up anymore."

She touched Ben's back, and he pushed away from the bureau to turn and face her. "I didn't know."

"Oh, don't get me wrong," she reassured him. "I was happy caring for the three of you; I just didn't like being left out of the fun. I feel like I haven't lived and—" She paused, knowing her next words might be hurtful. "And we both know how short life can be. I want to go with you and see this country and fire a musket and march in the rain. I want to live."

He tilted his head to the side and looked so much like Pa that it made her catch her breath. "But you could be killed out there."

Emily dropped onto the bed again and let her hands hang limp between her knees. "I know. But at least I will have lived a little, and I will have spent the time by your side."

Ben raked his hands through his hair and seemed to be thinking through all she'd said. With a burst of air from his lungs, he dropped his hands to his sides. "What if I took you home?"

"Would you stay there with me?"

He looked at her, defeated. "You know I can't do that. I must do my duty for my country."

Emily felt the certainty of her next words settle over her like a blanket. "And so I'll do mine."

Ben drew in a deep breath and let it go loudly.

"Pa said our family will always stand for what's right," she reminded him. "It's right that you serve and that I stand alongside you." Pa may not have wanted his only daughter on the battlefield, but he'd be proud of her for fighting to keep what was left of their family together. "Ben?"

He swallowed, then a half-hearted smile spread over his face. "Hand me that blade. You look like little Ada cut your hair."

Emily didn't immediately obey. Instead, she smiled back at her brother. "Thanks, Ben."

He pulled her against him for a hug. "Oh, Em, promise me you'll be careful. And smart."

"Of course I will," she promised. "But the name's Jesse."

Ben had arranged to have David buried in Congressional Cemetery first thing the following morning. As she sat in their room trying to eat breakfast, Emily was so filled with emotions that she wasn't able to eat the eggs, potatoes, and ham the boarding house matron had prepared for them and only pushed the food around on her plate until it was time to go.

Emily had not thought through what Mrs. O'Byrne would think of a boarder arriving as a woman and leaving as a man. Ben solved the problem by bringing her breakfast plate upstairs for her and later drawing the woman into a lively discussion about the Southern rebellion so that Emily, as Jesse, could sneak out the door unseen.

At the first purveyor they found, Emily purchased a brown

derby hat and men's brogans to complete her disguise. To his credit, the clerk did not pose a single question about the feminine laced boots that she arrived wearing. He simply went about the transaction as though he saw a man wearing women's footwear every day. She left the boots behind when they exited the store. As she stepped onto the sidewalk, she accidentally bumped into a fashionably dressed woman. Smiling, Emily tipped her new hat. "Pardon me, miss." The woman blushed and continued on her way.

When the woman was out of earshot, Emily nudged her brother. "Did you see that?"

Ben laughed. "I saw. Well done. Try lowering your pitch a bit next time."

After only a short distance more, Emily felt Ben's gaze on her, and she turned to find him studying her in a way that made her squirm. "What?"

He shrugged and made an obvious effort to look forward again, but his eyes kept sliding back to her. She stopped in the middle of the sidewalk to confront him. "What am I doing wrong?"

Ben glanced around and drew her out of the flow of pedestrians, nodding to a man and woman walking together on the opposite side of the street. "See that man? See how he holds his shoulders in a tight manner yet his lower body is loose, the movements freer somehow?"

She nodded, though she didn't quite understand his point.

"Now look at the woman on his arm. We can only guess what her lower body is doing under that skirt, but she seems to be carrying herself much more stiffly, as though she feels the gaze of the world upon her and she must not reveal her true self."

Emily raised her eyebrows and looked pointedly at her brother. "Since when did you become so poetic?"

Ben's ears turned pink, but he only shook off her teasing and stepped closer to Emily. With his eyes still on the couple and his voice lowered, he said, "You need to make sure you're moving like the man and not the woman. Or better yet, watch that single man over there. See how he swings his arms as he walks and places all of his foot on the ground with each step as though he's prepared for anything that comes his way?"

Emily nodded. "I see."

"Women take smaller steps, and they hold their arms closer to their bodies. If you're going to convince people you're a man, you need to loosen up, become bold. Oh, and pull your sleeves over your hands when you can."

They resumed walking, and Emily nervously tugged her sleeves down. "Why?"

"Your hands are small. They'll give you away."

Emily curled her hands into fists to hide them even further in her sleeves as she practiced walking like the men she saw, with long strides and loose hips.

Ben burst out laughing. "Okay, reel it in a bit. You look like you've been in the saddle for days and just got off the horse."

Emily was laughing now, too. For several blocks they continued this way, with Ben coaching her as she practiced moving like a man.

Their joviality faded the moment the arched sign over the cemetery entrance came into view. They both stopped short and took a deep breath, the weight of what they were about to do settling heavy upon them.

Congressional Cemetery was peaceful and well maintained. Flowers bloomed along the tree-shaded paths, and the hedges and grass were trimmed so that visitors could clearly read the names of the departed. Emily wanted to hold on to Ben's arm as they found their way to the cheaper and more crowded section where they would lay David to rest, but she refrained from doing so. Men did not cling to one another for emotional support.

A local chaplain awaited them at David's grave site and, when they were ready, stood at the head of the plain wooden casket and began to read in somber tones, "'The Lord is my shepherd; I shall not want...'"

Emily said the familiar words in her head along with the chaplain. With each word, her heart grew heavier inside her chest until she felt it a struggle to stand upright. David lay in that box. He would never again tease her. He would never marry and become a father. Emily would never play with his children nor be fast friends with his wife. How could she live her life without her older brother in it?

"'Surely goodness and mercy shall follow me all the days of my life, and I will dwell in the house of the Lord forever. Amen.'"

Somehow, Emily made it through the short ceremony and even managed to hold back her tears as she paid the chaplain for his time and for the burial. In silence, she watched the chaplain walking away, hoping she never saw him again.

Once he was gone, Emily reached out a shaking hand to Ben, and for several long moments, they held hands and stared at David's simple casket, knowing this might be the last moment they would be close to him. Washington was a long way from home.

Already, the war had taken two of her family. She'd do everything in her power to keep Ben safe. Even if that meant forfeiting her own life instead.

No matter what happened, she would make Pa and David proud of her.

It felt like only minutes since the chaplain had left when two workers arrived with shovels to lower David into the ground and cover him. Emily and Ben moved back to give them room, but they did not leave until the job was finished and the dirt smoothed over the top of the grave.

After the workers left, Emily knelt and laid a hand on the fresh soil. "I love you, David." She wanted to say more, but her words failed her.

When they finally turned away from the grave, the sun was

not even at its crest. They walked for a long while without talking. As they left the cemetery and blended into the crowds on the street, Emily's mind turned to something she had been considering since last night. "What do you think about joining the 9th Indiana? Pa and David's regiment?"

Ben's head swiveled sharply toward her. She stopped walking and turned to look straight into his eyes to show she was serious. "The soldiers there knew Pa and David. They could tell us stories about their last months."

"I would love that, but..." Ben seemed to be struggling to find the right words as his gaze searched her face. "Last chance, Em. Are you sure you can do this? You've seen how brutal this war has already been."

Emily nodded just as a little boy running along the sidewalk bumped into her. She and Ben were blocking the way. She nudged her brother's arm, and they fell into step again. "I think I can. I know I can. I'm not that different from you, you know."

They walked for several blocks without another word until finally Ben guided her toward a building and opened the door for her.

She didn't know what he was up to until she went inside the building and saw a ticket counter and a large board with several different cities and times listed on it. "The train station?"

Ben smiled and headed toward the counter. "We need train tickets if we're going to get to the 9th Indiana's camp, don't we?"

Chapter Nine

October 12, 1861: Union Army Encampment, Cheat Mountain, Western Virginia

*E*mily stood outside the surgeon's tent with trembling knees, trying her best to appear stoic. They had come all this way, had successfully found the regiment camped on Cheat Mountain in western Virginia, and had convinced the officers to allow them to enlist. The only hurdle left lay in the medical examination that Emily had not known would be required until now.

What would they do to her when the doctor discovered she was a woman? Several newspapers had reported on women like herself, and it seemed these women's fates were entirely in the hands of the commanding officer. At best, she would be sent home. Without Ben. At worst, she would be labeled a Confederate spy and hung.

A shudder went through her body, and she felt her bowels threaten to release. She held her breath and squeezed her eyes tight, willing herself to regain control. If she broke down into a weeping mess, they would discover her for sure. Her only hope was to carry on with this charade.

Ben, who was standing beside her at attention, swayed his

body toward her so his arm brushed against hers. She let go of the breath she held and filled her lungs deeply.

"Who do we have here?" Surgeon Meeker threw back the flap to his tent and strode out carrying a sheaf of papers. "We have two enlistees by the name of..." He brought his spectacles to his eyes and squinted at the forms they had filled out. "Wilson. Jesse, age nineteen, and Benjamin, age eighteen, of Stampers Creek, Indiana. Any relation to Calvin Wilson?" The portly man in uniform eyed them over his spectacles.

His white hair made him appear to be a friendly grandfather, but Emily wasn't fooled. She knew her life was in this man's hands. "Yes, sir," she answered, her voice cracking.

"What's that?" he nearly shouted. "When an officer asks you a question, you will answer in a manner that allows him to hear you. Now, I will ask again. Are you a relation of Calvin Wilson of Stampers Creek, Indiana?"

"Yes, sir!" both Emily and Ben barked back.

The doctor nodded. "Then it is with a heavy heart that I give you my condolences. He was well respected by everyone who knew him."

Emily nodded in thanks.

Surgeon Meeker dropped the papers onto the portable desk in front of his tent. "Let's get this over with." He crossed the distance to stand a foot in front of Emily. "Open your mouth wide."

She squeezed her hands into fists and complied.

"Close your teeth as if you are biting. Good. Good." He stepped back. "Now, jump up and down."

Emily wondered when he'd ask her to remove her clothing. After she'd jumped up and down to his satisfaction, the doctor placed one hand on the center of her chest and another on her back, thumping first one, then the other, listening through a stethoscope. Emily dreaded the moment he would feel the bindings under her blouse, but he dropped his hands and moved on to Ben without saying a word.

After the same examination of Ben, Surgeon Meeker returned to his desk where he unscrewed a pot of ink, dipped in his quill, and scratched his signature onto their enlistment papers. "You both are fit for service. Welcome to the Army."

Emily's relief was so great, she thought she might faint. She turned to Ben and found him smiling at her with equal wonder.

"Take these to Colonel Milroy's tent to be sworn in." Surgeon Meeker handed them their papers. "Dismissed."

They hurried across the dusty camp toward headquarters, staring in wonder at everything they passed. A-frame tents, Sibley tents shaped like upside-down cones, tents that had been fashioned into roofs for small, wooden cabins. Soldiers were everywhere, sipping from tin cups as they poked at a campfire with a stick, lying in the shade sleeping, wrestling on the ground with a group of onlookers, cleaning their firearms, playing musical instruments and singing, or playing games with cards or dice. All of this activity didn't even take into account the rows of men in the field beyond doing activities that made little sense to Emily. They looked to be walking around in circles to their officer's commands. From somewhere in the distance came the sound of gunfire, but no one seemed concerned about it so she assumed it was practice rather than a battle in progress.

As they neared the largest tent in the camp, she saw a group of uniformed men sitting on campstools around a rickety-looking table, upon which a map was laid out. One of the officers looked at them and then smoothly slid his hat off his head and over the map as though to obscure it from their view.

The man who seemed to be in charge, judging by the way the others looked to him, as well as by the shiny additions on his uniform, looked up as they stopped in front of him. He had short dark hair parted on the left and combed so neatly he looked as if he was on his way to church. His face was shaved except for a heavy mustache and a bushy strip of hair on the center of his chin. His critical eyes studied Emily and Ben. "These must be our new recruits."

The silence lengthened, and Emily realized they were expected to respond. "Yes, sir!" she answered, remembering to speak loudly.

An aide reached for their papers, looked them over, then handed them to the officer. "These seem to be in order, Colonel."

The colonel got to his feet and approached them. He towered over both of them and ordered them to raise their right hands. "Repeat after me. 'I, state your name, do solemnly swear.'"

"'I, Jesse Wilson, do solemnly swear.'"

Colonel Milroy gave the next line. "'That I will bear true allegiance to the United States of America.'"

They repeated the line and continued until they'd given the full oath. "'And that I will serve them honestly and faithfully against all their enemies and opposers whatsoever, and observe and obey the orders of the President of the United States, and the orders of the officers appointed over me, according to the rules and articles for the government of the armies of the United States.'"

As she spoke the words, tears stung Emily's eyes. These were the same words Pa and David had spoken six months earlier. The words filled her with pride. Finally, she would be doing something big with her life that wasn't caring for a home and family. She'd be doing something that few women experienced, and maybe she would make a difference.

As soon as the simple ceremony concluded, they were shown to the quartermaster's tent and given their uniforms, which consisted of a kepi hat with a horn insignia on the front, a blouse, an overcoat, a dress coat, a poncho, trousers, shirts, drawers, socks, and boots. They were also each given a haversack in which to store their rations, a knapsack to store extra clothing and personal items, a canteen, a half shelter tent, and two blankets, one woolen and one rubber. The quartermaster let them change into their uniforms in his tent—Ben turned his back to give Emily some privacy, which she appreciated—and then they stood before each other with their chests puffed in pride. Neither of their uniforms fit quite right, which Emily was grateful for, since it would aid in keeping her secret. But ill-fitting garments aside, they looked sharp as official soldiers of the United States Army. If only Pa could see them.

From there, they were shown to an open spot in a line of tents and told to make camp. They fastened their two half tents into a full tent that they would share, using the buttons and holes fashioned into them for that purpose.

Word got around camp that two new recruits had arrived, and soon they had several fellow soldiers hanging around. One of them, a lean, freckled man named Quincy Rawlings, even brought them an armful of wood and got a fire going in front of their tent. "Cook will give you a plate, a spoon, a knife, and a cup when you're given your rations at supper. Lose them, and you'll need to buy more from a sutler. You'll also want to be getting yourself a coffeepot and pan to cook in for when we're on the march. We're all on our own at that point."

"Keep your belongings stashed away inside your tent," advised Quincy's tentmate, a younger man who introduced himself as Willie Smith. "The creek is over there, so everyone from camp, even the camp followers, pass by here every day. If you leave anything lying around, it won't be there when you return."

Emily appreciated their advice. She'd seen the disorganized area on the other side of camp where the camp followers lived and was happy not to be among them, as had been her original plan. Pitching their tent in the orderly row with their fellow soldiers made Emily feel like she belonged. She had a purpose.

With their gear stowed safely inside their tent, they were free to relax, as the day was drawing to a close and duty would not start until morning. Emily dragged a log from a short distance away and used it as a bench in front of the fire where several men were regaling Ben with their stories of soldiering. Those that had known Pa and David shared memories of them that made Emily both laugh and have to fight to keep tears in check. She hid her emotions with a scowl.

As she sat at the fire with the other soldiers, Emily could almost believe she was one of them. She laughed at their jokes and knew not to believe everything they told her, for many stories were obviously greatly exaggerated. But then one man, a big-boned, beefy soldier a handful of years older than her, looked up from a letter he was reading and said, "Listen to this, boys. My wife sent along a newspaper clipping about a soldier in a New Jersey regiment who gave birth to a baby." At the exclamations of disbelief from the others, the man slapped his knee in delight. "Turns out it was a woman who disguised herself as a man and a soldier. Boy, they must be idiots in New Jersey."

"That's for sure," another man whose name she didn't know agreed between loud laughs. "Either that or they benefited from keeping the secret, if you catch my meaning."

That started several of the men backslapping each other and offering more crude suggestions. Emily laughed so she wouldn't stand out, but the talk made her nervous.

"If my tentmate were a woman," boasted one man in a voice tinged by a soft Southern accent, "you can bet I wouldn't get much sleep. Wouldn't be able to keep my hands off her during the day neither."

"But if anyone saw you, you'd look like you were buggering another man," his friend countered. "Or maybe you go for that kind of thing." His comment earned him a rough shove that landed him on the ground, where he collapsed into fits of laughter.

Emily looked at Ben and saw that he was thinking the same thing she was. She would be in terrible danger if any of these men learned her secret. She would have to be careful.

She'd been a man for a handful of days now, and she'd spent

all of that time watching and listening. She knew how to fit in, and she knew that now was a good time to display a new skill she'd been dying to try.

Silently, she sucked at her cheeks and drew all of the saliva in her mouth onto her tongue. And then, when the loudest of the men looked her way, she turned to the side and spat onto the ground beside her. To finish the performance, she spread her knees wide and leaned her elbows on them in a decidedly unladylike fashion. Even though she didn't catch the next joke, she laughed loudly along with the others.

Maybe tomorrow she'd have the courage to say a swear word or even try chewing tobacco.

She could hardly wait.

The next morning began early, but Emily was up before almost everyone else. She'd slept in her clothes, as they'd been told, so all she needed to do was put on her boots and coat and step out of the tent, leaving Ben still asleep. She knew she'd have to work extra hard to hide her true gender, and part of that meant bypassing the company sinks, as the latrine trench was called, to squat in the bushes far from curious eyes.

She found relief behind some shrubs a good distance into the forest and wondered how she'd manage later in the day when everyone was awake. She'd best limit her need by restricting how much she drank.

As she returned to camp, the bugle announcing roll call sounded, and she followed the rest of her company to the parade grounds, lining up between Ben and Quincy. Next to Ben was Willie Smith, and Emily was surprised to see them joking around like old friends. When had they become acquainted? Emily had been with Ben all last evening.

When her name was called, she forgot about Willie and turned her face forward to call out, "Present!" A thrill went through her whole body. She had never felt so alive in her life. Here she was, a woman, standing among men and serving her country.

She took to soldiering like a duck to water. Drilling—the strange formations she'd seen the men performing in the field yesterday—appealed to her sense of order. At one point when she turned to face right, as commanded, and found herself face-to-face with Ben, they'd both burst out laughing as he looked around and saw that he'd turned the wrong way. By the end of the morning drill, Emily understood every command and felt like she'd been following them her whole life.

Next, they went to a field where the rest of the company was to practice firing. Ben and Emily first had to go through training on how to properly load and fire their rifled muskets, although both had been shooting for years. Once they'd proven proficient in the task, the sergeant trained them how to fix bayonets and practice ramming them through a bale of hay over and over again. Every muscle in Emily's upper body ached from the exertion. Finally, the sergeant handed them each a cartridge box holding forty rounds and released them to the line with the rest of their company where they learned how to follow the multistep commands to load and fire together as a unit.

Emily had never had so much fun.

When it was time to transition from one task to another, Quincy Rawlings and Willie Smith teased Emily and Ben about being so green, but they also helped them know what to do and where to go. Soldiering, Emily decided, was like having dozens of brothers looking out for her instead of just the two she'd grown up with.

The reminder that David was not here made her heart ache, but she forced herself not to think of him. At least, she did not think of him during the day when there were plenty of other things to occupy her mind. As the sun started slipping behind the trees to the west, however, she found her thoughts going back to David and Pa and wishing they were both here, sharing this adventure with her and Ben.

As Ben joined Willie Smith at his campfire, Emily sneaked away into the woods to relieve herself. She had planned to wait until lights out, but she'd learned the previous night that being out of her tent and in the woods after "Taps" was a serious offense.

The woods around camp were ablaze with color so vibrant it seemed to glow even in the fading light. Interspersed between spruce and fir trees were all the warm colors of autumn— red, orange, gold, yellow. As Emily picked her way through the trees looking for privacy to do her business, dry leaves crunched underfoot and made it impossible to move without notice to anyone who might be about. But, she realized, this also meant that anyone else would alert her to their presence, so she felt reassured.

Once she'd gone far enough away from camp that she no longer heard the sound of the men laughing or playing the banjo or harmonica, she relaxed. Behind a large laurel shrub, she dropped her trousers and squatted, her relief immediate after holding it in for hours.

As she was finishing, a twig snapped nearby and she froze. Someone was there.

Frantic, she pulled up her trousers and fastened her belt as silently as possible. She didn't bother with tucking in her blouse and instead pulled her overcoat tightly around her. For the first time, she realized how foolish she was to walk away from camp without a weapon. Her sergeant had told her to always have it at hand, but she hadn't listened. Now she would pay. Anything and anyone could be out here: an animal about to eat her, a fellow soldier who watched her and now would use the knowledge of her true gender against her, a Confederate sympathizer about to put a bullet in her back… Each idea that came to her was worse than the last.

She hunkered down behind a tree and tried to find whatever

had made the noise, but nothing moved. The forest was hushed and growing darker by the minute. Safety could only be found back at camp, but if she turned and ran for it, she could be killed by whoever—or whatever—was out there.

Dizziness swept over her. With her eyes squeezed tightly shut, she drew in a deep breath and tried to slow her racing heart.

Leaves crumpled under someone's nearby footfall. Her eyes flew open.

Moving as slowly as she could to keep from making any noise, she turned to her right to peer around the tree trunk in the direction of the sound. What she saw made her gasp.

Not even ten feet away, a man dressed in a brownish-gray uniform crept through the woods, his musket in his hands, ready to fire, and his face turned toward the Union camp. She could see his face clearly. Thankfully, he wasn't looking her way and did not seem to know she was there.

The Confederate Rebel was thin and tall. His clothes hung from his frame in a manner that led Emily to think he'd recently lost weight. The Reb's face was tanned, and it had creases at the corners of the eyes and around the mouth in a way that might have been caused from a lifetime of working in the sun or, possibly, from long, hard months fighting this war. And he looked dirty. Hanging from his lanky body were a canteen, a knapsack, and a bedroll, all streaked with grime.

As Emily watched, the Reb moved stealthily through the woods past her until he disappeared down the mountain. For several long moments more, Emily did not dare move.

She must have sat there for a good twenty minutes, and it was only when she heard the bugle calling them to Tattoo, the final roll call of the day, that she was finally able to snap out of the paralysis her fear had instilled.

She ran back to camp as fast as she could, feeling certain that at any moment she would feel the burn of a bullet ripping through her spine. Imagined heat from the Reb's breath on the back of her neck spurred her feet faster until she finally burst out of the woods into camp. Willie gave her a funny look, and Emily realized how she must appear. Scared and secretive.

No matter what, she couldn't bring attention to herself or do anything that would encourage questions of any kind. Spreading her lips into a smile, Emily turned toward the parade ground and forced her feet to slow to a normal pace. As she did, she called back to her brother and Willie, "You coming? You don't want to be late!"

Chapter Ten

Present day: Woodinville, Washington

After Jenna went home and Kaia and Grams left to run errands, Larkin could not stop thinking about Jenna's suggestion that she find Sarah's brother and offer him some of Sarah's photos and other belongings. Larkin would have brushed off the suggestion if it wasn't for the wistfulness she'd always heard in Sarah's voice when she talked about Zach. She'd loved him, idolized him, and then felt betrayed by him when he'd left with their dad and made no effort to see her again.

Maybe Zach regretted that, and maybe he would like something tangible to remember his sister by.

Larkin settled onto her bed with Bowie and her laptop. She first tried Instagram and found a couple of people who might be Zach Faber, though she couldn't be sure. Switching to Facebook, she searched his name and, seeing one man who looked a lot like Sarah, clicked on his About page.

This Zach Faber lived in Walnut Creek, California, and worked for a tech company. He had gone to high school in Sacramento, where Sarah was from, and college at Stanford. Though there wasn't much else that could tell her he was the right Zach Faber, her instincts and the resemblance made her click on Messenger. She left a short message: *Did you have a sister named Sarah? Is this you in the photo?* She then took a picture with her cell phone of the photo of the two kids and attached it to the message. Before she could second-guess herself, she hit Send.

She felt nervous after sending the message. Was she doing the right thing in reaching out to him? Would Sarah be happy that she did, or angry?

When no immediate response came, Larkin decided to get her mind on something else. The diary waited on her nightstand next to Sarah. Perfect.

She'd been afraid of it until she'd read it again last night to her cousins and Grams, and now she was curious about what happened to Emily.

> *October 12, 1861: I am proud to say that I am now a private in the 9th Indiana Infantry, same as David was and same as Ben, who is with me. I was nervous, especially during the medical examination, but the physician only asked us to jump up and down and show our teeth. Maybe it helped that our new officers knew Pa and David. I have my Army-issued uniform and gear. There is a waterproof blanket made of cotton duck and coated on one side with vulcanized India rubber that promises to be useful indeed.*
>
> *Two days ago, while traveling here to western Virginia, I turned nineteen years old. I'm a new age and starting a new and exciting life. The only thing that would make this better would be to have Pa and David here with us. I am listening more than I am talking, and I'm learning fast. Ben is helping. His coughs and elbow jabs have saved me more than once!*
>
> *October 13, 1861: Boy, did I get a fright this evening! While in the woods to find some privacy for personal busi-ness, I spied a Johnny Reb. I thought that was the end of*

me for sure, but he did not detect me and I did not raise an alarm. I should have. I was greatly relieved to make it back to camp. It's curious. Before today, I hadn't thought that I'd have to shoot at actual people with wives, daughters, and sisters. Now I can't forget.

Larkin could relate to the moment of clarity when the enemy stopped being a faceless entity and materialized as a flesh-and-blood human with people who loved him. It was tempting to think about family at home in those instances and lose sight of the mission. That's why the ability to compartmentalize was essential in a soldier. It was too dangerous not to do so, both to herself and to her fellow soldiers.

The diary was making her feel agitated again, so she returned it to the nightstand next to Sarah and carried her laptop downstairs to make a pot of coffee. Kaia's talk last night about the hundreds of women who had disguised themselves to fight in the Civil War had intrigued her, and Larkin decided to search online to see what else she could learn about them. Maybe she could even find mention of Emily Wilson somewhere.

Her search of Emily's name came up with an actress, a professor, a musician, and a vlogger, but nothing on the Civil War–era Emily. She then searched the name Jesse Wilson and got much of the same.

She was about ready to give up on Emily/Jesse when Grams breezed in carrying a potted rosemary bush adorned with a red bow. "It's a madhouse out there. You were smart to stay home today. What are you up to?"

Larkin told her what she was doing and the dead end she'd already come to.

Grams gave Bowie a new chew toy. "You can try using my genealogy website account if you want. I have the full membership so you can search old newspapers and military records and all that." She set the plant on the table. "Here, let me log in for you."

Soon Larkin was diving into records on the genealogy website and was able to identify the correct Emily Wilson, thanks to an aunt of Sarah's who had done their family tree and allowed public access to it.

The only results for a Jesse Wilson came up with men who were clearly not the same person as Emily's alter ego.

Grams slid a plate holding a turkey sandwich and carrot sticks onto the table at her elbow. "You haven't eaten, have you?"

Distracted, Larkin thanked her but turned right back to the computer without touching the food.

Clicking through scans of old newspapers, Larkin searched both names and realized this was a more difficult task than she'd realized when every person ever mentioned in a newspaper with the same name came up as a result. She started wading through, zooming in to read the text carefully and not finding anything about the woman she was looking for.

"I'll never find her." Larkin sighed, looking up from her computer to find both Kaia and Grams puttering around in the kitchen.

"Oh, Kaia." Larkin had to blink and shake her head to switch her mind from the past to the present. "When did you get home?"

Kaia smiled. "Grams says you're researching Emily Wilson. What did you find?" She sat across the table from Larkin and took a bite of her own sandwich.

Larkin rubbed her aching eyes. "Not a lot. Where else should I look?"

Kaia considered the question as she chewed and swallowed. "I'd certainly want to see what the National Archives has on her. Since you have her name and regiment, you should be able to find her alias on Union Army rosters. You can also look for her in Confederate records in case she was ever taken prisoner, but chances of finding anything there are slim. When it became clear the Confederacy would lose, most of their records were destroyed."

"Thanks. I am so surprised that there are records of women serving, yet history teaches that women during the Civil War did nothing more than keep the home fires burning." Larkin took a bite of her sandwich and mulled it over. "You know, it makes me think that, although the U.S. government only recently changed regulations to allow women to fight in battle, there were probably women like Emily Wilson who did it all along. I mean, I personally know several women who were in firefights, myself included, in the Gulf War, Iraq, and Afghanistan long before we were officially allowed to be there."

Grams, busy emptying the dishwasher, finished drying a mug and placed it in the cupboard. "I think you'll find that women have been in all wars the United States has fought, and many of them found themselves in dangerous battle zones. They didn't make it into the history books, or their stories were changed to make their presence somehow shameful."

Larkin felt a familiar anger stir inside. She, and every woman she'd ever known in the military, had had to work twice as hard as a man only to earn half the credit. Or no credit at all. "People still make women's contributions out to be frivolous or shameful. It's bullshit."

Grams sent her a stern look. "I agree that it's aggravating, but you don't need to use that kind of language."

Larkin apologized, though in her head she was still cursing. "I need to find out more about all of these women. People need to know that we've always fought and that we matter. We need to be recognized for our contributions, the same as men."

"You should write a blog with their stories!" Kaia sat up, excited by the idea. "I'll help you set it up."

"Oh no, I couldn't do that." Larkin shook her head. "I'm not a writer."

"You don't have to be a perfect writer. Just tell these women's stories. People will be too interested to be judging your grammar."

Larkin thought about it. She had nothing better to do with her time, and she was already bursting to tell what she'd learned about Emily and Sarah Emma Edmonds to anyone who would listen to her. "Sure, why not?" She looked back at her computer. "I also want to find out more on some of these other women that you say served as men." She typed *Civil War women soldiers* into a search engine and dove back down the rabbit hole.

By that evening, Kaia had Larkin set up with a blog that was ready for her first entry, and Larkin had found several women to write about by searching the internet. She jotted notes on who to include.

The first was Sarah Emma Edmonds, whom Larkin found had published a memoir after the war about her experiences. Larkin found the book, *Nurse and Spy in the Union Army*, online and ordered it.

The second was Charlie Hopper, whom she stumbled across in a random article and whose story was corroborated on a couple different websites. Apparently, Charlie Hopper's real name was Charlotte Hope. After her fiancé was killed in a raid, Charlie Hopper joined the Confederate Army for the sole purpose of avenging her fiancé's death. She vowed to kill one Yankee soldier for each year of his life, for a total of twenty-one. Sadly, she herself was killed in a raid. Larkin scribbled down everything she could find on the woman.

Thinking of what Grams said about women always serving their country, Larkin widened her search and started finding evidence of women who fought in battles from colonial times and the Revolutionary War through all the wars to present day. Some of them disguised themselves as men, but some shouldered muskets and marched into battle wearing the skirts they had always worn. Some were enlisted in the military as nurses, and contrary to popular belief, they were not always safe behind the front lines but intentionally placed themselves smack-dab in the most dangerous areas so they could tend to the wounded, often taking fire and sustaining injury themselves.

The more she researched, the more Larkin's pride grew. These women were badass. Women had *always* been badass, and it was time the world acknowledged that.

By the time she went to bed late that night, Larkin already had Charlie Hopper's story posted on her new blog, with several more stories ready to go in the coming days.

For the first time in a long time, Larkin went to sleep feeling like maybe she wasn't a worthless waste of space. She had been one of these women. It broke her heart that she wasn't allowed to be a warrior any longer, but she had been one. And right up until that day in Kandahar, she had been a damn good one. As Sarah had been.

Thinking of Sarah, Larkin reached again for her laptop and pulled up her new blog. In the "About Me" section, she rewrote the information, dedicating the blog *To Captain Sarah Faber, the best friend any woman (or man) could want beside her in a firefight.*

Chapter Eleven

*T*hanks to Kaia mentioning Larkin's blog to her own readers, Larkin quickly got a following. People seemed to like the stories that she wrote of courageous and patriotic women. Some posts were even going viral on social media, including one about Prudence Wright's guard, an all-female home guard company in colonial Massachusetts. Personally, she loved Mad Ann Bailey's story. Ann, who was born in 1742, was paid by the Army to be an Indian scout and courier, which Larkin decided was equivalent to today's special operations.

She posted four stories that first week and was shocked when readers started leaving comments and even sending her emails. She ignored the trolls in favor of the majority who thanked her for the stories or shared their own connections to the stories—an ancestor who was a member of the guard, an elementary-school field trip where they learned about these women, that kind of thing. Some suggested new stories for her to research and write about. At Kaia's urging, Larking started a spreadsheet of all the women to keep them organized.

One email broke her heart. It was from a mother whose daughter had been killed in Iraq. She was a medic with the

Navy, riding in the second vehicle in a convoy from Bagram to Fallujah. When the lead vehicle hit an IED—improvised explosive device—she was one of the first to reach the injured marines. She pulled two out of the burning vehicle and was treating the third when she was hit multiple times by a sniper hiding in a nearby house. She saved three men but lost her own life on the medevac ride to the hospital.

Larkin burned with the need to ensure this woman was remembered. She shared her story on the blog and included a photo that the mother provided. That night, she had nightmares about IEDs and exploding trucks and voices calling out for help, but she wasn't going to allow that to stop her from writing the blog.

Soon, more parents, sisters, brothers, friends, and fellow service members were sending her stories of their lost loved ones. Each story helped to paint a bigger picture of all the women who bravely fought and died for their country. Each story was one more brick in the wall Larkin was building to tell the world that women are fighting, making a difference, and making the ultimate sacrifice, and they've been doing it all along.

Behind every story was a growing guilt that she wasn't writing the story most important to her—Sarah's story. But she couldn't. Sarah's story was tied so closely to her own that to talk about Sarah would mean talking about herself, and she wasn't ready to open up like that. She might never be.

Not all the stories she received were about women who were killed. Many were about women still serving. Stories about mothers who didn't see their young children for an entire year except through online connections, yet they reported to work every day because they had a job to do, and they did the job well. Daughters who carried on family military tradition by enlisting in the same battalion where their fathers or grandfathers had once served. Sisters who inspired younger brothers to shoot for goals higher than they'd previously imagined by never giving up despite the numerous obstacles put in their paths.

One Vietnam veteran wrote to Larkin asking if she would share her story. She had been an officer in the Women's Army Corps, or WAC, and had been tasked, along with a male noncommissioned officer, with helping the South Vietnamese train their own women's army corp. She did this despite the fact that the WAC did not provide her with adequate training, having eliminated vital programs such as weapons familiarization because, she was told, it was "a waste of time that failed to contribute to the image we want to project." That image was of wholesome and pretty young women in modest skirts standing behind the brave strong men, supporting them as the men did the *important* work. So, despite resistance from her superiors and sexist criticism of all women in uniform from the country as a whole, she trained herself and then trained hundreds of Vietnamese women.

In between all of this, Larkin continued to read Emily's diary. Some days she only managed a few entries before something Emily wrote sent her back to the internet to get more information. She was surprised at how easily Emily and her brother were able to enlist. They'd simply walked into camp and stated their intention. Their medical exam had been a joke. Larkin went online and discovered that the Wilson siblings' experience was not uncommon, especially in the first year of the war. Even though today's military was voluntary, people were turned away all the time for medical reasons, or for reasons such as having a visible tattoo on the neck or wrist. It seemed the requirements were much more relaxed during the Civil War, even before conscription started.

Larkin was happy to have something to do with her time beyond managing her own symptoms. She still felt the need to clear the house at night, and her nightmares still plagued her to the extent that she tried to drown them out with booze, but at least she had a reason to get out of bed every day. That was more than she'd had a month ago.

A few days later, Kaia cooked the Afghan meal she'd promised Larkin and invited Jenna and Evan over to share it. All afternoon, the scents of cardamom, mint, garlic, fried dough, and roasting lamb filled the house, although Kaia would not allow Larkin near the kitchen. She was so excited about giving Larkin this gift that Larkin didn't have the heart to tell her the smells were triggering memories that weren't all welcome.

Needing a break from the aromas as well as from her reading and blogging, Larkin decided to escape for a few hours and take Bowie for a walk. It was an uncommonly clear day for December, and she knew another might be months away.

Letting Bowie lead the way, she set off down the deck steps and across the grass to the trail that wound through the woods, past their old fort, to join with the neighborhood path that eventually merged onto the Tolt Pipeline Trail. The trail was a swath of open land about eighty feet wide with a dirt-and-gravel section in the middle that cut straight across King County and was popular with runners, mountain bikers, walkers, and even horseback riders. Larkin and her cousins had spent hours on the trail when they were kids, and coming here felt like stepping back in time.

Larkin heard the sounds of children calling to one another and the loud whine of a leaf blower starting up, evidence that she wasn't the only one feeling the need to take advantage of the break in the weather. Around her, though, the forest was hushed, which soothed her.

Although quite nippy, the air felt good on her skin, all full of moisture and oxygen so clean she almost wished she could strip off all her clothes and run naked through the woods, soaking it up.

She decided to turn west on the trail, toward the winery district in Woodinville. Larkin felt like a puzzle piece slipping into place as her feet followed the paths she'd walked for years.

Because it was a Saturday, the trail was busy with a wide range of people: a mom group with babies strapped to their chests or riding in backpacks, joggers with earbuds stuffed in their ears, middle-aged couples giving their dogs a long leash to explore, a couple of guys who raced by on mountain bikes. Three teenage girls on horses leisurely made their way out of a forested trail to the main trail and turned east. Larkin thought about going home to avoid the crowd, but knowing she would be on edge there, she kept putting one foot in front of the other. Bowie trotted happily beside her.

She spent the time looking at the houses, yards, and pastures she passed, and enjoying the rare sunshine that kept the chill of the wind from biting too deeply. As long as she kept studying the landscape, she found she could keep thoughts of Afghanistan at bay. Although there were mountains and forests in that country, Larkin had only served in the desert, where everything was a chalky-tan color. The green here, even at this time of the year, soothed her eyes and her soul.

Before she realized how far she'd gone, she found herself standing at the top of the hill that locals referred to as Heart Attack Hill, so named for its steep incline. When they were kids, she and her cousins raced each other up the hill. When that got easy, they'd raced up, down, and back up again. Usually Larkin or Kaia's older brother, Tanner, won, but occasionally Jenna had surprised them with a last-minute burst of energy.

From the top, Larkin could see down to the bottom where the city had newly installed a crosswalk stoplight on the busy Woodinville-Redmond Road. Although her view was blocked by trees, she knew the wine-tasting rooms, including her uncle's, were to the left. The district had grown from the first and only winery in the 1970s, Chateau Ste. Michelle, to now over a hundred wineries and tasting rooms, all of whom sourced the majority of their grapes from eastern Washington vineyards.

A glass of wine sounded like the exact thing she needed.

She started down the hill, stepping carefully so she didn't jar or further injure her bad knee. Bowie looked longingly down the hill as though she wanted to race ahead, but she must have sensed Larkin's pain because she didn't pull on the leash and sat patiently every time Larkin paused to rest.

Once Larkin reached the road, she realized her plan wasn't perfect. There were no sidewalks leading to the wineries from here. Cars zipped by nearly constantly, so walking on the road wasn't an option.

She peered across the road and saw that the trail continued past farmland to the Sammamish River and the paved biking and walking path running alongside it. If she took that route, she could make a loop back to the winery on the path and the side-walk along the road that ran east-west back to the winery district.

But that would add almost another mile, and her knee was already aching. She needed a break, and a glass of wine, before heading home up Heart Attack Hill. She could not manage another mile.

Larkin looked again at the road and the tasting rooms she could now see not even a quarter mile away. A narrow, dirt shoulder ran along the side of the road. It wouldn't be safe and one tipsy driver would be all it would take to end her, but she was willing to risk it.

Determined, she started walking, ignoring the cars whizzing past and keeping her own body between the road and Bowie.

When she arrived safely at the roundabout, she paused, searching the buildings on every corner for the sign announcing Uncle Matt's winery. There it was. Opposite corner.

She started across the crosswalk but had to stop in the middle as a car whose driver didn't see her nearly ran her over. "Watch it!" she yelled angrily, but loving the spurt of adrenaline that shot through her. She lived for that feeling. It's what had kept her alive in Afghanistan.

Outside the tasting room, she found a dog dish of water near the doors and a railing close by that she could tie Bowie's leash to. "Wait here, girl. I won't be long." She gave Bowie's neck a two-handed rub, then patted her on the head. "Be good while I'm gone."

The tasting room looked like a Pacific Northwest lodge, with natural wood and stone everywhere. Inside, she found a huge fireplace with a decorative metal screen in front of the crackling fire. Even though she hadn't felt cold during her walk, the warmth of the room wrapped around her, and she thought she might never want to leave.

She walked toward the counter looking for a familiar face. The only employee behind the counter was a woman she didn't recognize.

"What can I get you?" the woman asked, her long, curly black hair framing perfect skin and a warm smile. Her hair reminded Larkin of Sarah's, but she refused to linger on that thought.

"Whatever is your most popular white, please." As she waited, she thought about asking if her cousin or uncle was in, but then she changed her mind. If she saw them, fine. But really, she didn't feel like making small talk. The woman pulled the cork from a bottle and poured Larkin a glass, describing the wine as she did so. "Here you go. Enjoy."

Leaving some bills on the counter, Larkin carried her wine to the deep armchairs by the fireplace and dropped into one, stretching her aching leg out toward the warmth and sighing with pleasure. Taking a long sip of the wine—excellent, of course—she dropped her head back and closed her eyes. She wouldn't be able to stay long, or she'd be late for Kaia's dinner.

After a few minutes, the wine and the warmth got the better of her, and she felt herself sliding into sleep, unable to stop the descent.

Nahid's face swam before her, smiling in the cocky way he had that made him seem older than his twelve years. He laughed, said something in his native Pashto, then chased after his friends who were kicking a soccer ball in the street. "Bring me candy tomorrow, Captain Bennett," he shouted back to Larkin. "I will show you again my good English."

Larkin laughed and promised him candy tomorrow if he impressed her with the words he'd learned. She knew she'd give him the candy anyway, even if his new English words were vulgar swears he'd learned from the men in her squad. Heck, she'd give him candy for nothing. Nahid had become her friend over the four months that she'd been visiting the police station in his neighborhood. He was there every time, and he always greeted her with a mischievous grin.

She stood at the police station gates with two Afghan police officers on guard, watching the kids play. Suddenly, everyone except for her and Nahid disappeared. She called to him, but he didn't turn her way. She called out again, terrified that something was very wrong.

He turned toward her and started running straight for the gates, only he was no longer Nahid. He was a grown man wearing a white shalwar kameez with a brown vest and an unfastened green winter coat over it. On his head he wore a brown pakol hat. He looked at her as he neared, and his bearded face filled with hatred.

She lifted her weapon and yelled in Pashto, "Stop!"

He kept running, and now she saw that he held a SAW—an M249 squad automatic weapon—and it was pointed straight at her.

She yelled again for him to stop, but he ignored her. If anything, he ran faster. She pulled the trigger.

With a violent jerk, Larkin woke, spilling the wine still in her hand all over her pants. "Damn it!"

Realizing where she was, she looked around sheepishly. An older couple was cozied over a small table a short distance away, but they weren't paying her any attention. A group of women who must have come in while she slept were gathered around the counter, peppering the poor woman working there with dozens of questions and requests.

No one seemed to notice her. Larkin slowly released a pent-up breath.

The front door opened, letting in a gust of cold air and the words, "Aren't you a good dog! Where's your owner?"

Larkin realized the person must be talking to Bowie, which made her feel guilty for leaving her out in the cold. With a glance at the clock on her cell phone, she realized she needed to head home anyway.

She left her empty wineglass on the counter and turned to head out when one of the women called to her friend, "Anna, you've got to try this one!"

Larkin felt the ground drop away from her when she heard the name "Anna." Maybe it was the dream she'd just had still weighing heavily on her mind, but she could have sworn the woman had said Anahita. Not Anna.

Anahita. The one name—the one person whom Larkin refused to think about or talk about. To hear it here, in the last place she would have expected, hit her in the gut like a cannonball to the stomach.

Even as she fought to regain her breath, the vision hit her.

She was no longer standing in her uncle's tasting room, but on a dusty road lined on both sides with stalls and carts and tables loaded with goods for sale. Everything was covered in dust, but the shopkeepers did their best to beat the fabrics clean and wipe the grime from vegetables, fruits, jewelry, pots, and trinkets.

She kept one hand on her M4 as she and her team patrolled the street, letting the Afghan National Police officers lead the mission. Larkin walked ten meters behind Sarah and knew an ANP was five to ten meters behind her. The distance between them was intentional to reduce loss in case of an IED or suicide bomber.

Before Larkin even realized there was a threat, the ping of a bullet hitting the parked car beside her made her hit the deck. Crouched low, she shuffled around the car so that it was between her and where the shot had come from, and as she did so, she yelled, "Take cover!"

"Ma'am, are you okay?"

"Stay down!" she yelled back. Wait. She didn't know that voice. It didn't belong.

"Ma'am, can I call someone for you? An ambulance?"

The vision faded, and Larkin found herself crouched behind the armchair in the tasting room. Every single person in the room stared at her with a mixture of horror and pity on their faces.

The woman who worked there was leaning over her. Worry, and more than a little fear, stretched her features taut. "What can I do to help you?" she asked softly.

To her horror, Larkin's eyes welled with tears. She squeezed them tightly shut and managed, "Nothing. I'm okay."

When she thought she could stand, she got achingly to her feet and lifted her chin. With her gaze fastened on the front door to avoid eye contact with anyone else, she started in that direction. "Please excuse me."

She didn't wait for an answer, nor did she say anything else as she pushed into the cold air and found Bowie waiting for her. Her tail wagged in delight upon seeing Larkin, and the trust and love in her big brown eyes was nearly Larkin's undoing. She had to swallow twice before she could squeak out, "Come on. Time to go." She tugged Bowie's leash free and headed toward the trail.

Except, she didn't make it across the parking lot before she thought she heard a weapon fire, and she flinched. When she looked around, though, no one else had heard a thing. It was in her imagination.

One thing, she realized. One more thing and she would snap. She was strung so tightly that Bowie felt it. She was looking up at her and whining.

Defeated, Larkin sat on a curb in the crowded parking lot and pulled out her cell phone. "Jenna?" she said as soon as her cousin answered. "Can you come pick me up? I'm at your dad's winery."

"What's wrong?" Jenna sounded alarmed.

"I'll tell you when you get here. Hurry." She ended the call before Jenna could ask any more questions. As she waited, Larkin petted Bowie's soft fur, feeling as if the dog's steady presence was the only thing keeping her from a complete breakdown.

Time lost all meaning, but eventually Jenna pulled up in her black SUV and opened the back door for Bowie. Larkin wordlessly slid into the passenger seat.

On the drive to Grams's house, Jenna asked several questions, but all Larkin could manage was the single word "Flashback." She looked out the window and didn't say anything else. She was too busy coaching herself to hold it together.

"You can talk to me, you know." Jenna's voice was soft and understanding. "You don't have to bear it all by yourself."

Tears filled Larkin's eyes, but she didn't respond. She couldn't. She knew Jenna meant well, but she had no idea what Larkin was going through. She couldn't possibly know. No one could. No one had seen the things she'd seen or done the things she'd done. Jenna said she could bear it with her, but she couldn't. The burden Larkin carried was unbearable for anyone. She wouldn't put that on the people she loved.

"Thanks for coming for me," she muttered as they pulled into Grams's driveway and parked behind Kaia's car. "I should have known better than to go to public places." She got out and slammed the door to show she didn't need a reply. Opening the back door, she gathered Bowie's leash and led her into the house as Jenna followed behind.

"I'm back!" she called out as she slipped out of her tennis shoes and unhooked Bowie's leash. When she saw Grams, Kaia, and Evan in the kitchen with concerned looks on their faces, all Larkin could think about was to escape. "I, uh...I need a shower, but I'll be quick. I promise."

The warm spray of the shower helped wash away her anxiety. Her fear. Her shame. She stayed there for a good ten minutes, a record considering her Army training had instilled the habit of no more than three-minute showers. As she stepped out and dried off, she felt a little more like herself again. She slicked her hair back into the bun she'd mastered in the service and swiped lip balm on her lips. With a fresh pair of jeans and a warm sweater on, she didn't quite feel ready to face her family, but she knew she couldn't put them off any longer.

But as she came down the stairs, she heard them talking and she paused to listen. They were gathered around the kitchen island and talking in hushed tones. They hadn't seen her yet.

"Tiffany said she really freaked people out, yelling for them to 'get down' and hiding behind the chair herself." Grams must have called the winery. Larkin burned with embarrassment.

"I read those articles you sent all of us, Grams," Jenna said in response. "But I guess I didn't believe that's what Larkin's going through. You should have seen the terror on her face when I picked her up. It was like she'd witnessed something horrific. It scared me, but she wouldn't tell me what happened."

"I'm thankful she called you." Grams patted Jenna's arm reassuringly. "She has good days and bad days. All we can do is be here for her and hope the good days start outweighing the bad pretty soon."

Larkin sank onto the stairs and dropped her head into her hands. She'd had no idea her family was that worried about her, nor that they'd been noticing the extent of what she was going through. She'd believed she was hiding the worst of it.

She hadn't come home to drop all of her shit in Grams's lap, that was for certain.

Maybe she should leave. The inpatient PTSD program had helped. But maybe it wasn't enough. Maybe she should go back.

"Oh, Larkin, there you are." Grams shuffled to the kitchen table, carrying a stack of plates and smiling as though everything were normal. "We're about to sit down for dinner. I hope you're hungry, because Kaia has truly outdone herself."

Larkin decided to play along. She'd had enough of being the center of drama for the day. Plastering on a smile, she went the rest of the way down the stairs and reached the kitchen island at the same time the others broke into motion. Jenna and Kaia each reached for a dish of food as Larkin stuck her hand out toward Jenna's husband. "Evan," she greeted him. "Good to see you."

He smiled back as he shook her hand, and Larkin saw what had attracted Jenna to him. With chiseled cheekbones, a strong jaw, and an athlete's body, he was a good-looking guy who obviously took care of himself.

Soon the bustle of getting the food on the table distracted Larkin from the elephant in the room—namely, her—and she was able to sit with the others and act as if she were normal. She'd become good at acting, after all.

Kaia sat at the head of the table, her cheeks rosy from the heat of the kitchen, and presented every dish along with a bit of research she'd uncovered about the food and its history in Afghanistan. She lifted the lid of a large platter with a flourish. "This, I've discovered, is considered the national dish of Afghanistan. It's called Kabuli pilau." She hefted a large scoop onto Larkin's plate. "You said you ate it over there, right?"

Larkin looked at the heavily spiced rice and lamb dish and felt the memories push into her mind. "Yes, I did. Sometimes the local police officers would cook for us. This dish, or a version of it, was almost always included. It's delicious."

Although she knew the others wanted to hear her stories from Afghanistan, it was clear no one was willing to push her on it, and for that she was grateful. She was still raw, her senses dulled. She wanted to show her appreciation for Kaia's work, but it was all she could do to stay in her chair.

When Kaia presented a platter of bulani, Larkin reached for one of the fried pockets of bread filled with veggies. She ripped a piece off and dipped it into the ramekin of fresh yogurt that Kaia had placed at each place setting. "This was my favorite of all Afghan foods," she managed. "Especially the ones filled with potato and garlic." She took a bite and felt for a conflicted moment that she was standing on a Kandahar street. "Is this pumpkin?"

Kaia nodded, taking a bite herself. "And walnuts."

"I love it." Larkin ate the rest of the bulani hungrily and wished she could relax. As she ate, she tried to keep up with the conversation and even managed a question to Evan about work, though she wasn't able to focus on his answer. Her body felt like spiders were crawling under her skin, and she had to concentrate hard not to let her agitation show.

After the meal, Kaia asked, "I have dessert, but should we clean up dinner first and eat it later when we have room?"

"I'm afraid we need to be leaving," Evan said, his biceps bulging from his T-shirt sleeves as he pushed back from the table. Larkin was the only one who didn't protest.

"Evan, an extra half hour won't kill us," Jenna said. "Let's stay. I want to see what an Afghan dessert is like."

Evan scowled, not bothering to hide his irritation. The tension in the room made Larkin ache to escape, but she stayed put and watched as Evan drew his wife to the side and hissed, "I didn't want to come here tonight at all, but you made me. We've eaten dinner, and now we're leaving."

Jenna said something back, but Grams chose that moment to start making a racket with the dishes in the sink. Soon, Jenna was making the rounds with hugs and thanks. "That meal was phenomenal, Kaia. We should have it again sometime."

"I'm afraid the tea won't be any good cold, but I can wrap up some sheer pira and cardamom pastries for you to take home," Kaia offered.

Jenna made Evan wait long enough for Kaia to place a covered paper plate in her hands, and then they were out the door. Larkin, casting a glance at the clock to see how much longer until she could also escape, asked, "Is Evan always such a dick?"

The question made Kaia laugh. Even Grams bit back a smile. "Yes," Grams said as she filled a bowl with dog food for Bowie. "He has been that way for months now. Jenna won't tell me what's really going on."

"I know they've been fighting about starting a family." Kaia scooped leftover rice into a plastic container. "She wants so badly to be a mom, but he says it's too soon."

Larkin managed to last through the cleanup and dessert, and then she finally escaped upstairs to the solitude she so desperately needed. She felt like a reinforced door that had been bludgeoned by a battering ram for hours. The meal had indeed been delicious, but it had been too much for her on the heels of her flashback.

A bottle of gin helped her fall asleep. In her dreams she walked the marketplace. Over and over again, bombs exploded, bodies ripped apart.

"Sarah!" she screamed and jerked awake. Sweat covered her, and the blankets and sheets on her bed were in shambles.

Her bedroom door flew open and there was Grams, followed closely by Kaia, both in their pajamas, their eyes wide with panic.

"What's wrong?" Grams got to her first, switching on the bedside lamp and reaching for Larkin, who fell against her chest, sobs she couldn't hold back any longer pouring out.

"It's my fault," she cried. "It's my fault she's dead."

"No, it's not," Grams argued and rubbed her back. "You did the best you could. It was war. These things happen."

"You weren't there. You don't know," Larkin insisted.

"So, tell me," Grams urged. "Tell me what is hurting so deeply. Let me share your load."

Grams's words felt as if they scooped right into Larkin's chest and pulled her heart out of her body, leaving her weak and defenseless. "Anahita. I killed her, too."

She felt Grams's body stiffen. "Who is Anahita?"

"Nahid. The boy in the street. He was Anahita."

For several long moments Grams didn't say anything. She simply pushed Larkin's hair off her face and held her as she cried.

"Tell us, soldier girl," Grams urged again when Larkin's breath smoothed out. "Tell us what happened to you."

Larkin opened her eyes and saw Kaia sitting on the foot of her bed, tears running down her cheeks. Seeing her cousin's tears made the ache in her own chest grow. She never meant for her coming home to hurt anyone, yet that's exactly what she was doing. When would it stop?

She was so tired. Tired of hurting and tired of carrying her shame around, hiding it from the world as though ignoring it would make it go away when, really, it only grew stronger.

For a moment, she thought about lying, about saying she was fine, that it was only a bad dream. But her weakness won out. She wasn't strong enough to lie anymore. She deserved to feel their judgment and hatred once they knew the truth. She deserved to be punished.

So she told them, from the beginning, about the worst day of her entire life—the last day of Sarah's life.

"Sarah was frustrated when she learned her deployment to Afghanistan was going to delay her promotion to captain," she began. Pulling away from Grams, she hugged her pillow and stared at the wall she continued, "I was secretly happy, though, because as a first lieutenant she was able to attach to my company as a platoon leader. In Afghanistan, I saw her on a regular basis when I did my rounds checking on my platoons. I was there that day when Nahid first showed up."

She felt Grams shift so that her back rested against the headboard, but Larkin didn't look at her. She was being pulled back to that day so many months ago, and as she told Grams and Kaia the story, she felt like she was living it again.

There were about a dozen of them. Little Afghan boys who liked to play soccer in the street outside the police station. All were clean, well fed, and obviously cared for, though Larkin never saw their parents. The kids showed up after school and played until sundown, and they reminded Larkin of herself and her cousins running wild at Gramps and Grams's house all summer. As she emerged from the police compound with her team to go on dismounted patrol that day, the kids surrounded them with huge grins. When they discovered the soldiers were Americans, they insisted on practicing their English.

"Candy!" one of them begged, his little palm held open toward Larkin.

"Amrica," another boasted, pointing to the flag patch on her shoulder, twisting the name but obviously proud to know the country to which it belonged.

Larkin looked at Sarah, and they both grinned. They loved this part of their jobs, and they kept Jolly Ranchers and Tootsie Rolls in their pockets for this very reason. While the Afghan National Police grumbled under their breaths, Larkin and Sarah and the other Americans in the unit handed out candy and chatted with the boys.

It was always only boys. No girls. Girls were kept inside where they were protected and instructed on how to run a household.

One little boy pushed past the others to get to the front. He marched right up to Larkin, pointed to her name tape and sounded out what he saw there. "Buhn-net."

She smiled and handed him a watermelon Jolly Rancher. "Bennett. I am Captain Bennett."

"Captain Bennett," he parroted, flawlessly.

"What is your name?" She pointed to his chest. "Name?"

His eyes twinkled in delight. He puffed with pride, pointed to his own chest, and announced, "I am Nahid."

Surprised by his grasp of English, Larkin handed him another candy. "Nice to meet you, Nahid."

He popped the candy into his mouth where it bulged his cheek out as he answered, "Nice to meet you, Bennett."

As the patrol moved out, Nahid led the other boys back into the soccer game. Every time Larkin saw him after that, he was always at the head of the pack and the first to sound out new English words. Some of the guys in the unit liked to teach the kids American swear words, and the boys always giggled as though they knew they were being naughty. Nahid was bold and would say the words with confidence.

From that day on, Larkin kept an eye out for Nahid, and whenever she saw him, she made sure to stop and talk with him and share her candy. Sometimes he shared his naan with her. His smile was always ready and endearing. He was brash, loud, and funny, and she looked forward to seeing him every day she was in his neighborhood.

But then one day he wasn't there. When Larkin asked Sarah about him, she said she hadn't seen him for weeks. Larkin figured he must have been sick or needed at home, and she didn't worry until two weeks later when she stopped in again and he still wasn't there. Sarah had not seen him in all that time. No one had.

"Fahim!" Larkin called to Nahid's buddy as she waved him over and handed him a Tootsie Roll. "Where is Nahid?"

Fahim, wearing western-style jeans and a puffy jacket with a pillbox hat on his head, gave a nonchalant shrug of his shoulders. "Nahid *bacha posh*. Now Anahita. Married." Before Larkin could ask another question, he ran off to join the others.

The words made no sense. Larkin didn't speak Pashto or Dari, the languages of Afghanistan, so later she asked the terp what *bacha posh* meant. Her answer shocked Larkin and Sarah both.

Bacha posh literally translated to "dressed like a boy." It was a term given to little girls who were being raised as boys. The practice was, apparently, not uncommon in Afghanistan, where producing a son was the only way for a woman to gain respect from the community and her own family. Sons were revered because they were the ones who would inherit property and secure the family's future. Daughters were lost to their husband's family and were considered worthless until they produced a son of their own.

In families that produced only daughters, it was believed that dressing one of the girls as a boy would bring honor to the family and good luck so that the next child born would be a boy. Until then, or until the girl reached puberty, she took on the role of the family's honored son. With that change in status, she was able to live as a boy, running free in the streets, riding in the front seat of a car, sitting with the men, speaking her opinion, cutting her hair, and laughing out loud...all things denied girls. When she reached puberty, she was changed back into a girl and married off, every one of her freedoms stripped away in a single moment.

"But she's too young," Larkin protested after hearing all this.

The terp shrugged. "If she has started to bleed, she is not too young for marriage." The terp turned back to her work and forgot about Nahid/Anahita, clearly not as disturbed by the news as Larkin was.

Larkin stopped into that police station a week later, and when she asked, none of the boys had seen Anahita. Larkin had not been able to stop thinking about the poor girl. That day, the team planned a dismounted patrol of the local open-air market, and Larkin was happy to tag along, partly because she loved interacting with the locals and observing her officers in action, but also because she hoped to run into Anahita. Patrols like this one had the dual purpose of establishing a police presence in the community so locals felt safe and learned to trust the police, while allowing the ANP officers to pick up on any whisperings of insurgents in the area.

They were an hour into the patrol when they paused for the terp and some ANP to question a man with a suspicious package strapped to his motorcycle. Larkin felt comfortable leaving it to them and had turned toward a mango stand, thinking she should buy a couple to take back to the compound for Sarah, who had stayed behind. A voice she recognized spoke beside her, "*Asalaam u aleikum*, Bennett."

The voice was so quiet, she wondered if she'd imagined it. But, when she turned, a burqa-clad woman stood next to her. "Nahid?"

The blue head nodded and turned to look at a knot of women gathered together at the next vendor's stand, five yards away. In a low voice so no one would overhear, she said, "I am now Anahita. I should not be talking with a *khareji*, a foreigner. My husband would not approve."

"*U aleikum salaam*," Larkin responded to her original greeting, albeit delayed, with her hand over her heart as was customary. "Are you happy, Anahita?" Larkin kept her eyes on the mangoes, picking one up, squeezing and discarding it, continuing the motion over and over without thought.

"I miss Nahid." Anahita stopped, as though deciding whether to say more. "I do not like cooking and cleaning and being watched."

Larkin thought about this. In Anahita's place, she would be losing her mind. "Is your husband kind to you?" In the corner of her eye she saw Anahita's entire body shrink.

"No," she whispered. "I do not please him."

Larkin carefully set the mango down and clenched her hands into fists. "Does he hurt you?"

"Anahita!" a voice cut between them, making them both jump.

Larkin turned to find three women standing behind them, all wearing burqas matching Anahita's. The one in the middle was larger than the other two and clearly the woman in charge. She stood ramrod straight and a full step in front of the others. Although Larkin could not see their faces, not even their eyes, she could feel hatred and suspicion pouring from them. The middle woman unleashed a stream of Pashto onto Anahita, berating her. Before Anahita could say a single word, the woman grabbed her arm and led her away, quickly disappearing into the crowd of shoppers.

Larkin was furious. This poor little girl had been married off to a man who abused her, and overnight she'd gone from a fun, carefree soul to having her every move monitored.

Back at the FOB, Larkin asked the cultural experts and her Afghan friends what could be done for Anahita and learned there was nothing she, nor anyone, could do. Anahita was now her husband's property, and she must abide by his wishes. Pashtunwali, the way of living for Pashtun people, fiercely protected a woman's honor and that of her family. If Larkin, a foreigner, tried to intervene, she would dishonor all involved and Anahita would likely pay the price.

Four days later, one of the soccer players outside the police compound arrived with a note for Larkin. Sarah was there and read it, then got on the comm system to track Larkin down and tell her about it. The note was from Anahita asking Larkin to meet her in the marketplace the following day.

Larkin should have reported it up the chain of command, but she didn't. She told herself that Anahita was a harmless and lonely little girl who she might be able to help. Larkin was scheduled to stop into Sarah's station in the coming week anyway, so she arranged her schedule so she could tag along on their marketplace patrol the next day. Only Sarah knew Larkin was planning to meet Anahita.

The morning chill had already burned away, and heat was rising by the minute. The ANP were in charge of the patrol, and the Americans were there for support and backup. Altogether, there were six ANP, four guys from Sarah's squad, and Sarah and Larkin.

At first, everything went routinely. The stench of burning garbage filled the air as they stepped over gutters filled with rotting food and raw sewage. They made their way around locals carrying bundles of goods and handed out candy to the kids, all while keeping a hand on their weapons and being alert for threats or anything suspicious. It was a day like any other on the crowded street.

But then, something changed. Some unspoken message was delivered, or some secret signal released. Suddenly, the shoppers were hurrying away, and the vendors started closing their shops. Those with pushcarts dashed away so rapidly that many of them dropped merchandise but didn't stop to pick it up.

Larkin, Sarah, and the ANP knew what this meant. An attack was pending. The patrol went on high alert. The attack could come from a VBIED—a vehicle-borne improvised explosive device—coming their direction or already parked on the street awaiting a cell-phone signal to detonate it. Or it could be a rocket attack, snipers on the rooftops, or an insurgent wearing an S-VEST—a suicide bomb strapped to his chest. Whatever might be about to happen, it was their job to remove the threat before it caused damage and took innocent lives.

Larkin ducked against a building, using the corner as a shield between herself and the street. Everyone else found defensive positions of their own behind cars or mud walls or buildings. Peering around the corner, she scanned the street, the rooftops, everything within her line of sight, and could see no threats. But there was one. She had no doubt.

And then Larkin saw her.

A lone figure was walking toward them down the middle of the street. It was Anahita, fully revealed with no burqa or even a chador, dressed like a boy. She had a bomb strapped to her chest.

Tears streamed down her face and terror filled her eyes, but what really got Larkin were the purple bruises and cuts on her face and arms. She'd been beaten, and now she was being forced to die. Larkin didn't believe for a second that the girl was doing this by choice.

Larkin stepped into the street.

"Anahita," she called, signaling to the others to hold their fire. Slowly, she took one step and then another toward the terrified girl. "Anahita, let me help you."

Anahita saw Larkin, and her eyes widened even further. She stopped walking and turned her head to the left, down a side street. Larkin hoped the ANP officers noticed and would be heading that way, though she didn't take her eyes off Anahita to check. "What is this about?" Larkin called to her.

Anahita's terrified blue eyes turned toward Larkin again. Only a hundred yards separated them. Anahita took a shallow breath before replying, "My husband beat me for talking to a *khareji* in the market."

Larkin gasped for air, feeling like her lungs were sealed shut.

The girl was still talking. "I ran away from my husband and returned to my family's home, but my father sent me back. My husband beat me again and turned me out of his house. I returned to my father in shame. This is the only way for my family to regain honor."

This was Anahita's father's doing. An honor killing. Larkin had to save her.

Thinking through all of her training, Larkin searched for the right way to safely end this. Slowly, she took a step forward. Larkin was not trained in ordnance disposal, and she knew she was supposed to remain behind a barricade for her own safety and wait for the explosive ordnance disposal guys to take care of it. But there was no time to wait for them. Anahita's father could detonate the bomb at any moment.

That left one last option. She should take out the threat to minimize collateral damage. She should take out Anahita. Keep the bomb stationary and everyone else away from it.

But the girl was innocent. And she was Larkin's friend. It was because of Larkin that she was punished in the first place. There had to be a way to save her.

"Anahita," Larkin said, keeping her voice low and calm. "Can you remove the vest?"

The girl shook her head, fear pouring off her in waves. Her eyes begged Larkin for help.

"Do you have the detonator?" Larkin knew she didn't, but she asked anyway, both to be sure and to keep Anahita talking so she didn't succumb to panic.

Again, she shook her head, and a lock of auburn hair fell into her eyes. Her gaze slid to her left again. Somewhere over there her father had his hand on the button. Sweat rolled down Larkin's back.

"Bennett, take cover!"

Larkin was shocked to hear Sarah's voice so close to her. She turned and found Sarah kneeling behind a parked car only feet away, her M4 aimed at Anahita. "Hold your fire," Larkin ordered.

Sarah didn't lower her weapon, nor did she say another word. She simply got to her feet and moved toward Larkin. Before Larkin realized what Sarah was doing, she grabbed her arm and yanked Larkin back behind the car. Only then did she say, "Take cover, goddamn it!"

Neither had the chance to do or say anything else. The bomb detonated.

A solid wall of energy slammed into Larkin, throwing her to the ground. Pain ripped through her whole body. All sound ceased as her eardrums ruptured. The last thing she saw before she blacked out was Sarah landing on the gray ground beside her, her helmet missing and blood pouring from a gash on her head. Her eyes stared at Larkin sightlessly.

After that, Larkin was happy to close her own eyes and let go.

Larkin blinked and came out of the memory, surprised to find herself in her bedroom at Grams's house. Kaia was using the sleeves of her pajamas to wipe at her blotchy, wet face.

Grams was crying, too, and she had a tissue pressed to her mouth. She met Larkin's gaze and dropped her hand. Wordlessly, she slid under the covers with Larkin and wrapped her arm around her. "I'm proud of you, soldier girl," she said, planting a kiss on Larkin's temple. "You did the best you could."

"I should have done something different," Larkin argued, still holding her body stiffly, afraid to melt into Grams's embrace. "Because of me, Anahita died, Sarah died, two ANP died. If I hadn't talked with Anahita that day in the market, they would all be alive. If I'd listened to the cultural experts, if I'd alerted my chain of command, if I had done my job as I was trained, lives wouldn't have been lost. If I had done something, anything, to help Anahita out of her situation, maybe even she could have been saved."

"You can't think like that, sweetheart."

"I can," she insisted. "I have to. I caused their deaths. I am to blame."

Kaia crawled to Larkin's other side. She grabbed her hand and held it between both of her own. "No, you're not, Larkin. You did not detonate that bomb. You didn't kill anyone."

Larkin shook her head. Her therapist, doctors, and officers had all told her the same things, but none of them had been there. They did not know.

She was exhausted. After several long moments of telling Grams and Kaia she was fine and wanted to sleep, they finally believed her.

"Want me to sleep with you tonight?" Grams offered.

"Thanks, but no. I'll be okay."

Grams didn't seem to believe her, but she gave in and left with another lingering hug. Kaia hugged her, too, and whispered, "You are my hero, Larkin. You are so brave."

Larkin didn't respond.

When they were finally gone, she released a breath and tried to relax, but it was clear from the adrenaline still running through her body that she wasn't going to get any sleep tonight.

Her phone pinged and she grabbed it, hungry for something else to think about.

It was a message from Zach Faber, confirming he was Sarah's brother and he really wanted to talk to Larkin. He gave her his phone number.

Larkin shut her phone in the bedside drawer. She couldn't look at it right now. She couldn't think about Zach, or Sarah, or Anahita, or any of it. She picked up the diary lying on her nightstand and dove back into that world, hungry for an escape from her own.

October 24, 1861: My body is growing stronger (although leaner) as is my confidence. With the men, I can speak my mind and no one tells me to be quiet or to leave them be. I find I am developing opinions and thoughts I never had the freedom to form before now. I did not realize what I was missing, and now that I have experienced others seeing me as an equal, I do not know how I will ever give that up.

I've quickly grown used to my daily schedule being marked by the bugle and drums, and I quite enjoy it. What will I ever do after the war ends when no one is there to play me awake, to supper, and to sleep?

October 28, 1861: We received news today that the first transcontinental telegram was sent from San Francisco to Washington. Isn't that something? There are also rumors in camp that the area where we are located, here on Cheat

Mountain in western Virginia, will soon become part of a new state. The residents in these parts are voting to break off of the Confederate state of Virginia and become West Virginia. Surely this war will be over before it is official, but either way, I'm happy to know the Union will be one state stronger soon.

I am worried about Benjamin and his friendship with our fellow soldier, Willie Smith. Perhaps I'm only being selfish and don't want to share my brother with a new friend.

Tonight, I will stand picket duty for the first time. If the enemy, or any other threat, appears, it is my duty to sound the alarm. Like any man, I am ready for this responsibility of protecting the lives of my fellow soldiers. And yet, I cannot help but hope it is a quiet night.

October 29, 1861: I've discovered that Ben's friend Willie Smith is a stand-up kind of man. I can see why Benjamin has chosen him as a friend. I think he and I will become friends as well. After all, soldiering can be lonely and one never has enough friends.

Chapter Twelve

October 28, 1861: Union Army Camp, Cheat Mountain, Western Virginia

Fifteen days had passed since she'd seen the Reb in the woods, and Emily could not stop thinking about him. She'd made a mistake by not reporting having seen him to her officers.

For several nights afterward, she'd lain awake, unable to fall asleep in fear the Reb would sneak into camp and kill someone. Or worse, she feared that by not reporting his presence to her superiors, they would all be attacked and it would be her fault.

Only now, two weeks later, was she able to relax. She couldn't make a mistake like that again. She'd been lucky this time. Next time, she had to do better. Not because she was a woman pretending to be a man, but because she was a soldier and she needed to perform her duties to the best of her ability.

But the Reb still haunted her. At the oddest times, such as when she stood at attention for roll call or when she was sweating over the shovel she was using to dig a new company sink, she found the man's face floating in her vision, almost as if he were standing in front of her.

It took coming that close to the enemy to realize they weren't a faceless mass of evil, but real living human beings with sisters and daughters and mothers waiting at home for them. By shooting at them, she would be inflicting pain not just on the rebel soldier, but on his innocent family at home.

Could she do that?

But, on the other hand, were they truly innocent? It was the Southern states who'd started this war, after all. They were the ones wanting to leave the Union, and they'd fired the first shot at Fort Sumter.

But still, women and children who had no say in politics would suffer.

Would either side truly be able to win this war when the losses cut so deeply and intimately?

The truth was, she reminded herself as she stuffed her diary into the bottom of her knapsack and hurried across the camp to fall in for the Retreat roll call, the Southern states were trying to tear the country apart, and it was her job to fight to keep that from happening. She had to fight. Not to kill, but to preserve.

"Gentlemen!" Captain Johnson's voice cut across the lines of men standing at attention, Emily among them. "We've had word of Confederate scouts in the area, so we are doubling the number of guards on picket duty for the foreseeable future. Company lieutenants have duty assignments and will inform you of your shift."

Emily felt her knees weaken at the mention of Confederate scouts. That's what the Reb she'd seen had been doing! Of course! He'd been spying on their camp to glean information, and someone else must have seen him poking around.

As the captain strode away, leaving the company lieutenants to address their units, she pulled her shoulders back and lifted her chin, ready to do her duty. First Lieutenant Mattingly took his place at the front of their company, Company D, and began reading the names assigned to the first relief, which would commence in three hours, as soon as the men were dismissed from Tattoo, the final roll call of the day. Ben's name was called, and he shot a look of concern to Emily. She waited to hear if her name was called, and when it was not, she did her best to send Ben a look that would reassure him everything was fine. This was the first time they would be separated at night, and Emily knew Ben was worried about leaving her to fend for herself.

Her name was called for second relief, which was from 10:30 p.m. to 12:30 a.m. While the camp slept, she'd be patrolling the perimeter in the dark with only a handful of other men and the occasional campfire for warmth and light. She was ready.

When they were dismissed, Emily and Ben made their way back to their tent. They'd gotten started digging a foot into the ground to form the foundation of the little cabin they planned to erect. It would include a fireplace, log walls with the chinks filled with mud, and their half-shelter tents and ponchos stretched over the top as a roof. Tonight, with the knowledge they'd be standing picket duty during the night, they agreed to take a break.

Supper call would sound soon, and to pass the time, Private O'Brien from the tent to the left of theirs got out his fiddle and started playing a lively tune. Emily moved toward her usual seat on a log by her own fire, but when Ben passed her to go sit next to Willie Smith at his fire, Emily changed course and followed. She dropped onto an empty stump across the fire from them and was surprised to hear Ben's warm laughter fill the air. When Emily glanced over, he and Willie had their heads together, and Willie seemed to be telling him a humorous story.

A stab of jealousy shot through Emily. Didn't Ben care that she sat here all alone? Did he prefer his new friend's company to that of his sister?

Two boys across the company street, who couldn't have been older than fourteen and certainly must have lied about their ages in order to enlist, took to dancing with each other to O'Brien's tunes. One of them, pretending to be a woman, held imaginary skirts out to his sides and curtsied, sending everyone nearby bursting into laughter. Everyone except Ben and Willie, who seemed to be deep in conversation. Emily tried to watch the two dancing boys, but her gaze kept sliding across the fire to her brother and his new friend. When had they become so close? Where was she when this happened?

She studied Willie Smith carefully. He seemed to be about their age, maybe a little younger since his face was still devoid of whiskers. His body was small, as were his hands, as was fitting a man not yet grown. His straight, sandy-brown hair was cut cleanly over his ears but a bit long in the front where it hung into his eyes. With thin eyebrows and thin lips, he looked pleasant enough.

And then something strange happened. Willie leaned over and laid his hand on Ben's arm. At first, Ben leaned into Willie as though he was eager for the touch, which confused Emily. She'd never seen two men touch each other in such a manner.

But then Ben did something that confused her even more. His whole body grew stiff, and he jerked his arm away from Willie before jumping to his feet. His face had lost all humor, and he looked as if he was going to say something in anger, but he just pivoted and stalked away, disappearing into the dark.

Emily watched him go and thought about going after him, but then she saw Willie looking at her, and on his face was as expression that looked like... Was it shame?

She felt everything inside her go still. Even the noises and commotion around her seemed to disappear. The image of her brother and his new friend leaning toward each other filled her mind, quickly followed by the memory of their first night in camp when the men were joking about men having relations with other men.

Emily squeezed her eyes shut and then forced them open again as the bugle called them to supper. The men who had been entertained by the dancing boys groaned at the interruption, but Emily welcomed it. She needed something to replace the thoughts and images in her mind.

Grabbing her tin plate and cup, she fell in to the line of men snaking toward Cook's shack. She could not see Ben anywhere, and she hoped he did not miss the meal. He'd need the fuel before reporting for picket duty. When it was her turn, she held her plate out to Cook for the ladleful of stew and a biscuit plopped on top. Although she knew the stew, made out of salt beef and desiccated vegetables, would not taste anywhere near as rich as the stew she made at home, she'd come to appreciate the hot meal after the long days of work. At the next large pot, another soldier filled her cup with hot coffee.

On her way back to her campfire, she spotted Ben in the chow line and felt her muscles relax. He smiled and waved at her and seemed his normal self. Maybe she'd imagined something there that wasn't.

She sat back down on her log and turned all of her attention to her meal. Ben was still in line, and no one else had joined her. At Willie's campfire, a man Emily did not recognize was telling a story of a skirmish he had been involved in during the Mexican War fourteen years prior. He, of course, made himself out to be the hero. Emily was only half listening, but then the man said something that reminded her of a story her father used to tell.

"We went charging straight down into that canyon where the Mexicans were hiding out." The man had a huge smile on his face that told the gathering listeners something funny was about to happen. "Everyone else in the squadron became chick-enhearted and fell onto their bellies along the rim with their weapons pointing down at us."

He shoved a forkful of beef into his mouth. "Wouldn't you know it, but my friend started a'hollerin' like there were twenty of us." He laughed and slapped his knee. "And it worked. Those Mexican boys got so scared they seemed to be popping out of every hole in that canyon like prairie dogs intent on running. But our boys up top took care of them."

Emily called over to the man, "Was your friend named Calvin Wilson? From Stampers Creek, Indiana?"

The man looked surprised. "He sure was. You know him?"

Emily studied him. "He was my father. He was killed at Laurel Creek."

The man was busy sopping up gravy with his biscuit, but at Emily's words, he paused. "I'm sorry to hear that. Come on over here, boy. Join us."

Emily hadn't made any real effort to make friends, knowing that she had to be careful with everything she said or did so as not to reveal her secret. But, after watching Ben and Willie grow closer, she knew that needed to change or she'd be all alone. She picked up her coffee cup and got to her feet as Ben arrived from the chow line. "Come on, we're joining our neighbors' fire."

The others at the fire shuffled around and left them two empty stumps. Emily sat next to her father's old friend, who introduced himself as Kurt Schafer. Ben dropped onto the stump next to Emily, causing disappointment to flash across Willie's face. Quincy Rawlings was there, too, as was another man she didn't recognize with red hair down to his shoulders. She nodded to him but turned back to Schafer. "I'm Jesse Wilson. This is my brother, Ben."

"I'm happy to meet you both. Your father was a good man, and I'm sorry for your loss."

Emily nodded her thanks, and saw Ben do the same. This close, she could see that Schafer had a scar angling from the corner of his nose down to below his ear.

Schafer introduced the redhead as Donald MacGregor.

"Where are you from, MacGregor?" Ben asked as he tucked into his meal.

"Glasgow, lad," MacGregor answered, his thick accent giving him away as a recent immigrant. "In Scotland. I've been here two years, and I served with your father and your brother, God rest their souls."

"You've lost a brother, too?" Schafer asked them. When they told him they had, he shook his head. "That's a shame, but a testament to your family that you two are now here serving in their place."

MacGregor's next question sent a lightning bolt of fear through Emily.

"I thought for sure Calvin Wilson said he had two sons and a daughter, yet I've met three sons now."

Emily could not stop herself from looking at Ben, who was looking back at her with panic on his face. They had not considered there might be pitfalls to joining their father's regiment. How stupid of them! She had to think of something fast, before she made MacGregor even more suspicious.

Ben, recovering faster than her, laughed and shook his head as he said, "I always wondered if Pa thought we were one person, being only ten months apart and all." He looked squarely at MacGregor. "Our parents had three sons. Our sister, Emily, is at home with our aunt and uncle."

"Ah, my mistake." MacGregor finished off his meal with a final swipe of his bread across his plate. He washed it down with the contents of his cup as Emily watched, her stomach still churning.

"All this meal needs now is a good smoke." Schafer set his empty dinner plate aside and pulled a pipe out of his jacket pocket, which he lit with the glowing end of a stick from the fire. As smoke rose, he closed his eyes and gave a moan of pleasure.

"Hand that here," MacGregor ordered. He had drawn out a pipe of his own and, after the stick was handed over, was soon puffing away.

"I've got something better than a pipe," Willie Smith said with a mischievous grin as he drew his hand out of his coat to reveal a flask. "My own sweet mama's applejack recipe. Who wants some?"

"But we have picket duty," Emily reminded them.

There was a momentary pause before the men burst out

laughing. Emily looked to Ben for help, but he quickly looked away from her, biting back his smile in the process.

Quincy Rawlings, wiping a tear from the corner of his eye, told her, "Nothing ever happens on picket. Besides, it would take a lot more than Willie here is willing to share to have any ill effects."

Every man held out his cup, including Ben. He shot Emily a look that told her she'd better join in or risk being ridiculed further. She drained the rest of her coffee and stuck her cup out toward Willie.

Once the cups were filled, Emily watched as the other men downed their portions, noting how they smacked their lips and obviously found the drink pleasing. Encouraged, she followed suit, putting the cup to her lips and throwing her head back so all of the liquid would go straight down her throat.

She felt as if she'd swallowed flames. Sweet flames, but flames all the same. Without anything else at hand to wash the flavor away, she felt the heat rising until she had no choice but to cough. Her stomach revolted at the strong liquid, and she swallowed hard to keep it down.

Schafer saw it all. He pounded her on the back and laughed until his eyes teared up. "First applejack, huh, boy?" He didn't wait for an answer but kept on laughing and slapping her back, which was actually helping a bit.

At first, she panicked, thinking she'd just made a huge mistake. But then she realized he thought of her as a young boy and didn't think it odd that she had not yet tried alcohol. She started laughing, too, relieved and not at all offended at being the butt of his joke. "Guilty as charged," she admitted.

Ben had not reacted as she had to the powerful alcohol, and she wondered if he had gotten his hands on liquor in the past. She sent him a questioning look, but he only shrugged and reached out to take the pipe MacGregor passed to him.

Emily's shock deepened as she watched her brother expertly

smoke the pipe, clearly not for the first time. Ben raised his eyebrows and wordlessly offered the pipe to her.

A quick glance confirmed that all eyes around the fire were on her. Wondering if she'd regret it, she took the pipe from Ben, put it to her mouth, and inhaled.

Her lungs spasmed, and she coughed. Smoke poured from her mouth and her nose, burning as it went and making her cough all the more.

That sent everyone into peals of laughter until Willie took pity on her. "You've got to draw in a little at a time," he explained. "As you get used to it, you can take more."

Emily had had enough for one night and handed the pipe back to Ben, who took another drag before passing it to MacGregor.

Willie, his face turned toward the fire, asked, "You ever seen a tobacco field before?"

Most of the men shook their heads. Willie continued, "It's green plants as far as the eye can see with slaves with rags on their heads bent scattered throughout." He shook his head. "And an overseer whipping anyone he thinks isn't working fast enough."

"Is it true this war is about ending slavery?" MacGregor asked as he whittled a stick into a sharp point.

Quincy shrugged in answer. "Partly so, I reckon."

"I'm no' here to free negroes," MacGregor grumbled. "I'm here to preserve our Constitution. For all I care, they can sell off all the slaves to pay for this war and then do the same to the abolitionists. The institution has been working just fine all this time, and we should leave it alone. Anyone protesting and fighting against it is only stirrin' up trouble."

Emily had heard Uncle Samuel grumbling like MacGregor on many occasions. She'd never been able to say anything in response to her uncle, but now that she was a man, she felt the need, and the freedom, to speak. "What if you were born with black skin, MacGregor? Wouldn't you feel differently about slavery?"

The man let out a sound of disgust. "And what if I was born a pig? Wouldn't I want to avoid being Sunday supper?" He shook his head. "Your argument is stupid, boy."

Emily felt her anger rise. She'd never personally known a black person, but she had never believed they were less than human. It was illegal for black people to live in—or even visit—Indiana, but occasionally some who did not know better traveled through. On one such occasion when a handful of black folks walked past their farm, Pa had offered them fresh water and food for their journey. It wasn't until Emily got older that she realized they were probably escaped slaves on their way to Canada. Another time, Uncle Samuel had come across an escaped slave resting by the creek and chased him off with his shotgun, yelling that he was lucky he didn't sic the dog on him. Ever since, Emily had promised herself she'd be like Pa and not Samuel if given the opportunity. She would help.

She tried to keep emotion out of her voice. "Why is it stupid? Explain it to me."

MacGregor dropped his hands to his lap and stared at her like she'd lost her mind. "Because everyone knows the negroes aren't as smart as white folk. Their brains are closer to those of farm animals than to ours."

Emily had never heard that before, so she waited to see if anyone else would refute the statement. When no one did, she could not stay silent. "That can't be true. I've read of free black folks in northern states who have become doctors and business owners. No pig or cow could accomplish that."

MacGregor went back to whittling, clearly bored with the subject. "They must be the exception."

Schafer, sitting next to him, grunted and jerked his head toward the path to the river. "Speak of the devil."

They all turned and saw a black family of camp followers walking past carrying water jugs.

Emily had seen many camp followers but had not interacted with any of them. Some followers were family members of a soldier, as she would have been. Others made their living selling goods or services such as cooking or laundry washing to the soldiers. Some were prostitutes who welcomed men with coins into their tents. As far as Emily could tell, the followers represented all of America in the colors of their skin and the languages they spoke. As for this particular family, Emily didn't know if they were former slaves or free persons.

"Hey, darkie!" MacGregor called to the father. When he stopped and looked toward their fire, MacGregor called, "Yeah, you. Come over here and entertain us. There's a three-cent silver in it for you."

The man hesitated, but then he set down the jugs he carried and crossed the dusty street to approach their fire, his worn hat hanging limply in his hands. "Yes, sir, what can I do for you?"

MacGregor waved a coin in the air. "Show us something you can do."

Emily watched the man eye the coin before looking back over his shoulder to his wife, who held their baby in one arm with the other wrapped around her two older children. All but the baby watched with wide eyes.

The man faced MacGregor again, and Emily saw a careful mask come over his face, as though he was used to hiding his true self. He dipped his head. "I can do a real fine dance, sir."

MacGregor slapped a palm on his knee. "It's decided. Someone play a tune for this darkie."

O'Brien got out his fiddle and started playing "Camptown Races." The black man lifted both hands in front of his face and started clapping along, providing a beat. He stomped his feet, and soon his whole body was moving, knees lifting, arms waving. The man's wife watched him, stone-faced.

Emily felt paralyzed. She should stop this, but how?

When it was over, MacGregor flipped the coin in the air, and the man caught it before hurrying back to his family.

Emily hated that she'd sat there and done nothing. Before the man got too far away, she called to him, "That was real nice dancing. Thank you, sir!"

The black man turned back to her long enough to dip his head in acknowledgment before rushing his family out of sight.

The men around the campfire were silent.

Finally, Willie Smith broke the silence. "That was a low thing to do, MacGregor."

"What?" the Scotsman said. "I paid him!"

"You treated him like a slave. Like his only purpose is to serve us white folk."

MacGregor took a long drag on his pipe and blew it out in Willie's direction. With a smirk, he reached into his pocket. "Here you go, boy. I can see you're wanting a coin for yourself." He flicked it across the fire to Willie, then got to his feet and sauntered away.

A few of the other men laughed. The coin dropped into the dirt. Willie's face was dark as he watched MacGregor go.

A bugle call pierced the evening air, and men all through camp groaned. It was time to line up yet again for one last roll call before they were to prepare for bed and be in bed when "Taps" played at nine. It also meant it was time for Ben to report to picket duty.

Emily did not complain about the call. She was quite happy to move away from that conversation. As she headed toward the parade ground, she fell into step beside Willie.

Now she understood why Ben liked him.

As it was only two hours until her picket duty, rather than going to sleep, Emily lay awake in her tent thinking through all that she'd experienced in the last months. It nagged at her that Aunt Harriet was likely worrying about her and Ben and wondering what had happened to them. No one had written home with the news of David's death either.

No one had written to David's girl, Nancy.

She and Ben owed it to the people at home to tell them David had died, and how, and that she and Ben were safe. But she worried that if she wrote home and told the truth about her disguise and subsequent enlistment, Uncle Samuel would notify the military authorities and have her arrested and sent home. Emily wasn't ready to go home. At least not until the fighting was over and she could bring Ben with her.

Her thoughts drifted back to the black man who had danced for them this evening. It was the closest she'd ever been to a black person, and tonight was the first time she'd seen the kind of treatment even free black people received from white folks. It made her feel ugly and dirty. She could only imagine how the man and his family had felt.

Pa had made her understand the importance of fighting to preserve the Union, but now she was also starting to understand the importance of fighting for the abolishment of slavery. Human lives were at stake. How could anyone possibly be on the side of the Confederacy when slavery was so morally wrong?

She must have fallen asleep because, before she knew it, she was being shaken awake by the corporal of the guard, whispering that it was time for picket. She passed Ben as he returned to their tent, and he clasped her hand in his, as men do in greeting. Obviously fatigued, he trudged off to sleep for the night.

Emily reported to her post, a good distance from camp in the woods. It was dark, but from where she stood, she could see light from a few fires in camp piercing through the gloom. With the full moon filtering through the canopy, she felt confident that if anything moved, she'd see it. The light also made it easier for her to see the other guards nearby. Willie Smith was stationed a hundred yards west, and another soldier she didn't recognize the same distance in the other direction. Knowing they were nearby kept her from feeling completely alone. She pulled up her collar to ward off the cold and leaned her back against a tree trunk as she waited to see if anything would happen.

The first hour was quiet, with only the occasional hoot of an owl or rustle of some night creature in the underbrush. Emily found she did not mind, and even started to enjoy, being one of only a few awake because life in the Army meant she was never alone. The solitude felt peaceful, and she might have forgotten she was in a war if not for the ever-present knowledge that Confederate scouts had been seen in the area. She figured the Reb she'd seen was long gone by now, but that didn't mean others weren't lurking about, and that thought kept her wide awake, her gaze constantly searching the shadows.

At first, she thought her active mind was playing a trick on her. But then she realized something was definitely jostling a shrub a short distance from her. Was it a Reb?

She'd been resting against a tree, but now she jumped to her feet and aimed her musket at the bush. "Who's there?" she called, not loud enough to alert the camp, but loud enough for the spy in the bush to hear her.

The movement paused, causing her heart to ratchet up even more so now she could hardly breathe. "Show yourself! Hands up!"

Another sound caught her attention, and she turned to find Willie running toward her, his own weapon at the ready. "What is it, Jesse?"

"I don't know. Something's in that shrub." She had to admit, she felt better with Willie there, even though her training had ensured she knew what to do.

The bush rustled again. Willie jerked his weapon into position, and together, they slowly approached the bush. Emily made sure that with each step she took, she avoided stepping on a twig or dry leaf that would give away her position. The darkness was her cover.

Emily motioned for Willie to go one direction around the

bush while she went the other. When they were both in position, Emily drew a deep breath, cocked her weapon, and hissed, "Come on out, Reb. We've got you cornered."

A furry body about three feet in length darted out of the bush and came straight at her. Emily could not hold back a scream, but she was able to silence it almost immediately. A small white face looked at her and then darted away, and in that moment, Emily realized it wasn't a Reb at all, but a possum.

Willie saw the possum at the same moment Emily did, and after the animal had disappeared again, they both looked at each other and then broke into laughter.

When he finally caught his breath, Willie said, "You didn't even give him time to play dead! I think your scream scared him more than he did you."

His comment sobered Emily right up. Men, in her experience, did not scream. Had she just revealed herself to Willie? She grunted in a manner she hoped sounded like a man. "He did scare the socks off me, that's for sure. Thanks for coming to my assistance."

Willie slapped his back. "Anytime, Jesse. You'd do the same for me."

With that, Willie returned to his post and Emily to her tree, feeling that now Willie wasn't only Ben's friend. He was her friend, too.

Chapter Thirteen

*L*arkin hid out in her room all day Sunday and spoke to Grams and Kaia in monosyllables—and only when they opened her bedroom door and asked a direct question. She knew she was being infantile, but she felt so raw and exposed from revealing her greatest shame to them that she might as well have been a bloody pulp of flesh left to shrivel in the hot sun.

She'd talk to them eventually and apologize, but for now she had to be alone.

On Monday morning, she lay in bed and listened as Kaia left for work, then fell back asleep. An hour later, the creaking of the floorboards in the hall outside her room woke her again, and she heard Grams talking to Bowie, telling her to watch over Larkin while she was out at her meeting.

The house was empty, and Larkin was sick of her bedroom.

Bowie lay right outside her door, and when Larkin stepped out, she jumped up with her tail wagging, deliriously happy to see her. If only humans gave this kind of unconditional love, Larkin thought as she rubbed Bowie's fur. If only humans didn't mess up so royally and make it difficult to be loved.

Downstairs, she had some toast and tea and set herself up at the kitchen table with the diary and her laptop and notes, with a plan to look for evidence of Emily Wilson's service. Larkin knew, without a shadow of a doubt, that if not for this diary, she'd be in a dark place right now. Maybe she would have even found more pills, or another way to end the pain.

Sarah had given her the diary exactly when she needed it most.

Larkin paused and then rejected that idea. No, Sarah hadn't chosen to give Larkin the diary. Not now, anyway. If she'd known how she would die, she wouldn't have given Larkin anything.

Guilt, regret, and sorrow gathered in Larkin's chest and made the toast she'd eaten feel like thorns in her belly. She had to stop thinking about it. She needed to focus on Emily Wilson instead.

And so she opened a browser and dove in, hoping to find something more about Emily beyond what the woman had written in her diary.

She looked for information on the 9th Indiana Infantry and discovered that one of the men in the regiment had become somewhat famous as a journalist and author in the years after the war. Ambrose Bierce had been eighteen years old when he enlisted with the 9th Indiana and had served the Union Army for nearly four years. Many of his full works were available for free online, and Larkin pored over them, especially his Civil War writings, in hopes of finding Jesse, Ben, or Willie mentioned. None of them were. Discouraged, she switched back to the online newspapers site that Grams had told her about.

And she found her. After reading through countless pages, Larkin finally found Jesse Wilson in a Nashville newspaper, the *Daily Nashville Union*. She could hardly believe her luck, but there it was, the name Jesse Wilson as plain as day. Even more, the article specified the 9th Indiana Infantry as Jesse's regiment. It had to be Emily.

Shaking with excitement, Larkin zoomed in and read the entire article.

ARREST OF A WOMAN IN SOLDIER'S UNIFORM—Yesterday, Provost Marshal Alvan C. Gillem detected a woman in soldier's attire who goes by the name of Jesse Wilson and claims to be a private in Colonel Moody's 9th Indiana Infantry. She reportedly enlisted alongside her brother and served during the initial occupation of our fair city as well as in battle at Pittsburg Landing. Refusing to give her proper name, the young woman was arrested and sent to the city jail. We mention these facts as a part of the history of this war, let what may be said of the propriety of such conduct in a woman. This reporter must admit, however, she makes a fine-looking soldier.

The thrill of finding concrete proof of Emily's service made Larkin want to dance. But that feeling was tempered by the implied criticism of Emily by the article's author. To blatantly question Emily's propriety because she was conducting herself as a man made Larkin want to scream. Not only that, but Emily was reduced to nothing more than her appearance, as so many women still were today. Sure, societal expectations were different in the nineteenth century, but Larkin could practically feel the thumb grinding Emily and all women into the dirt. No wonder Emily felt such freedom when people thought she was male.

Larkin carefully read all articles in the *Daily Nashville Union* for the days following, looking for further mention of Jesse Wilson, but did not find any. She seemed to disappear after being thrown in jail.

Maybe Emily herself will tell me in the diary. Larkin laid her hand protectively over the leather-bound book on the table beside her, promising herself she'd read more tonight.

For right now, however, she wanted to dive into the battle mentioned in the article. Pittsburg Landing. She'd never heard of it.

She typed the name into a search engine, and the first entry that came up was for the Battle of Shiloh. She'd heard of that battle. Who hadn't?

Clicking on the link, she quickly found that Pittsburg Landing was the name of the place on the Tennessee River where the battle took place. As she read further, she learned that the battle later became known as the Battle of Shiloh after the name of the one-room log church in the area.

The more she read, the more her heart sank. The Battle of Shiloh was the deadliest battle in American history up to that time. After this battle, the American people realized that not only was the war more devastating than anyone had anticipated, but also there would be no quick end to it. The end, in fact, did not come for another three bloody years.

The joy she'd felt at discovering Emily in the newspaper was gone. In its place was a feeling that something bad was about to befall this real-life heroine. Something even worse than being discovered.

As she reached for Emily's diary again, a text message pinged on her phone.

The text came from an old friend from the service whom she hadn't heard from in a while. Not since before her last deployment, in fact. Larkin smiled upon reading her friend's name and swiped in order to read the full text, eager for news.

But the news wasn't good.

Hey, Bennett. Sorry I haven't been in touch. I heard about what happened to you, and I'm real sorry. Hope you're doing okay. I'm here whenever you want to talk. But right now, I have bad news. Griffin shot himself last night. His wife found him in their garage. I'll let you know when the service will be.

Larkin dropped her phone. *No. No, no, no, no, no. No!* Not Griff. He was one of the good ones. One of the guys who wasn't threatened by a female senior officer. He did his job professionally and honorably, and she would have trusted him to have her back in any firefight. But more than that, Griff was her friend. They'd done their first deployment together. He'd been by her side when they were ambushed the first time while performing route security between Bagram and Kabul. He had a four-year-old son and a baby daughter. Why had he killed himself?

She knew why. The same reason she'd attempted it. Because war fucked with a soldier's mind. Because at war a soldier saw and did things that changed her. Because while deployed, a soldier had a purpose. Her presence meant the difference between life or death for her buddies. Every single day she knew her job, and she performed those duties to the best of her ability. And then she came home and looked around and saw that her friends, family, and community had no clue what was going on over there. No one here cared, and it made her whole life feel pointless. They didn't care that people were risking their lives for their freedom. All they cared about were who tweeted what to whom and what celebrity was having an affair. It was all bullshit.

Her whole body was shaking, but Larkin couldn't seem to move. All she could do was stare at her phone where it had dropped onto the table.

Soldiers got home and realized they'd changed, yet their loved ones expected them to be the same. As if facing mortality on a daily basis was normal. As if watching friends die was normal. As if dedicating your life to your country and that service changing who you are at your very core was normal.

White-hot fury shot through her, and she shoved her laptop off the table, not even flinching when it broke into pieces and the screen shattered. Grabbing the next thing at hand, Emily's diary, she hefted it as hard as she could across the room, where it smashed against the post at the bottom of the stairs. It, too, broke into two pieces, but Larkin didn't care.

She tilted her head back, closed her eyes, and screamed as loud as she could. Bowie barked at her as though she were a stranger. Maybe she was. At times like this, she felt like a stranger even to herself.

"Larkin!" Grams appeared in the kitchen doorway holding grocery bags, her face panicked.

Larkin screamed again, and shouted, and raged against everything that had been pissing her off—the Taliban, the stupid shit at the Pentagon, PTSD, Congress for not doing its job, the Army for messing her up and then pushing her out, Sarah for dying, Griff for dying.

She crumpled onto the floor. "God damn it!" The steady beat of her forehead on the hardwood felt good.

Grams's arms wrapped around her, holding her tight. "Shh… You're not alone, Lark. I'm here. I've got you."

"It's all fucked up," Larkin whimpered, her anger draining into sorrow so deep she felt her chest caving in. "So fucked up. It's not fair."

"No, it isn't," Grams agreed. "It's not fair. But I've got you. I've got you, Lark."

Larkin leaned into Grams on the cold floor and sobbed. The tears felt like they'd never stop, and for once, she didn't try to shove them down.

When Larkin woke, it was dark outside and the house was quiet. The only lights on were the undercabinet ones in the adjoining kitchen that gave a soft glow to the room. She realized she was lying on the couch under a fuzzy blanket that had been tucked all around her like Grams used to do when she was a kid.

Grams.

A greasy ball of shame flowed through Larkin and she closed her eyes, willing herself to wake from this nightmare. Grams didn't deserve the burden Larkin was forcing on her. She had had enough heartbreak in her own life; she didn't need Larkin's, too.

Where was Grams?

Larkin's heart twisted when she saw Grams curled up asleep in Gramps's old recliner. Tears spilled onto Larkin's cheek, surprising her. She'd thought she was all cried out. Grams had protected her, watched over her as she slept. Grams had told her she was there for her, and she'd meant it.

Larkin pressed both hands to her face and silently wept. *And Griff. God, Griff. His poor wife and kids.* The pain was too much.

The sound of keys in the door filled the room, and Larkin jerked her hands off her face, unwilling to be caught crying. She shoved the pain down. Kaia tiptoed into the room. When she saw Grams asleep and Larkin crying on the couch, she stopped, her face a mask of dread. "What happened?"

Larkin shook her head. "Nothing. Everyone's okay."

Grams startled awake. "Larkin?"

"I'm here, Grams. Kaia, too. Everything's fine."

"Oh." Grams patted her chest. "What time is it? I should be starting dinner."

"Six thirty," Kaia answered, dropping her purse on a chair. "I just got home. What's going on here? You two feel okay?"

Grams put the recliner back into upright position. She opened her mouth to answer, then shot a look toward Larkin. "Lark? Are you okay?"

Larkin shrugged, wondering if she'd ever be okay. But right now, she was better than she had been. "Yeah, I'm fine." She shoved off the blanket, her joints aching as if she were coming down with the flu. "Let me help with dinner."

"What's all this?" Kaia stood at the base of the stairs, staring at the floor.

Larkin remembered throwing Emily's diary. "Oh my god."

Horrified she'd broken Sarah's treasure, she rushed over and knelt down, hardly registering the shock of pain from dropping too quickly to her bad knee.

The cover of the book had broken into two pieces. Next to the diary lay a yellowed scrap of stained cloth and a metal ring. Had they fallen out of the book? "What in the world?"

Kaia sat on the bottom step and picked up the ring. "It looks like it's engraved. Grams, will you turn on the lights?"

Grams flicked the switch, then shuffled toward them, moving like she was stiff and achy. Larkin swallowed, knowing she was to blame.

"It says 'Willie Smith, 9th Ind. Inf., Co D,'" Kaia read. "Who's that?"

"You sure it doesn't say Jesse Wilson?" Larkin took it from her to see for herself. Sure enough, the name was Willie's. "Willie was another soldier in Jesse's unit. They were becoming friends in the section I last read."

Grams reached for it. "Isn't that something," she murmured, more to herself than not. "I've read about these but have never seen one. I think it's an identity ring, worn so if the wearer is killed in battle, their body can be identified."

"Like dog tags?" Larkin sat on the floor and stretched her leg out, her knee twinging.

"Exactly."

"And what's this handkerchief?" Kaia handed the cloth to Larkin.

It was about eight inches square and made of what was probably once soft, white cotton but was now yellowed and stained and stiff with age. It was entirely edged with a hint of scalloping done in red thread with the rounded corners gently ruffled. The red thread continued in an embroidered pattern all around the circumference of the square with tiny dots making lines and diamond patterns. In one corner were the embroidered initials ODE.

"I don't know," Larkin answered. "I haven't read anything about it in the diary. I almost hate to touch it and risk ruining it. Look at this tiny stitching."

"Who is ODE?"

Larkin shook her head. "No idea. Those aren't Emily's initials, so it must have belonged to someone else. I wonder why she had it?"

Grams also had her head bent over the cloth. "Is that brown stuff what I think it is?"

Larkin gently spread the handkerchief over her lap and looked closer at the brown stains over the monogram that nearly obscured the red letters. "It's blood." Her heart pounded.

"Did Sarah ever mention any of this?" Grams asked, handing the ring back to Larkin. "I can't imagine her family would give something so precious away."

"You're right." Larkin got stiffly to her feet. "I think it's time I call her brother."

She gathered up the diary pieces, handkerchief and ring, and then she grabbed her cell phone from the table, surprised she hadn't thrown that, too. Limping upstairs, she shut her bedroom door and made the call.

He picked up after two rings.

"Zach Faber? This is Larkin Bennett. Sarah's friend."

A long silence stretched over the line. "Thanks for tracking me down. I can't believe she's gone." His voice cracked.

Larkin's heart started to thaw toward him. "Yeah, me too." She squeezed the ring in her fist. "She, um, she talked about you. Told me you were her hero when she was a kid."

"She said that?"

"Yeah." Larkin took a breath. "Until she never saw you again." Larkin fell silent as she realized she was trying to push some of her own guilt and shame onto Zach. But he deserved it, didn't he? He'd abandoned Sarah.

Before he had time to come up with lame excuses, Larkin

twisted the knife deeper. "Why didn't you try to contact her all those years?"

"I, uh…" He cleared his throat and started again. "I was a stupid kid when our parents split up and I went to live with Dad. Sarah was so little… I thought she wouldn't remember me, or want anything to do with me. Our mother didn't. She was furious that I chose Dad over her, and she told me she never wanted to see me again."

Larkin sucked in her breath. "Wow. She was a real piece of work, wasn't she?"

"Yeah, although I didn't realize how much until she drank herself to death a few years ago."

Larkin thought about all the stories Sarah had told her of the hell she'd experienced living with her mother, who had never gotten over her husband leaving her. "Sarah missed you. She felt that you and your dad abandoned her."

Zach let out a breath. "Yeah, I guess we did. I always thought I'd make it up to her someday. It's too late now, isn't it?"

"Yeah." Larkin fell silent, not sure what to say next. Her gaze fell on Sarah's urn, and she quickly turned away.

"Tell me about her," Zach urged, his voice pleading. "You were her best friend, right? You were there when she died?"

The pain of that made Larkin close her eyes, and for several long moments she couldn't speak.

"Larkin?"

"Yeah," she finally managed. "She was my best friend. Like a sister."

He made a sound like "Hmm" and Larkin wondered if he took that as a dig at him, though she didn't mean it that way.

"I have her stuff," she told him. "Some old pictures of you as kids. Do you want me to send them to you?"

"Yes, please. I don't have any."

Larkin jotted down his address. "There's something else," she told him. "Did you ever hear about an ancestor of yours who left her diary of the time she dressed as a man and fought in the Civil War?"

He chuckled. "Yeah, my grandmother read it to me when I was about ten. She left it to Sarah when she died, and I remember Sarah carrying it around with her for months like a security blanket. And this was even before she could read!"

Larkin smiled, imagining tiny Sarah hugging the diary. "I found the diary in Sarah's things and am reading it now. I can see why it inspired her so much."

"Is it why she joined the military?" he asked, his voice sounding sad. "I wasn't surprised when I'd heard she did."

His question reminded her of their graduation and commissioning ceremony when Sarah had hoped her family would show, but they didn't. Larkin decided not to bring it up. "Yeah, that's what she told me." Getting to the point, she said, "Look, I found something interesting in the diary today. A handkerchief and identity ring that were hidden inside. I guess I...I don't know...I guess I feel like I shouldn't keep something so valuable. Is there someone in your family who I should send them to?"

Zach paused for a moment before saying, "I'd love to see them someday, but if Sarah left her things for you, you should keep them."

Relief swept through Larkin, and she realized she didn't want to part with the items. She was becoming as attached to Emily as she'd been to Sarah. As she fiddled with the ring, she asked, "Zach, did your grandmother tell you anything about Emily's friend Willie Smith? I get the feeling he was special to Emily, and now that I've found his ring, I'm certain of it."

"You mean you don't know?"

"Know what?"

Zach chuckled. "I don't think I should tell you. Give you the fun of discovering it on your own."

"Tell me."

"No, I'm definitely going to let you discover it on your own."

Annoyed, Larkin had to take a deep breath. Zach wasn't a suspected criminal she was interrogating. If he didn't want to tell her, she couldn't make him. "At least tell me this. Do you know who ODE was? The initials are embroidered on the handkerchief I found."

"My guess would be it's connected to Willie Smith, but I really have no idea."

"Oh." For some reason, Larkin had hoped this one phone call would answer all her questions. Now she was eager to get back to the diary. "Look, I'd better get going. I'll send those pictures to you ASAP."

"Thanks. Hey, Larkin?"

"Yeah?"

He was quiet, and she could hear a TV on in the background. "Do you think I could call you sometime? I missed my chance to know my sister and was hoping, maybe, you could tell me more about her."

Larkin squeezed her eyes shut as tight as she could. "Yeah, that would be okay."

"Thanks." He hung up.

Larkin dropped her phone on the bed and looked at Sarah's urn. Larkin had been a coward. She should have told him she had Sarah's ashes. She should have told him it was her fault Sarah was killed.

"I just talked to your brother," she said. "He's not so bad. He misses you." Maybe he even regretted the fact that he never made any effort to know Sarah when she was alive.

Larkin looked at the pieces of the diary lying on her bed alongside the other items and felt deep shame for damaging Sarah's book. "I'm so sorry, Sarah. I'll fix it, I promise."

She inspected the broken pieces and saw with relief that the diary pages weren't harmed, nor was the back cover. Only the front cover had broken.

But when she looked closer, Larkin realized it hadn't broken at all. The book had been crafted by someone with the skill to carve out a hollow compartment in the leather-wrapped wooden cover. They had then used another thin piece of wood, also wrapped in leather, to fit exactly on top in a manner so tight that the seam between the two pieces looked like a decoration rather than a separation. The other decorative lines on the leather cover helped with that illusion. As Larkin pushed the cover back into place, she realized Emily likely had needed to use a knife or other flat instrument to pry the cover off when she needed to open it. The tight fit was what assured the secrecy of the compartment.

As she marveled at the diary's construction, Zach's words came back to her. There was something Larkin didn't know. She couldn't wait another second to find out what that was. Forgetting she'd offered to help with dinner, she lay down on her bed and continued reading.

December 12, 1861: The three of us, Benjamin, Willie (with whom we've grown as close as brothers), and I, have become quite comfortable with camp life and almost forgot we were here to engage in war. The truth has made itself known today as we marched to Allegheny Mountain in preparation for battle tomorrow. At dawn we will attack the Confederate camp there. I am not too proud to admit I am scared, but I am greatly comforted knowing I will have my two dear friends by my side. We each will ensure that we all survive.

Word has reached camp that the Confederacy has claimed both Missouri and Kentucky. It seems likely we will be ordered south to Kentucky in the near future. After today's long march, I hope the order is delayed.

As winter has settled over us, it has also brought illness. Daily fatigue duty involves burying those who have died from their disease. It is a gruesome task that reminds me how lucky David was to have died in a hospital with us at his side. We are doing our best to maintain our own health. Even Ben and Willie are avoiding the company sinks in favor of the woods behind our tents. Whenever possible, we collect our own water, taking care to be upriver from those exhibiting illness. I also make certain Ben eats the vegetables he is served, poor though they may be. Even desiccated (or desecrated, as the boys call them) vegetables are better for the body than none at all.

No bugle is sounding tonight, due to our proximity to the Confederate camp. I find I miss hearing it as I lie down to sleep.

Chapter Fourteen

December 12, 1861: Near Allegheny Mountain, Virginia

T he night they encountered the possum while on picket duty
marked the beginning of Emily's friendship with Willie.
He was smart, funny, and most of all, kind. Emily saw what had
drawn Ben to their fellow soldier, and in the six weeks since,
they'd become a close threesome. They ate meals together,
lined up for roll call together, and whenever given the choice,
volunteered for fatigue duty together. It was as though Emily
had two brothers again.

The only dimness in the light that was their friendship was
Emily's growing concern about the relationship between Ben
and Willie. Quite simply, the two men shared a physical closeness that was unnatural.

So far, Emily thought she was the only one who'd noticed
their soft glances when they thought no one was looking, or
their tender touch of a hand under cover of darkness, or the
way their bodies would lean toward each other when sitting
or walking together. If one of them had been a woman, Emily
would have thought they were falling in love. But they were
two men! This kind of thing wasn't done and could even
prove dangerous.

At first, Emily had been jealous, for the bond they were building between them excluded her. She did not want anyone, even her dear friend, taking her brother away from her. Nor did she want her brother taking away her new friend.

But then she truly looked at her brother and saw how happy Willie made him, and Emily knew nothing else mattered. And so she started to help them. Her presence had saved them many times already from being caught. Last evening, she had come upon them at their fire, sitting closer together than men normally do. Knowing other men were right behind her, Emily had insinuated herself right between the two, plopping herself on the log in a way that forced Ben to scoot aside. Willie's ruddy cheeks told her she'd arrived just in time.

This morning, as she was kicking dirt onto their campfire, Emily had glanced up and seen Ben and Willie walking back to camp through the forest where, she presumed, they had gone to fill their canteens from the river. They must have thought they were still out of sight because—and Emily had to admit it shocked her—they were holding hands. With a quick glance to ensure no one else had seen them, Emily did the only thing she could think of to break the two apart. She called to Ben, "Get a move on, Benjamin! You still need to pack your bedroll."

The two sprung apart so fast that it looked like they'd been stung by a bee. Emily knew she'd have to speak to Ben soon. They were growing careless.

Tonight they were too exhausted after the long march to Allegheny Mountain to do anything more than lay out their bedrolls and heat their rations in the large fry pan Emily had purchased from a sutler on robber's row with funds from her soldier's pay. They'd brought their half tents with them, but all agreed the effort of setting them up for one night was wasted, even if the temperature dropped below freezing. They would sleep under the stars beside the fire. As Ben started supper, Emily took their coffee pots to the nearby stream to fill up. When she returned, she set them in the coals to heat.

"I'm beat," Quincy Rawlings said as he shuffled to their fire and eyed the chunks of salt pork Ben was frying. "If you cook my supper, I'll share two apples my sister sent me, and some cinnamon, too."

Ben accepted the bargain, and Emily's mouth watered as she thought of the sweet dessert that was to come. Cooking was one thing she had never enjoyed, not like Aunt Harriet and most other women she knew, and she was happy that Ben took over the duty tonight. She poked at the fire and watched as he added Quincy's pork and potato ration to their pan.

"Since you're cooking our supper, I'll cook dessert," Willie offered, accepting the apples, spice, and fry pan from Quincy, who turned to lay out his bedroll in line with theirs.

Emily poked at the fire and watched Quincy. He was a fine-looking man, she realized. He hailed from up near Muncie where his family had a dairy farm, and he looked every bit the farm boy, all lean and freckled with arms strong from lifting hay and carrying milk pails. He often sat with them in the evenings, telling stories or playing cards, and Willie said he was a courteous tentmate back at camp.

Maybe after this war was over, Emily mused, she could settle down with a man like Quincy. They would work their farm together and raise a family of their own.

Emily poured coffee into the bubbling water and stirred it with a stick as she thought about becoming a wife. It was expected of her, of course, but she'd much rather be the one out with the animals and the crops, making decisions, instead of the person left at home over a hot stove, minding crying babies.

Maybe she should continue to live as a man after the war. She'd already proven she could convince people she was one. She'd helped Pa on the farm enough to understand the work and knew she could do that job as well as she soldiered. What did she need a man in her life for, anyhow?

Her gaze drifted to the other side of the campfire where Willie was holding out a tin plate for Ben to fill with pork and potatoes. Anyone else watching would not see the connection between them, but Emily did. There was an invisible tether between the two that was as real as any rope would be. Her heart twisted upon seeing them together for although she knew their feelings would bring them trouble, those feelings were deep and true.

That was what she needed a man in her life for. Someone to look at her like she was his whole world. Someone who made her feel more important than anyone else in the room.

Quincy finished unloading his gear and sat on the ground with a groan, stretching his fingers to the fire. "I don't know about you boys, but I can't wait to see my Minié balls slam into a Reb or two tomorrow. It's been too long since we had a fight."

Emily exchanged a glance with both Ben and Willie. "This is going to be my and Ben's first skirmish. Got any advice?" The sun dipped below the trees, and a cold wind pierced her overcoat. Emily reached for the tin plate that Willie held out for her, eager for the warmth it would bring her body. She shoveled in a square of pork and chewed slowly to savor the saltiness.

Quincy accepted his plate. "Keep your head down, aim low, and reload as fast as possible." He forked a huge bite of potato into his mouth, fanning his tongue as it burned.

Emily smiled and hunched her shoulders forward, reveling in the heat rising from her plate. She could fire and reload four times a minute, which was fast, and she could certainly keep her head down. It was the part about shooting people that she wasn't so sure about.

"We'll prevail tomorrow," Willie said, handing Emily his empty cup for some coffee. "I feel it in my bones."

"I hope you're right," Ben said. He shot Emily a look that

conveyed his concern. "I've already lost enough of my family. I don't aim to lose more."

They were roused before dawn, not with a bugle call, but by officers going quietly around camp, kicking men's feet and grunting, "It's time."

Breakfast was a hurried affair, eaten cold with stiff and trembling fingers. They were instructed to pack everything and to line up for roll call within ten minutes.

Two men from their company had disappeared during the night. Emily did not know either of them, but she knew desertion was a serious crime. If caught, the men would likely face a firing squad made up of men from their own company. The knowledge cast a heavy pall over all gathered. Every man kept silent as final instructions were given and they began the short march up Allegheny Mountain under cover of darkness. Frost crunched underfoot. Their breath looked like smoke.

Emily fell into step between Ben and Willie, with Quincy on the other side of Ben. No one spoke as they followed the Stars and Stripes up the mountain.

When they neared the Confederate camp at the top, they were quietly ordered to fan out through the forest and be ready to fire into the clearing where the Rebs slept in their winter quarters. They would attack imminently.

The sky lightened and Emily saw that much of the forest had been cut down, leaving stumps and brush to maneuver around. There would be little to hide behind when the Rebs started shooting.

Before Emily was ready, the bugle sounded the order and the entire line of Federal soldiers started running. Emily, Ben, and Willie joined in, keeping their places in line, and soon they could see that the Rebs weren't asleep after all.

The sun was starting to come up over the mountains to the east. A shaft of light speared the clearing and illuminated a row of gray uniforms with weapons pointed straight at them. All at once, the bangs and pops of musket fire filled the mountain, followed soon after by the loud boom of artillery. Smoke drifted on the cold air, obscuring her sight. A stump near Emily shattered from a Rebel shot, and she flinched as splinters hit her face. She dropped to her knee and leveled her rifle, forcing herself not to think of the gray line as men, but as an evil force trying to kill her and her friends.

She was able to fire and reload and fire again for what felt like hours, occasionally rushing to another location for better cover or back to the supply wagon for ammunition. Twice she dragged a fellow soldier who had been hit back to where those assigned to nursing duty could help him, but she always returned to her post.

And always, always, she kept track of Ben and Willie's locations. She only lost them one time, when she found herself at a bit of a distance from her comrades. As she was standing up to advance, a Johnny Reb surprised her by popping up from behind an earthwork that she'd thought abandoned. For one timeless moment, she stared into his wild eyes, unsure of what to do next. Even the sounds of the bugles and drums and the screams of the wounded faded away. All she knew was the youthful face of the man in front of her. He was too young to grow a beard, and his dirt-smudged cheeks still showed the pudginess of youth. When his countenance of surprise shifted to hatred, Emily knew she would be taking her last breath unless she fired first.

She fired.

The Reb's mouth dropped open in shock, and she watched as he looked down at the blood spreading across his chest. He stared at her in surprise, as if asking why she had shot him. Then he pitched forward and landed on his face in the dirt.

Nausea rolled through Emily as she reloaded. Her limbs felt

heavy and slow, as if she were trying to run through mud, and she knew she would remember that boy's face forever. But, right now, she needed to continue to fight and to stay alive.

Hours later, the sun was high in the sky and Emily's arms ached from the constant strain of loading and firing. Her canteen had run dry, and her mouth felt as if it were shriveling up like the garden in a drought from the powder that inevitably got into her mouth when she tore the paper cartridges open with her teeth.

"Fix bayonets!"

Emily's breath hitched. The order had come from the opposing side. She had only seconds before she'd be facing steel blades. Shaking, she hurried to fix her bayonet.

"Retreat! Retreat!" someone shouted, and Emily looked up to see a line of Rebs running straight at her with bayonets glinting in the winter sunlight. Fear slammed through her so swiftly that she almost couldn't move. She dropped the shot she was trying to ram into her barrel and turned to run for safety.

"Ben! Willie!" she called as she ran. "Fall back!" Up ahead, she could see the mounted officers galloping behind the lines, motioning the soldiers toward them as they took aim and fired over their heads on the Rebs coming up behind. "Retreat!" one of them hollered.

Emily stopped running after she passed Colonel Milroy and his horse, turning back to make sure Ben and Willie were retreating. She fell into step with them as their forces ran down the mountain.

Finally, at the base of the mountain where they'd camped the night before, they were ordered to halt. Emily thought the officers of her regiment must be concocting another attack plan and it would only be a matter of time before they were ordered to charge up the mountain again.

As she waited, Emily sat on the cold ground, exhausted. A tremor swept through her body, and she realized she hadn't eaten for several hours. If she was going to return to the fight, she needed fuel. With the call to march coming at any moment, she didn't have time to build a fire and cook, so she settled on a square of hardtack, which might be all her sour stomach could hold right now anyway. She'd discovered through trial and error that she could not bite through the rock-hard bread, so instead, she sucked on one corner until it softened enough to scrape off with her teeth.

Willie dropped down next to her and sat with his hands hanging between his knees. Emily could smell him and knew she probably stank equally as bad. Willie's face was streaked with black powder. "I don't think I could lift my musket again to save my life. You'll have to save me if the Rebs come after us."

Emily nodded, feeling much the same. "Don't worry. I only have to throw this hardtack at our attacker's head, and he'll be gone from this world."

They fell into an easy silence, too exhausted for further conversation. Emily watched Ben carefully as he returned from filling their canteens, worried how the battle had affected him and wondering where his energy came from that he could perform even that simple chore. He did not seem harmed in any way from the day's fighting. In fact, under all the soot and dirt covering him, his face was alight with joy. His teeth gleamed white when he smiled at her. "That was something, wasn't it?"

Emily thought of the man she'd killed and could not force an answering smile, no matter how hard she tried. She nodded.

"It sure was," Willie agreed, his face lighting up at the memory. "I didn't expect so many of them up there."

"I know!" Ben handed Emily her canteen and plopped down next to Willie.

The two of them continued discussing the battle, but Emily had lost interest. With the hardtack hanging out of her mouth, she dug her diary out of her knapsack. She found, however, that there were no words to adequately describe what had happened to her. Battle was something men talked about and wrote about all the time, but Emily now knew the reality was very different. So much more terrifying. And yet, exhilarating. Brutal, yet life-affirming. And sad.

So very sad.

The image of the man she'd shot filled her mind again, and she closed her eyes. *Forgive me*, she begged him silently.

The bugle sounded, calling them to fall in, and soon they were on the return march to their permanent camp at Cheat Mountain. Rumors and speculation flew through the ranks.

"There's no doubt in my mind we conquered those Rebs," one man boasted. "Why, I took down at least thirty of them myself!"

Emily did not know how he knew that because shots were flying in all directions during the firefight. Except for the one, she had no idea if any of her shots had hit anyone.

"I think we were lucky to get out alive," said another man. "Those Rebs knew we were comin', and they were ready for us."

"Did we win?"

"Of course we did."

"Nah. We lost this one, boys."

Emily listened and concentrated on putting one foot in front of the other. The face of the Reb she'd shot would not fade from her mind. She carried him with her with every exhausting step. For the first time, soldiering was something she no longer wanted to do.

When they finally reached camp at Cheat Mountain after dark, she didn't have the energy for anything more than to wrap herself in her coat and rubber blanket and lie down on the ground to sleep, too tired to care if she froze to death during the night.

Sleep claimed her, though her dreams were filled with the sounds of gunfire, artillery explosions, the cries of men as they lay dying, and the image of a Southern boy's face as she shot him dead.

In the morning they were told they had fought honorably and courageously, but the victor was indeterminable. Both sides had large numbers of casualties, and unfortunately, the Rebs remained at the top of Allegheny Mountain.

That sounded like a loss to Emily's ears, but she kept her opinion to herself. She felt much improved after a night's rest, except for a heaviness hanging about her that she could not shake off. She went about her duties as always, drilling, firing practice, fatigue duty that involved collecting wood and water, digging entrenchments, and working construction on a new blockhouse, but she could not quite get back to her old self. Nothing was as fun as it had been before the battle.

It wasn't until Retreat roll call before supper that Emily heard the news. Quincy Rawlings had been injured so severely in the battle that the surgeon had been forced to remove his right leg above the knee. He was being sent home.

"Come on, brother," Ben said as he came upon her sitting in front of a cold fire. For once, Willie wasn't with him. "Let's rebuild our tent while we wait for the call to supper."

Emily pulled her heavy thoughts back. Ben shook out his half-tent and attached it to the one he pulled off her pack, using the buttons and holes along the sides. Though she wanted to do nothing but rest, she also wanted a warm place to sleep tonight, so she forced herself to her feet to help him.

They'd finished constructing their new shelter only a week ago, just in time for the freezing nights that descended over camp. The money they'd paid to a soldier in camp who had been a mason before the war had been well spent. Using stones Emily and Ben carried from the river, he'd constructed a fireplace and chimney that kept their little tent cabin warm.

They'd stretched their half-shelter tents over a framework

of sapling rafters to form a roof, with the gables covered by their rubber blankets. When they'd been ordered to march to Allegheny, they had taken down their half-tents and blankets, and now they needed to put it all back.

Having finished fastening the tents together, Ben flung the fabric over the rafters. Emily grabbed for it on the other side and set to work tying the corners and sides to the stockade walls. When they met at the back of their little cabin to fasten Ben's rubber blanket to the gable there, he looked around and, in a low voice, said, "I've been thinking. What if we invited Willie to share our shelter with us now that Quincy is gone? More bodies in one cabin would be warmer."

Emily's fingers froze, and she looked at her younger brother in disbelief. Was he asking her blessing to share a bed with another man? His expression gave no answer, so all Emily could do was make her voice carefully neutral when she asked, "Where would he sleep, exactly?"

A flush crept up Ben's neck. His gaze slid away from hers to focus on the knots that he seemed unable to tie. "It would be a simple matter to construct an elevated bunk. Some of the cabins have four men in them. Three of us should be quite comfortable."

Emily looked around to make sure no one was within earshot and lowered her voice. "Ben, I see you've developed feelings for Willie, and I see he feels the same." She laid her hand on his arm to get him to look at her. "While I admit that I'm surprised by it, I can see he makes you happy. What I'm worried about, though, is that if others find out, they won't understand and they'll hurt you. Or, worse."

Ben's eyebrows drew together, and he looked confused. "Why would anyone hurt me?"

He wasn't making this easy for her. She took a deep breath. "Haven't you heard the way the men joke about bedroom matters? The few times anyone has mentioned sexual relations between two men, it was clearly said with disgust, hatred even. I don't want you to be the target of all that."

Ben's mouth was twisted to the side, and he was biting his lip as though trying not to laugh. Emily grabbed both of his upper arms and put her face right in his. "It's not funny! You're putting yourself and Willie in danger if you continue this way!"

Rather than making him understand, her words seemed to amuse him further. And then he did the most surprising thing. He pulled Emily into a hug. "Oh, Em, I do love you. You are something else."

Emily hadn't realized how much she'd missed physical contact. Back at home she'd hugged Ada, Harriet, Pa, or one of her brothers nearly every day. It wasn't since David died, in fact, that she'd been hugged, and now that Ben held her, she didn't want it to end. She closed her eyes and held him a moment longer.

But she needed to make him see her point. Regretfully, she pulled back to face him again. "Ben, don't you understand what I'm saying to you? You must end your relationship with Willie before you are discovered."

Ben's eyes still gleamed with delight as he said, "I love Willie, Em. I truly do."

Emily looked at the ground and searched her mind for a way to make him see her point. Ben reached out a finger, which he placed under her chin to tip her face up. His expression softened. "You do know Willie is a woman, don't you?"

Emily reared back and stumbled over an exposed root. "What?"

At her exclamation, Ben shushed her and pulled her back behind their cabin. With all the commotion in camp and music coming from a handful of different groups, she doubted anyone had heard her. Still, she lowered her voice again to be certain no one but Ben heard her words. "Willie is a woman? You're not lying?"

Ben shook his head. "She's the same as you."

Emily felt as if she'd been hit by a lightning bolt. How could she have not seen the truth? How had she missed all the signs? Because now that Emily thought about it, there had been several. Willie's small hands. The way he cut off his laughter as though embarrassed by its unusually high pitch. The way he rubbed dirt on his chin, which Emily had thought was due to absentmindedness but now realized was intentional to look like the shadow of a beard.

Right on the heels of the realization came an unexpected feeling of betrayal. Why hadn't Willie trusted Emily with the secret?

Shame filled her. Emily hadn't trusted Willie with her secret either.

"So what do you think?" Ben cut into her thoughts. "Can I invite her to share our cabin now that she doesn't have a tent-mate? We can protect her."

A new thought came to Emily's mind. "Don't you care about the impropriety of that? I mean, what about her honor?"

Ben's eyebrows shot into his hairline, and he rolled his eyes. "Since when do you care about propriety, Miss Trousers?"

Emily blanched at the truth of his words, and then a burst of laughter escaped her. She was being ridiculous. She shook her head and reached to tie the final knots on their cabin. "Yes, I think it's a good idea to have Willie join us. But"—she paused, nervous—"does she know...about me?"

Ben nodded. "I told her you're a woman, too, if that's what you're getting at."

A shot of anger swept through her. How long had Willie known the truth about her? "That wasn't your business to tell, Ben. You should've asked me first."

He ducked his head. "I know. I'm so sorry. It slipped out after I discovered her secret." Here his face flamed, and Emily wondered what they had been doing when the truth was discovered. Clearly, however, Ben wasn't going to share that bit of the story with her. "I wanted to reassure her that I wouldn't give her away."

Emily pinned him with her gaze. "That's a bit ironic, don't you think?"

Again, he looked ashamed, which mollified Emily. "You're right," he admitted. "I shouldn't have said a word. I won't make the mistake again. I promise."

She nodded. "See that you don't." Then, to show him she held no hard feelings, she gave him a little shove toward camp. "Go invite her, I mean, him—we must still use that pronoun—to join our tent, and I'll hunt up some timber for another bunk."

"Thanks, Em." Ben pulled her into another quick hug before dashing away. Emily shook her head in wonder as she went in search of an ax to fell the trees she'd need for Willie's new bunk. Improper or not, it was probably better for the couple to have a private place where they could relax their guard so they didn't slip up in the presence of others.

Their cabin would now be cozier with three of them in it. So why did the idea of Willie joining them make Emily feel so lonely?

Later, after Willie's bunk was built, her few possessions moved in, and dinner was eaten, the three friends finally had time to relax around the fire outside. Emily couldn't help but feel awkward around Willie, now that she knew her secret, and she realized both Willie and Ben were probably feeling awkward, too, or else they would have gone inside to escape the cold. The tone of the entire camp was subdued tonight. She heard no music, and most of the men were writing letters or staring silently into the flames of their campfires.

Ben cleared his throat. "I wonder if the man who killed Pa was in battle yesterday." He poked at the fire with a stick. "I'd like to know he got his due."

Emily wondered what due was coming to her for the boy she'd shot. She swallowed hard.

They all stared into the flames, lost in their thoughts. Emily thought that was all they were going to say about the battle, but then Willie quietly asked, "Did you hear that horse scream when the shell hit him?"

Emily shuddered, remembering. It was a sound that had haunted her all through the long cold night, and she was not looking forward to a repeat tonight. "Some of the men say we should sew our names onto our clothes. To identify our bodies if it comes to that."

Only the sound of the popping and crackling of the fire greeted her announcement. After a long moment, Willie got up and went into their tent. She reemerged carrying a small pouch and raised her eyebrows. "Well? Go get your housewives, and let's get it done."

Emily got to her feet and went inside to dig her sewing kit, called a housewife by the soldiers, out of her pack. Ben followed close behind her.

Willie was still standing by the fire, and she had both hands on the still-fastened top button of her coat. She looked at Emily with a half smile. "Perhaps we should do this inside, where it's warmer."

Emily realized it wasn't a matter of warmth that prompted the suggestion, but the need to keep their secrets. Removing their coats, something Emily never did except to sleep at night, could risk revealing their true forms under the thin Army blouses they wore.

"Yes, good idea," she answered, turning back to their tent. "Let's go inside." She pulled aside the rubber blanket that served as their door, just as Ben was coming out. "We're going to work inside," she told him.

The smile on Ben's face did not reveal if he understood the reason she wanted to work inside, but he was clearly delighted at finally sharing his personal space with Willie. The look he sent her could have melted wax. "I'll go collect some wood for the fire so we'll be plenty warm."

Emily and Willie each removed their overcoats and settled side by side on Emily's bunk. As they set to work sewing their names into their collars, Emily spoke hesitantly. "Do you bind your...yourself? To look more like a man?"

Willie shook her head. "No need to. As long as I keep my coat or jacket on, no one can see anything. My mother and sister are equally as...um, lacking." She laughed good-naturedly.

Emily laughed along with her friend. She'd lost weight since enlisting, which reduced the size of her bosom some, but she still required the bindings. "Consider yourself fortunate. My bindings are too hot and too restrictive. There are times I swear I might faint for the lack of a deep breath."

They were still laughing when Ben came in. "What's so funny?" he asked as he crouched in front of their tiny fireplace to build up the fire.

Emily and Willie looked at each other and broke out in another fit of giggles. The topic was much too personal to share with a man, even Ben. When he turned back to them with a quizzical look on his face, they both laughed harder. "What?" he asked.

Emily took pity on her brother and forced herself to stop laughing. "It is nothing," she told him. "Truly."

Emily changed the subject. "Willie, tell us about your home in the Nebraska Territory. What's it like there?"

Willie smiled toward her handiwork, but her mind was clearly on her home as she said, "It's beautiful. You would love it. Both of you. All wide-open sky, rolling wheat fields, and prairie. You think the horizon is going to stretch on forever, but then a mountain pops up out of nowhere and it's the most beautiful thing you could imagine."

Emily could almost see what Willie described. "What about your family farm?"

Willie nodded and used her teeth to cut the thread. "My family grows wheat and corn, which my father sells in Omaha to traders who take it down the Missouri. My older brother is talking about getting into the cattle business, but when I left, he hadn't done anything about it yet."

"You've mentioned him before," Ben said, the sewing completely forgotten on his lap where he sat on the ground by the fire. "Tell us more about him."

"His name is Terrence. He's five years older than me and has a wife with a baby on the way." She fell silent for a moment and, in a quiet voice, amended, "I suppose by now the baby must be about a year old."

Emily didn't like to see her friend sad. "Do you have other siblings, or is it just you and Terrence?"

Willie nodded. "I have a younger sister." She hugged her coat in her arms. "She was the only one I told before I left." Abruptly, she dug through the coat on her lap until she found what she was looking for in an inside pocket and held it out toward Emily. "She gave me this so I would not forget her. It was her favorite."

Emily stuck her needle into her coat and set the whole thing aside so she could take the offered handkerchief from Willie with the reverence it deserved. She spread the square of cotton over her lap and studied the fragile design.

The border was made of tiny red stitches in a subtle scallop design. Inside of this were tiny red dots in a band about a quarter inch wide. Next to the band of scattered dots was a row of red dot clusters forming diamonds, laid end to end all the way around. The entire pattern was repeated, scattered dots and diamond dots, and finished with diamonds even smaller, made of only four red dots. Stitched into one corner were the initials ODE. Emily pointed to the initials. "Are these your sister's?"

Willie nodded as she took back the handkerchief, as though

it pained her to be out of contact with it for too long. "Yes, her name is Olive."

Emily wondered about the other two initials. "Is Smith a name you chose when you enlisted?"

Willie nodded but did not offer her real family name.

Ben said, "Olive must be real special to you."

Willie blinked several times and resolutely returned to her sewing, even though her name was finished on her overcoat. Emily thought she wasn't going to respond, but then Willie said, "Yes, she is. She helped me concoct my plan and new identity when I decided I needed to leave home. If not for her, I wouldn't be here, free."

"What do you mean, free?" Ben asked, doing his best not to appear too interested, but Emily saw he was barely breathing in anticipation of Willie's answer.

Willie kept her eyes on her needle and thread, up and down, creating a design after her name that looked like a sheaf of wheat. "My father arranged a marriage for me that I did not want." She blushed. "The man was a neighbor whose first wife had died, leaving five children. He was thirty years my senior."

Ben nodded, and tension visibly drained off of him. "So you had to run away to avoid the marriage?"

"Yes, and I'm sure I broke my poor mama's heart in the process." She fell silent as she took several stitches. "The only way I could survive on my own was if I took on the identity of a male. Otherwise there would be no jobs available to me."

Emily understood this well. The only jobs available to an unmarried woman were domestic worker or schoolteacher, neither of which paid enough to support oneself. The other option, prostitution, was too horrible to think about.

Willie let out a loud sigh. "The rest you know. I enlisted, and here I am."

"Do you think you'll go home after the war?" Emily asked her, thinking about their own home in Indiana.

"Oh, most assuredly." Willie's voice lost the melancholy tone and became animated. "I want to own my own farm there. Maybe even have a cattle ranch like my brother."

"Near your family?" Ben asked.

"If they'll forgive me for leaving."

Later, after Tattoo, the three of them settled for the first time together in their tent for the night. Emily lay quietly and listened to the mournful sound of a bugle playing "Taps." As the drummer beat a few single, isolated beats at the end, she turned over onto her side and whispered, "I'm happy you're with us, Willie. And I'm happy you two have each other."

"Thanks, Jesse," came the whispered reply out of the darkness. "I'm happy, too."

A rustling sounded, and in the lingering light of their dying fire, she saw Ben's hand reach to the newly built bunk above him, where Willie clasped it in a momentary squeeze.

Emily shifted again to stare at the dark canvas above her, wishing it was only Ben here and she could tell him how scared she'd been at Allegheny. But telling him would likely only make him want to send her home.

"Em?"

She startled, surprised he'd use that name in front of Willie. "Yeah?"

"I'm happy you weren't hurt in the battle."

She had to draw a deep breath before she could trust her voice to remain steady. "Yeah, me too." She waited a moment and then, softly, she said, "Good night."

"Good night, Em."

Chapter Fifteen

Present day: Woodinville, Washington

December 13, 1861: I wonder, when I die, will I see the face of the person who kills me and feel only pain and hatred toward him? Or will I see the face of God as His welcoming arms surround me and feel nothing but His love, as Aunt Harriet says happens in Heaven? Does God welcome those who have taken the lives of others?

I took a man's life today. Possibly more than one, but one I know for certain because we were face-to-face and if I hadn't killed him first, I would not be here writing these words. He was young. He was a person with a family waiting at home.

When I sleep, he is there. Taunting me, laughing at me, begging me to spare him. Blood, screams, terror, all the horrors of battle fill my dreams and make me wake often. I feel covered by that man's blood.

I love most things about being a soldier, but I despise the killing.

Larkin closed the diary and sat for a long time with her eyes closed, remembering the first time she'd taken a life. It had been necessary, she knew. And doing so had likely saved countless other lives. But still, it had eaten away at her. She knew exactly how Emily Wilson had felt. Killing changed a person.

For the past week, ever since the winery fiasco, Larkin hadn't left the house. Not even to go for a walk with Bowie. Griff's suicide had hit her hard, and her nightmares and flashbacks were taking her over.

She wasn't doing well. She'd called her therapist and talked with her for an hour—promising yet again to find someone local to see on a regular basis but knowing she wasn't going to—and came away from the call feeling no better. She knew how to cope with her symptoms. She knew to identify her stuck points—the strong negative beliefs she held that were problematic—as they entered her mind and how to change them. She knew to name her emotions so that she could process them rather than avoid them or let them become consuming. She knew to confront her trauma, whether it was memories from Afghanistan or losing Griff, and process through it, challenging the assumptions and false beliefs she attached to the events. She even knew that yoga and meditation and deep breathing helped.

But it all felt like bullshit.

All she wanted to do was distract herself by reading Emily's diary, and when the words started to blur, she shifted to the new laptop she'd ordered after ruining her last one to try to find anything connected to Emily on the internet. And when all that became too much, she drank, slept, watched *Doctor Who* reruns, and drank some more.

Reading Emily's account of the Battle of Allegheny Mountain both thrilled her and shook her. She was so proud of Emily for standing strong with the men and proving she was fit to be there, but she knew too well what it actually felt like to have bullets whizzing past, each with the intent to kill.

Larkin had never been afraid of a firefight and had taken part in many, but now that she no longer had her weapon, the account of the battle reminded her how vulnerable she really was.

Lives were taken so easily by bombs, bullets, accidents, or one's own hand. How did anyone manage to go about their lives in this world and not feel scared shitless? And pissed off by that?

Larkin was angry, that much was certain. And when she read Emily's accounts of the bad dreams plaguing her since the battle, she knew there was a good chance the poor woman had also suffered from PTSD. But of course it wasn't called that back then. Soldiers presenting with symptoms of PTSD during the Civil War era were said to suffer from melancholia, soldier's heart, or, absurdly, insanity. Sufferers in World War I were diagnosed with shell shock. In World War II it was combat fatigue, battle fatigue, or even the victim-blaming "lack of mental fortitude." Vietnam veterans were told they had post-Vietnam syndrome, as if that meant anything.

Trauma messed a person up, no matter what time period they lived in. That's what Larkin knew for certain.

Did reading the diary of a traumatized woman trigger her own symptoms? Larkin didn't know, but she wasn't about to stop. She knew to take it in small doses.

That was why today she'd let her cousins and Grams drag her away from it all and to the mall for some Christmas shopping.

Maybe *insanity* was an accurate diagnosis after all, she thought as she stood in the busy center court and surveyed the mass of humanity pushing and shoving past one another. Why else had she agreed to come here? This was a mistake. She could not handle crowds like this. Too many people, too much commotion, too much noise, too many potential threats.

On the balcony above them a line of parents and children snaked around the atrium and down the opposite wing of stores, all of them waiting to see Santa, who presided over a mock North Pole workshop. A stage was set up to one side of the center court, and on it, a middle school band screeched out "Here Comes Santa Claus." Larkin eyed the instrument cases stacked along the back of the stage, knowing any of them could contain an IED. For that matter, any package carried by any one of these shoppers could contain an IED. Puffy winter jackets could be hiding suicide vests.

"I want to go to Nordstrom to look for a sweater for Mom," Kaia said. "Who wants to come with?"

"I'll come," Jenna said. "Maybe I'll find something for Evan's mom there." She turned to Larkin and Grams. "You two coming?"

Larkin didn't answer. She was too busy watching a group of teenage boys who were following some girls much too closely. Were they going to harm them? Grams laid a hand on her arm.

"I think Larkin and I will find a quiet spot to get a cup of coffee. You two go ahead, and we'll meet up later."

Larkin let Grams pull her along as she did her best to watch each and every person around them—up ahead, in the stores they passed, sitting on benches, and leaning against walls. Soon, Grams gently pushed her into a chair in the back corner of a coffee shop. Larkin sat, grateful Grams knew to give her the seat that put her back against the wall.

Eventually, the cocoon of the coffee shop eased her tension, and Larkin was able to focus on a conversation with Grams. She updated her on the latest sections of Emily's diary and on her search for Emily in other records. "Basically, I'm not getting far," she admitted, sipping the peppermint mocha Grams had set in front of her.

"What can I do to help?" Grams offered. "I've done a lot of genealogy research and can navigate the various sites."

"Let's sit down together tomorrow and see what you can come up with." Larkin was distracted again. A woman wearing a niqab had entered, pushing a toddler in a stroller.

It wasn't the woman's clothing that made Larkin uneasy. She'd found far more innocent women during her searches than not, and she'd befriended plenty of women who dressed similar to this one. No, what made her uneasy was the fact that she was the exact height and size as Anahita. Even her eyes looked the same. They were the same light blue as the sky on a hot summer afternoon. This woman's eyes were rimmed with eyeliner, and her lids were painted a dusky rose color. That alone should have differentiated her from Anahita, for Larkin had never seen the girl wear makeup. But still, for a moment, Larkin's stomach jumped into her throat.

As she watched, the woman ordered a box of apple juice for her son and spent a minute trying to stab the tiny straw into the hole as the toddler screamed and kicked his miniature Nike shoes against the stroller. When she finally handed it to him, he grabbed it with both hands and settled back with a look of adoration at his mother.

Anahita had never gotten the chance to be a mother.

"Larkin?" Grams asked. "You okay?"

"Uh, yeah. I'm fine." She forced her gaze away from the woman and back to her coffee. No, she would not think about Anahita. She would not go there. Not today. Today she was supposed to be having a nice shopping outing and nothing more. She gripped her cup between both hands and plastered on a smile for Grams. "So, Grams, what do you want Santa to bring you this year?"

The Anahita look-alike accepted the iced latte the barista handed her and stuck it into a cup holder on the stroller, presumably to drink later when she wasn't so covered up. She said something to her son, and they left the store. Larkin watched until she disappeared, her heart still yearning for Anahita.

Chapter Sixteen

December 25, 1861: Union Army Camp, Cheat Mountain

*T*he regiment settled back into camp life so smoothly that one might forget they had partaken of battle earlier in the month. But Emily could not forget. Every night she faced the Rebs again, and every night she shot that poor boy over and over. Sometimes it took all night long to kill him. The worst was when she shot a Reb in her dream, and after the smoke had cleared, she was looking into her own dead face. Or Ben's. Or Willie's. One time, the face even belonged to her little cousin Ada.

She had taken to volunteering for night guard duty to give Ben and Willie privacy, but mostly to avoid her dreams. It helped some. When she dozed during free moments throughout the day, the dreams did not come, and she was able to find her rest that way.

When Christmas morning dawned, others in camp were as excited as children. For many Union soldiers, St. Nicholas came in the shape of a Christmas box delivered by express mail from home. Although Emily, Ben, and Willie never received packages and knew none would be coming on this day, they did catch the joy in the air. When called to Reveille, some men in another company were so high on anticipation of the day that they launched into singing before roll call. Soon, nearly every man gathered had joined in, including Emily, and their voices filled the morning air with the tune "O Come, All Ye Faithful," followed immediately by "One Horse Open Sleigh."

No quarter was given in honor of the holiday, and drilling and fatigue duty commenced per usual. After Retreat sounded late in the afternoon, however, a swarm of men raced for the express wagons that had arrived with the mail. Emily, Ben, and Willie returned to their tent.

"I think we need a Christmas tree," Ben announced as they rested their weapons against the wall. "I'll go find something suitable while you two find a way to decorate it." He caught Emily's eye and gave her a wink.

She was startled to feel the sting of tears and an overwhelming rush of heat in her throat. As much as she'd tried to hide it, Ben must have noticed how the battle had affected her and was trying to cheer her up. She'd always loved Christmas, and when she'd first seen a drawing of a Christmas tree in *Harper's Weekly* several years ago, she had made a nuisance of herself until Pa had given in and gotten them one. They'd had a Christmas tree every year since, and Ben knew it was Emily's favorite part of the holiday, after the special meal, of course. But that was not an option in camp.

"We have no candles or ribbon or nuts or cakes," Willie announced unnecessarily. "What can we possibly find to decorate the tree with?"

Emily went into their tent and started poking through their meager possessions. Socks? No, those would hardly look festive, what with the holes in the heels and toes and ripe smell emanating from them. Minié balls or cartridges? She rejected that idea as well. First of all, it would be too dangerous in the chance that the tree caught on fire, and second, they would likely get in serious trouble for misuse of ammunition.

What could they use?

Her gaze landed on her haversack. Three days' worth of hardtack was stacked inside, more than she could possibly eat. If Ben and Willie also gave some of theirs, the hard biscuits might look like the cakes and cookies they used at home on the tree. She grabbed all but two.

What else?

The only thing left was a packet of desiccated vegetables and another of salt pork. After months of the tough meat, she could stand to forgo that particular ration for a few days.

Willie laughed when she saw the salt pork, but she dashed inside and emerged a moment later with her own rations. Ben returned carrying a spruce tree as tall as his shoulders. He dug a pit into the ground in front of their tent and stuck the trunk of the tree into it, using dirt and rocks to prop it upright. When he was finished, he stepped back and proudly announced, "We have a Christmas tree."

Feeling lighter than she had in weeks, Emily began arranging her hardtack on the branches. Like at home, she started to sing, "Silent night. Holy night…"

Willie and Ben joined in the singing, and all three of them continued decorating the tree. When Emily laid chunks of salt pork on a branch, it sent Ben into a fit of laughter so intense, he was bent over double with his hands on his knees.

They were all laughing as Schafer and MacGregor walked up, carrying boxes in their arms. "Merry Christmas," Schafer greeted them, a quizzical look on his face. "What is the joke?"

Ben simply pointed at the tree, and when Schafer saw the chunks of gray meat that were its decoration, he let out a loud guffaw.

MacGregor did nothing more than shrug as he sat on a stump. "In the spirit of Yuletide, we thought we'd share our boxes with all of ye, seeing as how your relations are not so generous."

The kindness of the gesture sobered everyone. Willie shook

her head. "That is considerate of you, but there is no need." Emily saw that her gaze was firmly fixed on the fruitcake in MacGregor's open box.

Emily nodded. "Your families sent those to you. You should enjoy them."

"There is more here than we could possibly enjoy on our own," Schafer assured them. "Besides, it gives me joy to share with you." As though that decided the matter, he pulled out a bottle of brandy. "Who wants a drink?"

They all did, and soon all five were passing around the bottle and taking swigs of the burning liquid in between bites of the fruitcake and walnuts from MacGregor's box.

Looking for more treats, MacGregor dug through his box and pulled out a book with a sound of disgust. "I don't know what my wife was thinking when she included this in my box. At least it will make good kindling."

He moved to toss the book onto the fire but Emily saw the title, *Uncle Tom's Cabin*, and stopped him. "I'd like to read it, if you've a mind to let me have it." She had heard of the book by Harriet Beecher Stowe, and its examination of slavery.

MacGregor shrugged and handed it to her. The call for supper sounded, and they all got to their feet to retrieve their plates and cups.

As they joined the chow line, they discovered another stir of excitement rippling through the ranks. "Captain's wife is here, and she's handing out gifts!"

Speculation on what the gift might be spread like wildfire. Some guessed blankets, others socks. One man, his hands buried deep in his pockets, hoped for gloves.

When it was their turn at the soup pots, they were given a serving of fresh beef and buttered peas along with their usual coffee. The line continued to where the captain and his wife were standing together in front of a wagon loaded with boxes.

The captain's wife was young and beautiful in a green

velvet dress and burgundy cape. Her blond hair was drawn up and pinned under a black hat, but a few curls had escaped to frame her delicate face, her cheeks tinged pink from the cold. Balancing her plate and cup on one arm, Emily raised her collar, pulled her cap lower, and tried to hide as much of her hands as possible in her long sleeves. Would the captain's wife recognize a fellow woman in her or Willie? Was this the moment their ruse would be discovered?

As they edged closer, Emily saw that the woman had an air of sadness about her. She was smiling as she placed a fresh apple and a homemade molasses cookie into each soldier's open hand, but the smile did not reach her eyes. Those were often shifting to the side where her husband was conversing with a fellow officer. Emily sensed an intense longing there.

But oh, how the woman was on the receiving end of attention from the enlisted men! Emily could not help but smile as one man after another nearly tripped over himself when confronted by the first woman any of them had knowingly seen in months.

Unbidden, the memory of Teddy Hobson and his marriage proposal came to mind. He was the only man who had ever acted anything like these men around Emily. She knew she was no beauty like the captain's wife, but she was not unpleasant upon which to gaze. Frankly, the men made themselves look silly, preening and blushing in front of the woman. Emily would much prefer a man who treated her kindly and respected her mind equally as much as, if not more than, her appearance.

Suddenly, it was Emily's turn at the front of the line. Fear flared hot inside her, and she felt her face flame. Ducking her head, she reached out for the apple and cookie. The captain's wife placed both in her hand without a word, and Emily mumbled, "Thank you, ma'am," and hurried after Ben without waiting to see how Willie fared.

Dark had settled, and a cold breeze blew through camp with the scent of coming snow. They agreed to eat their dinner indoors and soon were settled inside around the fireplace. Even MacGregor and Schafer joined them, and as they ate, they all shared stories of Christmases past.

When Schafer left to report for guard duty, MacGregor also left, no doubt to join another group gambling on cards. That left the three of them, and now, out of sight of any others, they all relaxed. Ben sat on his bunk with Willie close beside him, their fingers intertwined.

Emily remained on the dirt floor near the fire and watched them for a moment, wondering what their future held. Would the war end soon, and if so, where would they live—Indiana or Nebraska? Would they start a family? Would Emily be there, too?

She'd been thinking a lot about what she wanted when the war ended. Hopefully, that came sooner than the end of her enlistment period of three years. She didn't want to think about how over two and a half more years of soldiering was going to be like when she was already tiring of it. Sure, she loved the freedom she felt as a man, but she was starting to see that a soldier wasn't really free at all. Every moment of the day was dictated, and anyone who dared to do something against the rules was severely punished. Emily couldn't even decide for herself when to eat, when to sleep, where to stand. It was only with careful planning, and Willie's help more than once, that she was able to sneak into the woods every morning and night to relieve herself.

Willie had become vital to Emily in ways she hadn't expected. While Emily loved being a man, she was surprised to find that having another woman around helped to ease the difficulty of Army life. She was sure the men felt as miserable as she did, but they handled it differently. Maybe it was simply that they were more used to dirt, grime, stink, and discomfort than she was. Or maybe the pressure of always having to guard her secret was what was wearing her down. Whatever it was, having Willie to quietly commiserate with helped.

"I've been waiting all day to give you two your Christmas

presents." Ben dug in his trousers pocket and pulled out something small. "I got the idea a few weeks back when we sewed our names onto our coats."

He handed something to Willie and then held his hand out toward Emily. "It's not much, but I hope you like it."

As Emily held the object toward the light of the fire, she realized it was a ring.

"It has my name on it!" Willie exclaimed.

Emily looked closer at hers and saw that inscribed on the outside of the narrow band was the name *E. Jesse Wilson* along with *9th Indiana Inf. Co D.* "Oh, Ben, how did you afford this?"

He shrugged. "I don't got much else to spend my pay on so I asked a sutler to get them for me. Go on. See if it fits."

The ring was small, but it fit perfectly onto her pinkie finger. Now, barring the chance her hand was shot off, her body could be identified. The thought dropped her into the darkness lingering over her since the battle, but she refused to let Ben see her melancholy. She formed her lips into a smile. "Thank you, Ben. That was kind of you."

"Did you get one for yourself?" Willie asked as she admired the ring on her own hand.

"I did." Ben dug into his other pocket and withdrew a third ring, which he slipped onto his own finger. "Someday our grandchildren will look at these and know we honorably served our country."

Emily got to her feet and went to sit on the bunk next to her brother. She picked up his hand and intertwined her fingers through his as she leaned against his shoulder. On the other side, Willie did the same.

As they sat together and waited for the bugle to sound, calling them to Assembly and Tattoo, they watched the flames and held one another close. "I have all I want for Christmas," Emily told them, her heart full. "I have my brother and my new sister with me tonight."

Ben squeezed her hand, and Willie reached over to pat her arm.

"You know," Emily said, "it's funny that I had to become a man before I finally got a sister."

"Except she's a man, too," Willie joked.

"You have a point," Emily said. "Another brother, then."

Ben chuckled. "My dear Willie, I, for one, am grateful that you are indeed not a man."

Willie lifted her face to smile at him, and Emily felt a pang in her heart. "Excuse me," she said as she got to her feet, doing her best not to look at the two lovebirds. "I need to...um...go. I'll see you at Tattoo."

She darted out of the tent and sucked in the cold night air to keep tears from falling. She'd be glad when this emotional day was over.

A snowflake drifted down and landed on her nose, quickly followed by several more. As she watched, the snow came faster and faster, and she held her breath, watching the beauty of everything around her being blanketed by a layer of white perfection.

Even in war, peace finds a way.

Chapter Seventeen

Present day: Woodinville, Washington

December 25, 1861: It is Christmas Day. If we were back at home, we would be eating roasted turkey. Oh, my mouth waters thinking of the mashed potatoes and gravy, roasted brussels sprouts, and soft dinner rolls warm from the oven! I cannot complain, however, about our Christmas rations. Here we ate fresh beef and peas with real butter. The captain's wife visited camp and gave every soldier a fresh apple and a molasses cookie. I felt sad for her. She seemed lonely. I feel sad for us, too, on this day when families gather together. Without Pa and David to share in the holiday joy, today should have been a day like any other. I feel their absence keenly. I must, however, focus on what I do have, and those are a brother and a ~~sister~~ second brother in Willie. They are all I need.

Ben and I don't get boxes from home, of course, but neither does Willie. It seems he had a falling out with his family, and they don't know where he is. Knowing this, I am doubly grateful that we found him. He can be part of our family.

Others shared the contents of their boxes with the three of us, which was kind. With the Christmas boxes came newspapers, and word has spread through camp that Queen Victoria of England has lost her husband to typhoid fever. Even though she is not American like me, nor involved in this bitter war, I feel a kinship with her. Is the entire world in mourning?

*L*arkin gripped the diary in both hands, her heart racing. Emily had clearly written the word *sister* when talking about Willie and then crossed it out. Could Willie have been a woman, too? What were the chances that two women disguised as men served in the same regiment?

She had to know for sure so she texted Zach Faber: Willie was a woman, right? That's what you wanted me to discover on my own?

His reply was immediate, even though they hadn't had any contact since their phone call. Bingo! Fascinating, huh?

Totally! Before she could second-guess herself, she added, Merry Christmas!

You too!

Larkin set her phone aside and wished she could return to reading the diary. Now that she knew Willie was a woman, everything was different. Willie's relationship and interactions with Emily and Ben meant different things.

Another realization hit her. This was why Zach had suspected that the handkerchief had something to do with Willie! If it didn't belong to Emily or Ben—which it surely didn't with initials so different from their own—then it must belong to the only other person they'd been close to, assuming a new relationship didn't appear in the diary later. This was a good lead to go on. ODE must have been Willie's initials, for surely Willie Smith had not been her real name.

Larkin was dying to keep reading, but she couldn't. She'd promised Grams she wouldn't hide up here all day, and even though crowds made her nervous, it was time she joined the family downstairs. Today was Christmas, after all.

Maybe she could take a few moments to go through Sarah's things. She did promise Zach she'd send him some items. But as she stared at the boxes, she realized the task still felt too daunting. She probably shouldn't have made the offer.

A burst of laughter floated upstairs, and Larkin grudgingly admitted she was stalling. Consoling herself with her plan to blend into the background and avoid conversation as much as possible to avoid a freak-out, she left her room.

The entire clan was there, even Uncle Matt who'd had to sit in his car on Snoqualmie Pass for two hours on the drive over while crews performed avalanche control. Everyone wanted to hug her and welcome her home, but they all kept their conversation light and short. She knew she had Grams to thank for that.

Larkin was especially grateful that everyone tried not to overwhelm her when her own mother failed to keep conversation light. It came when they were all settling around the table for dinner. Larkin sat across from Kat, and as she laid her napkin on her lap, her mother asked, "So, Larkin, have you found what you're going to do with your life now that your indentured servitude with the government is over? It's about time you put your college degree to use, if you ask me."

A hush fell over the room until Grams asked, "Who wants some green beans?"

As everyone dug hungrily into the dinner of prime rib and twice-baked potatoes, Larkin ignored her mother's question and kept her eyes on her own food. Somehow, she made it through the meal without snapping at her mother or giving in to the tension in her body that made her want to scream and run out of the room.

After the dishes were cleared, everyone gathered in the family room to open presents. It was all Larkin could do to stay rather than quietly escape upstairs. The heat and commotion were getting to her, as were the fake smiles and overly encouraging comments.

She tried to feel excited over the spa gift card her parents gave to her. Likewise, with the set of journals from Kaia, the yoga mat and video from Jenna, and the new pair of jeans and sweater from Grams. But Larkin felt nothing. Numbness filled her chest and spread through her body, and she couldn't manage even a flicker of interest in any of it.

Last Christmas, before they deployed, Sarah had given Larkin a new pink scarf to wear as a head covering when working with Afghan locals. Larkin had loved that scarf and had worn it nearly every day.

The scarf was gone now. Like Sarah.

She got up to pour herself a whiskey and Coke, flicking her gaze to the clock to see how much longer she was going to be forced to pretend. Too long.

"Oh my goodness, you shouldn't have done this!" Grams's exclamation caught Larkin's attention. Grams was holding a piece of paper and a full-color brochure on her lap. Her eyes were bright with unshed tears, and she held a wrinkled hand over her mouth.

"You deserve this, Mom," Kaia's mom told her with a rub of Grams's shoulder.

"We know it's what you've always wanted to do," Kat added. The satisfied look on her face told Larkin the gift had been her idea. "You've put in so many hours studying your ancestry that we figured it was time you went to Scotland yourself and visited the places where your grandparents once lived."

Grams was shaking her head, still overcome.

Uncle Matt cleared his throat. "All you need to do is choose your travel dates, and we'll get everything else lined up, including first-class seats on British Airways for you and whoever you want to take with you. They're the kind of seats that recline into a bed. You'll love it."

"I hear you should go in July when it's warmer," Larkin's dad said as he got up to pour himself a drink. "Or August if you want to see the Royal Edinburgh Military Tattoo and you don't mind the crowds."

"Yeah, but doesn't Scotland get midges in the summer?" Kaia's mom asked, the bells on her Christmas sweater jingling. "I've heard they can drive a person crazy."

"I don't care when I go," Grams said. "I'm thrilled to go at all." She was looking around the room at all the faces of her family, and her own face reflected the love she felt. When she got to Larkin, however, something flickered in her eyes and her smile looked strained. "Perhaps I'll wait to book the trip for a little while," she told her children as she carefully set her gift on the end table beside her. "You know, so I can fully research where to go and what to see."

Everyone started chiming in with their thoughts of what Grams should do in Scotland, but Larkin didn't hear any of it. All she saw was the mask Grams had drawn over her face when she'd remembered Larkin and all she was going through right now. Larkin knew Grams was afraid to leave her alone. She was afraid Larkin would hurt herself if she wasn't here to stop her.

Larkin stared at her feet and let her hair form a curtain around her face. Grams wasn't wrong. Some days she was the only thing holding Larkin together. The last thing Larkin wanted was Grams postponing the trip she'd dreamed of her whole life—but she had to admit that she really didn't want Grams to go. How selfish was that?

Her aunt collected the discarded wrapping paper to stuff into a garbage bag while the others refilled drinks and set pies and cookies out for dessert. Larkin took advantage of the commotion and snuck up the stairs to her room.

She needed a break from herself, a break from her problems and her mistakes and her weaknesses. She needed Emily Wilson's world.

With her back against her headboard and her new computer on her lap, she opened Grams's genealogy site account. She should figure out who Willie Smith had really been. Surely there weren't that many people living in the Nebraska Territory with those initials at the time. She could figure out her real name, and she could contact any descendants, learn more about Willie and Emily and their time as Union soldiers. Maybe she should even offer to give them the handkerchief and ring.

Even knowing she was getting way ahead of herself—for she could be totally wrong about the handkerchief belonging to Willie—she proceeded with the search anyway. She hadn't felt this excited about something in a long time. Going off the initials on the handkerchief, she started with the federal census in 1860 for all residents of Nebraska Territory with a last name beginning with the letter E.

After a confusing series of clicks and searches, she found over 164,500 records. Narrowing it down a bit, she revised the search parameters to the last name E and got 657 results. But when she looked closely at the results, she found that, somehow, all the letters of the alphabet were represented, and her only choice was to wade through each one looking for a name that might fit. When she got a few pages in, she realized the census year was not only 1860, but all years up to 1865. Somehow, she'd messed up the search. She felt out of her league.

A burst of laughter from downstairs reminded her of the party she was avoiding. She closed her eyes and took a deep breath to soothe the anxiety stirring in her gut and turned again to the search on her screen.

Making sure to specify only the year 1860 and inputting the letter E in the last-name field, she hit Enter and waited. But she got zero records. Backing up, she did not specify an initial and hit submit again. This time, 49 records popped up.

But when she searched through them, none of the last names began with the letter E.

Frustrated, she searched for a genealogical society in Nebraska and, finding one, shot off an email on their general contact web form asking if there was someone she could hire to help with her research. Grams had offered to help, but she'd been busy with holiday preparations and Larkin didn't want to put more on her plate.

Setting the computer aside, she drew Emily's diary out of the nightstand drawer to read more. First, though, she took the handkerchief out of its hiding place in the cover and studied the embroidered initials covered all these years ago with bloodstains. Who was ODE? And, whose blood was this?

January 9, 1862: I had grown complacent, though that has now changed. Did I really think we would serve our entire enlistment in camp? It saddened me to take down our half-tents, roll my blankets, and pack my haversack with rations for three days. Although we three are still together, the impermanence of marching and temporary camps reminds me that this could change at any moment. We are at war, after all. That war has sent us to Fetterman, Virginia, where we have been ordered to wait until we receive further orders. No one knows how long we will be here. I am cold and wet, and I miss our cozy tent on Cheat Mountain.

February 19, 1862: Orders came in, finally. We are on the march to Louisville, Kentucky, to meet up with another regiment for a final march to Nashville, Tennessee. Forts Henry and Donelson have been taken by our side, which means the Federals now control major rivers in the Confederate state of Tennessee. As Nashville is that state's capital as well as its commercial hub, it will be a boon for the Union when we also take it.

I find I do not mind marching. It fends off the cold and allows me to see areas of our great country I otherwise would not have had the chance to ever see. My feet have never hurt so badly in my life, not even when the mule stepped on my foot three summers ago. It helps to keep my feet, socks, and boots dry, but I can't control the rain so it's not always possible. I'll never take shelter and a warm fire for granted again. Or a bath, for that matter.

Residents in the areas through which we pass are suffering. Army foraging efforts, on both sides, have stripped them of their farm animals and winter food stores. They stand beside the road and beg us for food as we pass. I have nothing to give them. Guards must march alongside the wagons, or else the civilians would attack and steal the Army provisions.

Morale is high after we received the news of Grant's victories at the two Tennessee forts. Surely the tide has turned in the Union's favor, and we now need only one major battle to end the war. A new song has reached us, and the soldiers often sing it while on the march for it makes us feel that God is on our side, or rather, that we are doing His duty. "Glory! Glory! Hallelujah! His truth is marching on." It makes my heart doubly glad that the lyrics were penned by a woman, Julia Ward Howe.

February 25, 1862: Nashville is the first large city I have seen with my own eyes in a secessionist state. It appears untouched by war, if one ignores the thousands of Union troops patrolling the city and the many businesses and homes that have been vacated by their secessionist owners. General Buell has accepted the city's official surrender, and now our duty will be to hold the city for the Union side. I am curious to see what that will entail.

Sad news is being reported in the newspapers. President Lincoln's young son, Willie, has died of the same brutal affliction that took David from us. I know how it feels to lose a cherished family member, but a child? My heart aches for President and Mrs. Lincoln.

Chapter Eighteen

February 25, 1862: Nashville, Tennessee

To Emily's surprise, her company was billeted in one of the finest buildings in all of Nashville—the Tennessee State Capitol building. It was certainly the grandest building Emily had ever set foot in. The Capitol building loomed over the city on a high hill, its Grecian columns visible for miles. Limestone flooring and marble columns inside created a cavernous feel enhanced by the lack of furnishings and drapery. No one could agree on whether the secesh had taken the furnishings with them as they fled the city, or if the building was so new, it had never had any to begin with. Emily, Ben, and Willie were quartered in a small room in the basement near the newly created armory and shared their room with three other men.

Their days varied but were always full. Some days their duty was together, some days apart, but always they came together in their little room to share stories of duty that was very different than it had been in western Virginia.

Their first few weeks of Nashville occupation involved building beds and converting city schools, homes, and churches into hospitals, many of which were quickly filled after skirmishes and battles in the surrounding area. They also were tasked with guarding supply depots along the major railway lines running through Nashville and along the Cumberland River. Without careful guarding, secesh residents would either steal the goods intended for the Army, or sabotage and spoil the food and supplies.

Tall buildings packed tightly together on well-formed streets was a mightily different sight than the trees and hills she'd grown accustomed to, and Emily enjoyed the change, especially since the city was firmly in Union control and she did not have to fear Confederate bullets. She imagined that Nashville—with its fine brick homes, stately architecture, and tree-lined streets—must surely be one of the finest cities in the nation. The weather felt mild compared to the mountains of western Virginia, and she fancied herself visiting this city again someday on holiday long after the war was over.

Emily's favorite duty in Nashville was when she was posted somewhere in the city to enforce martial law and to keep the peace. This meant checking civilians and military personnel for the necessary passes that allowed the bearer to be in that particular location. It was an opportunity to talk with all sorts of people, and she found she enjoyed their stories. The only downside of the post was that it sometimes meant standing stone-faced as schoolchildren or even young women in hoopskirts and bonnets spat on her and called her names.

With each passing day, Emily saw more black folks from the surrounding countryside enter the city and ask the first member of the Federal forces they came across where they might be safe from their former masters. She was slowly reading the copy of *Uncle Tom's Cabin* that MacGregor had given to her, and she pretended that every man she helped was Tom and every woman, Eliza or Cassy. Already a large contraband—the name given to escaped slaves—camp was growing on the outskirts of the city. Some contraband worked for the Union Army, building various structures and fortifications around the city. Some contraband, Emily had heard, were returned by Union Army commanders to their owners. Her heart broke to think of the courage it had taken to run away in the first place only to be sent back.

One afternoon, she was guarding the corner of Summer and Spring Streets where General Buell had his temporary head-quarters in the St. Cloud Hotel. As was happening more and more with each passing day, a young black family—a husband and wife, likely not much older than Emily, and their two small children—approached her. The father pulled off his slouching cap and looked at her feet. "Beggin' your pardon, sir. Can you tell us where to go? Where we're safe?"

Emily wondered what the man had endured that had put such a fear into him that he couldn't even look at her. His wife stood proudly beside him, but she, too, pointed her gaze to the ground. Only their toddler looked straight at Emily and smiled. Emily smiled back, remembering when Ada was that age. Proud she knew the answer to his question, Emily pointed to the west. "Take this street about five blocks until you reach the railroad depot. From there—"

"Jedediah, what are you doing here?"

By the way the man flinched, Emily realized with dawning horror what was happening. This poor family had just been discovered, probably by the very person from whom they were running. Before the loud white man drew close enough to hear her, she whispered to the family, "Go. I'll stall him."

Turning to face the finely dressed man with a full beard, Emily pasted on a smile to hide the revulsion she felt. It was people like him who were responsible for this war. Men like him had killed Pa and David. Through gritted teeth, she greeted him, "Good afternoon, sir. How may I be of service?"

The man's stovepipe hat hardly moved as he craned his neck to look past Emily. "Go on, Jedediah. Git back to Belle Meade right now, and I won't punish you."

Emily glanced back to see Jedediah duck his head in a manner that told Emily he was well acquainted with a whip. He held on to his family and was pulling them with him along the sidewalk, edging away from their former master, still with his eyes downcast. "Meaning no disrespect, sir, but we won't go back. We're here to get free." He grabbed his older daughter's hand and, together with his wife who was holding the baby, took off running down the street in the direction Emily had indicated.

"Hold on! Get back here!" the white man yelled, his face turning red. He took a step forward, but Emily blocked him.

Holding her musket across her chest, she dropped all pretense of civility. "Sir, do you have a pass?"

For the first time, the man looked at the Union soldier in front of him, but his gaze quickly returned to the now-empty sidewalk where his slaves had disappeared. "Why would they want to run away? I treat them kindly." He shook his head, confounded. "All of my slaves are happy at Belle Meade. They're like family."

Emily's muscles twitched, and she almost whacked the butt of her musket into the man's face. "Apparently not, sir," she managed to grind out in response. "Your pass?"

The man distractedly pulled the slip of paper from his coat pocket and presented it to her. Emily took her time inspecting the pass and saw it was good, but the image of that innocent family was still fresh in her mind. She ripped the pass into bits and dropped it on the sidewalk.

"What do you think you are doing?" the man gasped, his face darkening in anger.

Emily smiled at him innocently. "Go on. Git back to Belle Meade, and I won't punish you for owning human beings."

The man gaped at her, clearly shocked to have his own words used against him. She simply lifted her musket. Blustering, he turned and walked away toward the riverfront, the opposite direction from that taken by the black family.

Once he'd disappeared, Emily felt the strength drain out of her, but soon it was replaced by a sense of elation. Where had her courage come from? In helping the former slaves, she was doing something that mattered. She'd joined the Army to stay by her brother's side, but inside her was growing the heart of an abolitionist.

A week after arriving in Nashville, the entire regiment held its first dress parade in the city, which meant taking a bath (something that had proven tricky for Emily and Willie, but they'd managed by sneaking away to a private bathhouse that cost them two whole dollars each) and donning their full uniforms. They'd marched along the city streets and stood at attention on Nashville's Public Square for their commander's review. Captain Johnson had promised them passes for tonight if everyone made him proud.

Emily and Ben were the first to return to their room, having been near the front of their company in the parade. As Emily traded her formal overcoat for her more casual blouse, Ben leaned his head out into the hallway. He was acting so secretive, Emily knew that if there was a door, he would have closed it. He whispered to Emily, "I have some news."

Emily leaned toward him. "What is it?"

An angelic smile spread across Ben's face under the beard he'd grown since they'd left Cheat Mountain. "I'm going to ask Willie to marry me." His eyes sparkled with his secret joy.

A stab of worry shot through Emily. "But, Ben. How is that possible?"

He shook his head impatiently. "No, I don't mean now. I mean, I'll ask her now but we'll marry after the war is over." A dreaminess came over him. "I love her, Em. I really do."

The news did not surprise Emily. She'd seen them growing closer and closer, and she knew Willie felt the same as Ben. "I'm still worried, Brother. Your relationship could expose her secret. You need to be very careful."

"Be careful about what?" asked Private Yardley as he came into the room and let out a loud fart. Emily had never shared quarters with anyone as vile as him, nor as dangerously inquisitive.

She recovered the fastest. "Oh, being out tonight on leave. I hear local secesh have taken to guerrilla warfare and are attacking Union troops in the streets." She shot Ben a look.

Ben nodded. "I think we'll be safe as long as we travel in pairs or larger groups. Right, Yardley?"

Yardley sucked in air to loudly form a collection of phlegm in his throat, which he spat onto the gleaming limestone floor. With his dirty boots on, he dropped full-length on his bottom bunk and crossed his arms behind his head. "Personally, I'd be happy getting into a fight with those lowlifes. I wish I had some civilian clothes to wear so that I could get away with more than my blues allow."

Emily and Ben exchanged a glance. They were saved from having to respond when the rest of their roommates filed in, Willie among them. General chaos filled the room as they all readied for a night of freedom.

"Some of us are going to Smokey Row tonight. College Street." Private O'Brien's face turned redder than his hair, and if the others had not already known this was the address of the fancier bordellos in the nightlife district, his blushing would have given it away. "Any of you boyos want to join us?"

Yardley and Jacobs, their other roommate, agreed. Emily had been trying to think of a way to give Ben and Willie a night alone together, in whatever way possible, and decided this was as good a way as any. Besides, how could she explain a reluctance to visit a brothel without raising suspicions? She'd blend into the crowd, and no one would be the wiser. "I think Ben and Willie already have plans, but I'll join you."

Ben's head snapped in her direction, but she ignored him. She could handle herself.

"What are your plans?" Jacobs, a nice boy from Ohio, asked Ben and Willie. "Maybe I'll go with you."

Willie retied her boot, a bored look on her face. "I was thinking of visiting the Adelphi Theater. I hear *Follies of a Night* is playing this evening."

"Seriously?" Yardley scoffed. "That is what you choose to do on your night off duty?" He got to his feet and headed for the door. "If you change your minds, you know where to find us. 154 College Street."

Jacobs shot Willie an apologetic look and hurried after Yardley. O'Brien used both hands to slick back his hair as he followed them out. The big sister in Emily could not stay silent, however, and as she waved goodbye to her brother and Willie, she warned, "Be careful!"

"The same to you!" Ben called back, sounding as though he was strangling on all the words he wanted to say.

Emily laughed as she hurried to catch up to the others on their way up the narrow stairs. What could go wrong?

Plenty. Plenty could go wrong, Emily realized an hour later as she watched a red-faced O'Brien disappear up the carpeted stairs with a buxom woman, followed closely by Jacobs with a woman of his own who looked like she could be someone's grandmother.

Emily had chosen a plush seat in a corner of the bordello's front room, where she hoped to remain invisible until her friends finished upstairs and they could all leave.

Although she'd come to the Army knowing about the activities of men and women behind closed doors, her education on the matter had grown exponentially over these last months. Men who were away from their wives and sweethearts had a way of talking around campfires that she'd bet most women never heard in their lifetimes.

But knowing what activities went on here, she had not

expected the bordello to look anything like this, like an upper-class society parlor during a dinner party.

All of the women wore fine evening gowns—admittedly, many gowns came only, shockingly, to the wearer's knees, and several necklines were cut scandalizingly low—and their hair was piled on their heads in the latest fashion with feathers or faux jewels adorning their curls. The men, most wearing Union uniforms but some in gentlemen's evening wear, conversed with one another and the women on topics as mundane as the weather or the movement of troops in the eastern theater. Alcohol flowed freely, though not cheaply, and tuxedoed black servers weaved among the guests, offering refills and fancy pastries. A string quartet played in one corner loud enough to be heard throughout the main floor, but not so loud as to make conversation a challenge.

The room itself was quite possibly the most lavish one Emily had ever seen. The furnishings were all of the finest workmanship and crafted from gleaming woods she couldn't begin to name. A richly carved marble mantel supported a flower arrangement that erupted from its gold vase in a riot of color and scent. Emily wondered where the flowers could have possibly come from here in the middle of winter and war.

The seats and cushions on the chairs and settees were made of fine velvet or floral jacquard, all in rich greens, golds, and reds that made each piece feel like artwork. A lovely wallpaper, lit by ornate chandeliers and sconces, depicted a country scene in leaf green and rose pink. Several elaborately framed portraits or landscapes hung around the room, each seeming to be quite proper upon first glance. It was upon second glance that Emily found herself looking away in haste from the naked and cavorting figures displayed there.

As Emily studied the lace doily on the gleaming accent table next to her, someone slapped her hard on the back, bringing tears to her eyes.

"What do you say, Wilson?" Yardley asked as he propped his hip on the arm of her chair. "Which girl has caught your eye?"

Emily had thought up her excuse on the walk over. "Oh, I'll wait for you boys here. I don't have the necessary funds."

"Nonsense!" Yardley sipped from the delicate champagne saucer he held in his hand as he surveyed the room. He pointed with the glass to a woman coming down the stairs on the arm of a disheveled-looking soldier. "I bet she could show you a good time. Come on, I'll spot you the cash. How much do you need?"

Emily pushed Yardley's wallet away from her face. "No thanks. You go on."

"No, no. I insist." He forced three Tennessee dollars into her hand. "I bet you're still a virgin, aren't you, Wilson?"

She felt her face flame, but she refused to back down. "So what if I am? I've got a girl at home I'd just as soon wait for, if it's all the same to you." She shoved the money back at him.

He refused to take it, and she let it drop to the floor. Yardley's face pinched, and he looked ready to explode.

"Now, boys, if you have money to throw around, I'll take it off your hands."

It was the woman they'd seen on the stairs. She was shorter than Emily by several inches, and her curves were threatening to spill free from her fuchsia-colored gown. Despite having just been upstairs entertaining a customer, she appeared fresh as the morning with every hair in place and her kohl-rimmed eyes and berry-stained lips unsmudged. Those red lips spread wide and revealed a row of crooked but clean teeth. She stopped directly in front of Emily and looked her up and down with her hand resting on her cocked hip. "What do you say, sweetie? You look like you could use a woman's touch."

Emily's mind raced. How was she going to get herself out of this with the least amount of embarrassment to all involved, but mostly, without revealing her secret? "My friend Yardley here has the cash. He'd be happy to take you upstairs."

The woman turned her charm on the soldier beside her. "Shall we proceed, Private?"

Yardley licked his lips in anticipation as his eyes hungrily surveyed the poor woman's half-exposed bosom. "Absolutely," he told her, bending to retrieve the fallen money from the floor. "But you must first see to my friend Wilson here. It's his first time." He took the woman's hand in his own, kissed the inside of her wrist, and laid the three bills on her palm. "Show him how a real woman pleases a man before he goes home to a life of boring tumbles with the miss he plans to marry."

Emily squirmed. Did all men think this way? "No, no. I won't take your money, Yardley. You go on."

The woman took the matter into her own hands by tucking the bills into a pocket in her skirt, wrapping both hands around Emily's arm, and drawing her away from her protective corner. "Don't you worry none, sugar. You're in good hands with me."

Emily tried to pull away, but the woman held on tighter. All the way up the stairs, she talked to Emily in her sweet Southern twang, saying things that made little sense and reminded Emily of her pa talking to a skittish colt. At the top of the stairs, Emily looked down into the parlor one last time and saw Yardley watching her with a leering grin on his face.

The bedroom was dominated by a huge four-poster bed dressed in rose silks. Emily stayed close to the door. "Look, you seem real nice, but I can't do this."

The woman laid her fingertips on Emily's neck and slowly drew them down her arm. "Don't be nervous, sweetie. I know you're young, but you have nothing to be afraid of. I'll take care of you. All you need to do is relax."

Emily pushed the woman's hand away and tried to think of a way to get out of this without revealing the truth. "Look, ma'am..." She paused. "What is your name, anyway?"

"V. A. White, but you can call me Vee." She leaned back against the bureau and thrust her breasts out.

Emily looked away and pointedly studied the pinstripes on the wallpaper. "Miss Vee, I appreciate your efforts, but I am not interested in your services." She moved toward the door. "Keep the money."

She had her hand on the doorknob when she felt herself spun around and enveloped in soft skin and the scent of night jasmine. Lips clamped onto her own, tasting of mint.

Emily froze. This was the first kiss she'd ever received in her entire life, and it shocked her to be coming from another woman. Of course, the woman thought she was kissing a man, but still, the strangeness of it all confused Emily.

Vee's lips softened and started to move in a way that actually felt nice. Was this what it was like to kiss a man? Emily's eyes drifted closed, and she forgot herself in the sensation of intimacy she had never known.

But then she felt the touch of Vee's tongue inside her mouth, and she was reminded of where she was, and who she was. Emily put her hands on Vee's shoulders and stepped back roughly. "No. I cannot."

But Vee would not be swayed. She reached for the buttons on Emily's trousers and undid the top one. She would have continued with the rest had Emily not grabbed her hands. "I cannot be more serious. Stop."

Vee dropped her hands so they hung limp at her sides, and her head drooped. "What did I do wrong?"

Now she'd done it. "It's nothing you did, I promise." She refastened her button and straightened her blouse. "It's just that I...you see...I..." She struggled to come up with a plausible excuse and finally settled on the one she'd tried with Yardley. "I want my first time to be with my girl back home. After we're married. You understand."

Unfortunately, that seemed to renew Vee's efforts. She stepped toward her. "I can show you how it's done so that you please your girl beyond her imagination. You won't be dishonoring her, but rather, you'll be doing it for her." She reached up and placed both palms on Emily's chest.

They both froze.

Vee's palms flexed, and she pressed harder. Mortified, Emily felt all energy drain from her. Her ruse was up.

For one cold moment, Emily felt a plan forming in her mind. To protect herself and her secret, she would do what she needed to do. Even if that meant harming this poor woman. Holding absolutely still, Emily waited to see what happened next, for that would determine her own actions.

As though unsure of what she was feeling, Vee's hands slid down Emily's body toward her trousers again. Emily stepped back before those exploring hands found what they were looking for. Or, rather, found the absence there.

"You're a woman." It wasn't a question. Nor an exclamation.

All of her senses focused on this one moment, and Emily knew she was about to do something she could not take back. Swiftly, Emily grabbed Vee's wrists and held them so tightly she saw the woman flinch, though she hid it behind a saucy smile. Emily shoved her face into Vee's. "If you tell anyone, I'll kill you. Do you understand?"

To her credit, Vee did not struggle to get away. She did not appear at all afraid of Emily, and even started to laugh. With her hands still in Emily's grip, she moved her arms as though to spread them wider and Emily let her, curious to see what she was up to.

Vee spread her arms wide, taking Emily's wide as well, and her gaze inspected Emily's body. "I noticed you were feminine, but I thought it's because you're so young. How old are you anyway?"

"Nineteen."

"A year older than me." She twisted her hands out of Emily's grasp and walked around her, inspecting her all the more. "What's it like to be a soldier?"

Not sure what she was up to, Emily shrugged. "It's all right.

I work as hard as any man, and I do my duty better than a lot of them."

"Aren't you scared?"

"At times." She thought about it a bit more. "All the time when the Rebs are shooting at us."

Vee completed her walk around Emily and looked closely at her face. "Have you killed anyone?"

Emily swallowed and looked away.

Vee nodded. "In battle or to protect yourself?"

Thank heaven she hadn't had to resort to that for her secret. Not yet, anyway. "In battle."

Vee didn't blink. "How do you maintain your disguise?"

"We soldiers sleep in our clothes and rarely bathe, though I've swum in a few rivers fully clothed." Still not entirely certain she could trust this woman, Emily took the seat Vee offered on the edge of the bed, making sure she was close enough to Vee to stop her if she ran for the door. "I find that if I act like a man, everyone sees a man."

Vee climbed on the bed with her and sat cross-legged with her back against the headboard. She suddenly looked young and nothing like a lady of the night. "Do you curse and fight and gamble and do all the things we women aren't supposed to do?"

Emily relaxed. She nodded and burst out laughing at the eager delight that crossed the younger woman's face. "And I march through rain and mud and sleep in the snow and sometimes have nothing to eat but hardtack full of vermin."

Vee's face took on a look of consideration. Finally, she said, "But you can't deny your freedom is better than living like this." Her arms indicated the room and the knowledge of what she did here to survive.

That sobered Emily. "Yes, I think it must be better than this." She asked, "How did you come to be here?"

Vee looked at her lap and fiddled with a loose string on the bedspread. Emily opened her mouth to apologize for the intrusive question, but Vee started telling her story. "I had a beau back home, named Joe. Lordy, was I head over heels for that man. I would have followed him to the ends of the Earth if he asked it of me."

Emily shifted so she was more comfortable. "What happened?"

Vee continued fidgeting with the string. "I bore his child, and when he found out, he left town. Some say he joined the fight against Northern aggression." She shot a look of apology to Emily.

"Whatever happened to him," Vee went on, "he was gone, and I was an unmarried mother. My family took my daughter from me, and I don't know what they did with her. They disowned me." She finally raised her face and looked at Emily as though daring her to condemn her as so many others had done. "I made it here, and I'm surviving on my own without them. I don't need them."

Knowing her next words had the power to inflict even more wounds on this tender creature, Emily thought about how to best respond. "You seem to be successful at your profession."

"I'm saving to buy a house of my own. I won't be doing this forever, you know."

"I didn't think you would." Although she hadn't thought about it at all.

"How much do you make soldiering?"

The question surprised Emily, so she answered honestly. "Thirteen dollars a month, plus one set of clothes per year and daily rations."

Vee scowled. "That ain't much."

"No, but I have freedom to say what I want and think what I want, and most days I'm happy under the sky and stars doing work that feels important. Plus, I get to be with my brother and our best friend."

Vee thought that over. "Maybe I should enlist, too. Wouldn't that be something?"

They were startled by a hard rapping on the door and a male voice calling, "Customers are piling up, Vee. Finish and get downstairs."

A wave of scarlet moved up Vee's chest, neck, and face. For the first time since they started talking, she seemed embarrassed by her line of work. "Thanks for talking to me, Private. I don't have many friends, you know."

Emily took her hand and gave it a squeeze. "My name is Emily, and I hope our paths cross again someday when this war is over. I don't have many friends either."

Vee bounced off the bed. "I better go boast of your manly prowess to your friends downstairs if I'm to be helping you keep your disguise."

Downstairs they found Yardley, O'Brien, and Jacobs all standing by the door, impatient to be on their way to the saloon they planned to visit next. Vee clung to Emily's arm all the way down the stairs, and then, as they joined her fellow soldiers, she took Emily's face in her hands and gave her a deep, passionate kiss. When she pulled back, Emily knew her face must be as pink as Vee's dress but she didn't say anything as the men whooped and slapped her on her back.

"Come see me again, soldier. Many times." Vee winked at Emily, and as she turned to walk away, she lightly tapped her palm against Emily's backside, sending the men into another round of cheers.

Emily smiled her thanks to her new friend and then lost sight of her as the others pulled her out of the brothel amid congratulations and questions. "You have to tell us everything," O'Brien begged as they turned toward the river. "What was she like?"

Emily smiled. "A gentleman does not kiss and tell."

Chapter Nineteen

Present day: Woodinville, Washington

*L*arkin spent the day after Christmas at home alone while Grams and Kaia went shopping. Rain poured steadily all day, and Larkin was quite content to stay inside with Bowie, who never judged her, never pitied her. She flicked on the gas fireplace, made a fresh pot of coffee, and listened to the rain pound on the roof as she settled at the kitchen table with her laptop. This search had become an obsession. Larkin was fully aware that obsessive work was another symptom of PTSD, but she wasn't about to stop. Others may judge her for it, but the research was holding her together.

Emily had not written much in her diary about her time in Nashville, and Larkin was curious about it, so she looked up the Union occupation and was surprised to see search results come up for a big battle in that city. It took her a moment to realize the battle wasn't in 1862, but two years later. The reason Emily did not write about a Nashville battle when she was there was because there hadn't been one. After Fort Donelson fell to the Union side, Confederate generals knew Nashville would be the next target so they pulled their forces out of the city. Nashville's Mayor Richard Boone Cheatham met Union

General Buell under a flag of truce, and Union forces peacefully took control.

Curious to see if she could find more on the movements of Emily's regiment, Larkin spent time searching and clicking on links, reading whatever came up. That's when she realized Emily would soon be heading into the Battle of Shiloh. The warring emotions of curiosity and dread battled inside her until curiosity won out and she opened Emily's diary once again.

March 26, 1862: I have never been more miserable in my life. Our march seems endless. Every hill we crest, we see nothing but more hills in our path. Everything is soaked through since we've had more days of rain than not. Ahead of us in the column are miles of other soldiers stirring the mud into a sticky soup as deep as our knees in places. Each step is difficult with all the blisters and open sores on my feet. Holes in my boots grow bigger each day. Each mile is daunting, yet we pass them somehow. At least twelve a day.

I think I could march in my sleep. Maybe I do, since I can't remember big gaps of time. We've been assigned to General Buell's Army of the Ohio in Bull Nelson's Fourth Division and Hazen's 19th Brigade. Colonel Moody leads our 9th Indiana. Word is we are marching for Savannah, Tennessee, where we'll join General Grant's forces and proceed south to Corinth, Mississippi, to seize control of Confederate railroad lines.

Several battles have been occurring elsewhere, and I know it is only a matter of time before I again face the Rebs. The Union conquered the Confederacy at Pea Ridge, Arkansas. But northeast of there (and my present location), our forces were forced to retreat from the Shenandoah Valley and are amassing in Washington to protect the Capital. Ironclad ships battled for hours in the waters off Virginia. What a sight that must have been! Though the war continues, I stand firmly on the right side of this conflict and know the Union will prevail.

Trees are starting to burst open with new leaves, and early flowers have pushed into the light of day. Surely this new beginning is a sign from Heaven that our country will soon have its own new beginning with all states reunited. I hold on to that hope, even knowing that each day could be my last. I have Ben and Willie beside me, and that's all I ask.

Chapter Twenty

March 15–April 7, 1862: South Tennessee

*E*mily could have happily served out the rest of her enlistment in Nashville, but on the fifteenth of March, orders came in directing them to march southwest to Savannah, Tennessee, where they were to join forces with the Army of the Tennessee and confront the Rebels in northern Mississippi. They set out from Nashville late in the day on a southwesterly course and were told to be on alert for secesh along the way who were itching for a fight.

The men also had their eyes out for food in fields and cold cellars to supplement the poor rations they were given on the march. They found that most had been cleaned out long ago.

On the first day, Emily, Ben, and Willie laughed at the soldiers who had grown soft in Nashville and had to shed weight from their packs. Discarded clothing, cookware, books, and all sorts of items littered the roadsides and sank into the mud, becoming unrecognizable after muddy boots, wheels, and hooves tromped over them. By the third day of marching, Emily could take it no longer and had to step out of line to lighten her own load.

She could not give up her half-tent or rubber blanket, not with this rain. In fact, she'd developed a strong attachment to her rubber blanket and would not let it leave her sight. It was the only thing keeping her dry on the march and warm at night. In a way, it was the closest thing she had to a home.

Nor could she discard her overcoat, for she needed the extra layer for warmth. It might have been spring, but the nights were still cold. Her ammunition, musket, and haversack of food were essential, of course, as was her diary. What could she possibly let go?

Digging deep in her knapsack, her hand touched the book MacGregor had given her at Christmas. She'd carried it with her all the way from Cheat Mountain and had finished it days ago, but she was hoping to read it again. Uncle Tom and Eliza and all the others felt like old friends. How could she possibly give them up?

The book was a brick, though. There was no denying it. She had to leave it behind.

After laying it as far away from the road as she could, and under cover of a rhododendron bush in hopes that it might survive the rain and be a gift for some unlucky soul traveling the same road, she also tossed her fry pan, figuring she could share with Ben or Willie until she bought a new one later.

She didn't dare shed any clothing, for not only did it protect her from the elements, but it was her disguise and she could not risk that being her undoing. The only things left were the stack of letters she'd taken from David's pack and her family Bible. Since the letters were written in her own hand, she decided she could let them go. She set them on top of *Uncle Tom's Cabin*. As she moved to place the Bible there as well, she realized she still hadn't been able to bring herself to record David's death. She stuffed it back inside her knapsack next to her diary.

With her pack only a little lighter, she resumed her march and soon caught up again with Ben and Willie in the slow-moving line.

Excitement came on the fourth morning when they reached the Duck River and found the bridge on fire. While the officers and engineers discussed what to do, the soldiers got in a much-needed break, many of them hunkering under trees around hastily built fires and boiling water for coffee. Some took the time to pitch tents and fall asleep wrapped in their rubber blankets on a bed of mud. Emily waited long enough to warm her insides with a cup of weak black coffee before she wrapped herself in her coat and blanket and fell asleep with her knapsack as a pillow.

She was soon roused, however, with orders to ford the river and make camp on the other side. The commanding officers had decided it would take too long to build a pontoon bridge. Emily didn't mind. Wading was her only means of bathing, for what it was worth, and she was wet already from the rain. They were ordered to hold their muskets and cartridge boxes over their heads to keep them dry as they crossed, but Emily managed to hold her knapsack up as well. If her diary got wet, it would be ruined. It was her last link to Pa and worth saving, no matter what it took.

With thirty-seven thousand troops to get across, along with the wagons, animals, and artillery, the process took all day, and they camped on the opposite shore that night. Emily's aching legs and blistered feet welcomed the respite, and she was grateful for a break in the rain and a roaring fire that helped dry everything out.

By sunrise the next morning, they were back on the march. The terrain they covered was all rolling hills, knobs, and valleys interspersed with creeks and gullies. Wide meadows and fields were bordered by hardwood forests with occasional stands of pine. It was beautiful country—or it would have been, had the weather been pleasant. The road on which they marched took them through small towns and across vast plantations. Emily knew hundreds of slaves had fled their masters for the safety of Union-occupied locales such as Nashville, so she was surprised to see slaves working those fields. If only she could've gotten within earshot of them, she would have urged them to flee.

To pass the endless hours, the soldiers talked as they marched. A popular topic of conversation was what they planned to do after the war. "I'll return to the farm, no doubt about it," Ben told them before launching into a long reminiscence on the buildings, their crops and animals, and the neighbors who lived nearby.

Emily stayed silent as Ben talked. She wasn't so sure that she wanted to return to Stampers Creek after the war, because that meant returning to a life without the freedoms she'd become accustomed to. Aunt Harriet might be more accepting, but Uncle Samuel would have her hide the moment she set foot back on the farm, and then he'd beat her again for wearing men's trousers, and then a third time when she spoke her mind. Men had all the power in this world, and now that she'd tasted that power, she wasn't ready to give up even a small slice.

"What about you, Willie? Will you return home to Nebraska Territory?" O'Brien asked after telling them all about his dairy farm.

"I long for Nebraska," she told them wistfully. "But I don't know if that's the place for me after a falling-out I had with my family a while back."

Ben was eyeing her closely, as though this was the first time they were discussing where to live after the war. "Nebraska is a large territory. If that is where you want to settle, it's what you should do."

Willie marched silently for several steps before she replied. "If I save my pay, I might be able to buy some land and build a house and farm there."

"I'll go with you," Emily found herself saying. "Owning my own land sounds like a fine way to live out my days."

Ben looked at her sharply, and Emily knew he was full of questions he wouldn't dare ask with the other soldiers nearby. She took pity on him and offered, "I'm not so sure Indiana has anything for me to return to, other than you, Brother. Why don't you come to Nebraska with Willie and me?"

A flush crept up Ben's neck, and a small smile tugged at his mouth. Emily could see the idea was growing on him. She bumped her elbow against Willie's arm and grinned. "The three of us could be neighbors. What do you think of that, Willie?"

Willie nodded, though her gaze was on Ben. "I'd like that."

The march to Savannah should have taken nine days but it took more than twice that, and they finally arrived late on the sixth of April. Although they'd been looking forward to a day of rest, what they found was a full-scale battle in progress on the other side of the Tennessee River.

Emily, Ben, and Willie gathered with the rest of their regiment on the bank of the wide, brown river and looked across to where a swarm of Union blue amassed on the opposite bank from the unseen battlefield farther beyond. Although the setting sun and all the smoke in the air made it difficult to see, the river appeared to be rimmed in blue.

"Are they all injured?" Willie asked no one in particular. "There must be several hundred men sitting there."

Emily watched officers on horseback riding back and forth along the river. They were too far away to hear, but they seemed to be calling to the men huddled under the overhanging bank. "You don't think they are cowards, do you?"

"They sure seem to be hiding from something," Ben answered, his eyes glued to the opposite shore. "The wounded are those lined up at the landing and being carried onboard the steamships."

As they watched, one steamer pushed away from shore and chugged to the middle of the river, so full of wounded men that even the open decks were packed with them. Cries and moans echoed across the water.

Two Federal wooden gunboats, the *Lexington* and the *Tyler*, positioned with their cannons pointing toward enemy lines, kept up a continuous assault. Their cannons boomed and their shells shrieked, and each one sent a shudder of fear through Emily. She wanted to cover her ears and run far away from all this misery and terror. The battle must have been worse than any other, or so many men wouldn't be cowering on the riverbank. She wanted nothing more than to turn around and march back to Nashville. Or anywhere. As long as it was far from here.

She looked at Ben and Willie. Fear etched lines onto both of their faces, and Emily felt words forming on her tongue—*Let's run away from here.*

But she did not speak, and she did not run. She'd made a promise to serve her country, and so she would. She would stand proudly beside her brother and Willie and all the others, and she would fight because that was what was asked of her. Most of all, she would fight beside Ben and Willie and protect them.

By the time it was their turn to be ferried across the river, night had fallen and a storm had blown in. As Emily stepped onto the muddy ground at Pittsburg Landing, she found herself face-to-face with a bloodied Union soldier, his eyes wide with fear so palpable that Emily's entire body shook in response. He tried to shove past the disembarking soldiers to board the steamboat himself. From out of the darkness appeared an armed guard who forcibly shoved the terrified soldier away. Sickness settled into Emily's gut. What horrors awaited them over that bluff?

Despite her fear, her training kicked in, and she marched with her regiment up the embankment. As lightning flashed, she saw they were in a wide field bordered by a forest lined with soldiers lying on their bellies with weapons pointed into the dark. It was so dark, in fact, that Emily had to stay close to the heels of the man in front of her to avoid taking a wrong turn. She reached back and held Ben's hand, worried of being separated from him.

Despite the rolling thunder, pounding rain, booming cannons from the gunboats, and the cries of the wounded lying somewhere out in the night, no one spoke above a whisper. The enemy might be hiding in the shadows.

"Get what rest you can," Colonel Moody ordered via whispers

that were passed down the line. "No fires. We move out before dawn."

They dropped to the ground and quietly dug cold rations out of their haversacks. No one bothered to lay out a bedroll. Instead, they wrapped their rubber blankets around themselves and got as comfortable as possible in the cold and rain, and tried not to think of the guns that could be pointing at them.

Whispered rumors spread through the line as men on the outskirts of their huddled regiment encountered men from Grant's army who had been in that day's battle. Someone said that Grant himself had been shot, but someone else reported he'd only taken a tumble from his horse and was now commanding the action on crutches. No one knew how many Confederates they would face, but the answer was certainly in the thousands, although that was the same number claimed to have been killed already. Tales of walking across a carpet of dead bodies emerged, and Emily wondered if they were still out there in the dark, forgotten. Some said the Union side had won the day's battle; most said they'd lost. All agreed it would continue when the sun rose.

Emily tried to sleep, but her nerves were frayed and she could not manage more than a few minutes at a time. When the call to assemble came, Emily felt even more achy and tired than she'd been at the end of the march. Still, she dropped her knapsack in a pile along with the rest of the regiment's, taking a precious few minutes to stuff her diary into her damp chest bindings for fear of losing both it and the money she stored in the secret compartment. At the last second, she also slipped her inkpot into her pocket. With her haversack, canteen, and full cartridge box strapped to her body, she took her place in line, musket in hand.

The regiment moved southward through Dill Branch, expecting at any moment to encounter their opposition. Emily knew what to expect from battle, but that knowledge did nothing to ease her anxiety. The waiting was harder than the actual fighting would be, and she wished they could get on with it.

Blessedly, the rain had stopped, and the eastern sky was starting to fill with color, promising a beautiful spring day. Everywhere she looked, vibrant green leaves sprouted from their buds, promising the return of life.

That's when Emily realized there was little else alive in these woods, other than the soldiers walking beside her. No birds sang in the trees; no squirrels chased one another in the branches. There even seemed to be an absence of insects. Everything was still, silent, and holding its breath.

As she rounded a clump of trees, Emily was startled to find a body lying on the ground. At first she thought it was an enemy lying in wait to shoot her, but then she realized the man wore Union blue. She let out a quick rush of breath and was about to ask him what he was doing, when Ben, walking next to her, nudged him with his rifle butt.

The soldier did not move. Ben nudged him harder until he managed to roll the body over onto his back.

Emily retched. She turned away and stumbled blindly from the body, knowing she would never be able to forget the sight of the man whose face had been shot off, leaving a gaping, rotting hole in its place. The only thing that told her there had once been a face there was the remaining row of teeth and a tongue lying blackened in the gore.

She did not stop running until she emerged from the woods, uncaring if she stumbled right into a Confederate line.

Thankfully, no Rebs awaited her on the other side of the Branch, and when Ben and Willie caught up with her, she was at least able to breathe again.

That is, until the breeze shifted and she caught hold of the scent filling the area. The stench of decaying flesh made her gag yet again, and her eyes filled with tears. Only now did she realize that what she'd thought were mounds of earth scattered around the field were actually bodies left lying where they'd fallen in the battle the day before. They lay in every conceivable position, marked with horrific wounds that no person should ever have to see and no body should ever endure.

"You can't think about it, Jesse," Willie told her, placing a sympathetic hand on her back. "Only think about what we're here to do."

The idea that she might inflict such damage on a person sent a shock of horror sliding again through Emily's body.

The face of the Reb she'd shot at Allegheny Mountain flashed into her mind, and her own chest felt carved out.

"Fall in!" came a bark down the line.

She squeezed her eyes shut and forced herself to think only of Pa and David. If they could give their lives for this cause, so could she.

When she opened her eyes, both Willie and Ben were with her, watching her carefully. For them, she would fight today. She could kill Reb after Reb to stop them from hurting these two. "Come on," she said to them, hoping she looked stronger than she felt.

They hurried to take their places in the reassembled line. Their 9th Indiana was on the right flank of Hazen's 19th Brigade, with the 6th Kentucky and 41st Ohio filling the line to their left. Emily continued the march south over the fields, cringing every time she had to step over a body or, worse, a detached limb. "Don't think about it," Ben said, echoing Willie. "Think only about staying alive yourself and doing your duty."

"What duty?" Emily could not recall why this awful war was even being fought. It was senseless.

"To fight to preserve our great Union!" Ben answered, looking annoyed.

Emily nodded numbly. Of course she wanted to preserve the Union, and she'd also come to realize that she fought to stop the spread of slavery into new states and territories, if not abolish it altogether. But right now, as she marched south on the battlefield and saw more dead bodies than she ever thought she'd see in her lifetime, she knew she would be running screaming from the battlefield if not for her brother and best friend. Today she was fighting solely for them.

They marched past two deserted log cabins that had once been someone's farm. Bullet holes riddled all four walls of each. Spreading out behind the buildings was a newly planted field with only a few tender green shoots poking up through the mud. The rest had been crushed to oblivion. A shot rang out, shattering the early morning quiet, and Emily dropped to the ground along with the rest of the line as a bullet whined past her.

"Fire at will!" Colonel Hazen shouted from atop his horse.

Emily fired into the line of trees across the field. Without looking to see if her bullet hit its mark, she grabbed another cartridge from the box hanging at her side, tore it open with her teeth, rammed it into the barrel with the rod, and fired again. Over and over she fired, advancing forward across the field when ordered, and doing her best to keep track of Ben and Willie at all times.

As Emily advanced toward the trees, she could make out the butternut color of the Rebs' uniforms and the glint of their musket barrels as they lifted them to fire. A cold stillness filled Emily's body, and she found she no longer cared what damage she inflicted on those men. She was happy to put a bullet through a skull or two, or several, in order to stop them from doing the same to Ben or Willie.

For what felt like hours, they fired at the line of Rebs in the trees. As Emily grabbed her last cartridge, Ben shouted, "I'm going back for ammunition!"

Emily took her shot and raced after Ben to the supply wagon parked near the cabins. As they filled their boxes, Ben looked at her, his eyes glassy. "Where's Willie?"

Emily looked back toward the line and saw their friend running toward them through the smoke. "Here she comes!" she yelled, relief making her voice crack.

Ben grabbed her arm, his eyes wide with fear before his gaze jerked toward the other men at the wagon. Only then did Emily realize she'd used the wrong pronoun. They covered the slip by grabbing cartridges and helping Willie refill her box, while Emily carefully watched the other men. No one paid them any mind. Relieved, and with their cartridge boxes now full, Emily turned with her friends back toward the line, pausing to squeeze her brother's upper arm. "Be careful, Ben."

He gave her a quick glance. "I will. You too." As Willie took off, he ran after her and Emily brought up the rear. When they were all three back on their bellies, Ben hollered, "Take that, filthy Rebs!"

The fighting continued. With shot after shot, Emily lost all track of time. When the Confederates retreated, she jumped to her feet with the rest of the line and chased after them, bursting through the forest and into another field, this one with cotton on one side and peach trees on the other. The trees were full of pink blossoms. Emily was shocked that such beauty could exist here in this hell.

Emily pushed out all other thoughts but those of loading, firing, protecting Ben, protecting Willie. She felt like a machine, cranking through the motions of her job without emotion. She had a purpose, and she was fulfilling it. Her senses were full of noise—beating drums, screaming wounded, booming artillery—and smells—sulfur, decay, sweat, smoke. Her sight narrowed to the pinpoint of where she aimed her shots.

An enemy bullet slammed into the tree right next to her head and sent splinters shooting painfully into her face and neck. She slapped her palm against her cheek and drew it back to find it covered in blood. The sight renewed her anger, and she yelled her rage as she took aim and fired again.

Suddenly, a great commotion arose as their line ran forward. She got to her feet and followed, reloading as she went.

Along with the rest of her regiment, Emily burst out of the

forest into a bare field and abruptly stopped when she saw the artillery on the other side of the field pointing right at her. Going by instinct, she dropped to her belly and took aim as Willie rolled to the ground beside her.

As she fired, she wondered where Ben had gotten to. He wasn't on the other side of Willie.

She raised her head higher, hoping to spot him, but grapeshot flew over her head and slammed into the trees behind her, making her dive back to the ground again.

"Where's Ben?" she yelled to Willie between shots.

"I don't know. I saw him heading that way." Willie jerked her chin to the right before lining up the sight on her rifle and firing. "I'll go look for him."

"No, wait—"

Emily did not have time to get her warning out before Willie jumped to her feet and was immediately hit in the stomach. Her face filled with confusion as she dropped her rifle and pressed both hands to her abdomen. Before Emily could react, another bullet hit Willie, the impact sending her sprawling onto her back.

"Willie!" Emily screamed. Horror held her in its clutches for one frantic moment, and she couldn't move, couldn't even breathe. And then suddenly, everything slammed into her all at once. All the noise, the revolting smells, the taste of gunpowder and blood in her mouth, and the sight of Willie lying on her back, too still.

"Ben!" Emily cried. Tearing her eyes from Willie, she searched for him. "Ben! Where are you?" She couldn't see him anywhere.

Frantic, Emily scooted over to Willie, trying to keep her own head down in the process. Willie was still breathing. Relief flooded through Emily, sending strength she didn't know she had through her body. She had to get Willie to safety. "I've got you, Willie. We'll get out of this. Just hold on."

With little regard for the bullets still whizzing past them, Emily slung her rifle over her shoulder and out of the way.

She reached under Willie's shoulders and lifted her upper body enough to drag her into the copse of trees behind them. She dragged her inert body over fallen logs and corpses until she was sure they were well away from the line of fire.

"Stay with me, Willie," she ordered as she propped her against a tree, twisted off the cap of her canteen, and brought it to her friend's lips. "Drink some water. You'll feel better."

Willie turned her face away and moaned in pain.

Emily forced herself to look at Willie's wounds. The one on her head, the one that had likely pushed her to the ground, looked like the bullet had skimmed along her skull. Although blood flowed down the side of Willie's face, it didn't look serious enough to kill her. Gently, she poured water from her canteen over the cut to wash out the dirt and debris.

She turned her attention to Willie's stomach, knowing this would be the worst of the wounds. Willie's hands were red from all the blood pouring from her body.

Emily gently pulled Willie's hands away from the wound. A hole several inches wide seemed to be pumping out dark red, almost black, fluid. Emily had never felt so powerless in her entire life. "Hold on, Willie. I'm going to find you some help. Hold on."

She started to get to her feet, but Willie's hand clamped onto her wrist. "Don't go."

Emily stared at her friend, whose face was turning a sickening gray color, and the skin around her eyes and mouth a ghastly blue. "Willie?"

"No use," Willie managed. "Dying."

"No!" Emily grabbed Willie's shoulders and shook her, hoping it might jar life back into her body. "You aren't dying. I'll find a surgeon, and you'll make it through. I need you to make it. Ben needs you."

With obvious effort, Willie tugged at her finger. It took Emily a moment to realize she was pulling off the identity ring Ben had given her at Christmas. "What are you doing? You need that for…" She didn't need to finish her sentence. They both knew what Willie needed the ring for, and they both knew today would be the day it would be needed.

Still, Willie pulled the ring off and pressed it into Emily's hand. "Give Ben. Tell him…" She coughed, a deep bubbling cough that made her struggle for breath. "Love him," she finally whispered.

Emily sat and pulled Willie against her. "I'll tell him," she promised through her tears. "I'll tell him you love him. He loves you, too, you know. As do I. You are the sister I never had and always wanted."

Willie made jerking movements, and her breathing quickened.

"What is it?" Emily asked, hating to see her friend in such pain.

Willie patted her chest. "Handker…"

"You want your handkerchief?" It seemed like a silly thing to want at a time like this, but Emily was not about to refuse her friend anything. Gently, trying to avoid moving or jarring her any more than necessary, Emily unbuttoned the top button of Willie's coat and reached to the pocket inside. She felt a piece of paper, which she ignored, and the scrap of cloth she was looking for.

"Here," she said, pressing the handkerchief into her friend's limp hand. "Here's your handkerchief."

Willie would not take it and instead pushed it back to Emily. "Take to…sister. Tell…sorry." Her eyes were closing as strength flowed out of her.

Emily's breath caught, and she fought to hold back the sobs that threatened to burst out. Words failed her so all she could do was nod.

Willie's hand closed over Emily's and squeezed with what little strength she had left. "Thank you…" Her eyes closed, and her hand went slack.

"No!" Emily squeezed Willie's hand. "Not yet. Don't die. I need you!"

But Willie's chest refused to lift with breath. Her hand refused to squeeze back. She was gone.

The sounds of the battle came roaring back so strong they nearly slammed the breath out of Emily, too. She gulped for air. She gathered Willie into her arms and held her, as though doing so would keep her soul from fleeing. With each boom of artillery, she flinched, but she did not move away from her friend.

She stayed holding Willie for as long as she dared, feeling her warmth drain away. When it was clear that Willie was long gone, Emily laid her friend back against the tree until she could return and give Willie a proper burial.

Carefully, she slid Willie's ring onto her own left pinkie finger and folded the bloody handkerchief into a tiny square, which she tucked into her chest bindings alongside her diary. "I'll take your handkerchief to your sister, Willie. I promise," she swore aloud. "I'll tell her your story and how bravely you fought. I'll make them proud of you."

That's when a sickening realization hit her. She didn't know Willie's last name. She didn't even know in what town in Nebraska her family was from. The only information she had was the three initials embroidered on the handkerchief: *ODE.* What did that stand for? How could she possibly find Willie's family in all of the Nebraska Territory when she didn't know their name?

Her friend was barely gone, and already Emily had failed her.

With her second promise to Willie burning in her heart, Emily searched the battlefield for Ben. As she left Willie's body to return to the line, her fellow soldiers ran past her in retreat.

"They've got us in a crossfire!" a man she didn't know yelled as he sprinted past, his eyes wide with fear. "Retreat!"

Emily ignored him and kept searching for Ben. She asked

every soldier who passed if they'd seen him, but most seemed not to hear her. Others simply shook their heads as they ran. The sounds of battle moved away, and she focused on nothing but finding her brother.

Dreading the worst, she searched the faces of every dead man in blue that she passed, but none was her brother.

Suddenly, someone grabbed her arm and spun her around.

"Where the hell are you goin'?" O'Brien yelled at her, his face black from musket powder and his eyes glazed. "Colonel Hazen's disappeared. Whitaker has ordered us to fall back to the wheat field and regroup."

"I have to find Ben," she yelled back. "Have you seen him?"

"No." O'Brien shook his head and released Emily's arm. "He's probably back at the field, where we should be." He disappeared through the trees, leaving her to her own fate.

Emily turned to follow him when a bullet whizzed by her so close she felt heat as it passed her ear. She dropped to the ground and reached for her rifle. Terror filled her when she realized she'd left it with Willie's body.

With no way to fight back, she was as good as dead.

She started crawling in the direction O'Brien had gone, doing her best to stay low to the ground. She needed to stay alive. Ben needed her. Willie needed her to fulfill her promise.

Five feet in front of her lay a dead soldier. His rifle lay on the ground next to him. Relieved, Emily crawled faster and was reaching for it when something sharp jabbed into her spine.

She froze. Her mind raced through her options: whip over and grab the weapon from her assailant, lift her arms in surrender, lie and wait to be shot.

"Move and yer dead." The gun barrel dug deeper into her back. "On behalf of President Jefferson Davis, I take you prisoner of the Confederate States of America." The voice had a Southern drawl mixed with what sounded like a Spanish accent. "Turn over, Yank, and keep your hands where I can see 'em!"

Emily did as she was told and found herself at the mercy of a solitary Confederate soldier. Anger tore through her. No! She couldn't be captured. She needed to find Ben.

Before the Reb could anticipate her move, she rolled quickly to the side, intending to jump to her feet. But the Reb was faster. Pain exploded on the side of Emily's head as he bashed her with his rifle butt. "Don't be stupid, Yank," he warned.

Fear seized Emily. She couldn't die right now. She had to get to Ben. "Please don't kill me!" she begged as tears blinded her. She didn't care how weak she looked to this Reb. She just needed him to release her.

The rifle jabbed her in the center of her chest. "On your feet."

Emily did as she was ordered and saw that only she and her captor remained in the clearing. "Please, I need to find my brother."

"So? We all have brothers."

Emily felt an unfamiliar hatred slide through her, and for the first time, she knew she could kill with no remorse. "You're never going to win this war. You disgust me." She spit the words at the man.

The Reb threw back his head and laughed, and Emily realized he must be insane. Only an insane person would find something to laugh at on this day.

When the Reb regained control of his mirth, he winked at Emily and smoothed his mustache with two fingers. "Think what you want, but who seems to have the upper hand right now?" He winked at her, sending a fresh wave of hatred through her.

"You there! What's going on here?" A Confederate officer rode toward them atop a chestnut mare.

The Reb's smile dropped. "Got myself a prisoner, sir!"

The officer stopped beside them, his gaze skimming over Emily. He turned back to the Reb. "Good work, soldier. What's your name?"

The Reb stood straighter. "Lieutenant Harry T. Buford, sir!"

"Take him back with the others, Lieutenant Buford," the officer ordered. "Then rejoin the line." He rode off.

"Yes, sir!" Lieutenant Buford jerked his head to the left, indicating to Emily which direction to walk. With a nudge from his rifle barrel to get her moving, he fell into step behind, the rifle poking at her when she slowed and removing all hope that she'd be able to escape.

Emily marched where she was ordered, saying nothing more. As they passed dozens and dozens of bodies, she realized that no one knew these men's names or what had happened to them. No one knew about Willie.

And now that she was captured by the enemy, no one would know what happened to her either. Ben must be frantic right now, searching for both her and Willie among the regiment. He would find neither.

Chapter Twenty-One

Present day: Woodinville, Washington

April 8, 1862: I must write fast before they see me. Don't know where I am—somewhere in northern Miss., I think. I am a prisoner of the Confederacy, captured by a Reb by the name of Lieutenant Buford whom I burn to hunt down and kill. I'll write about that in a moment, but first I must write about Willie.

We fought with honor. We stood shoulder to shoulder with our regiment, and we served our great country as was asked of us. We knew we could be killed. We'd known all along. But I truly believed I could protect Willie and Ben. I truly did. I thought if I was quick enough to reload, if my aim was sure, if my love was strong enough...I could keep them alive. But I was wrong. Willie was killed. Shot in the gut.

I've never been so scared in my life, or so angry. She was the best friend I could have ever asked for. She was going to be my sister. Ben wanted to marry her. We already felt like we were family. But I failed to protect her, and now she's gone. I didn't even get a chance to give her a proper burial because a damn Reb took me prisoner. I should have followed orders and retreated when told, but I had to look for Ben. For that I'm not sorry.

In her last moments, Willie gave me the handkerchief her sister had given to her, and she asked me to return it to her family and ask their forgiveness. I will fulfill this promise if it takes me to my last breath. She had a paper in her pocket with the handkerchief. Did it have her family's name and address? I will never know. I will never stop looking for them. I would do anything for Willie. She also gave me her ring, which I will return to Ben. Oh, how I dread telling him she is gone.

Wherever I am, we marched late into the night last night, our hands tied together like hogs for the roast. By the position of the sun this morning, I know we are marching south from the battle. We've passed through cotton fields, onion fields, small towns, and past isolated shacks with a handful of children staring at us from the front yard. All the while, I'm searching the faces of my fellow prisoners hoping to find Ben. What if I never find him?

When I see Lt. Buford, the Reb who took me prisoner, I'm going to kill him.

But first, I need to find Ben.

*E*ven though she suspected it was coming, reading about Willie's death hit Larkin hard, and she had to put the diary aside for several days. She filled those days with research, reviewing each and every one of those 164,500 federal census records from Lancaster County in 1860. She obsessively read each entry, searching for a family with a last name starting with the letter *E* and a daughter around Willie's age, and another with a name that began with *O*.

At least she now had confirmation that the handkerchief had belonged to Willie. Or, rather, to her sister. Emily had promised Willie she'd find her family and give her sister the handkerchief, but Larkin knew she'd failed because it had remained in Emily's possession until her death. Larkin froze as another realization came to her. Emily died in possession of Willie's ring, too. Why hadn't she given it to Ben?

Instead of thinking of that, she focused on the handkerchief. It must have tortured Emily to search for her friend's family and not find them. Nothing, Larkin knew, hurt worse than a broken promise to a friend.

Like the promise Larkin had made to Sarah to always have her back. Or to scatter her ashes in California.

Emily may have failed in her promise to Willie, but Larkin could fulfill it now and had, in fact, already started trying. She had modern tools at her disposal. Surely Larkin could find the right people and their descendants.

As Grams, Kaia, and Jenna visited friends over the holiday break and went to New Year's Eve parties, Larkin spent nearly every waking moment on the internet, searching for census records, inspecting digital archive records, following leads that always led nowhere, but following them just the same.

She'd spent half an hour the day after Christmas on the phone with a genealogist in Nebraska who agreed to help Larkin's research, for a hefty fee, and from then on, emailed with the woman every day, giving her an update on the places she'd looked and asking if there were any new leads. So far, all she'd found was the enlistment record for Willie Smith of the 9th Indiana Infantry. The hometown listed for Willie was not in Nebraska, but La Porte, Indiana. They decided that Willie must have lied about this since La Porte was the town where the three-year regiment of the 9th Indiana was mustered into service. Willie had likely falsified her hometown in order to protect her identity.

Larkin pulled the ring out of the diary and inspected it, hoping for a flash of insight or a vision from beyond, anything to tell her where to look next.

No visions came, so she slipped the ring onto her right pinkie finger and decided to take a break. Her promise to send Zach some of the photos she found in Sarah's boxes had been nagging at her like a toothache, and after learning of Emily's promise to Willie, the idea of returning items to a soldier's family member held a new kind of urgency.

Larkin grabbed a box and set it on her bedroom floor, sat down beside it, and took a deep breath. "Here I go, Sarah," she told the urn. "Please be gentle on me."

She sliced opened the box and smiled at the first item she saw, a woobie. The official name for the blanket was "poncho liner," but everyone called it a woobie. Made of three-color camouflage pattern nylon with polyester filling, it served as shelter, blanket, pillow, and emotional security while out in the field. Larkin and Sarah and everyone they'd ever served with had loved their woobies. Apparently, Sarah had loved hers so much she'd failed to turn it in when she was supposed to. Holding it on her lap, Larkin felt the warmth it provided and thought back to all the nights one like it had kept her warm. Too many to count. Sarah's woobie would have a new home on Larkin's bed.

As she draped the woobie over her shoulders, Larkin recalled the passage in Emily's diary where she talked about how her rubber blanket felt like her home. The rubber blanket must have been the woobie of the Civil War.

Smiling, Larkin reached for the next item in the box, a stack of envelopes with a rubber band around them. She inspected the top one and was surprised to see it was addressed to Zach Faber with Sarah's return address at JBLM. There was no postmark.

Knowing she was probably invading Sarah's, or even Zach's, privacy, she pulled the notebook paper out of the envelope anyway. It was dated a year ago November, right about the time their deployment had been announced.

Guiltily, Larkin started to read...

Dear Zach,

It looks like I'm heading back to Afghanistan. As soon as I heard, I thought of you. We haven't talked in eighteen years, though I saw you at Dad's funeral. I sat in the back and left early. I don't know why I went. I guess to make sure he was really dead. To me, he died when I was six years old when he left and never looked back.

You left me, too. I know you were only sixteen and just trying to survive, like I was, but I thought you'd come see me again. I thought you'd come back and save me from Mom's abuse. Did you even know how she changed after the divorce? She drank a lot, cried a lot, slept a lot, hit me a lot.

I convinced myself you didn't know, or you would have saved me from her. To think you abandoned me the same as Dad did hurt too much to accept.

Did you? Did you abandon me? Did you think about me at all?

It took a lot of courage for me to send you and Dad the invitations for my college graduation and Army commissioning ceremony. Why didn't you so much as send a note? I looked for you that day.

I don't know why I'm writing this letter to you. I'll probably never send it. I guess knowing that I'm about to return to a war zone that not everyone comes home from is making me think of what I'd regret. I'd regret not fixing my relationship with my brother.

But I'm too scared to contact you. It's easier not to try than to be rejected again.

I still love you,
Sarah

Larkin closed the letter and slipped it back in the envelope, her throat clogged with emotion. She'd never known Sarah yearned for her brother like this. She flipped through the rest of the stack and saw they were all letters to Zach, all unsent.

Zach had seemed like a nice guy on the phone, but why had he never reached out to his little sister? Would it have killed him to pick up the phone and call her once and a while?

Sarah had died with that pain. The knowledge broke Larkin's heart.

Right on the heels of that hurt came anger. Zach Faber needed to know what he did. He needed to suffer, the same way Sarah did for so many years.

Larkin should send the letters to him and make him see what he'd done to his sister. Better yet, she should take them to him in person and force him to read them as she watched so she could be sure he felt Sarah's pain.

Yes, that's what she would do. She'd take these letters down to California, and she would present them to the one person who could have taken away Sarah's pain but hadn't. She'd make him say he was sorry. That, like returning the ring and handkerchief to Willie's family, might make Sarah happy. And then, just maybe, Larkin could stop feeling so damn guilty.

She spent the rest of the day sorting through Sarah's stuff and putting together a box of things to take to Zach. Some items, such as the letters, were meant to hurt him. Others, like the photos, she would give him if she decided he'd earned them. He'd have to do a lot of groveling to Sarah's ghost if he expected to get anything more than the letters.

When she was done, Sarah's service memorabilia and clothes were safely stored in Larkin's closet. Her stuffed sea turtle and woobie had new homes on Larkin's bed. A stack of photos that would mean nothing to Zach, but meant everything to Larkin, was tucked safely in Larkin's drawer where she could look at them when she wanted. The rest were in a single cardboard box waiting to be lugged down to California.

Satisfied she had a plan, Larkin pulled Emily's diary out again, snuggled under the woobie with Sarah's turtle, and went back to reading.

> *April ?, 1862: I don't care any longer. About anything. Except Ben. I care about Ben. I pray he is alive. I pray he is safe. He's not here, I looked. This horse barn where we're locked up reeks. Horse shit, human shit. No room to lie down. I stay in my corner. Should've written to Harriet. Should've stayed home. Should've run when I had the chance. Maybe I'll die here.*

Chapter Twenty-Two

April 12, 1862: Corinth, Mississippi

*E*mily jerked awake when someone kicked her boot and snarled, "Get up. They're moving us."

She'd fallen asleep wedged into the corner of a horse stall with her knees hugged to her chest. Her muscles refused to cooperate as she tried to stand, and she lost her balance, falling into the man next to her, who shoved her back. She would have fallen if not for the rough planks of the stall, and she came away with several splinters in her arm and palm.

A burning feeling filled her lungs and she coughed into her bent arm, hearing a rattling sound along with it. Phlegm filled her mouth, and she spat it into the soiled hay at her feet. In the middle of the night she'd woken feeling like she was being burned alive. She'd realized quickly that she had a fever, and also that there was nothing she could do about it. They hadn't had clean water to drink since they'd all been shoved into this barn four days ago and little food beyond the dry bread and half-rotten potatoes served once a day.

With little notice of anything else, Emily shuffled along with the others and allowed herself to be herded out of the barn and onto a waiting railroad car with the other prisoners. As soon as she was on board the filthy cattle car, she found herself another corner and promptly fell back asleep.

She drifted in and out of sleep during the journey. During the two occasions when they were forced to change trains, she found herself being half carried by two other soldiers. She was grateful for their help, although she was so ill she wouldn't have blamed them if they'd left her to die in the train car.

But then she'd remember Ben, and she'd find a new well of strength that helped her to hold on. She needed to stay alive so she could find him, give him Willie's ring.

As she was half carried off the train for a third time, she heard someone say they were in Tuscaloosa, Alabama. Her head pounded too much for her to care.

The next time she came out of her delirium, she found herself being hoisted out of the back of a wagon and carried into a brick building that echoed inside with all the men's footsteps and voices. She was blessedly placed on a cot and covered with a scratchy blanket, and she fell again into the relief of sleep.

She did not know how long she slept, but nearly every time she woke, she found the same black-haired man sitting beside her, bathing her hot face with a wet cloth or forcing broth between her cracked lips. Each time she drifted back to sleep, it was with Ben on her mind. She needed to stay alive so she could find him. He must be so worried about her. Did he know about Willie?

Finally, she woke feeling enough like herself that she could think straight. Everything came rushing back, and remembering her diary and Willie's handkerchief, she weakly lifted a hand to her chest bindings.

Her hand touched the blanket and shirt covering her chest, but instead of finding the tight bindings with the lump of a book under them, she found soft flesh. Her eyes flew open in alarm.

"Now, now, don't go getting yourself worked up," a voice said. Emily turned and found the man who'd been nursing her.

He was plain-looking with a dark complexion, dark wavy hair, and full lips. For some reason, the man wore his blue forage cap, and on it, she could see the crossed sabers indicating a cavalry unit. His smooth face revealed him to be young, younger than herself. "You've nothing to worry about."

"Where…" Emily had to pause to sort her jumbled thoughts. So many questions battled inside her mind that she was impatient to give voice to all of them, but she settled on the most important. "Where are my things?"

"Your diary? It's right here." The man lifted it from the floor and tucked it into Emily's hand. "The guards read it but must not have found anything of interest in there. We weren't too sure you were going to make it. The prison commander even called the town doctor to come see you and a few of the others."

A doctor had examined her? Had he stripped off her chest bindings? They must know the truth of her gender. But that didn't make sense. She turned her head and found herself in a large open warehouse full of other Union soldiers. Confederate guards holding muskets were stationed at various points around the cavernous room. The corner where she lay in her cot must have been designated the infirmary because it held the only beds in sight. A dozen other ill or injured men lay beside her, being tended by Union soldiers still covered in battlefield muck and dried blood. The nurses were, apparently, fellow prisoners.

Through Emily's muddled mind, one question became clear: If her secret had been detected, why was she still imprisoned with the men?

And they'd read her diary. She closed her eyes and searched her memory for anything she might have written that would incriminate her. All she could think of was the entry when she'd written about Willie's death. She'd used the pronoun *she* for the first time, but she'd also said Willie had died. Surely nothing she'd written would reveal her own true sex?

"I'll be frank with you," the man nursing her went on in a whisper, his eyes keenly watching her. "I know your secret."

Emily's breath caught and sent her into a fit of coughing. Her nurse helped her drink from a water glass and then lie back again. When she could breathe again, Emily watched him warily, knowing full well that her fate rested in his hands. She was prepared to give him anything, anything at all, in exchange for his silence. "What do you want?"

The man's expression did not change, and he stared at her for a long moment. "You've been here three days. I'm the only one who has tended to you."

Emily figured that was probably good news, unless the man intended to abuse his power. "Where are my..." She searched for a way to ask her question without revealing her secret to those nearby. "Where are the rest of my clothes?"

"Your *clothes* had to be removed to allow you to breathe and cough enough to clear your lungs. I removed them myself before anyone saw and covered you back up with your Army blouse. You'll find them under your mattress. When you're recovered, I'll help you put them back on when the others are sleeping."

The promise both comforted her and terrified her. What else did he intend to do to her when the others were sleeping? "Why are you helping me?"

"George," a man several beds over called out, and Emily's nurse turned his head. "Can you bring me some water?"

"I'll be right there, Harry," George answered before turning back to Emily. He seemed to be considering his answer for a silent moment, and then, with a quick nod of his head, he whispered, "Because I understand secrets."

Emily watched George walk away. Whatever his secrets might be, she was going to have to be very careful around him.

Through several long days and nights, Emily slowly recovered from her illness until she was left with only a lingering cough and general weakness in her limbs. Being cooped up like this was wearing on her as much as it was on the other men. Fistfights broke out daily, as did verbal arguments and petty bickering, though Emily stayed out of it.

When Emily was declared fit enough to move to the other end of the warehouse where the men slept in rows on the floor, wrapped in thin blankets, she was relieved to finally put some distance between her and George. That relief, however, ended almost immediately when she realized George had arranged a space for her to sleep next to him. Where, he said, he could keep her safe.

Safe? Emily wondered. *Or in his control?* She still had no idea why the man was helping her, and she feared what sort of payment he'd ask of her in return.

Prison life felt much like Army life in that she was always too cold or too hot. There weren't enough blankets to go around, nor enough food to satisfy anyone. Emily's belly ached constantly, and she didn't know if it was a lingering effect of her illness or simply hunger. Her clothes were still stained with dirt, gunpowder, and sweat from the battle but even worse, the front of her blouse was stiff with Willie's dried blood. Between nightmares of the battle, Willie's death, and Ben's voice calling to her, she often dreamt of a hot bath like the one she'd taken in Nashville before their dress parade.

With little to do to fill their time, the prisoners had taken to singing songs, playing what games they could in the confined space, and talking for hours on a variety of topics.

"I thought I'd be home by now," a grizzled middle-aged man from New York told them as he scratched his belly and considered the cards in his hand. "Hell, I'd promised my grandson I'd be home for Christmas, but that was nearly four months ago and I'm still here." He slapped a card on the overturned crate they were using as a table.

"I never thought it would be like this," another man said, his hands hanging between his knees as he leaned against a brick wall and watched the poker game in progress. "What we saw back there at Pittsburg Landing..." He shook his head, and several men around him did the same.

"They kept saying we just needed one big win in battle, and the Rebels would give up their fight." The bald man, also playing poker, twisted his head from one side to the other as though seeing beyond the walls of the prison warehouse. "It don't look to me like anyone is going home."

"Remind me, would you?" asked a soldier who was lying on the bare cement a few feet away from those gathered around the card game. "Why are we fighting this war? I thought it was to preserve the Union of our states, but it looks to me like all it's doing is tearing us apart."

"Don't fool yourselves, gentlemen," George drawled. "This war has never been about states' rights or Federal control or economic differences. We're fighting against the institution of slavery. Period. The Southern states want to preserve it because it's the only way they get rich, and they want to spread slavery across the country so their side of the argument is strengthened. The Northern states want to abolish it and keep it from spreading. That's all there is to it."

"You're wrong," protested an Irish boy. "I don't care one ewe's teat about slavery. I do care about preserving the strength of my new nation so that it can withstand threats from other nations."

"Oh, don't get me wrong, boys," George told him in a placating tone. "I'm not saying all that isn't important and an aspect of the conflict. What I'm saying is that when it's all boiled down, it's about Southern landowners needing slave labor to run their plantations so they get rich. And before you tell me again that I'm wrong because not all Southerners own slaves, know that those who don't are still fighting for slavery because it keeps

them above a whole lotta folks on the social hierarchy. They'd
die before finding themselves at the bottom."

"I'm not putting myself in front of a bullet for no nigger," a
man across the room called over, though Emily could not see
who he was. Others voiced agreement.

"If the negroes don't want to be slaves, why aren't they
fightin' on our side?" the card player from New York asked
George pointedly.

George appeared relaxed, but Emily could feel the tension
pouring from his body. "They aren't allowed to. The Union
Army has turned away hundreds."

That was news to Emily.

"Why, I heard the negro brain is smaller than ours," offered
the bald man. "They simply aren't as smart as a white person."

"I've heard others say that," Emily said, thinking back to
MacGregor and to all the evenings when Uncle Samuel had a
bit too much whiskey and got to talking. "But I don't think
it's true."

George grunted in disgust and got to his feet. "Just because
someone looks different from you does not mean he is any less
intelligent." As though he could not stand another moment of
the conversation, George walked away, shaking his head.

Emily was relieved to finally get a break from him, but something about him was nagging at her. He had already admitted
to having secrets, and now, after seeing him get so worked up
about slavery and colored people in general, she could not help
but wonder if he was connected to the community in some
way. He felt strongly on the matter, which could mean he
might be an abolitionist, or he might even have some African
blood in him.

As the other men went on discussing the differences between
whites and blacks, Emily watched George walk away. Sure, his
complexion was dark, but so were many of the men's here in
the prison.

Still, Emily felt almost certain she'd discovered George's secret. If he was truly part African, then being discovered serving in the Army as a white man must assuredly be as dangerous as being discovered to be a woman. Maybe even more so.

Finally, Emily had some leverage over George in the event that he tried to hurt her. She did not plan to use the knowledge unless he forced her to, but now she didn't feel quite so vulnerable around him.

Chapter Twenty-Three

Present day: Walnut Creek, California

Z ach Faber lived on the side of a hill in a house that looked new and big enough to sleep a handful of families. The sight of it pissed Larkin off more than she already was. She'd spent the entire flight to California steaming over how Sarah's family had treated her so poorly.

She parked her rental car and stalked to the huge front door, ready to put this arrogant prick in his place. Since he was the only member of Sarah's family still alive, he would represent all of them. She jabbed at the doorbell and waited, her arms folded across her chest.

A dog barked, and she heard a male voice talking to it, though she couldn't make out the words. The door opened and there stood Zach Faber, looking lean and tanned—in January—and healthy. He shared the same coloring as Sarah, all dark Italian or Eastern European. He was dressed in golf attire, and a large Doberman stood regally at his side. The sight of Sarah's brother made Larkin want to punch him in the face. His sister was dead, and here he was living this life of luxury.

"Can I help you?" His smile showed perfect white teeth. Of course.

"I'm Larkin Bennett," she announced, sure he would recognize her name. "And I have Sarah in the car."

Zach's entire body jerked as though he'd been shocked with electricity. He craned his neck to look behind Larkin to her rental car, his eyes wide.

"Her ashes, I mean," Larkin clarified, feeling warm satisfaction as he deflated. "I have some things I'd like to talk with you about. Can I come in?"

Zach nodded and a lock of black hair fell into his eyes. He absently shook it back with a toss of his head. "Yes, please. Come in. Don't mind Stormageddon. He's friendly."

Larkin didn't try to pet the Doberman, even with Zach's reassurances. He looked intimidating.

Zach led her to a sunroom off the kitchen, overlooking an infinity pool with a view across the entire valley. "Can I get you a drink? I have iced tea, coffee. It's probably too early for wine."

"Water is fine." Larkin sat on an overstuffed armchair. The dog jumped onto the couch opposite her and lay down, leaving a space for Zach to sit when he returned. A laptop waited on the coffee table, as though he'd been working before she arrived.

"Here you are." Zach handed her a tall glass of ice water with a slice of lime floating in it and sat on the couch. His free hand rested on the dog's neck. "So, Larkin. What brings you here today?"

Larkin looked at him for a moment without responding. He really did bear a strong resemblance to Sarah. Something around the eyes and lips. As much as she didn't want to admit it, Zach's eyes sparkled like Sarah's always did, as though life was a huge adventure and they couldn't wait to see what came next.

She had to look away to collect her thoughts. The letters. "As I mentioned to you on the phone a few weeks ago, I have Sarah's belongings. She left them to me when she died, and I've been going through the boxes of things she put into storage when she deployed."

"Yes, you said you have some photographs. Did you bring them?"

Larkin nodded. "We'll get to those." She drew the stack of letters from her bag. "I could've mailed the photos to you, but then I found these letters, and to be frank, I want to see your face as you read them." She shoved them into his hands and felt as if she were handing him a live grenade.

Confusion pinched his face as he saw his name on the top envelope, and then the dozen envelopes under that one. With a questioning look toward Larkin, he opened the top one and read it silently. It was the one Larkin had read. She'd never looked at the others because it felt like an invasion of Sarah's privacy, but she imagined they were all a version of that first one.

Larkin sipped her water and carefully watched him as he read. Her training had prepared her for this moment perfectly, she realized as she caught a flash of emotion cross Zach's face. His micro expressions, the way his shoulders stiffened, the nervous tapping of the foot he draped across the opposite knee. All of it conveyed the truth of how he was feeling, and Larkin saw it all. The man was in pain. He felt guilt. He felt sorrow. He felt shame.

Zach did not look Larkin's way the entire time he read through all thirteen letters. And when he was done, he kept his gaze down as he folded the last paper and slipped it back into the envelope.

Larkin decided to go for the jugular while he was feeling vulnerable. "Why did you abandon her?"

His reaction surprised her. Instead of getting angry or making excuses, he dropped his face into his hands and sobbed.

Tears filled her own eyes, and she had to clench her teeth together to hold them in check. She couldn't back down now. "So what if your parents treated her like shit. That didn't mean you had to do it, too." She took a breath and let it out slowly. With her voice calm, she went on. "She talked about you often.

She followed your social media pages and kept tabs on where you were, what you were doing, but she was too afraid to actually contact you. She couldn't take being rejected again."

Zach rose to his feet and stalked to the windows, his back to her. The dog watched him and whined.

Larkin didn't say any more. She'd made her point.

Just as she was thinking of letting herself out, he started talking, quietly at first. "I was a stupid kid when our parents split. Sixteen, thinking more about girls and sports than anything else. I knew Sarah was hurt when I chose to live with Dad and she wasn't given a choice, but I told myself she'd be okay. I thought a girl needed to be with her mother. I had no idea Mom would start drinking."

He turned, his hands in his jeans pockets. "Mom never forgave me for going with Dad. She hung up when I called, and she refused to let me in the house when I stopped by. Eventually I gave up trying."

"I don't think Sarah knew that."

He looked at the tile floor and chewed on his bottom lip. "I knew she went across the country for college and then joined the Army. I should have contacted her when she was free of our mother's clutches, but I thought it was too late. I didn't think she'd even remember me since she was only six the last time I saw her."

Larkin could see his pain. It was etched on his face, dragged down his body, and was coming at her in waves. No one could fake this.

Suddenly she wasn't angry any more, but her heart felt so heavy it was pulling down on her throat and making it hard to speak. "I, uh…" She took a deep breath and started over. "Want to see the pictures?" She drew them from her bag and handed them to him.

Zach returned to the couch and looked at the top picture, the one of the two of them as kids with their arms looped around each other. He bit his bottom lip. "She was such a cute kid. A pain in the ass sometimes, but I could never be mad at her." He went to the next photo and laughed when he saw it. "I remember this day! I saved for years to buy this car, and when I brought it home that afternoon, Sarah insisted on being the first person to go for a ride. She was so small she couldn't even see out the windshield, but she made me put the top down and turn up the stereo." He fell quiet but kept staring at the photo for several more minutes as though lost in the memory.

As he flipped through the rest of the photos, Larkin told him about their time at Norwich University together, about Sarah's various stations and deployments, and their vacations all around the world.

"Did she have a boyfriend?" Zach wondered.

"She had boyfriends off and on, but no one that stuck. It's difficult to maintain relationships when you're moving so often."

He set the stack on the coffee table next to his laptop. "Thank you so much for these. Seeing them makes me happy, and yet they break my heart at the same time." He blew out a heavy sigh. "I missed so much, and now it's too late."

Larkin watched him swallow and turn his head to look out the window, pain etched on his face.

"Do you want to see her? Her ashes?"

He looked unsure, but he nodded in agreement so Larkin went out to the car to collect the urn from the front passenger seat. Back inside the house, she handed the Himalayan salt urn to Zach as carefully as she would an infant.

He took it and held it to his chest, tears pouring down his cheeks. To Larkin, it looked like he was hugging his sister, and in that moment, she knew Sarah was actually here, in his arms. The pressure of her own tears grew to be too much, and she covered her mouth with her hands as tears flowed unchecked down her cheeks.

After what might have been an hour or only a couple of

minutes, Zach looked at Larkin with red-rimmed eyes. "Thank you." His voice was raw.

She nodded but could not speak around the clog of emotion in her throat. After swallowing several times and taking a deep, cleansing breath, she finally managed, "She asked that I scatter her ashes on a California beach and then leave the urn to dissolve in the ocean. She cared about the environment and didn't want to leave anything behind."

He smiled. "I like that about her."

She smiled back. "Yeah, me too." An idea came to her that felt so right, she was surprised she hadn't thought of it sooner. "I haven't been able to say goodbye to her yet, but maybe we can do it together?"

His arms tightened around the urn. "Do you mean...scatter her ashes today?"

She nodded. "Yes. I think she would like that. I know I'd like your company."

Tears filled his eyes again, but they did not fall. He nodded. "Yes. I'd like that."

Zach took her to a beach over an hour away where he, Sarah, and their parents had had a family picnic years ago, before their family had fallen apart. He told Larkin about throwing rocks in the ocean and how, even then, Sarah had a strong arm. "She made me explore the entire beach that day, and we stayed until the sun had gone down. It was our last perfect day together."

Larkin looked around. It was a small beach, rocky and gritty, but the closer to the water she went, the smoother the sand became until it was powder fine. The Pacific Ocean spread out blue and expansive in front of her. On the horizon, a bank of clouds was already tinted pink from the setting sun. "This is perfect, Zach."

A cold wind blew off the water and kept everyone else away. Larkin was grateful for that small blessing. The moment was a private one.

She carried Sarah's urn to the water, ignoring a wave that splashed over her bare feet. She took another couple steps forward, and the next wave hit her knees. The cold felt good. It reminded her she was alive. Sarah would never feel the cold of the ocean again, nor see the breathtaking moment when the sun dipped into the water and left a streak of golden light straight to the shore.

She held Sarah's urn to her chest and reached for Zach's hand. It felt natural to hold on to him and she closed her eyes, focusing on the warmth coming from Zach and wishing with everything in her that she could give that gift to Sarah.

She turned her attention to the weight of the urn nestled against her chest, knowing it would be the last moment she would have a physical connection with the best friend she'd ever had in her life.

But it wasn't Sarah any longer. Sarah was gone. "I miss you so much," she whispered aloud. In her mind, she added, *I'll watch over Zach for you, okay? He misses you, too.*

"Are you ready?" Zach asked gently.

She opened her eyes and nodded. She was ready.

She carefully pulled off the pink salt lid and looked for the last time at the remains of her friend. "Should we pour it out together?"

"I'd like that." Zach's hands joined hers on the urn and together they tilted it sideways until the gray ashes started falling to the water.

The breeze picked up some of the ashes and swirled them into their faces. Before Larkin knew what was happening, she'd inhaled the ashes and started coughing.

Zach was coughing, too, and they both looked at each other and burst out laughing. "I guess she'll always be a part of us, now, huh?" he said with a smile.

"At least a part of our lungs." She smiled, too.

With her heart a little lighter, Larkin turned back to the task at hand, and they poured out the final bits of remains and watched them swirl and sink into the water. When it was done, Larkin placed the lid back on the top and carefully set the urn on the surface of the water. It floated for a short moment before sinking.

As they turned to walk back to dry beach, Larkin again took Zach's hand. "I'm glad you were here for this. I think she's happy about it, too."

He squeezed her hand but said nothing.

They settled onto the sand and wrapped a blanket around them that Zach had brought from his car. The waves came in and washed back out, and with each one, they knew Sarah was being carried farther into the ocean.

They stayed there, watching the waves, until the stars came out and the ocean grew black.

On the drive home, they took a short detour and had dinner in Sausalito at a restaurant right on the water. They talked mostly about Sarah, but eventually the conversation turned to their own lives. Larkin asked Zach about his work as a program manager at a tech company and if he'd ever been married. He had, but said they'd both been too young and it hadn't worked out. They were still friends. He asked her about growing up in Washington and her Army career. Although he asked, she wasn't ready to talk about the bombing. She'd have to tell him someday that she was to blame for Sarah's death, but not today.

"Look, about the diary," she said as they walked back to his car. "I'd understand if you want to keep it in your family. Just please let me finish reading it. I'm trying to find descendants of Willie's siblings. I think they'd like to have the handkerchief and ring, don't you?"

"Yes, probably, and that's kind of you," he answered. "But I think you should keep the diary. I think you are the only person I know who could appreciate it as much as Sarah did, and she obviously knew that. Keep it in her honor and pass it down to your own children someday."

Larkin smiled at that. "Any daughters I have will want to be soldiers for sure after hearing about Sarah and reading about Emily and Willie. I think those three women would be quite proud of that legacy, don't you?"

He smiled and opened the car door for her. "I definitely do."

That night, Larkin stayed in a hotel in Walnut Creek, but sleep eluded her. She'd done it. She'd finally said goodbye to Sarah and scattered her ashes. But, she knew, Sarah was still with her. She'd always be with her.

As she lay there staring at the popcorn ceiling of the hotel room, Larkin's thoughts turned to Emily. In the last diary entry she'd read, Emily had been in the Confederate prison after Willie's death. She hadn't been given the chance to bury her friend. At least Larkin knew where Sarah's remains were. She'd cared for them herself for months, and tonight she'd released them to the ocean. All Emily had was the memory of leaving her friend's body on the battlefield. Had someone buried her? Had she been left to rot until she was unrecognizable? Had anyone prayed over her grave?

Those questions did not have any answers, she knew. But she could find out what happened next to Emily.

Larkin pulled the diary from her bag and read late into the night.

May 19, 1862: This prison is being decommissioned, and we are to be sent north and exchanged for Confederate soldiers in Union prisons. Finally, I can find Ben!

As I sit on this train on my way to freedom, I think of the souls who have never known freedom, and I am determined to see the end of the institution of slavery. Colored people experience so much that a white person will never truly understand. We need to listen harder, see more.

I am grateful to George Harris of the 8th New York Cavalry for nursing me back to health, though I hope today is the last I see of him. He has secrets, though I know not what they are. So many of these men hide a part of themselves away. Maybe it's what we have to do to survive war. No matter what the secret part is, it is all ours. It is all we have control over.

I am tired, but I am ready to do whatever I must to find Ben.

Chapter Twenty-Four

May 19, 1862: Confederate Prison, Tuscaloosa, Alabama

W hen I read your name," called the guard to the prisoners standing at attention, "you are to receive your papers and fall into line for the march to the railroad depot." They'd been woken with the news that they were being sent north. Loud cheers echoed through the warehouse, and now, two hours later, the tone of the room still felt jubilant. "Gordon, Jones, O'Neil," read the guard from the list in front of him, "Spencer..."

Emily stood at attention and waited for her name to be called. She could hardly believe her luck. She'd been locked in this stuffy, stinky building for over five weeks now—one of the men had been counting the days with hash marks on the wall—and had felt like she'd never see freedom again. Never see Ben again. As each day crawled closer to summer, the temperature in the building climbed, the stench of bodies with it, and many men had taken to going shirtless in the afternoons. Emily, obviously, did not have that option and worried that these close quarters were going to lead to the discovery of her secret.

The guard flipped a page over and read the next list of names. Emily cast a glance over her shoulder to George. Ever since the day Emily started suspecting George was part African, he had kept his distance from her, as though he'd known he'd made a mistake in speaking so freely. George's expression did not change as he met Emily's gaze. His eyes shifted forward again.

Emily turned forward herself, relieved that after today she might never see him again. He would no longer hold the power of her secret over her.

When her name was finally called, Emily made her way to the open door, where she collected her papers and took her place in another line waiting to march away from this dismal place. A quick pat reassured her the diary was safely in place in her bindings, the handkerchief and ring in its secret compartment. Amazingly, even her inkpot had survived all she'd been through and rested in her pocket.

"Do you think they'll let us go home?" asked the boy in front of her.

Emily shook her head. "They're sending us to the custody of the Federal Army. I'm sure we'll be returned to our regiments."

"Oh." The poor boy's face crumbled and he turned back around, but not before Emily saw his bottom lip tremble.

"Although I could be wrong," she added, hoping to cheer him. "Especially if you have an injury or are unfit for service."

She saw his shoulders straighten at that and knew she'd raised his spirits.

The jovial mood of the men continued all through the march to the railroad depot and the long ride north. Emily kept to herself and managed to write in her diary more than she'd dared while at the prison. For the rest of her time on the long train ride, which took all day, she alternated between dozing and staring out the window, watching the landscape pass by.

Several buildings near the tracks had been burned, and evidence remained of a skirmish. At one point, she thought she saw an Army encampment through the trees, but she could not determine if it was Union or Confederate. The farther north they went, the easier she breathed.

The sun sat on the horizon when they pulled into Nashville, and the Federal troops on board the train cheered upon seeing the United States flag flying at the station. They were free and back in the arms of their country. Now, finally, she could send a message to Ben.

"Welcome home, boys!" called the Union officer who greeted them on the platform as they stepped off the train. "It's good to have you back."

They were herded into formation and sent marching a good distance down the road to a camp outside of town, where they were to be quartered until processed back into their units or sent home. As Emily marched, she could not help casting a glance up the hill to the capitol building where she'd been stationed last time she was in this city. It felt like a lifetime ago since she'd been here, although it had only been two months. Only two months ago she'd been happy with Ben and Willie at her side, all of them certain they were going to beat the Rebs and then start a new life together in Nebraska.

She turned away from the white building and fastened her eyes firmly on the soldier in front of her so she would not see anything else that would remind her of what she'd lost. *Come find me, Ben. I need you.* She said the words like a prayer in her mind as her heart ached. *Where are you?*

The camp felt no different from the Alabama prison. Sure, she could look up at the wide-open sky, was given food three times a day, and could go to the privy without asking permission first, but she still did not have her freedom.

She'd posted a letter to Ben, in care of the 9th Indiana Infantry wherever they might be located now, but knew there was no guarantee it would reach him.

She watched as day after day more men were sent back to

their regiments, on to join new ones, or home to their families. All she could do was wait for her orders. When George Harris marched past her tent toward the train that would carry him back to his regiment, Emily copied the other men and called, "Go get 'em, George!"

George ignored her and kept his eyes forward.

Emily felt like she was dying, waiting to be sent somewhere—anywhere. Finally, finally, she was back with the Federal Army and she could look for her brother. She wanted to go to him today. Now. But every time she asked to be sent to rejoin her regiment, she was told to wait. When she'd offered to travel to wherever they might be on her own, she'd been denied and told to wait.

Wait for what? For orders.

What orders? Whose orders? The lack of information was infuriating. Didn't they understand? She had to find Ben. She had to be with him and protect him better than she'd protected Willie.

Willie.

Thinking her name was more than Emily could bear. Feeling sick to her stomach, she poured out the rest of the coffee she had been drinking and got to her feet to walk off the unwanted emotions threatening to spill over. She couldn't leave camp without a pass, but she could pace down the rows of tents and back again.

"Private Wilson?" An orderly was walking toward her, calling her name. "Private Jesse Wilson?"

"Yes, that's me," she answered. "Have my orders come in?"

The man did not answer. He stared at her with bored eyes until, finally, he said, "Your presence is commanded at headquarters." He smartly pivoted and marched away, not looking to see if she followed.

The wait was finally over. She would return to Ben today! Emily hurried to catch up to the orderly and stayed right on his heels the whole way to the one-room house that served as camp headquarters.

To her surprise, the room was full of officers in uniform. At least seven men turned as she stepped through the door, all scrutinizing her with narrowed eyes. No one said a word.

She stepped to the front of the desk in the middle of the room and smartly saluted. "Private Wilson reporting, sir!"

No one spoke. Floorboards creaked as one man shifted his weight. Another coughed.

Finally, the man behind the desk stood. "Private Wilson, I am General Ellington. This man to my left is Provost Marshal Gillem, and the man next to him is Dr. Hawkins, who will be performing a medical inspection of your person."

Emily took a step back, alarmed. "Whatever for? I assure you I am in good health." Her body grew cold. Had George turned her in before he left?

General Ellington wearily lifted a piece of paper from his desk. "It seems you may not be who you say you are. We received this letter from a man who says he is your uncle, claiming that you are a woman impersonating a man and a soldier. How do you respond to these charges?"

How had Uncle Samuel found her? She could not breathe. Her lungs strained to fill, but she could not manage to draw air into them. Flashes of light flickered in her vision, and she searched the room for a friendly face, an ally who might help her. Every man there had some version of the general's expression—lip curled in contempt, eyes full of disgust. Every man except the one standing in the corner wearing civilian clothes and scribbling on a pad of paper. His eyes looked delighted.

"It's a lie!" she finally managed. "Of course I am a man. I've been serving for seven months now, honorably I might add, including in the battles of Allegheny Mountain and Pittsburg Landing where I last saw my brother. I've also been a prisoner for the last several weeks. I've proven my worth. Please, I need to find my brother." Her hands shook so much she had to press her palms hard against the seams of her trousers.

The provost marshal cleared his throat. "Impersonating a man is a serious offense. Impersonating a soldier even more serious. The Confederacy has already sent spies into our ranks posing as soldiers, and there are women among them. If found guilty, spies are hung for treason. Do you understand?"

A tremble shook her entire body. "I'm not a spy!"

"So, you do admit you are a woman?"

"What? No!" She was becoming flustered and knew she had to calm down and think straight. "Look, Uncle Samuel is a hard man. I'm certain he was not keen on being left with all the work on the farm when my brother and I departed. This is his way of making me go home, that's all. Let me go, and I'll return home and clear this up. You won't be bothered by my family again. I'll see to it."

The general curled his lips so they disappeared into his beard and mustache. He studied her for another second, then gave a curt nod.

Before she realized what was happening, two men had grabbed her arms, restraining her. "What is the meaning of this? I am a soldier for the United States of America!"

"Until we have proof of your sex, you will forgive us if we don't take you at your word." The general got to his feet. "Doctor, we will step outside while you perform your inspection. How many men do you require to assist you?"

"Those two ought to do," the doctor answered, nodding to the two men holding her.

Emily struggled, terrified of whatever was about to happen to her. The men holding her arms twisted them, sending a stab of pain through her shoulders. She bit her lip to keep from crying out.

When the room had cleared of all but the three men, the doctor rounded the desk to stand before her. She was surprised to see he was a young man, no older than his late twenties, she would venture. A full head of dark hair melded into heavy patches of hair on the sides of his face with the rest shaved clean to reveal a strong jaw and full lips. When he smiled, she saw his teeth were straight and clean. Kindness filled his eyes and she knew if she'd encountered him anywhere else but here, she would think him handsome. "Now, Private Wilson, if that is your name. Let us get this over with, shall we?"

To her horror, he reached for the rope that she used as a belt and started tugging it loose. For the first time, she realized what he meant to do and felt her entire body light on fire with shame. "No, please," she begged. "Don't do this." She folded at the hips, trying to pull away from his searching hands, but the men holding her tightened their grips and prevented escape.

The doctor's gaze flickered over her face, and she saw a hint of regret there. "I'm only doing my job, Private." He finished undoing her belt and proceeded to unbutton her trousers.

Emily closed her eyes and wished she were anywhere but there. She'd even choose to be on the battlefield staring down a line of Rebel muskets pointed straight at her rather than endure this. When the doctor put his hands on either side of her hips to grab fistfuls of her trousers and yank them down, she could not silence a whimper.

The men froze. Emily, still with her eyes squeezed shut, felt a draft of cold air where no breeze should touch, and certainly no male eyes should either. Hot shame coursed through her, and she wished she could melt into a puddle and disappear through the floorboards.

"I'll be..." said one of the guards as though he'd never seen a female body before.

Emily's body buckled. She slipped free of the men's grasp and fell, her body folding to hide her nakedness. When she felt her bare bottom hit the cold, gritty floor, she felt the last of her control snap and she sobbed. Even as she tried to cover herself with one hand, she buried her face in the other and cried, knowing it was all over.

One of the guards tried to grab her arm and pull her to her feet, but the doctor stopped him with a command. "No, leave her be." To Emily, he ordered, "Cover yourself, madam, before the rest of the officers return, or your shame will be that much worse."

Horrified at the thought of more men seeing her most private self, she managed to get back on her feet and fasten her trousers. Without asking for permission, she stumbled into a corner and curled into a chair to await the announcement of her fate.

How had Samuel found her? The question would not stop battling around in her mind. His betrayal hurt. But the worse betrayal she felt was that done by these officers. To them, she was nothing more than a body. She wasn't a person. Certainly not a human worthy of respect and honor. Did they care that she had stood shoulder to shoulder upon the battlefield to defend her country? No. All they cared about was the sex organ between her legs, and upon confirming she was female, they now considered her worthless. Even now, as the men tromped back inside and were given the verdict from the doctor, no one cared enough to hand her a handkerchief to dry her tears. They looked at her with eyes full of disgust.

"It seems we have ourselves a bit of a dilemma," the general said to her as he settled back into his chair behind the desk. "What should we do with you?"

"I bet she doesn't even have a brother," one man said, his voice full of innuendo. "Probably followed a lover into the Army and then serviced the entire regiment."

Most of the men laughed, including the doctor. The general just sighed. When the laughter died down, he turned to Emily. "What is your name?"

"Jesse Wilson," she answered, refusing to give them what they wanted.

"Jessie? As in Jessica or Jessamyn?"

"Just Jesse."

"Your uncle's letter says your name is Emily."

She looked him straight in the eyes and said, "My name is Jesse."

His eyebrows rose in disbelief, but he let it go. "Jesse, what can you tell us of your movements in the U.S. Army?"

Emily looked at him, then at the other faces in the room all staring at her, and realized that if she did not answer their questions, they might follow through on their threat to have her hung as a spy. She swallowed and dropped her feet to the floor. She ached to hide away, but she forced herself to meet the general's gaze squarely. He was the only one who had not laughed at her. "After our older brother, David, died of typhoid last summer, my brother, Benjamin, and I enlisted in his old regiment, the 9th Indiana Infantry. It was our father's regiment, too, you see, before he was killed at Laurel Mountain. We wanted to do our duty to our country, same as Pa and David. I can fight the same as any man."

She told them all she could remember of the last seven months, with the exception of any mention of Willie. She would not be the one to tarnish Willie's memory in anyone's mind. As far as these men were concerned, Emily was the only woman to have ever served.

"And then you brought me here today," she finished. She clasped her hands together. "Please, sirs, I beg you. Please allow me to return to my regiment. I need to find my brother. I don't even know if he is still alive."

The general shook his head. "I will not send you back to the field. You can no longer impersonate a soldier, do you understand me?"

Emily had to look away from his accusing glare. She had not been *impersonating* a soldier. She had *been* a soldier. "Yes, sir."

"And furthermore, if I allow you to walk out of here a free woman, you will do so wearing the proper garments of your sex, do I make myself clear?"

He must no longer suspect she was a spy. Relief made her

nearly start sobbing again, but she swallowed it back and nodded. "Yes, sir."

"Now," the general said, planting his palms on his desk and addressing his men. "See that she is escorted to a cell at the city jail, where she is to be held until which time a decision and the necessary arrangements are made."

"But, sir," Emily interrupted. "What about my brother? I need to find him. He is the last of my family!"

The general seemed to soften at that and held up a hand so the men escorting her would pause. "Miss Wilson, your brother was killed in battle at Pittsburg Landing. After your uncle was notified of his death, he wrote to us asking about you. That's how you came to our attention."

Emily tried to draw in a breath, but she found her lungs would only accept small sips of air, and each one felt like blades of ice slicing up her insides. Ben was dead. Before she broke down in front of these heartless men, she turned and walked on her own volition toward the door, the two guards at her sides.

"Oh, and, Miss Wilson," she heard the general call after her. "Here is a letter from your aunt. You can read it once you're settled." The guard to her left took the folded paper and tucked it into his coat pocket.

Numbly, Emily went where they took her, no longer caring what happened to her.

The city jail was nothing like the Confederate prison where she'd been confined in Alabama. This prison reeked of mold, rotting food, and human excrement. It held civilian prisoners including thieves, murderers, prostitutes operating without a license, and a number of black men whose crimes she could not determine. After being searched and having her possessions, including her diary containing Willie's handkerchief and ring, taken from her, she was shoved into a barred cell with two very foul-smelling women.

"This is where you belong," the guard sneered, "with the other whores." The keys clanged as he turned them in the lock, and then he shoved something through the bars. "I'm s'posed to give you this. Not that you're smart enough to read it." He dropped the paper and walked away.

Harriet's letter. A part of Emily wanted to leave it lying in the dirt, but then she remembered that Harriet had always been kind to her. It was Samuel who had turned her in. She picked up the letter and moved as far away as she could from the other women. One of them whistled at her.

"Y'all sure got spunk, traipsing around in that getup," said the older one with white hair. "Take that from your man, did ye?"

When Emily didn't answer, the other woman, who sported a black eye and a green bruise on her cheek, said, "I bet she stole the uniform so she could blend into the camps and work her way through the men, tent by tent."

"Oh, now isn't that a sweet idea?" the older woman gushed. "If I was ten years younger, I'd do the same thing myself. Take the goods to the customers, I say. Is that what you were doing, dearie? When you got caught?"

Deciding her best course would be to ignore them, Emily sat on a filthy cot. Exhaustion rolled over her like a wave. *Ben was dead.* How would she bear this pain?

"If you're going to be like that," huffed the younger woman, "we don't want to talk to you either!" She turned her back to Emily and reached her hand over to clamp onto the other woman's shoulder, making her turn away, too.

Forcing herself not to think about all the offensive things that might be lingering on the cot, Emily lay on her side and unfolded the letter from her aunt. Tears stung her eyes when she saw Aunt Harriet's familiar handwriting.

Dear Emily,

I hope we don't get you in trouble by asking the Army to find you. I've been so worried, and when we learned about Ben, I was desperate for word of you. We did not know where you two had gone or what had happened to you! Upon learning that Ben enlisted, I had a feeling that's what you did, too, since you wanted to go with your pa and David when they left. But the war is no place for a woman!

I'm sorry to tell you that home is not as you left it, my dear. Your uncle was furious when he found you and Ben gone. The burden was too great for him alone, and he was forced to sell off most of the north fields. As soon as this war is over, he says he will sell the entire farm and move us back to be near his family in Virginia. You are welcome to come home and live with us, and move with us when we go, but I must be honest and tell you that your uncle is not too keen on you after what you've done.

I pray every night that you are safe. Write to me as soon as you receive this. Please know I love you very much. Andrew and Ada also send their love.

With God,
Harriet

Emily cried as she folded the letter, knowing she would never return to Indiana. There was nothing left there for her.

"Hey, you!" A male voice jarred her out of her misery. A mean-looking guard stood there, rubbing one hand absently up and down one of the bars of her cell. The way he was staring at her made her uneasy, and when he licked his lips, she felt her skin crawl. She drew her legs up to her chest and hugged her knees.

"Why don't you stand up and let me see your purty uniform?"

"No," she spit out, a greasy uneasiness filling her stomach.

"I bet you know how to make a man happy, now don't you? How 'bout you come over here so we can talk? You need a friend in a place like this, you know."

Emily didn't doubt it, but she had a feeling this man would be no friend to her. "No, thank you," she told him, knowing she shouldn't anger him. "I'm exhausted and need to sleep."

"Come on, darling, it'll just take a minute."

"I know how to make you happy," purred the black-eyed woman across the cell as she stepped toward the bars, hips swaying.

The guard's smile widened. "I bet you do."

Emily ignored them and closed her eyes. She'd never before hated being a woman like she did now.

She'd never before been entirely alone like she was now.

Chapter Twenty-Five

May 27, 1862: City Jail, Nashville, Tennessee

*E*mily lifted the skirts she'd been forced to put on, hating that they tripped her as she climbed the short flight of steps into the provost marshal's office. The corset and bodice of the dress fit her snugly and felt much like her chest bindings had felt all these months, so they didn't bother her. The sleeves of the dress, however, bothered her very much. They were fitted to the elbow and from there became layers of lace to her wrists, all of it so confining and bothersome she struggled to lift her arms more than waist high. She'd have to rip the darn things off if she wanted to shoot her musket.

But, of course, that wouldn't be happening. Not for the Army, at least.

"Miss Wilson, please approach."

Emily tore her thoughts away from her misery to look at Provost Marshal Gillem where he sat behind a banged-up wooden desk with his back to the windows overlooking the stables behind the jail. A uniformed guard stood in the corner, at attention.

Colonel Gillem regarded her over a pair of wire-framed glasses and, judging by the curled lip and arch between his eyebrows, clearly did not find the dress a flattering change from the uniform he'd last seen her wearing. She fully agreed with him. To make the matter even worse, she hadn't had her hair trimmed since the last time she was in Nashville over two months back. It hung over her ears and curled against her neck in an unkempt manner that did not flatter her, no matter what gender she embodied, but seemed even less attractive when paired with women's clothing.

Obeying the marshal's order, she crossed the stone floor, hating the ridiculous pointed-toed, heeled shoes she'd been forced to wear. She'd take her old boots over these any day. When she reached the desk, she kept her head lowered and hoped she looked meek and humble so he would take pity on her and let her go.

"Miss Wilson, it is my duty to inform you that all charges against you have been dismissed and you are free to go, on the condition that you will never again don men's clothing nor impersonate a soldier."

"I *was* a soldier." The words slipped from her mouth before she could stop them. "I didn't impersonate anyone."

He cleared his throat loudly. "Regardless, you will henceforth conduct yourself in a manner befitting a young lady, or there will be dire consequences. Is that clear?"

She nodded.

"I said, 'Is that clear?'"

Emily lifted her chin and glared at him with all the fury she felt but knew she could not unleash. "Yes, sir."

He gave a curt nod. "Very well. Your possessions will be returned to you at the clerk's desk. You are free to go."

Numbly, she allowed the guard to lead her to the front office where she was handed her diary and the ring she'd been wearing when she was arrested, which she jammed onto her right pinkie. "What about my clothes?"

The clerk shook his head. "You're wearing them."

She didn't bother to say anything more. She simply turned

and walked through the door onto the street with no idea where she was going or what she would do next.

Ben was dead.

Drawing on all the training she'd received as a soldier, she swallowed her pain and forced herself to walk down the street as though today were a normal day and she were a normal woman, though neither could be further from the truth.

It was nearly noon, and the morning rain that had pounded on the jail earlier had given way to a blue sky and sun that was rapidly drying the streets and ripening the stench of horse manure and unwashed bodies. The only place Emily could think of to get away from the press of people, horses, carts, and carriages was the river, so she headed that direction.

She realized her mistake when she reached the bank of the Cumberland River and saw the crush of activity as steamers were lined up to receive or deliver goods and passengers. It was a beehive of movement, and Emily felt out of place and in the way.

As a woman, that's all she was now—a superfluous thing, always in the way.

If she were truly a man, she could look for employment doing any number of things. As a woman, her only options were to work as a servant tending to someone's home and children. Or she could be like those girls calling from the second-floor balconies on Smokey Row to the men below, offering their bodies in exchange for money.

The first profession sounded equally as offensive as the last to Emily's mind. After tasting freedom, she did not want to go back to having to answer to someone else for her every move.

But with no family left, how was she going to survive?

No family. Angrily, she yanked off her identity ring and threw it into the Cumberland River, where it sank out of sight in the brown, swiftly moving current. She had no one left to care what happened to her. No one left to care about her identity when she died. For one tantalizing moment, she considered following her ring into the depths of the river, and never coming up again. It would be so easy to lie in the water and let herself drift away.

But she was too much of a coward for that.

Defeated, she turned her feet north on Front Street and started walking, not caring where she went and not caring what anyone might think about a young woman walking in this rough neighborhood unescorted.

Ben was dead.

Her stomach cramped, and a sob tore from her mouth. Nonetheless, she kept walking. She knew if she stopped, the pain might catch up to her and swallow her whole. She had to keep moving, moving, staying ahead of it because if it caught up to her, she…

She didn't know what would happen. She simply knew she could not bear it.

She walked for hours, blindly turning corners and crossing streets, unmindful of the danger of carts, wagons, horses, and mules. Her legs and feet ached, but she was used to the pain, and it felt better than the pain in her soul, so she encouraged it by walking uphill, and down, and back again.

It was her fault Ben had been killed. She had talked him into leaving home. She'd promised him she'd keep him safe and he'd believed her, trusted her. She was supposed to stay by him that day, but she'd gotten caught up in the fighting and she'd lost track of him. Because of that, he'd been shot.

She would have stepped in front of the bullet that got him if she'd seen it coming. She would happily have taken his place. Willie's, too. They should both still be alive and planning their wedding and the children they would have together. She should have been the one killed.

But she was being selfish. She would not wish the pain she felt on anyone else, and if she had died, then Ben would be here suffering.

She hoped he wasn't suffering, wherever he was. A soul feels only love after death, right?

She was alone now. Her entire family was dead, and she had no one. No reason to keep moving. Why was she even trying?

She stopped, and a man bumped into her. He scooted around her with a tip of his hat and a "Pardon me, miss," but Emily barely noticed.

What was she going to do now? She had no home to go to, no means of income. Little money.

Worry shot through her. Did she have her money, or had the jail guards stolen it?

She jammed her hand into the hidden pocket in her skirt where she'd stashed her diary.

She looked around for a secure place where she would not be seen by pickpockets or other unscrupulous characters, and realized she was near the capitol building, where they had been quartered back in February. It felt so long ago.

The building sat stately on top of the hill with all slopes leading up to it a warren of cart tracks, footpaths, and Army tents, all guarded by the soldiers standing atop the barricades that had been constructed around the gleaming limestone building. There was nowhere she could check the contents of her diary without being seen. No shrubbery or walls to duck behind.

And then she remembered St. Mary's Church, only a block away, where she'd attended services the Sunday after arriving in the city back in February. She hurried there with the diary clutched in both hands. When she reached the brick building, she ran up the steps and inside.

Emily immediately realized her mistake. She'd forgotten the church had been converted to a hospital. Beds lined the walls and made two rows down the center of the building, all filled with what looked to be gravely ill men.

"Hello, miss," came a friendly greeting from a soldier carrying a basin of water. "Can I help you?"

She backed away, "No, no thank you. I…I took a wrong turn."

She hastened back out and spotted a nook to the side, just outside the church doors and shielded from the street by a brick wall. Quickly, she ducked into the secluded space and, with a last glance to confirm no one was paying her any attention, opened the diary's secret compartment.

Relief flooded through her. Willie's handkerchief and ring were still there, as was the stack of currency she'd stashed away at every payday while in the service of the Army, and the money she'd taken from David's knapsack all those months ago. She was grateful she'd had little to spend her money on, because it would keep her alive until she figured out what she was going to do. She would have to be careful to stretch it as far as it could go.

Casting another furtive glance around her, Emily withdrew a couple of bills and securely tucked the rest back inside the diary, slipping it into her skirt pocket.

The afternoon light was fading as she returned to the street. Night would soon be upon her, and she needed to find a place to sleep.

She took to walking again, her legs and feet protesting every step. The ill-fitting shoes she'd been given had worried blisters on both feet that felt like they were oozing blood. As she neared the Public Square, she could not keep her memories at bay. Was it only two months past that she'd stood here in this square for the dress parade, shoulder to shoulder with her fellow Union soldiers? She had felt so much pride that day in her ability to serve her country and do it so well despite being a woman.

With Ben on her right, she'd stood at attention for what felt like hours with her eyes glued to the stately Nashville City Hall and Market in front of them. The building stood three stories tall with an additional level in the form of what looked like two stone guard or bell towers on the top. Without turning her head, she'd moved her eyes to see what she could of the rest of the square and remembered being impressed by the fine architecture, with many of the buildings standing four or five stories tall. They should have made her feel small, but on that day, they'd only made her stand straighter and lift her chin, feeling all the pride of her station.

Pride goeth before a fall. That had certainly been true for her.

Pushing her memories aside, she made her way past City Hall and Market, seeing for the first time that a long extension came off the back, filled with merchants hawking their wares, though most were shutting down for the day. Past the great colonnaded block that was the Courthouse, she spotted what she was hoping for—a dusty sign proclaiming the three-storied building fronted with balconies to be the City Hotel.

Feeling like something was finally going her way, Emily found the entry door on the side of the corner building and saw she was on the street that had once led to a suspension bridge across the Cumberland. The bridge had still been smoldering back in February when she'd first arrived after retreating Confederates had set it afire. Now there was nothing but a wooden sign stopping pedestrians from walking right off the high bank and falling into the water.

The hotel entry was a tiny space so small Emily could have stood in the middle and touched all four walls, if her tight sleeves allowed her to raise her arms that high, of course. Cooking smells wafted through the air, and a flight of scuffed stairs disappeared up to the right. A bell hung from the wall beside a closed door with a sign inviting guests to pull it should they require assistance. She gave the thin rope a yank.

Heavy footsteps announced the proprietor's arrival before the door was thrown open and a harried-looking woman appeared, wearing an apron and holding a chubby baby on her hip. "Oh, hello," she said with a smile. She pointedly looked behind Emily, as though expecting a husband or other escort. Upon finding none, she lost her friendly facade and raised one eyebrow at her. "What do you want?"

"Good evening," Emily began, showing her best manners to

disabuse the woman of her obvious assumption. "I am in need of lodging and have cash to pay for it. Do you have a room?"

The woman didn't bat an eyelash. "No, sorry, we're all full." She closed the door, and Emily heard the slide of a lock being firmly secured.

Defeated, she retraced her steps to the Public Square and looked around, hoping for another option, or another idea. When none came, she stopped a gentleman passing by with an armful of rolled papers. "Excuse me, sir, but could you point me in the direction of any nearby hotels or inns?"

His face held questions as his gaze examined her, but he succumbed to good manners and pointed. "The Union Hotel over on Market Street. Second building on the left." He tipped his hat and continued on his way.

She must look a fright, she realized, if people were assuming she was a woman of questionable morals. She raised a hand to touch her short hair, realizing she should have asked the provost marshal for a hat. All the shops were closed now, and she would not be able to buy one until morning.

The burn of shame propelled her across the square to the hotel. She wanted nothing more than to lock herself away in a room and hide from the rest of the world. The Union Hotel, however, also did not have any vacancies. The kind man there directed her to Mrs. C. Lankford's boardinghouse, but Mrs. Lankford also turned her away.

What was she to do now? She had nowhere to go, and she was in a town crawling with soldiers looking for female companionship. And, apparently, she looked the part.

Her stomach clenched. If she had her musket, she might be able to protect herself, but she'd been stripped of that and left with only a dress that didn't allow her to raise her arms enough to fight off an attack.

Simply standing on the street alone at this time of the night would make anyone think she was a working woman.

A working woman. That was it! Emily knew a working woman who might feel sympathetic enough to her plight to help her. The prostitute at the bordello the other men had dragged her to down on College Street. What was her name? Bea? Lee? Vee! That was it. Vee. Vee White.

With her head held high, projecting as much confidence as she could muster, Emily walked the three blocks as fast as she could and marched right up to the grand front door of the bordello. No gentlemen were coming and going yet, and it took a few moments for anyone to answer.

When the door finally opened, a graceful, middle-aged woman wearing a blue gown stood there looking at her quizzically. "I'm afraid you have the wrong establishment, my dear," she told her kindly after looking Emily up and down. "Perhaps you should try Madame Emaline's down on Front and Broad Streets. She might have a place for you."

Emily placed her hand on the doorjamb. "Wait, please. I'm looking for a friend of mine who works here, Vee White. Is she available? I'll only take a moment of her time, I promise."

The woman's head tilted to the side. "She does not work here anymore. Up and disappeared one morning, and we've never heard hide nor hair of her since. Left us short a girl, that's for certain."

Tears stung Emily's eyes, and she looked down at the stoop to hide them from this kind woman. What would she do now? Where could she find safety? *Damn this cursed dress.* If she were still in men's clothing, she had no doubt she would already have secured lodgings and would be enjoying a hearty meal at this very moment.

The woman studied her, and just when Emily started to turn away to retreat back down the steps, she opened the door wider and said, "Why don't you come in? I'll see to it that Cook gives you something to eat and a warm place to rest for the night. In the morning, we can see if there might be something we can do to help each other."

Emily's stomach growled so loudly in response to the offer of a warm meal that even the woman heard it, and she smiled. "That decides it. Come in."

Emily had no intention of discussing future employment with the woman, but she was not about to turn down the offer of a safe place to sleep tonight. She followed the woman down the back stairs to the kitchen, where she was handed a chunk of bread and a bowl of stew by the cook. The other woman disappeared upstairs. The delicious aromas curled around her, and completely forgetting her manners, Emily lifted the bowl to her chin and spooned the broth in like she'd never had a proper meal before.

With her stomach finally full, she sat back on the bench and looked around. The cook was bustling about the room, aided by two young girls setting delicious-looking cakes and sweets on shining silver platters to be carried upstairs. Other plates held nuts and dried fruits, and some held sliced meats and cheeses.

Emily could not remember the last time she'd seen this much food in one place. Not even back home in Indiana had they feasted like this, except the day after Mama died and all the neighbors brought food to the house to comfort them.

But this wasn't mourning food. This was celebration food.

Emily stared at it all in wonder, feeling like she'd slipped out of her time and into another for, surely, food like this wasn't available during wartime. Where had it all come from?

When Cook saw her staring, she snapped her dish towel in the air and ordered, "Come with me. I'll show you where you can sleep tonight. It's best if you stay out of the way, and whatever you do, do not go upstairs or Madam will have your hide, and mine too."

She led Emily to a room off the kitchen no bigger than the pallet on the floor that would be her bed for the night. It looked like heaven to Emily, especially since it had a door she could lock and know she would be safe.

As soon as Cook left her with an oil lamp, she kicked off her shoes and set them next to the closed door. The sound of voices from upstairs told her customers were starting to arrive, and she wondered if they would keep her awake. She lay on the pallet and drew a single blanket over her, needing nothing more since the heat of the kitchen warmed the room nicely. She planned to close her eyes for only a moment and then take some time to write in her diary, but sleep claimed her.

Emily woke some time later to the sound of a particularly loud thud from upstairs. She held still and listened, wondering if there was something wrong, when the sound of women's laughter filtered through the floorboards to her tiny room. Reassured, she turned the lamp down to plunge the room into darkness before falling right back into a fitful slumber.

Her dreams were convoluted with disjointed images. First there was Ben, imploring her with desperate eyes, "Why didn't you protect me?" Emily did her best to tell him she was sorry, but he disappeared.

Then came Willie, gasping in pain as blood flowed out of her. "Find my family," she begged.

"What is their name?" Emily yelled to her, but Willie could not hear her. "What is your sister's name? Where do they live?" She kept shouting the questions, but Willie only moaned in pain.

Images of soldiers laughing and playing card games were over-laid with her memories from the battlefield of dead men staring with sightless eyes at the sky with chunks of their heads missing and their brains oozing out. She found herself standing all alone in the middle of a field with an entire company of Rebs running at her full tilt with bayonets, hatred in their eyes. She had no weapon and could only brace herself for the impact that never came, though she felt she stood there all night.

"Why didn't you protect me?"

"Find my family!"

"I'll kill you, you bloody Yank!"

303

Suddenly, there was Uncle Samuel sitting in Pa's rocking chair on their front porch, rocking back and forth, back and forth, laughing at her. "You thought you could make a difference? You're a lousy, worthless woman! Not good for nuthin' but making babies, that's for sure." Rocking, rocking, back and forth, his laughter digging straight to her soul.

"Why didn't you protect me?"

"Good for nuthin'!"

"Help me. Find my sister!"

"Lousy, worthless woman!"

Emily jerked awake and, for a long, frantic moment, thought she was still in the jail cell with that creepy guard leering at her. When she remembered she was in the bordello, she rolled over and turned up the wick on the lamp, wondering what time it was.

Her head pounded, and her eyes felt like they were full of dirt. Her body did not feel rested and, in fact, felt as though she'd been marching all night long. Her throat was parched.

When she cracked her door open to see if anyone was up and about in the kitchen, she was surprised to find a shaft of sunlight streaming into the room from a window high on the wall over the worktable. Cook was kneading dough on the floured surface, and her two young helpers were sitting on the other side of the table eating their breakfast porridge.

"Good morning," Emily said as she stepped from her room. "Can I bother you for a drink of water?"

Cook nodded toward the pail and dipper sitting near the hearth. "Cups are on that shelf over there. Help yourself to porridge if you're hungry."

She was. After slaking her intense thirst with three cups of water, Emily filled a bowl with the porridge and sat next to the little girls, leaving the cook plenty of room to roll out her dough.

"Are you the new girl?" asked the little girl beside her, her mouth full.

Emily tried to figure the girl's age. She couldn't have been any older than eight or nine, and the other girl was probably a year older than that. She wondered if they would one day have to work upstairs to earn their keep. "No. I needed a place to sleep, so the madam let me stay."

"That's not what she told me," Cook grunted as she arranged balls of dough in a cast iron skillet.

"Oh. Well." Emily did not know what to say to this.

"What's your name?" asked the second girl, her big brown eyes full of curiosity.

Emily opened her mouth to say "Jesse" but stopped. That life was over. Starting again, she answered truthfully, "Emily. What's yours?"

"I'm Christina, and this is my sister, Julia. She's seven, and I'm nine. We work here."

Emily bit back a smile and formally nodded to the two girls. "I'm pleased to make your acquaintance."

"Hurry and finish your breakfast, girls. We need to get to the market before all the fruit is gone, if there's even any to be had." Cook carefully laid a clean dishcloth over the rolls and set the pan on the hearth to rise. To Emily she said, "I thought you might be needing a bath, which you can take while we're gone. No one will disturb you. The upstairs girls all sleep in. There's hot water in that pot there and cold in the barrel." She pointed out everything Emily would need and hustled the girls up the stairs.

The house fell into silence, with the only noises coming from the crackling fire in the fireplace and noise from the street filtering through the window. The idea of a bath brought the sting of tears to Emily's eyes, and she quickly grabbed the large tub from where it hung on the wall and filled it with water.

As she lowered her aching body into the tub, she did weep, even though she had to bend her knees to her chin to fit and the water didn't even come up to her belly button. It felt heavenly, and when she started rubbing the cake of soap Cook had left for her across her grimy skin, she wondered how she had gone without this for so long.

When she was finally clean, she dried off and put her dress back on. Although the dress was much better than her filthy uniform, she still wished for the rough trousers and shirt. Her life would be so much easier if she continued to live as a man.

The thought reminded her that the woman sleeping upstairs was going to wake up and expect to discuss the possibility of employment with her.

If the job was to work down here with Cook, Christina, and Julia, that would be one thing. But Emily knew that wasn't the job she would be hired to do.

She finished dressing and looked around, trying to figure out where her bathwater should be drained. It was too heavy to lug up the stairs and out the door to the street by herself. Should she take it up by the bucketful? That would take too long. She did not want to risk being here when the madam woke up.

With a whisper of apology to the cook, she left the full tub where it sat near the fire. Grabbing a hunk of bread from the half-eaten loaf she found in the bread box and tucking it in her pocket, she tiptoed up the stairs and out the door.

As she had the day before, Emily walked aimlessly as she tried to come up with a plan. As the sun rose higher in the sky, she found inspiration eluding her. Nashville was clearly a military town, and though martial law had long ago been lifted, troops still marched through the city, and nearly every block had some sort of military-occupied building, be it a hospital, officer's quarters, prison, Union storehouse, or barracks. The civilians in the city went about their business as normally as possible, but clearly, the city was not running as it would in peacetime and paying jobs were scarce. Paying jobs for a respectable woman were certainly nonexistent.

Discouraged, Emily considered returning to the brothel.

Would the work be that bad? She'd have a place to sleep and food to eat.

But then she heard a paperboy calling the day's headlines. "Lincoln signs the Homestead Act into law!" the little voice announced over the din of horses and carriages and pedestrians pushing past. "One hundred sixty acres to any U.S. citizen willing to farm the land! Read all about it!"

Emily did not want to waste a nickel that could be put to better use than on a newspaper, but she did it anyway. She propped her back against the brick building behind her and read the announcement as fast as she could, excitement building.

According to the article, President Lincoln was allowing United States citizens to file applications for a parcel of land in the western states and territories. Once the homesteader lived on the land for a minimum of five years and showed improvement to the land, he could file for a patent and the land would be his, free and clear.

Even better, the act allowed women to take part. The only thing holding Emily back would be her age. She would turn twenty in October, still a year shy of the required twenty-one years.

She could not wait a year. She'd have to lie about her age.

Reading further, her heart sank when she read that no claims could be filed until January 1, 1863, still eight months away. What would she do until then? Her money would not last nearly that long, and she would still need funds to travel to Nebraska and get a farm up and running.

The excitement she'd felt drained out of her like water from a leaky bucket. She was back to where she'd started.

Tucking the paper under her arm, she continued to walk and think, hoping she'd stumble across something, anything, that might help her.

Night was falling, and Emily still had found no place to sleep and no respectable businesses or homes that wanted to hire a woman without references. She knew her appearance did not help her effort, even though she was clean from her bath that morning. Her hair was shaggy, and her body had become lean and muscular during her months of soldiering. She did not look like a woman anyone would want in their homes. But she would not return to the bordello.

She turned her feet away from Smokey Row and the tightly packed buildings of downtown to walk north, past Public Square and farther. The neighborhood quickly became residential, with the houses spaced farther apart, allowing for yards and fences and little gardens bursting with plants. Her stomach growled as she thought about the vegetables growing there. She'd eaten the bread she'd pilfered from Cook hours ago.

As she walked down one packed-dirt street, she heard a mother call her children in for supper. Through the window, Emily watched the domestic scene inside unfold as the children plopped onto chairs at the table, their parents at either end.

Emily's gaze slid to the path worn into the grass alongside the house and knew it led to a garden in back. She could see it from where she stood on the other side of the street.

If she was careful, she could make her way back there and find something to eat in their garden while the family was occupied. Surely some greens or a few peas could be picked without the family noticing their absence.

Before she could change her mind, Emily lifted her chin and walked across the street as though she belonged, hoping not to draw any neighbor's eye. As soon as she reached the yard, she hurried to the shadows alongside the house and paused, willing her heart to slow its frantic beating so she could hear if anyone sounded an alarm.

The neighborhood was quiet, with only the sounds of barking dogs and the occasional horse and wagon passing on the busier street a block away.

With a deep breath, she moved alongside the house to the backyard where the sight of a bountiful garden rewarded her efforts.

Ignoring the mud, she dropped to her knees and started pawing through the plants, shoving whatever looked ripe into her mouth. The deliciously bitter taste of green beans was sweetened by tiny early strawberries.

As she was digging her fingers through the soil in hopes of finding a small new potato, she saw a flash of movement in the corner of her eye. She froze. The movement came again, and she turned to see what, or who, was in the yard with her.

Laundry. It was only laundry hanging on the line, swinging gently in the breeze. She could have melted to the ground in relief. With a chuckle for how scared she'd been, she finished digging up the potato, and then dug out two more for later, which she shoved into her pockets.

With her stomach finally satisfied, she climbed to her feet and was about to return to the street when an idea struck her.

Hanging from the line were two sets of men's clothing, including breeches, shirts, socks, and even a cotton jacket.

With another glance at the house to make sure no one was looking, she crossed the yard and took the items she needed from the line. In their place she clipped bills she pulled from her diary to cover their cost. With the goods bundled to her chest, she darted back to the shadows alongside the house, where she would be screened from the street by a huge hazel alder shrub. Moving quickly, she kicked off her shoes and stripped off her dress, dropping it to the ground. As she slipped into the man's breeches, she found they fit better than the uniform she'd been wearing for the last several months. She would still need to roll up the bottoms, but she was not at risk of them slipping off her hips without a belt. The shirt fit as well, but this she removed again and started ripping the second shirt to use as her chest binding.

Voices on the street made her move even quicker. Finished,

she gathered her dress into a bundle, for she wasn't quite ready to be rid of it. It might be needed. Or she could sell it, at the least. She grabbed a clump of dirt and rubbed it on her jaw and chin like she'd seen Willie do, hoping it would look like she needed to shave. Finally, she reached for her shoes to put them back on, her heart sinking when she remembered they were clearly women's shoes.

The street was quiet again. She'd be safe to duck out of the shadows now. But those blasted shoes! With nothing else to put on, she slipped into them and unrolled the legs of the breeches enough to cover the shoes as much as possible. That would have to do.

Feeling like herself again, she moved to the front corner of the house and leaned out just enough to see the street. Empty.

With a deep breath, she straightened her back and crossed the short front yard as quickly as possible, her gaze firmly forward, and headed back toward downtown.

The farther she moved away from the house, the more she could relax. Only when she'd gone several blocks was she able to turn her mind back to the problem of where to sleep for the night. As a man, she had more options.

But, then again, did she really want to spend money on a place to sleep when she should be saving it for her land claim? The night was fairly warm, after all. She was used to sleeping on the ground. She didn't have a blanket, but the dress could suffice.

She passed an abandoned two-story brick building, no doubt the former property of a secesh who had fled the city when the Union Army arrived. It had an inset porch that, with no lamp lit, appeared as dark as a cave. She could curl up there and no one on the street would see her.

She darted up the steps and rapped sharply on the door. When no one answered, proving the building was abandoned as she'd thought, she relaxed. With that, she lay on her side in the corner with the dress over her as a blanket and waited for sleep to claim her.

From her vantage point she could see the street, and she idly watched people pass by, mostly men on their way to the saloons and brothels on Smokey Row. None of them gave her a passing glance.

She was starting to doze off when a strange sight made her sit up. Two children crept along the street, one a black boy of about nine years of age and the other a little blond girl who looked to be Ada's age, about six. The boy followed a step behind the girl, as though he were her servant, and did not say a word as the girl planted herself in the path of two men in uniform and turned her wide eyes up to them. "Please, sirs, could you spare a coin? I'm a poor little orphan with no place to live, and I'm very hungry." She let out a heartrending sob.

Emily was digging in the pocket of her dress for her diary, intending to draw out some money to give to the kids, when she saw a third child, a boy with hair matching the girl's, dart out from the shadows, pick the pockets of both soldiers, and disappear before they even knew he was there. The three children were clearly working together.

"Now, now, little one," said one of the soldiers. "Don't get all worked up. We'll help you." He reached into his pocket and, finding it empty, got a confused look on his face. "Wha—"

The girl and her friend took off running. The soldiers gave chase, but they were no match for the small children, who disappeared around the corner.

Emily chuckled as she lay back down, impressed by those kids. They would, undoubtedly, survive this war just fine on their own.

And so would she, she decided, curling onto her side. She was going to be fine, too.

Chapter Twenty-Six

Present day: Woodinville, Washington

May 29, 1862: There is no use pretending anymore. My charade is up with the Army. I am again in men's clothes and am doing my best to play the part of a civilian man now.

I was betrayed by Uncle Samuel. I underwent the most shameful inspection of my most private person and was thereafter discharged, after a night in the city jail. I am so angry, but that is not what I want to think about right now. Something even worse has happened. I received news that Benjamin was killed in battle at Pittsburg Landing. He has been gone all these weeks, and I did not know. How did I not know? Did he die before Willie, or after? Are they together now in Heaven? Was he scared when it happened? Did he suffer, or did it happen quickly? Oh, I hope it happened quickly for I cannot bear the thought of my brother dying alone and in pain.

Ben, I am so sorry I wasn't with you. I am so sorry I failed to protect you. I am so sorry that we enlisted in the first place. I would beg your forgiveness, but I am unworthy of it. You deserved so much more.

Dear God, how am I to go on?

I reckon I don't have a choice.

Since being released, I've slept in a brothel and on the street. I never wrote here about Vee, so I will do so now. Back in February when we were posted here, I had the unique opportunity of seeing the inner workings of a house of ill repute. Details are not necessary, but I came out of that place with a new friend and a softer heart toward women like Vee who have fallen so far due to no fault of their own. Vee said her name was V. A. White and she was kind, so when I found myself back here in Nashville and needing help, I thought of her. Alas, she is no longer employed at that bordello, and I was unable to determine where she went. I hope she is alive.

I did have some good news. Lincoln has signed into law a homestead act for which I am eligible, or will be upon my twenty-first birthday. I'm considering following through on the plan I made with Willie and Ben, even though they won't be with me. Why can't I go to Nebraska Territory and settle there myself? I see no reason not to, and so that is what I will do. Being there will also help me look for Willie's sister and return her handkerchief to her. Why can't I remember her sister's name? Why can't I remember if Willie ever told me her family name?

How am I supposed to fulfill my promise to her? Maybe I won't be able to, but my chances are higher if I'm in Nebraska. So, somehow, I'll find my way there.

*L*arkin's heart felt pulverized as she read Emily's diary and saw how the woman blamed herself for her brother's death and struggled to see a path forward under the weight of that guilt and the weight of her promise to Willie. To Larkin, Sarah was her Ben and Willie combined. Larkin was trying to find her way forward in life while dragging guilt and obligation along with her. And most days, she did not have the necessary strength.

Larkin had flown home from California on Sunday morning, and Grams had picked her up from the airport. On the drive back to Woodinville she'd told Grams about Zach and how they'd released Sarah into the ocean. Her emotions caught up with her and exhausted her so much that, when they arrived home, she crawled into bed and slept for two hours.

When she woke, she'd pulled the diary out to read more. But now she needed a break. She set the diary aside, thinking about Emily's struggles. They were timeless. Even now, over a hundred and fifty years later, female veterans faced many of the same challenges that Emily did: being seen as inferior because of her gender, not being able to find work after being discharged from the military, earning less than men, becoming homeless.

It really pissed Larkin off that her country had barely evolved in all those years. Women today were doing the same jobs as men, both in the military and out of it, and still being treated as second-class citizens. The constant battle was exhausting, and right now, Larkin was too tired to fight it.

Like Emily, Larkin was wandering aimlessly with no viable future. The diary wasn't going to occupy her forever. She would eventually need to get on with her life. Find a new career. Venture into a job world that had nothing to do with the military, which was all she'd ever known.

The thought of it made her want to throw up. She'd never considered doing anything but serving her country. It had been her life's mission and her purpose. And now it was gone.

She groaned, hating the pit her thoughts were pulling her into. Determined to get her mind on something else, she opened her blog and read through some of the comments readers had left.

They wanted more. She hadn't posted a new entry in over three weeks, and readers were asking whose story would be next.

To appease them, she pulled out one of the books she'd ordered online about the women who served in the Civil War and flipped through the pages, looking for someone interesting. A name caught her eye and she looked closer. George Harris. Didn't Emily write about a George Harris?

Larkin picked up the diary and searched for the passage. There it was. On May 19, 1862, Emily wrote about the soldier who'd nursed her back to health at the Confederate prison and gave his name as George Harris of the 8th New York Cavalry. She hadn't seemed to trust him much.

Turning back to the reference book, Larkin found that the name and regiment matched. It had to be the same person. And *he* had actually been a *she*, and Emily hadn't known. What were the odds?

Shaking her head, Larkin read more about George Harris. The book said her real name was Maria Lewis, and not only was she pretending to be a man, but she was African American and had successfully fooled everyone into believing she was white. What made this even more impressive was that she served before African American men were allowed to enlist. That didn't happen until after the Emancipation Proclamation on January 1, 1863. After the war, she was even chosen as a member of an honor guard who presented the War Department with seventeen captured Confederate battle flags. Maria, as George, was only discovered to be a woman and African American after the war ended, and she sought help in finding a new life as a free person from Northern abolitionists. No one knew what came of her after that.

Larkin felt a thrill when she posted the entry about Maria/ George to her blog. In her post, she also shared information she'd learned about African Americans serving in the war. Once black men were allowed to enlist, they were paid only ten dollars per month compared to the thirteen dollars white soldiers received, and of that, only the black soldiers had to pay three dollars for clothing. White soldiers received a clothing bonus. Black soldiers, disgruntled by the announcement of lower pay for equal service, wanted to leave the service but were not allowed to do so. Many chose to protest by refusing to accept any pay at all until the discriminatory policy was reversed. This caused them and their families great hardship, especially as white-run charities in the North turned away black families.

It wasn't until June 1864 that Congress passed a law granting black soldiers the same pay as whites. Besides pay being discriminatory, all African American regiments were segregated and led exclusively by white officers. If a black soldier was captured by Confederate forces, his treatment was brutal and usually fatal. Maria Lewis had defied so much in posing as a white man, and Larkin held no doubt that if the woman had been discovered, she would have been severely punished. But still, she served.

Pride in this fellow soldier she'd never met helped ease Larkin's funk, and she decided to track down Kaia and Grams and see what they were doing the rest of the day.

She found Kaia in the kitchen cooking what looked to be yellow pancakes in a cast iron pan on the stove. The smell of maple syrup and coffee filled the room and reminded Larkin she hadn't eaten since breakfast. "Hey, whatcha makin'?" She opened the fridge to look for leftovers.

"Johnnycakes," Kaia answered as she pushed her bangs back with her forearm, a spatula in her hand. "I'm playing with some old Civil War recipes. These were popular because they didn't use flour or sugar and could be topped with syrup, molasses, or jam."

Larkin peered closer at the pan. "If there's no flour in them, what're they made of?"

"Cornmeal." She flipped the pancake over.

"Where's Grams?" Larkin asked. Nothing in the fridge looked appetizing, so she closed the door.

"Woodinville Heritage Society meeting." Kaia took a plate out of the cupboard and placed the johnnycake on it. "Here, eat this."

"Woodinville has a heritage society? How much heritage can

the town possibly have?" Larkin slathered butter on the cake and drizzled the maple syrup Kaia had warmed over it.

"The area was first settled by the Woodin family back in 1871 and became an important location for the logging industry. Sure, the history is nothing compared to towns in Europe, or even the East Coast, but I think it's great the society is preserving all it can."

"1871, huh?" Larkin cut a bite of cake and stuck it in her mouth. It tasted a bit like cornbread and was perfect as a comfort food. "That's during the Reconstruction Era. I wonder if they were veterans." She shook her head, wondering why every thought she had was either about the Civil War or military service in general.

Kaia shrugged. "Grams might know. So, how was it?" She motioned toward Larkin's now-empty plate.

"Delicious." She held the plate out for another. "When you're done, do you want to get out of here? Go for a drive or something?"

Kaia's eyebrows shot into her hairline, but she didn't question why Larkin suddenly wanted to get out. "That sounds great. Any chance you might be up for a movie? The theater in town now has reclining chairs and an ICEE machine in the lobby."

Larkin laughed, knowing the frozen slushy Coke drinks were Kaia's weakness. She wasn't sure how she'd do being stuck in a dark theater with strangers, but she surprised herself by agreeing. "Maybe Jenna's free and can meet us there."

She was, and Larkin successfully sat through the entire romantic comedy without her symptoms being triggered once. She was so happy about this small success that, when it was over, she suggested they walk to Red Robin for burgers.

Her cousins agreed, and together they crossed the street and went inside the restaurant, debating the whole time about how long it had been since they'd last been to the restaurant that was always their first choice as kids.

In the booth next to them, two male police officers were finishing their meals, and Larkin couldn't help but stare at them. Several MP friends she'd served with who had separated from the Army had decided to become civilian police officers. She'd never thought about doing anything other than military police, but now that she was forced to consider a new career, she wondered about it for herself.

In between perusing the menu, ordering, and chatting with her cousins, Larkin kept an eye on the officers. At one point, a mom with a little boy about four years old came up to the officers. "I'm sorry to interrupt," she said to them, "but my son says he wants to be a policeman when he grows up. He wanted to meet you."

The officers, one tall and thin with a graying mustache and the other looking fresh out of the academy, smiled at the boy and asked him his name, which set him off on a long story about his toy police cars. The scene reminded her of all the hours she'd spent chatting with Nahid and the other boys in Kandahar.

The boy was still chatting and sharing the older officer's french fries when a beep rang out, followed by a voice announcing a crime in progress. Both officers set down their burgers and dropped bills on the table.

Larkin watched the officers stride out the door and felt with certainty that she did not want their job. She didn't know what crime they were rushing off to, but she knew it could be anything from teenagers shoplifting at the nearby bookstore, to a traffic accident, to a break-in. The thought of responding to any of those exhausted and depressed her.

It all seemed so petty compared to protecting the safety and security of the nation's military forces. Not that military police didn't deal with pettiness. But still, it felt different.

"So tell us, Larkin." Jenna's voice cut into her thoughts. "How was California and Sarah's brother? Was he a jerk like you expected?"

Larkin had to force herself to pay attention to the conversation at her own table. She shook her head. "Actually, not at all. I think both Zach and Sarah were victims of their parents' problems. Their mother, especially, was a train wreck."

As they ate, Larkin told them about Sarah's mom and all the ways she'd failed her daughter. "You both know I don't see eye to eye with my own mother, but all I needed was to hear a story about Sarah's mom to remember that my own isn't so bad."

"Was she why Zach stayed away from Sarah all those years?"

Larkin nodded. "I think their mother killed any relationship they might have had, and then they were both too hurt and afraid of rejection to reach out. It makes me so sad to think of what Sarah missed out on."

"So you like him, huh?" Kaia had a bright glint in her eye as she asked the question.

"Not like that." The thought hadn't crossed Larkin's mind. There had been too many other emotions in play during her visit. "But yeah, I do think we could be friends."

Jenna and Kaia exchanged a look, and Larkin knew they were matchmaking. She ignored them and finished her burger.

"What's the latest with your diary research?" Kaia asked as she bit into a fry. She turned to Jenna. "She says Emily was discovered and kicked out of the Army. She's thinking about going to Nebraska to find Willie's family."

Jenna leaned toward Larkin. "Does she go?"

Larkin shrugged. "I don't know yet, but even if she did, she never found Willie's family or the handkerchief wouldn't still be in the secret compartment."

"Have you gotten any closer to finding them?" Kaia asked, sipping another Coke.

"I found a family that might be hers, and I'm waiting for the genealogist who's helping me to look into it and call me back. Urlich and Elizabeth Ellery were living in Washington County, Nebraska Territory, in 1860 with a fifteen-year-old daughter named Olive. No mention of an older brother. If it's Willie's family, it means that she left home before 1860, long before the war started. Her enlistment records give her hometown as La Porte, Indiana, but we think she made it up since that's the town where the 9th Indiana mustered in."

With a far-off look on her face, Kaia finished her burger and wiped her hands on her napkin. "Try widening your search for those names in earlier censuses."

Larkin shook her head. "1860 was the first year that Nebraska was included in the Federal census, and the territorial census was pretty spotty before that."

Kaia nodded. "Yes, but try looking at records from other states. Since Nebraska was only newly being settled at that time, maybe the Ellery family came from somewhere back East. They might show up, with Willie included, somewhere that you don't expect."

Larkin thought about it. "And if I find them earlier, with Willie, I'll know for sure what their names were and can then find the family later in Nebraska or wherever they ended up!"

Kaia grinned. "Exactly."

"Excuse me," a voice said, and Larkin looked up to see an older couple with matching silver hair standing by their table. The man pointed to Larkin. "I noticed your T-shirt. Does your husband serve in the Army?"

Larkin had forgotten she was wearing her Army PT shirt. She knew exactly what was happening, and it made all the commotion of the restaurant fade away. Even her vision narrowed so that all she saw was the man looking through her, as though she wasn't a human herself, but an accessory to some man who owned her. She couldn't possibly be the person who had earned this Army shirt, could she? She was only a woman, after all.

She pinned the man with a look she usually reserved for suspects she was questioning. "I am not married."

The man still didn't get it. "Oh, your father, then?"

Kaia must have felt Larkin's anger because she spoke up, pointing to Larkin as she did so. "She's the one who served. She did two deployments to Afghanistan."

Surprised, the man looked flustered for a moment, and then he thrust his hand into her face. "In that case, let me thank you for your service, my dear." He smiled as if it had all been a joke.

Larkin couldn't bring herself to shake his hand. She'd lived a scenario like this too many times, and she was sick of it. She slapped his hand away and got to her feet so she could look right into his sexist face. "It's not funny, you asshole. I risked my life every day I was over there, and my best friend lost hers in service to this country. Morons like you"—she stabbed her finger into his chest—"don't see us. To you, women in the military are fluff and decoration. You dismiss our contribution and overlook us as if we're invisible, and I'm sick of it. Sarah didn't die so that idiots like you could forget she ever lived."

The man gaped and his wife started tugging on his arm, trying to pull him away from the unhinged veteran. Larkin had had enough. She turned away from them and saw that everyone at the nearby tables was staring at her with varying expressions of horror and pity on their faces.

She ran out of the restaurant and across the street, not bothering to wait for the crosswalk sign. When she reached Kaia's car, she fell against it and took several deep breaths, trying hard to get herself under control. But a sob escaped, and that was all it took for her to break down completely. Why was everything so hard all the time?

"Lark, it's okay." Kaia was suddenly there, and she laid a hand softly on her back. "That guy was an asshole. You were right to get angry with him."

Soon, Jenna joined them and she, too, tried to make Larkin feel better. When Larkin's tears finally dried, she wasn't in the mood to talk. "We should get going."

They said goodbye to Jenna and drove home in silence. As

Larkin came into her room, her eyes went immediately to the spot on her nightstand where Sarah's urn had sat these last weeks. It was empty. She'd forgotten she'd let her go, and the reminder now felt like she was losing Sarah all over again.

Did any part of Larkin's old life remain?

Chapter Twenty-Seven

May 29, 1862: Nashville, Tennessee

S unlight woke her early, and Emily grimaced as it speared into her pounding head. All night, she'd dreamt she was fighting a battle, chasing and shooting at a Reb with no face, and always missing. At one point she came upon Ben sitting on a log in the woods as though he were at a Sunday picnic. But then, before she could say anything to him, his body was slammed over and over again with Minié balls that sliced right through him, leaving holes she could see through. He did not fall off the log but simply sat there and said, "You killed me, Em."

Emily rubbed her eyes, wishing she had water to help wash away the dreams and the awful heaviness they left in her.

Her little cave of a porch was now fully illuminated with the morning sun, and passersby were casting her curious glances. Taking as little time as possible, she pulled her diary from the dress pocket, tucked it into her chest bindings, and rolled the dress into a ball that she crammed into a corner of the porch where she could find it later. Ready for the day, she started down the street with no destination in mind, snacking on the raw potatoes as she went.

After only a few minutes, the difference in how she could

move through the world was obvious. No one stared at her like they'd done when she wore a dress, their expressions full of judgment. As a man, she could slough off the forced mantle of shame that was put upon women, as though their very existence was something for which they must apologize.

She was once again a man with all the freedoms that gender enjoyed. She intended to enjoy that freedom to the fullest, starting with a visit to the place where no respectable woman went: the saloon.

Smiling, she yanked open the door to the first saloon she came across, on Front Street. Already, card games were in progress at a couple of tables, or maybe they were still going from the night before. At one table, a man slept with his head in his arms. Someone had placed a daisy into the back of the man's breeches so that it looked like it was growing out of his backside. For some reason, it reminded Emily of the two soldiers in camp who had danced together one evening, taking turns being the woman and sending the other men into gales of laughter at their antics.

She missed that life. Sighing, she turned to the barkeep, who was wiping the countertop with a rag and eyeing her curiously. "Can I help you?" he asked in a friendly manner, his long mustache wiggling.

Emily dropped onto a stool at the end of the bar. "Do you serve breakfast here?"

"Sure do. Want coffee while you wait?"

She did. Soon she was happily slicing into a slab of ham with eggs, grits, greens, and a buttermilk biscuit the size of her palm filling the rest of the plate. She knew she should save her money, but she needed energy if she was going to figure out how to get to Nebraska.

As she ate, she watched men come in, slam back a drink, then saunter out again, likely on their way to work. The man with the flower in his breeches woke up and hollered for coffee, which the barkeep hustled over to give him. One poker game finished up, and the men shook hands before parting ways and disappearing through the door into the bright day outside. The other poker game looked like it could go for several hours more.

"Hey, boy!" called a gruff man at the poker table. "Yeah, you. Want to join us? We just lost a man." He nodded to the man heading out the doors with shoulders drooping.

Emily normally would have turned down the invitation, but she missed being one of the men. She missed playing cards with Ben, and she missed sipping on Willie's applejack. Even knowing this poker game would not be the same as sitting with her friends and would not bring them back, she got to her feet and crossed the room. Promising herself she'd quit when she was ahead, she said, "Sure, I'll play. Deal me in."

The hours passed without much notice. She played hand after hand, winning some and losing some and generally coming out even, she figured. She drank the whiskey that appeared in front of her from time to time, and she took breaks to visit the privy in the yard out back, but she kept returning to the game, enjoying how it made her forget everything else. As she played, she did not think about Ben or Willie or being discharged from the Army. She did not think about where to find work or how to get to Nebraska, or what she'd do until she could make a claim on land there. She simply played the cards in her hand.

When she got up to visit the privy for the countless time, she was surprised to see the sun had gone down. She'd played all day.

The unsteadiness of her feet attested to the fact that she'd also drunk all day. She giggled. What would her father have said about this? She giggled again. Alcohol may be sinful, but it sure made her feel better.

As she returned to the game, she noticed two of the men she'd been playing with were gone, and two new faces scowled in their place. Shrugging, she nodded her greetings to them and picked up her cards, ready for another round.

It was clear from the start that these two were men she had to be careful with. She didn't worry, though, as she knew how to handle them. There'd been some of their kind in her regiment, always causing trouble, never owning their responsibilities. She played the game fairly and kept her conversation limited. And yet, the two men, especially the older, scruffier one, seemed to grow angrier with each hand that they lost and with each drink they swallowed.

By the fourth round, Emily made the decision to excuse herself from the game and return to her sleeping porch. It was a good time to stop, before the men grew violent and while she was ahead in her winnings. That's one thing Ben had taught her, to know when it was time to quit.

"That's it for me, fellas," she said, tossing her cards on the table. "If you will excuse me, I bid you good night." She rose from her chair.

"Hold on one cotton-pickin' minute." The gray-haired man clamped a weathered hand over her wrist. "You cheated!"

Emily reared back. Never in her life had she cheated at anything, unless one counted disguising herself as a man—was that cheating? Still, she'd never cheated at cards, and she never would. "I most certainly did not!"

"Now, now, Walt," the barkeep said, appearing at Emily's side. "Don't go getting carried away. You lost fair and square."

Walt jumped to his feet, knocking his chair over behind him. His young friend followed suit and pushed up his sleeves as though getting ready for a fight. "I saw him touch his hand to his chest. He's hiding cards in his shirt. Go on, search him if you don't believe me!"

Emily backed away. "I promise you, I did not cheat, and I don't have any cards. They're all right there." She pointed to the table. When she noticed her hand shaking, she quickly drew it back and stuck it in her pocket. Catching the barkeep's eye, she pleaded with him, "Believe me. I'm not a cheater."

The barkeep tilted his head toward the door, clearly telling her to leave before things got worse. She didn't need to be told twice. She pivoted and made a beeline for the street.

"Where's he goin? Stop him!"

"How 'bout you boys let me get you another round on me?" the barkeep was asking as Emily dashed through the door.

The street outside was busy, even though night had fallen. Knowing the men might follow her despite the barkeep's efforts, she crossed to the other side and tried to blend into the crush of men making their way to their evening entertainment. She headed in the direction of the deserted house.

When she reached the quiet street where she intended to sleep, only a block away from her porch, she thought she'd escaped them. But then she heard footsteps coming up fast behind her. She was turning to see who it was when a fist slammed into her stomach and her body exploded with pain.

"What's the matter, boy?" the younger man from the saloon yelled in her ear as she doubled over. "Can't take what you got comin' to you?"

The man's beefy fist slammed into the side of her skull, propelling her to the ground. Her head hit the brick sidewalk with such force she saw an explosion of light behind her closed eyes. She curled into a ball with her arms wrapped around her head and waited for him to finish, but the man was far from done with her. He kicked her ribs, and through a haze of pain, she wondered if her bindings would hold her bones in place.

"Stand up and fight like a man! Or maybe you ain't a man, seein' as how you can't even defend yerself." *Kick.* "What's wrong with you, huh?" *Kick.*

"He's a baby who should be home with his mama," came Walt's voice now. "What am I sayin'? I bet you're a deserter, aren't you? Deserters deserve to be hung."

Emily had never felt such pain in her life. She fought to catch a breath and to see through the blurry vision that came with her pounding head. She wanted to get to her feet, to fight or run away, she wasn't sure, but her body wouldn't cooperate.

"I said, get to your feet, boy!" One of the men grabbed the front of her shirt and lifted her. As he did so, her shirt tore and the cool night air hit her skin above her bindings. "What in the...? Walt, look at this!"

Emily tried to cross her arms over her chest, but one of the men roughly shoved them out of the way and she was too weak to resist. She found herself again sprawled on her back, but this time she was lying in the dirt and filth of the street. She had to blink several times to see clearly, and what she saw stopped her blood cold. A blade wavered in front of her face.

She tried to roll away, but the men held her down. All of a sudden, the blade sliced through her bindings. One of them grabbed her diary and tossed it aside, and then he roughly grabbed her breast, squeezing it so tightly that she cried out in pain. He whooped with delight and squeezed again.

"We got ourselves one of those Amazon women. A regular Joan of Arc herself, all dressed up like a man and picking fights."

"Let's show her what real men do."

To her horror, she felt her trousers being tugged down her hips and she was roughly pushed over onto her stomach with her face being ground into the dirt. She squeezed her eyes tight and bit her lip until she tasted blood, terrified of what they were going to do but having no way to stop them.

Calloused fingers grabbed her bare backside and she screamed, hating that they could hear her weakness but unable to keep quiet. She closed her mind off from what was about to happen to her body and drew into herself, waiting for it to be over.

Through the fog in her mind, she heard the younger man's voice yell, "Walt, get down! Where'd that come from?"

Emily forced the rest of their words from her attention. It was the only way she knew to survive their abuse.

But then, she realized no one was touching her any longer.

Afraid to hope, and too hurt to move, all she could do was lie still and wait to see what happened next.

She jerked as a small hand touched her cheek. "You need to get up," whispered a young voice right into her ear. "They're going to come back when they realize those were just rocks we was throwin' and no one was shootin' at 'em." Emily felt her arm tugged. "Come with us. We'll help you."

Emily squinted through the pain and found the little blond girl from the street last night and her two companions. The pickpockets. She forced herself to her knees and finally to her feet where she hastily put her clothing to rights, shame burning through her entire body.

When she took a step, her knee buckled, and she would have fallen had the older boy not been there to grab her. The other boy, who couldn't have been older than eight, moved to her other side, and together they helped support her as she limped slowly behind the little girl.

She didn't know where they took her and, in fact, could not have retraced her steps because she paid no attention to their route. All she knew was when they finally let her lie down, the relief was so great that tears flowed from her eyes. "Thank you," she managed before losing consciousness.

Even before coming fully awake, Emily felt her entire body throb with pain. She tried to sink back into oblivion, but then she remembered the two men who had beaten her, and her eyes flew open, afraid of what she was going to see.

She'd expected to find herself lying in the street, or maybe on the abandoned porch where she had slept before, but she was in neither place. Confused, she tried to sit up, but a sharp pain in her ribs halted her movements and told her they were likely broken. Sucking air through her teeth, she eased back down and turned only her aching head to look around.

She seemed to be in some sort of shed or small barn. Sunlight filtered through the few cracks between boards that had not yet been stuffed with wadding. Someone had covered her with a blanket and that, combined with the clean straw that was her bed, made her quite comfortable, pain notwithstanding.

"Oh good, you're awake."

A little girl with hair so light it was almost white, yet hanging limp with grease, popped into the shed, and Emily recognized her as one of the street kids she'd seen picking pockets. She wore a simple yellow dress with blue flowers on it over a pair of brown trousers and sturdy black shoes. She reminded Emily of her cousin Ada.

Her memory rushed back. The kids had saved her from those men. Where were the two boys who had helped her here? Wherever *here* was.

"We were really worried about you," continued the girl as she reached for something above Emily's head. From the sounds, it must have been a bowl of water. "How do you feel?" The girl gently placed a cool, wet cloth on Emily's forehead, smoothing her hair away as a mother would for a child.

"Not well, to be honest," she said, answering the girl's question and following it with two of her own. "Where are we? Where is your family?"

The girl settled onto the ground at Emily's side and crossed her legs "We live here. Don't worry, no one knows we're here, and no one saw us bring you here either. All the family I got left is my brothers, and they'll be back soon."

The girl sounded like an echo of Emily's own words after Pa died. Before Ben... She swallowed back the agony of remembering and forced her attention to the girl and the feeling of the cool cloth. From the tender way the girl administered to her, Emily knew she must have recently had a mother. "What happened to your parents?"

The girl's tiny shoulders shrugged. "They died. Papa was shot by the Yanks, and after our slaves ran away, Mama worked all by herself with only us for help until she got sick and died, too."

Emily acknowledged the girl's unspoken pain with a close-lipped smile. "I lost my parents, too," she told her.

Just then, two bodies burst into the small room, filling it with energy and noise.

"Did you see his face when I started crying?" laughed the younger boy, the one who looked like the girl. "Boy, was he a sucker!"

The older, black boy laughed and grabbed onto the younger boy's shoulder as though needing his support to remain upright. "I was so scared when he grabbed you, but then I couldn't believe it when you started wailing! Real tears, too!"

They dissolved into a fit of giggles that Emily could not resist. She smiled at the boys and waited for them to notice her.

"What'd you get? I'm hungry." The little girl was unamused by the boys' antics and simply stared at them with big brown eyes.

The black boy looked at the girl, and then his eyes shifted toward Emily. When he saw her watching him, his laughter faded. Suddenly serious, he opened the burlap sack he carried and looked inside. "We got a loaf of bread, some strawberries, and two eggs."

The girl held out her hands. "Hand them over. Our guest must be starving."

The black boy scowled in Emily's direction and handed the sack to the girl, who disappeared outside with it. The younger boy took his sister's place on the ground next to Emily. "What's your name? Mine's Isaac, and he's Gabriel." He moved his skinny arm to indicate the black boy still rooted in place near the door. "Our sister is Nellie."

"Thank you for taking care of me, Isaac. You too, Gabriel." Emily smiled at the boys even though the effort split her swollen lip open and she tasted blood. "My name is Je…" She stopped, realizing the kids knew she was a woman. They'd also put themselves at risk to help her. She owed them the truth. "My name is Emily."

"Why are you dressed like that?" Isaac asked, his round face full of questions. "I ain't never seen my mama dressed like a man."

"Because I'm all alone in the world now, and I've found I am safer as a man and can find better-paying work as one."

He nodded as though nothing would surprise him. "What happened to your family?"

"My mama died when I was about your age, and my father was killed in battle," she told him, watching out of the corner of her eye as Gabriel took a seat on an overturned crate in the far corner near the door. She could tell he was as curious as Isaac but afraid to come too close to her. "Then my brother David died of typhoid. After that, my brother Benjamin and I enlisted in the Army. That's when I started pretending I was a man." She stopped, wondering if she was telling them too much.

"Where is Benjamin now?" Gabriel asked, though his scowl showed he hadn't intended to voice the question.

"He was killed in battle at Pittsburg Landing. His fiancée, too."

Isaac leaned forward, his eyes wide. "You tellin' me there was two of you dressed like men?"

Emily nodded, then told them the story of how she and Willie had met and the three of them became fast friends. "Willie was like a sister to me."

Nellie came back in carrying a plank of wood with their breakfast on top. She'd fried the eggs and sliced the green tops off the strawberries. "That's like us," she said, setting the make-shift platter on the ground between Emily and Isaac. "We aren't really kin with Gabriel, but he's our brother just the same."

Emily's heart turned over upon hearing the love in her voice. To her, the difference in their coloring was clearly irrelevant. They were siblings, and that was the end of it.

Oh, Willie, she thought, *I wish you were here.*

And then she remembered. "My diary!" Frantic, she tried to sit up to look for it, but the pain in her ribs stopped her, and she cried out. With shallow breaths, she eased back down.

"What are you fretting about?" Isaac asked, staring at her as if she'd lost her mind.

"I lost my diary. I need to go look for it." She tried to ignore the pain and get up, but only got as far as rolling to her side before she had to stop and rest, her breath coming in gasps.

"We'll go look for it after breakfast. You need to rest, and you need to eat." Nellie gently pushed on her shoulder until Emily gave in and lay back down.

It was gone. Her diary and all her money, but even worse, Willie's handkerchief was gone. She'd failed her friend so miserably. She'd lost everything.

Tears rolled down the sides of her face and into her ears, but she did not wipe them away.

"Come sit with us, Gabriel." Nellie was busy ripping the bread into four equal chunks. She used one to carefully scoop up some of the fried egg. She held her offering toward the oldest boy. "Get it while it's hot."

Gabriel joined them and hungrily bit into his breakfast. When Nellie tried to hand her a share, Emily turned it down, knowing she could find her own food later.

Nellie wasn't having it. "Take it, Emily. You need food so your body can heal."

"Yeah, take it," urged Isaac. "It's not much, but it's fresh."

Gabriel had finished his egg and bread and was reaching for a strawberry. When his gaze met Emily's, he did not say a word, but he nodded as though giving her his permission. Reluctantly, but also feeling ravenous, Emily tried again to roll over and managed this time to get onto her side and prop herself on one elbow. She took the offered food, bit into it, and nearly wept at how good it tasted.

"There's a lady in town," Nellie told her around a mouthful of bread, "who sometimes gives us food and blankets. She says they are building an orphanage and that she'll see to it we get two of the beds. But we're not gonna go." She slid a glance toward Gabriel.

"Why not? You'll be safe there, and you won't have to steal your food."

"Because they won't take Gabriel," Isaac told her matter-of-factly. "On account of him bein' a contraband."

So, Gabriel had been a slave. She looked at the boy and was surprised to see he did not seem sad at being rejected by the orphanage but, rather, resigned. "But he needs to be cared for the same as the two of you," she protested.

Nellie shrugged. "They don't want any negroes. Only white children."

"So what's Gabriel supposed to do?"

Isaac lifted his chin as though preparing for a fight. "He stays with us, that's what. We'll care for each other."

Emily's heart twisted again, and she didn't know if it was simply in response to the love these three clearly felt for one another, or in envy of their relationship when she had no one.

When the food was gone, Gabriel pulled out a canteen stamped on the side with the letters CSA, for Confederate States of America. He took a swig and passed it to the other kids who also drank before passing it to Emily. She drank, seeing the irony of drinking out of a Reb's canteen when only a few weeks past she'd been shooting at them.

Completely spent, she handed the canteen back to Gabriel and eased herself back to the ground, feeling a wave of heat that hinted at the possibility she might be becoming feverish. She closed her eyes and waited for the food to bring her body strength.

The kids must have thought she'd gone to sleep because they started talking about her in whispers.

"How long is she going to be here?" Gabriel's voice. "It takes all we got to feed ourselves. We don't need another mouth around."

"She's hurt, Gabriel," Nellie reminded him in her tiny voice that gave away her young age, no matter how mature she acted. "She has no one else to care for her."

"How do you know? She probably has folks back home wherever she came from."

"She told me. She's all alone."

The kids fell silent, and Emily drifted off to sleep.

Her dreams were tangled and fraught with danger. She could hear Ben and Willie calling to her for help, but she couldn't reach them.

But then it was Gabriel, Isaac, and Nellie standing on the battlefield with dead bodies lying all around them. They held hands and stared at the horizon as if waiting for someone. Their parents? Emily called to them, but they couldn't hear her. They stood there, motionless except for the wind blowing Nellie's long blond hair across her face and her skirt around her little legs.

Suddenly, Emily was back in the thick of battle, chasing after a Reb. No matter how far she ran or how many shots she fired, he wouldn't die. She kept running and firing, but the bastard wouldn't die.

And then she was with Willie, who hung onto her hand and begged, "Find my sister. Tell her I'm sorry." Her eyes pleaded with Emily even as blood ran down her face, turning it into a grotesque mask.

"How?" Emily begged her. She was holding on to Willie's hands even though she felt the flesh drain away through her fingers until she was left holding nothing but bone. "How can I find your sister? I don't know your real name!"

Chapter Twenty-Eight

June 6, 1862: Nashville, Tennessee

*I*t took a week of being cared for by the children before Emily felt strong enough to emerge from their little hut. She was plagued by nightmares and, even a few times when she was awake, by visions of men with guns bursting into the room and shooting at her and the children. She was sure the kids thought she was out of her mind, but they did not say a word about it. They simply went about their routine of melting into the city and returning with pilfered food that they cooked and ate together, sharing stories and helping each other as best they could. She told them about Willie and Ben. They told her about living on the plantation and how they'd walked into town and found this shack.

While awake, Emily had a lot of time to think. She thought about her promise to Willie that she'd tell her family what had happened to her, and how there was no way she could possibly fulfill that promise. Her friend had enlisted as Willie Smith and, to Emily, that's who she'd been. She'd never thought to ask her real name, and now it was too late. All she knew were Willie's sister's initials: ODE. Did that mean Willie's real last name started with an *E*? Could Emily go to Nebraska and start knocking on the front door of every family there whose name started with *E* and eventually find them?

Nebraska. The word filled Emily with a sense of wonder. Willie had described the wide prairie in such vivid detail that Emily could see it in her mind: the blowing grass, the rocky outcroppings, the bison and cattle and chickens and goats. Emily loved the idea of homesteading there, but could she do it? Could she really go there and build a life all on her own?

It was a question she pondered greatly during those long days, staring at the rough boards of the little hut while twisting Willie's ring on her finger. She could spend the rest of her days as a man and get along well, but did she want to? A part of her, a large part, still hoped to get married and have children.

But, conversely, could she give up all the freedom she had living as a man? No. She could answer that question, at least. She would never again settle for a life where her every action, even her thoughts, were controlled by someone else. From now on, no matter where life took her, she would live on her own terms. If that meant living by herself on the prairie with no husband and no children, so be it.

She was really starting to like the three kids caring for her, and when she wasn't worrying over her own future, she spent hours trying to come up with a plan to help them. That line of thought always brought her back to the look on Gabriel's face when Isaac had said the orphanage did not want him. He'd looked resigned. Where Emily had expected hurt or rejection, she'd seen only acceptance. At nine years of age, he was already acquainted with a world that did not want him and could not even see him as human.

But then she had a new realization. Gabriel didn't need to be accepted into the orphanage. He didn't need pity and charity. He needed a family, and in fact, he already had a family with Nellie and Isaac. Emily envied them. Their relationship was so close that the two younger kids had turned their backs on safety and comfort in order to stay with Gabriel, as Emily had done to be with her brothers. The way the kids worked together to survive, and yet were willing to help her, a stranger, inspired her.

She'd had that closeness before, with her own family and then with Ben and Willie. She wanted it again. She wanted a family again. Maybe she'd already found them.

But, of course, that was impossible. The kids were thieves. They smelled like they hadn't bathed in months. They squatted in a shack on property whose owner could return any day and evict them. They squabbled. They manipulated people to get what they wanted.

And still, Emily looked at her future and saw them in it.

On the morning when she finally felt strong enough, she bound her chest with a strip of cloth the kids gave her, tucked in her mended shirt, and promised to return that evening with food after securing a job for herself.

Standing together in the dirt yard to say goodbye, the deserted main house blindingly white in the rising sun, all three had smiles on their faces that told Emily they were up to some mischief. "What are you hiding behind your back, Nellie?"

"We was talkin'," Isaac said, looking older than his years, "and we decided you don't look right."

Emily blinked. "What—"

"We got you a hat," Gabriel blurted out, jamming an elbow into Isaac's side. "We thought it could make your disguise better." Nellie brought the hat from behind her back with a flourish and held it up to Emily. She was nibbling on her bottom lip, betraying her fear that Emily wouldn't like the gift.

The brown bowler hat drooped in Nellie's hands. Sweat stains darkened the felt where it had once sat on some man's head, and the smell of tobacco smoke fouled the air around it. The hat had clearly been stolen, but Emily knew her only choice was to accept the gift in the spirit it was being offered, or risk offending her hosts. She smiled at Nellie as she took the hat and plopped it on her own head. "Thank you. It is exactly what I needed."

The little girl beamed.

All day, Emily walked the streets, stopping at every business she came across and asking for work. It quickly became apparent that the city was firmly in the hands of the Federal Army and most industry was in support of the Union cause. Buildings that had once housed grocers or hotels were now hospitals or barracks or storehouses for Federal goods.

Enlisting again was out of the question. Not only would they not accept her back, should they determine her true identity, but she found she did not want to reenlist. The fight had gone out of her when she'd lost Ben and Willie. All she wanted now was to live a quiet life of her own and turn her attention to the future, as much as she could in a country ripped apart by war. But even more than that, when she now thought about secessioners, she saw in her mind's eye the innocent faces that waited for her back at the hut. She would never fire upon them.

She applied for work at several stables, offering to tend the horses and tack, but every one refused her. On College Street she found a bakery emitting scents that made her mouth water. When she knocked on the door and asked for work, telling the baker who answered that she'd been baking bread all her life, he only scrutinized the still-healing bruises on her face and turned her away.

At a carpenter's shop on the corner of Spring and College streets, she tried to apply for a job as a laborer but was told only Federal troops worked there. When asked why she wasn't fighting for the Union, she made up an excuse about being physically unfit for service which, of course, implied she was also unfit as a laborer. She quickly retreated before any more questions were asked.

At the St. Cloud Hotel, she asked for work washing dishes or laundry and was turned away yet again. Over and over, she got the same response: the work was only for Union soldiers, or there was no work to be had in the first place.

Night was falling, and she gave up. Disheartened, she turned in the direction of the hut, without the food she'd promised.

And then her luck turned. As she passed a boardinghouse, she happened to glance in the open door to the kitchen and saw a chicken roasting on a spit over the fire, its juices running over the crispy flesh and dripping onto the hot coals beneath. The delicious aroma made her light-headed.

She stopped and leaned against the building. She'd seen no one inside, but that didn't mean the room was deserted. Someone could be just out of sight.

No sounds emerged from the warm kitchen, and Emily knew if she was going to act, she'd have to be quick.

With a request for a cup of water ready on her lips, she stepped into the room and looked around. It was bare, furnished with a scarred wooden table, two cane-backed chairs near the fire, and pots, pans, tubs, and utensils lying or hanging around the room. A pot of potatoes boiled in the fire next to the chicken, and a pan of biscuits sat on the table, ready to be placed over the coals. No one was in sight.

She quickly grabbed the cloth from over the biscuits and wrapped it around the chicken so she could slide it off the spit without burning her hands.

Holding the chicken to her chest like an infant, she sprinted from the room and onto the street, eager to share this treasure with the children.

"Hey! Come back here!"

Emily started running, turning corners and dashing down alleys to evade anyone who might be chasing her.

Lying in bed all week had taken its toll, and she soon found herself winded and her ribs sore. Stopping to catch her breath, she peeked around the corner to see if anyone was chasing her and was relieved to see no one seemed to by paying any attention to her.

After several more breaths, she pushed away from the brick

wall and headed for the kids' hut, this time at a slower pace. A warm chicken right off the fire was going to fill their bellies and fuel them through another night.

As soon as she skirted the abandoned house and made her way into the yard where their little hut huddled against the back wall, she heard the kids arguing.

"You shouldn't have taken that, Gabriel!" Nellie's voice. "It isn't yours!"

Emily paused to listen.

"She's right, you know," Isaac put in. "You need to give it back."

"But she'll be cross with me, and I...I like her." Gabriel sounded defeated. After a beat, Emily realized the "her" being discussed could only be herself.

To give them warning, she retraced her steps and intentionally kicked a rock so it banged against the water pump, making a clanging noise. The kids' voices cut off.

She pushed open the ramshackle door, and acting as though she hadn't heard a thing, she held up her prize. "We're having chicken for dinner!"

Amid moans of delight and cries of "That smells so good!" they gathered in their circle on the floor to eat. Gabriel revealed a loaf of bread he'd obtained, and Nellie and Isaac proudly presented two potatoes they'd dug up in an abandoned garden and baked all afternoon in a pit they'd dug in the yard.

When the chicken had been picked clean and their bellies were full, Emily took a deep breath and confessed, "I didn't find a job today. I don't think there are any for me here."

The announcement was met with silence. Nellie shrugged one shoulder. "No matter."

Isaac took out a coin purse he'd lifted off someone and upended it onto the ground. He and Gabriel started debating what they would buy with the four coins lying in the dirt.

"You know," Emily said, interrupting them, "I've been

thinking of going to Nebraska Territory and making a home-stead claim. My friend Willie was from there, and she said it's a grand place to live."

The boys nodded at her and went back to inspecting their coins. Nellie dug her fingers into the dirt.

Emily had been thinking all day about heading for Nebraska and taking the children with her. She knew it was a mad idea, but she couldn't let it go. The kids had helped her. Maybe she could help them in return. "What do you think about going with me?"

All three heads snapped up to look at her suspiciously.

"Why?" Isaac asked.

Emily shrugged. "Wouldn't you like to get away from this war? Go to a place where you could play in the sunshine and grow your own food?"

Gabriel's eyes narrowed. "You going to be a farmer?"

"Yes."

"And we'd be your slaves?"

Emily gasped. A quick glance confirmed that the other kids had been thinking the same thing. "No, not at all! You'd be my family. We'd be farmers together. Look out for one another."

The kids exchanged glances, and then Emily felt something shift in the air.

"How would we get there?" Gabriel, ever the thoughtful one, was already thinking through the logistics.

"I don't know," she admitted. "If we had money, we'd take a steamer upriver or a train. But since I lost my money when those men attacked me, and I can't find work, I don't know how we'll get there. Walking would be dangerous, but it might be the only way."

Nellie twisted her mouth in a way that showed she was think-ing hard.

"Did those men take your money?" Gabriel asked, his voice low as though he was afraid to ask the question.

Emily shrugged. "I'm not sure. It was hidden in a diary I kept here." She touched a hand to her chest where her bindings were. "I remember one of them tossing it aside, but then it was lost."

Isaac and Nellie were both staring at Gabriel with stern expressions. Gabriel squirmed, and his eyes would not meet hers. "Miss Emily," he finally croaked. "I didn't mean to take it. I picked it up when we found you, and when I saw it was a diary, I thought I should read it before giving it back to be sure you were trustworthy."

"You can read?"

He nodded, his face still turned to the ground. "Mistress Alice taught me when she taught Isaac. Told me to keep it secret from the master, or we'd all get in trouble."

"That's wonderful!" She turned to Nellie. "Can you read, too?"

The little girl shook her head.

"We'll start working on that."

Gabriel crawled the short distance to his pallet in the corner and withdrew something from under his blanket. When he returned, he held Emily's diary. The sight of it made her gasp.

"I shouldn't have taken it." He shoved it at her.

Emily could not hold back tears as she took the book from him. "I thought it was gone for good." She ran a hand lovingly over the cover, thinking about the day Pa had given it to her and all the days it had kept her company in camp.

"There was no money in there," Gabriel insisted, his voice loud. "I swear it!"

She placed her hand over the cover protectively and smiled at the boy. "Let's see about that, shall we?" And then, not bothering to hide her actions from the kids, she unwrapped the leather thong, popped off the cover to the secret compartment and felt a rush of emotion upon seeing Willie's handkerchief tucked safely inside. Her money was there, too, but all she had eyes for was the handkerchief.

She lifted it reverently with both hands, her heart tugging upon seeing the brown stains from Willie's blood. "This is the handkerchief I told you about from Willie. See her sister's initials?"

"What was her sister's name?" Nellie asked, her finger lightly tracing the letters.

Emily shrugged. "She told me, but I can't remember."

"I bet it was Ophelia, or Octavia," Isaac insisted.

"Or Odette," Nellie said, getting in on the game.

Gabriel didn't say anything about the handkerchief. He was too busy staring at the money. "Is that real?"

Emily lifted the cash out and saw it was all there. Now her future did not look so bleak. "It sure is." Then, after the kids each had a chance to inspect it up close, she said, "What do you say? Shall we go to Nebraska?"

No one said a word, but clearly a lot of communicating was going on through the looks the kids were giving each other. Emily held her diary and waited.

Finally, Gabriel scooped the four coins from the dirt and held them out to her. "Add this to the collection. We're going to need all we can get if we're to become farmers in Nebraska."

Emily couldn't help herself. She gave a whoop of joy. Wide smiles spread across the children's faces.

When she calmed, Emily shared the rest of her plan. "I was thinking I would go back to wearing a dress, and we could tell people I'm a widow and you're my children. Would that be okay?"

Nellie bounced up and down. "Oh yes!"

Gabriel scowled. "No one is going to believe you're my mother."

Emily couldn't refute his statement. "That doesn't matter. People can keep their thoughts to themselves."

"Besides," he insisted, "you're too young to be our mother."

She hadn't thought about that and stopped to do the math. He was right. She would have given birth at the age of eleven in order to have a nine-year-old.

Gabriel must have read the truth on her face because he

announced, "We'd best say I'm your servant. People would believe that."

Emily ached for the boy. "You're right," she admitted. "But as soon as we arrive safely in Nebraska, you'll be my son and we're a family. Got it? I don't care what anyone says."

"And we won't be your slaves?" Gabriel asked again.

She shook her head and looked him straight in the eyes. "No. I admit we'll all have to work hard if we're going to survive on the prairie and run a farm all by ourselves, but all four of us will equally share in the rewards. Agreed?"

Gabriel's lips twitched with a smile he was trying to hold back. He nodded solemnly, but his eyes shone.

"Do we call you Mama?" Isaac asked shyly.

"Do you want to?" She knew the kids had only recently lost their own mother and might not want a replacement so quickly, but both blond heads nodded. "Then I think you should."

Seeing the light go out of Gabriel's eyes, Emily nudged his foot with her own. "What's got you down?"

He shrugged but remained silent.

Nellie piped up, "He wants you to be his mama, too, but you can't."

Emily crawled over to Gabriel and put her arm around his shoulders. "Whether I'm old enough or not, I'd be honored to be your mama. Or, if you insist I'm not old enough, I can be your older sister. What do you think of that?"

He leaned into her. "That sounds nice."

Emily looked at her new little family and felt her heart threaten to burst open. "We'd better start making plans."

Chapter Twenty-Nine

Present day: Woodinville, Washington

June 6, 1862: This past week has been a difficult one. I was beaten, lost my diary, and was nursed back to health by three street kids. My diary was returned to me. I healed. I've been out looking for work and have not found anything. Newspapers are full of stories of battles from the Peninsula Campaign but I find myself tuning out, turning away. I cannot fight for my country any longer. My country does not want me. Never mind that I lost everything to this war, never mind that I lost my father, brothers, and best friend. No, all the officials see is my sex and that I am inferior, so they turn me away. Good riddance. Let them fight their bloody battles without me. I am done giving everything for a country that does not value me.

From now on, I'm living life on my terms.

June 7, 1862: Those street kids I mentioned earlier have become quite dear to me. Gabriel is the oldest at nine years of age, though his experiences have aged him to double that. He is a whip-smart black boy who works hard to keep his little family together. Isaac is eight and was once, I gather, the son of the family who owned Gabriel, though you wouldn't know it. Those two are as close as any brothers I've known. The youngest is Nellie, who is six. She is spunky and brave and not afraid of anything, it seems. They saved my life, both that night on the street and by giving me a new reason to look forward to the day. They are my new family.

Lincoln has abolished slavery in Washington and all U.S. possessions. Some say it's a matter of days before it is abolished in all territories. It looks like George was right. This war is, at its core, about slavery. The Federal side must win so that our country can be reunited and slavery abolished in all states. I know this now more than ever every time I look into Gabriel's eyes. That sweet, strong boy deserves the freedom to make his own choices in life, and he deserves, at minimum, the same respect his two siblings receive for no other reason than the color of their skin. I cannot rejoin the fight, but I can help this one former slave and his adopted siblings, for they are helping me in equal measure.

*E*mily's description of her time with the three orphans gave Larkin an idea. If the kids had given Emily a new purpose in her life after the military, maybe Larkin could find similar purpose. She was far from ready to start a family of her own, but she could be a mentor to a child. The military had taught her a lot of valuable skills in working with people, and she'd always enjoyed mentoring opportunities. She would be perfect for the role.

A quick scan online squashed her hopes as swiftly as they'd risen. Mentors were people who had their lives on track. It was all Larkin could do some days to get through the day. Who was she kidding? She didn't have any experience with kids, and what made her think anyone would trust their daughter to a woman who had gotten the only kid she'd ever befriended beaten and killed by her own father?

No, Larkin was not mentor material. She'd probably mess up

anyone who came into her life. She had absolutely nothing of value to offer anyone.

Plus, she was a liar. She'd known it when she was with Zach last weekend and had told him all about Sarah except for how she died. She hadn't expected to like the guy. She'd thought she could gloss over what she'd done, but the fact that he deserved to know the truth had been haunting her ever since.

Without pausing to allow anything to change her mind, Larkin picked up her phone and dialed his number. He picked up on the second ring.

"Larkin, it's good to hear from you."

"It was my fault," she blurted out. "I'm the reason Sarah is dead. You need to know that."

"What?" There was a sound, like fabric rubbing against the phone's speaker. "Hang on a minute. I'm at work. Let me go into an empty meeting room."

Larkin waited, not saying a word. She deserved to have this drawn out. Deserved for this to hurt.

"Okay, I'm back." Zach sounded worried. "What did you say?"

She perched on the edge of her bed and stared blindly out the windows. "I said that I'm the reason Sarah is dead. I fucked up, and she paid the price."

She told him all of it. The whole story of Nahid and Anahita. Of how Sarah had advised her not to interfere and to notify their superior officers of the situation, but Larkin hadn't listened. Of how Larkin had let her personal relationship with the girl blind her to her duty, and how Sarah had stepped in to stop her and lost her life doing so.

"I thought you should know the truth," Larkin finally said when the whole story was out.

Zach was silent for so long she might have thought the line had been disconnected, but she could hear him breathing. His breaths were short and fast, as if he was angry. As he should be. As anyone would be.

She waited for his pain and his anger.

"I, uh…wow," he said finally. "That's a lot to take in."

Larkin closed her eyes. Breathed.

Another voice sounded in the background, and Zach said, "Look, I can't really talk about this right now. I'll call you later tonight, okay?" He hung up.

Larkin let the hand holding her phone drop to her lap. Telling the story to Sarah's brother had been brutal, but she now realized she'd been hoping he would make her feel better, just as he'd eased the pain of scattering Sarah's ashes and saying goodbye to her. Larkin had been hoping Zach would excuse her and make it not her fault.

But it was her fault. Nothing, no one, could make it better.

Numbly, Larkin went downstairs looking for Grams. Grams always made her feel better about anything that ever happened to her.

But Grams wasn't there. A note on the counter said she was out running errands. Kaia was gone, too. Probably at work.

She had no one, so she reached for the next people on her list of friends: Jim Beam and Jameson.

With a bottle of each cradled to her side, she grabbed her rucksack and sweatshirt and slipped into her tennis shoes but didn't bother to tie them. She didn't know where she was going; she just knew she needed to get away from here for a while. She got in her car and drove east, toward the mountains.

The burn of the whiskey in her throat felt like the penance she knew she deserved, as though it was burning the story she'd spoken, searing it into her body so that it would forever be written in her flesh. A testament of her shame.

It would be so easy, she realized, to ignore the curve of the road. Rather than turning the wheel, she could keep it straight and sail off the pavement into the ravine. For one glorious moment she would feel like she was flying, weightless, free. And then she would slam into a tree, and she wouldn't have to feel anything ever again. She could join Sarah in the ocean.

The car shuddered as the right tires hit gravel on the side of the road, and she automatically corrected back to the left.

Her mother had begged her not to kill herself where Grams would find her. She would do it this way, where some stranger would pull her body from the wreckage and no one in her family would have to clean it up. Her mother's final wishes for her would be fulfilled.

Larkin raised the bottle of Jim Beam into the air as a toast to her mother. But then the memory came to her of Grams curled in Gramps's recliner watching over Larkin as she slept.

Grams would be shattered. Not even a year had passed since Gramps had died. Losing Larkin might be more than she could take.

Shaking, Larkin put on her blinker and turned onto the next side road she came to and immediately onto the dirt shoulder where she turned the car off. She had no idea where she was. All around her was dripping-wet forest. There were probably houses tucked in the trees, but she could not see any, and she felt all alone. Even the heavy gray sky pressed over her, making her feel as though there was nothing beyond her car.

She didn't know what she wanted to do, and she was tired of thinking about it.

She was so tired of everything.

She'd sleep. And when she woke up, she would decide what to do next. She crawled into the back seat with her two best friends, Jim and Jameson, and stopped thinking about anything else.

It was the cold that woke her. And an annoying tapping sound. A bright light shined right in her face and really pissed her off. Other than the light, it was pitch-black outside.

"What?" she yelled, holding her arm over her eyes.

"Open the door, ma'am," came a muffled response.

Larkin opened her eyes fully and realized she was in the back seat of her car with an empty bottle of Jameson cradled in her arm. And worse, staring at her through the window was an officer in uniform. He still shined his flashlight into her face.

Knowing this wasn't going to turn out well, she slid the bottle to the floor and took a minute to push her hair off her face and tuck it behind her ears. Her head ached, and her eyes felt like sandpaper. Then, reaching to lower the window, she realized it wouldn't go down with the car off and swore under her breath.

"Open the door, ma'am," the officer said, seeing what she was trying to do.

Obeying, she flicked the lock up and opened the door, shivering as a blast of cold air swept over her. She blinked. It wasn't as dark as she'd first thought. In fact, the eastern sky was starting to lighten, so it must be near morning. She'd been here all night. "Good morning, Officer. How may I be of service?"

"Would you please step from the vehicle?"

Larkin had been on the other side of this situation more than once on various military bases during her career. She knew she had no choice but to comply.

Making sure to keep her hands visible, she climbed from the car and stood leaning against it, hoping the officer hadn't noticed her swaying when she got to her feet.

"What are you doing here, ma'am?"

"I was...um...feeling sleepy so I pulled over to rest for a while." She was sure she'd heard the line from someone she'd interrogated at some point in her career. She hadn't believed it at the time any more than this guy seemed to.

"How much have you had to drink?"

Larkin mentally crossed her fingers. "Not much."

"Uh-huh." His expression didn't change. "So, you didn't actually drink that bottle I saw you holding?"

"What bottle?" She turned as though to look for a bottle, but the movement made her dizzy. "Oh, yes, I remember now. Hmm." She really didn't know what to say, and her brain refused to click into gear.

"What is your name, ma'am?"

Knowing she was caught, Larkin hung her head. "Larkin Bennett, sir."

"Larkin Bennett, I'm going to need you to give me your car keys as well as your identification and vehicle registration." He opened the car door for her and waited for her to produce the requested items.

She was feeling nauseated and shaky and wanted nothing more than to go back to sleep, but she knew she had to be careful. He could arrest her for DUI, public intoxication, or some other charge. Or, he could take pity on her and simply take her to the station to sleep it off.

"I need you to come with me, Ms. Bennett," the officer said, reaching for her elbow to escort her to the cruiser parked behind her own car, the engine still running. She had no choice but to go with him.

The back seat smelled funky, but the warmth of the heater welcomed her, and she did not care about anything else. As the officer got on his radio and called in the location of her car, she realized he had not read her Miranda rights to her. She wasn't being arrested.

Relieved, she leaned against the car door and let sleep claim her once again.

Chapter Thirty

S he'd disappointed Grams before—like the time she'd stolen a ten-dollar bill from Gramps's wallet when she was eight, or the time when she was twelve and locked Kaia and Jenna out in the rain because she was mad at them—but this time she'd reached an all-new low.

At the police station, she was led to a row of chairs and allowed to lie down as they called Grams to come get her.

Grams said little to her at the station and even less on the drive home. Larkin tried to apologize, but Grams ignored her and turned the radio up louder.

When they got home, all Grams said was, "Why don't you go wash off your night and then go to bed. We'll talk when you wake up."

Larkin nodded like a recalcitrant child and did as she was told.

Her dreams came strong and fierce. She was back in Kandahar, standing in a crowd of children begging for food and candy and money, but this time the Afghan police captain didn't send them away with angry words. He instead fired his AK-47 into the crowd, tearing through their fragile little bodies like paper targets at a gun range. Larkin screamed for him to stop, but her cries went unheeded. And then, she looked down and saw that she had been the one firing on the kids. Her rifle had a spray of blood over it.

When she looked up, the children were gone, and so were the rest of the police, both American and Afghan. Only Larkin stood on the dusty, smelly street, and walking toward her was a figure wearing a blue burqa. Larkin knew who was beneath that heavy cloth. She knew *what* was beneath that heavy cloth.

"Stop!" she shouted. But the figure kept walking toward her at a slow and steady pace.

"Anahita, stop!" she shouted again. The figure kept walking.

Larkin pleaded for her to stop over and over again, and then, in the corner of her eye, she saw movement. When she looked that direction, she saw Sarah there, walking toward Anahita with her M4 assault rifle raised. "Sarah, stop! Go back," she yelled now, but Sarah did not hear her.

Suddenly both of them were directly in front of her—both Anahita and Sarah—their faces stretched in ugly expressions of contempt. "Your fault," they said in unison. "You did this."

Larkin slapped her hands over her ears to drown them out, but their voices got louder and louder until she felt they were inside her skull, driving her mad.

And then the noise stopped. She held herself still, listening for movement. When she opened her eyes, she was no longer on the street, but sitting on a colorful floor cushion, sweets and tea spread before her on the *desterkahn*—a large plastic table-cloth on the floor where food was served. Anahita sat across from her wearing a dress bursting with colors to rival the floor cushions and a green chador pulled back to reveal her short, amber hair. When she saw Larkin staring at her, she smiled a sad, knowing smile. "Tell my story, Bennett. Don't let them forget me."

Larkin jerked awake and immediately regretted the movement because it set the room spinning. For several long moments, she lay completely still with her arm over her eyes, waiting for the room to stop and her stomach to settle.

The dream had felt so real. She could still hear Anahita's words ringing in her ears.

Tell my story. Don't let them forget me.

She had told Anahita's story. She'd told it to her family and to Zach, and each time it had only hurt more. What did Anahita want? What did Sarah want?

The surge of emotions roiling through her stirred up her stomach, and her mouth began watering in the painful way it always did when she was about to vomit.

She lurched from the bed and made it into the bathroom just in time to throw up into the toilet.

After her stomach was emptied, she felt too weak to move, and she did not trust her stomach not to heave again, so she lay on the bathroom floor between the toilet and the bathtub, every nerve in her body sensitive and aching.

When she woke, she found a bath towel draped over her, and she didn't know if she'd pulled it over herself or if she had Grams to thank.

The familiar greasy sludge of shame oozed over her at the thought of Grams seeing her like this. *Damn.* For months she'd been trying to hide the darkness inside her, but it kept leaking out anyway and dragging the people around her down with it.

Why was she hiding? Who did she think she was fooling? No one, that's who. There wasn't one person she could think of who was fooled by Larkin's act. Certainly not Grams, not her parents, not Kaia, not Jenna. Not even Zach Faber anymore.

She might as well tell the whole world the truth. Lay herself bare. Share her shame with everyone so that when she took herself away, no one would miss her. They'd be relieved.

With that decided, Larkin crawled out to her bedroom and opened her laptop. Without thinking about what she was writing, she poured out the story of Nahid, Anahita, and Sarah. Every painful word of it.

Without revising or editing, she posted the story on her blog. It was her penance. It was her explanation.

It was her goodbye.

The ringing of her cell phone woke her, and she answered without thinking.

"Larkin, it's Zach. Sorry I didn't call you back last night like I said I would."

Larkin's eyes flew open. She'd fallen asleep on the floor. Hearing Zach's voice now, when she was still feeling sick and vulnerable, sent a surge of panic through her. She did not have the strength for another battering on her heart. This was going to hurt, and there was no way to protect herself from it. She pushed herself up so she was sitting with her back against the bed. Her heart was racing, and she thought she might vomit again.

"Anyway," he said, sounding confused that she hadn't spoken. "I, uh, I thought over what you told me, and I wanted to let you know that I don't blame you. I don't think you could have done anything differently."

"I could have shot Anahita before Sarah got too close to the bomb."

He sucked in his breath, and Larkin knew she'd surprised him.

"I could have done my fucking job and not gotten involved in the first place," she added.

Zach was silent for a beat. "Look, Larkin. I admit I didn't know Sarah, but from what you've told me, and from what I've heard in your voice and seen on your face, you are a person who cares about people. You only wanted to help that girl, and sure, it went wrong, but that doesn't mean you were wrong to try. In fact, I know you expected me to hate you once you told me the story, but actually, it made me like you even more. I can see why Sarah loved you."

"But, Zach—"

"No buts, Larkin," he interrupted. "You've given me the greatest gift I could ever hope for by bringing Sarah back to me. After that day on the beach with you when we said goodbye to her, I've felt a sense of peace that I never knew was possible. Thank you."

That surprised her, and she was happy to hear he felt this way, but she knew the truth. She knew there was no fixing what she'd done. "Look, Zach, I don't think you understand."

"I think I do, Larkin," he said softly.

His tone wasn't argumentative, nor was it cajoling. It sounded like he was stating a simple truth. Maybe that's why she believed him. It was as though he was so certain of his words that she could do nothing else. "Oh. Okay."

"And there's something else," he went on. "I want to help you look for Willie Smith's family and return the handkerchief and ring to them. I never connected with Emily the way Sarah did, but ever since you told me about all that, I feel like she's important. I want to help you fulfill the promise she made to Willie, and I think it would make Sarah happy if we do it together. What do you think?"

Larkin thought about her plan. She'd posted the story with the intention of taking her life afterward. If she hadn't fallen back asleep, would she be gone now? If Zach hadn't called when he did, would she have woken up and gone through with it?

An unfamiliar sense of calm came over her, and she could've sworn Sarah was sitting on the floor beside her. Did Larkin want to keep living? Keep searching for Willie's family? Accept Zach's offer of help?

Yes. Yes, she did. For now, at least. "I'd like that, Zach."

"Okay." His laugh sounded self-conscious. "With that, I should probably get back to work. But let's talk more tonight.

Or whenever you have more time. I want to hear everything you've done with the project."

Larkin agreed and they hung up, with her feeling more than a little shocked at the turn of the conversation. Zach didn't blame her for Sarah's death. How could that be?

She thought over everything that had happened in the last twenty-four hours and realized that, had she succeeded in driving herself into a tree last night, she wouldn't have been here today to take Zach's call. She would have died thinking that he hated her when, really, he sounded as if he wanted to be her friend. She'd be a fool to throw that away.

Picking up her phone again, she called her therapist. The moment she got on the line, Larkin said the three words she now knew she should have been saying all along. "I need help."

Chapter Thirty-One

July 1862: Nebraska Territory

*B*y stretching Emily's cash and the kids' pickpocket earnings as far as they could, she and her new little family traveled by steamship down the Cumberland River to the Ohio and then up the Mississippi to Quincy, Missouri. From there, they traveled by train to the very end of the line at St. Joseph, Missouri, where they bought passage on another steamer up the Missouri River to Omaha, Nebraska. The farther they traveled from the war, the easier Emily breathed.

Luck was on their side during their last steamer ride up the Missouri when a young married couple from Omaha befriended the young family and, after Emily admitted she had no idea where they would stay once they arrived, invited them to be their guests. Emily was about to gratefully accept when she remembered her agreement with Gabriel, that once they reached Nebraska he would be her son and not her servant.

With a deceptively serene smile, she asked the couple the one question she could think of that would reveal their true natures. "That is a kind offer, and I do thank you, Mr. and Mrs. Goss. But before I accept, I must make certain that your invitation includes all *three* of my children."

The couple exchanged a surprised glance, and then their eyes sought out Gabriel, who was sitting with his siblings near the window, watching the riverbank of Nebraska pass by. "Why, yes," Mr. Goss said with a warm smile as he stretched his arm across the back of his wife's chair. "I do believe we have room for all four of you. You and your daughter can sleep in the guest room, and your two sons can sleep in the adjoining bedroom. Our room is across the hall. Does that suit you?"

Relief came so suddenly that Emily found she could not speak around the lump in her throat. There weren't many folks who would view her new family without judgment, yet the Gosses did. Emily knew her smile must be blinding, but she could not pull it back. She took Mrs. Goss's hand in her own. "I did not know what we would do in Omaha with dwindling funds and no place to stay. Your invitation is generous, and I promise to repay you one day."

"Nonsense," said the kind woman as she patted Emily's hand. "You'll be doing me a kindness by showing me how to raise children. I have no experience, and it's something I'll need to know soon." She placed her free hand on her still-flat stomach.

Emily silently laughed at the idea that she—so new to the role—would have parenting advice to give, but outwardly she gushed, "That is wonderful news. Congratulations!"

And so, upon disembarking from the stern-wheeler *Cora*, the new little family followed Mr. and Mrs. Goss into a cramped carriage that carried them across town to their temporary home in Omaha.

With the Gosses' help, Emily and the kids became acquainted with Omaha. Whenever she could fit it into conversation, Emily inquired of her new acquaintances about families in the area with a name starting with the letter *E* who had two daughters and a son. Only once had she received an introduction to such a family but was disappointed to find all three children were school-aged and couldn't possibly be Willie's family.

Even though the Gosses so generously provided them with two bedrooms, most nights the boys ended up in Emily's room, where they fell asleep on the floor in front of the fireplace. Emily always welcomed them because she knew why they were there. Every single one of them suffered from nightmares. Their cries in the night echoed Emily's own, and told her of the traumas they had endured.

Gabriel's cries were the most heartbreaking, and often Emily would leave her bed to gather him into her arms. The memories plaguing him were more than her impotent reassurances could conquer, but she continued to try, night after night.

Caring for the children gave Emily something to focus on other than her own trauma and loss. But on the nights when her dreams became too much, she always woke to find at least one of the children snuggled against her, holding her like she held them during nightmares. They belonged to each other now, all four of them, and Emily vowed to protect them for the rest of her life.

Slowly, they collected supplies for their new home, including clothing, weapons, farm tools, and building materials, almost all of it offered freely by their new friends, or on credit using the Gosses' good name as a character reference with promises of payment as soon as the crops Emily planned to plant started selling.

While Omaha was a lovely little town, Emily knew she wanted to be out on the prairie. She wanted to live the rest of her days gazing upon the land that Willie had described to her so vividly all those nights by their campfire and during all those seemingly endless miles of marching. She wanted to be free to wear trousers if she wanted, or dresses if that fit her fancy, with no one making a comment on the matter. She wanted the children to run free like she and her brothers had when she was young. And so, after a long conversation with the children to be sure they agreed, Emily bid farewell to their new friends and packed up the wagon she'd bought on credit, along with a horse and oxen, with a promise to send payment as soon as possible.

Following the wagon train roads, they headed west along the Platte River with an eye always searching for a place they could call home.

They found it nearly ninety miles from Omaha, west of the tiny town of Columbus along the north side of Loup River where it bent like a horseshoe.

"Is this it, Mama?" Isaac asked, standing on the buckboard with his hand shading his eyes. "Is this our new home?"

Emily breathed deeply of the scent of prairie grasses and wild-flowers baking in the sun. Then she climbed down and reached back to help Isaac and Nellie as Gabriel jumped down on his own. "I think so. What do you think?"

Isaac smiled at her, showing a gap where he'd lost a tooth during their journey. "I like it here."

"I do, too," Nellie chimed in. Then, grabbing her brother's hand, she said, "Come on, let's go see the river."

"Be careful!" Emily called as they ran off, loving how she sounded like a true mother. Loving even more how the kids could run and laugh as though their young lives had never seen hardship.

A warm hand slipped into hers, and her heart caught in her throat. Giving it a squeeze, Emily looked down at Gabriel. "What do you think? Should this be our new home?"

He seemed to be considering the question in great depth. Then, to her surprise, he asked, "Do they have plantations here? And slaves?"

Emily had to swallow before she could answer him. "No. The people of Nebraska Territory voted to make slavery illegal here. You'll be safe. I'll make sure of it."

Gabriel sighed, and his entire body seemed to relax as though he was letting go of a great weight. He lifted his chin and asked, "Can I go play, too...Mama?"

Unable to speak around the stinging in her throat, Emily nodded and watched as he ran off to join the other two who were throwing rocks into the river.

"I made it, Willie," she said aloud, feeling the warm wind carry her words away. "I'll make you proud, dear friend, and I promise you, I'll never stop looking for your family."

She swore she felt a hand touch her cheek, and she gasped. With tears falling down her cheeks, she whispered, "I miss you, Willie. Take care of my little brother for me, okay?"

And then, with a shuddering sigh, she, too, went to throw rocks in the river.

Chapter Thirty-Two

Present day: Woodinville, Washington

July 29, 1862: We found our homestead today. Tomorrow we start building the foundation for our cabin. Already, Gabriel is acting more his age. Freedom has lifted the weight of fear off him. We have a lot of work ahead of us, so I won't have much time for writing in my diary anymore. Thank you, Pa. You had no way of knowing how much I would need this book to get me through, but that's what it did. Give Mama and David and Benjamin my love. I know all four of you are watching over me and the children. We'll need you. Take care of Willie, too. You would have loved her as a daughter. Don't you worry none about me, you got that? I miss you all more than I can convey, but I have a reason to get up every morning with a smile on my face, and that's all I've ever wanted. That reason is calling me right now to tuck them into bed, so I must put down my pen. Soldiering was hard, but I would do it all again because it led me here to my new home and my new family. It gave me the chance to prove I am as strong as any man, and it showed me that I can overcome any challenge put before me. I served honorably, Pa, and that's something I'm proud of.

   Even if nobody knows.

April 7, 1928: Grandma Emily died today after a long and happy life. We found it fitting that she passed away on April 7, the same day that Willie and Ben died sixty-six years earlier. I have no doubt she is with them now, all sitting around their campfire and telling stories.

Grandma didn't write in her diary once she and the kids settled in Nebraska. I think it was her way of moving forward with her life. Maybe she even found peace. Either way, I'm writing this now so all of her grandchildren and their children will know the rest of her story.

Emily and the children successfully homesteaded their land and were given the deed in 1868. They were happy there, the four of them. When Nellie got married in 1874 and moved out west with her new husband, Emily decided to go with them, settling in Sacramento, California. It was in Sacramento that she met her husband, John Haydon, who was also a Civil War veteran. They were very happy right up until his death in 1916.

To all of Emily's descendants, please safeguard this diary so that Emily will always be remembered. She was a strong and loving woman who did something not many other women have done. May we all grow up to be strong like her.

*L*arkin closed Emily's diary and held it against her chest, wishing she could keep reading Emily's story. What was their life like in Nebraska? What was the man she fell in love with like, and did he treat her right? What kind of people did the kids grow up to become? She wished she could talk to Emily and ask her if her bad dreams finally left her alone, or if they plagued her throughout her life. She wished she could ask what she'd done to look for Willie's family.

One thing that seemed certain was that writing her experiences in this book had helped Emily through her war trauma. Larkin did not know if Emily was ever healed, but at least she was able to process and cope with the effects of that trauma, which Larkin now knew was vitally important.

Her therapist had told her right from the beginning that she would feel better once she told the story of that day in Kandahar, but Larkin had resisted. Talking about it felt like she was teetering over a bottomless black pit that would suck her down and suffocate her.

What she hadn't realized was that she'd needed to go down into that pit so she could emerge out the other end, free from the fear that had controlled her. She finally told her therapist the story, and then she'd told it again, and again, and she was finally starting to get some distance from it. She could feel that one day soon she might be able to shrug off the chains that bound her to what happened and see it as a time of her life that was in the past and no longer controlling her. She hoped so, at least.

Her weekly group therapy was helping, too. She regretted resisting going for so long.

Now that she'd finished Emily's story, she saw for the first time how similar Anahita's story was to Emily's. Both needed to become a male in order to be seen as an equal. Both lived in the role splendidly. Heck, even Larkin herself had something in common with them. In order to be taken seriously in her role as a military police officer, she'd had to learn to express more of her stereotypically male qualities and suppress the female ones.

She hadn't meant to ever share the story on her blog. She blamed being hungover and her nightmares for that. But now she was so grateful it had happened. The predominant reaction to the story was compassion. That fact both surprised Larkin and tore her defenses to shreds.

The road to healing still stretched before her, but she felt she finally had her feet on the right path. She was heading to a better place—one where she could function in her community and live a mostly normal life.

And she was never going to drink again. Grams had given her

a stern talking-to after that morning at the police station, and her therapist had also made her realize she had a problem. She was on day nineteen of her sobriety and, although each day was a struggle, so far, they were all victories. She'd take them one at a time.

When her phone rang, she didn't have to look at it to know it was Zach Faber calling her, as he'd done nearly every day.

His words stopped her breath. "I found Willie's family."

Chapter Thirty-Three

Present day: Shiloh National Military Park, Tennessee

*L*arkin stood in the waist-high grass next to Zach and stared up at the huge stone memorial to the 9th Indiana Infantry. In the distance she could hear the booming of cannons and the cries of soldiers as reenactors commemorated the anniversary of the Battle of Shiloh at several locations within the park. She'd been nervous about coming to the Shiloh battlefield because her deep connection with Emily made her wonder if being here would be too much. It was where both Willie and Ben had been killed. Or, maybe, the sounds of the mock firefights would trigger a flashback.

So far, though, all she felt was an intense reverence.

"It's strange to think the three of them stood right here on this field that day in 1862," Zach said, turning away from the obelisk to gaze at the forest bordering the edge of the field. "Confederate soldiers were in those trees firing at them. People were dying all around them."

Another cannon went off, and Larkin jumped. *Nothing but pretend*, she reminded herself.

She took a deep breath and imagined the scene when Emily had been here, on the second day of battle. Like an overlay over the peaceful wheat field and forest around her, her mind's eye placed a line of Federal soldiers standing beside her and swarms of gray uniforms in the trees, light flashing from the ends of rifles as they fired, smoke obscuring everything. Emily must have been terrified and more than a little frantic, knowing the two people she loved most in the world were in the line of fire, too.

Larkin stared toward the trees. Until the 9th Indiana pushed the Confederates back, they were sitting ducks here, with little to give them cover.

But, Larkin knew, strength came in numbers, and the regiment had fought shoulder to shoulder, and they had prevailed. They did push the Confederates back that day, and by the end of it, the Federal Army had won.

But Emily herself had lost. Lost everything. Her brother, her best friend, her job, and eventually, her identity. Had it been worth it?

"It's time, Larkin," Zach told her, interrupting her thoughts. "We'd better head over there."

Larkin nodded and fell into step beside him as they walked out of the wheat to the shorter grass and their car parked on the paved road a short distance away. The five-thousand-acre park was beautiful and lovingly preserved. Monuments had been respectfully erected at every notable location commemorating the regiments, officers, movements, and deaths from the two-day battle. As they drove, they passed a company of reenactors marching in file alongside the road.

They drove to the visitor center at the top of the bluff over Pittsburg Landing, where Emily and her regiment had landed that wet, terrifying night. The visitor center was a redbrick building with yellow wooden trim and four huge yellow columns out front. Larkin, her family, and Zach had gone through the exhibits and watched the film inside earlier, and now their destination was the large white tent on the grass beside the building with people streaming inside.

Standing near the entrance with nervous expressions was a middle-aged couple who could only be Nathan and Karen Ellery. They were holding hands and watching everyone who entered the tent as though they were looking for someone.

"Mr. and Mrs. Ellery?" Larkin asked as she and Zach approached. As smiles spread across their faces, she stuck out her hand. "I'm Larkin Bennett, and this is Zachary Faber. It's so good to finally meet you in person."

Over the last two months, she had spoken with them on the phone and through emails. Nathan, a direct descendant of Willie's brother Terrence, told them that Willie's family had never heard from her after she'd ran away from her arranged marriage. After three years and the war waging with no end in sight, they figured she was most likely dead. They'd followed their dreams west to Oregon where they became cattle ranchers.

"I can't thank you enough," Nathan told her as he clasped her hand between both of his own. "You've solved a family mystery, and more than that, you've made Wilhelmina into a hero."

Willie's true name had been Wilhelmina Ellery. Larkin was delighted to learn the name meant "strong-willed warrior," which she figured was exactly what Willie had been. As they continued making small talk, Larkin studied the tall, thin man with sandy-brown hair and wondered if Willie had looked like him. "She fought for her country, Mr. Ellery. She was a hero."

With a satisfied smile, he nodded. "If either of you are ever in Portland, I hope you'll stay with us. I'm also supposed to let you know that you have a standing invitation to visit my cousin who still works Terrence Ellery's cattle ranch in eastern Oregon."

"I'd like that very much." The uniformed park superintendent was waving at her. Larkin motioned toward him. "It looks like Mr. Northcott wants to get the program started."

As she entered the tent, Larkin felt engulfed by gratitude. In the rows of white folding chairs sat Grams, Larkin's parents, Kaia and Jenna, Zach's cousins, numerous people from the local community, and several veterans of all ages, many of them in uniform.

They were here to present the Shiloh Battlefield Visitor Center with Emily's diary, along with Willie's ring and handkerchief. A new exhibit would open in the summer, centered on these items, and would present the stories of several women who had fought in the war and finally honor them as they deserved. Larkin was bursting with pride.

At the microphone, she told the audience about the diary and about Emily and Willie, and then she stepped aside so Zach could talk about Sarah, who was so inspired by these two Civil War women that she'd become a warrior herself and given her life for her country.

As Larkin stood beside Zach and listened to him speak, she noticed a movement in the back of the room. When she looked that direction, she saw a young blond soldier standing there wearing the blue uniform of the Civil War Union Army. Slung across his body were a knapsack and canteen and, on his shoulder, a musket with bayonet attached.

But then the soldier looked directly into Larkin's eyes, and a jolt of recognition shot through her. Before she could place him, though, he reached up, tipped his kepi hat to her, and walked back out of the tent, a graceful smoothness to each step. The reenactor was, fittingly, a woman.

Later, at the catered reception Larkin's parents had surprised her by insisting on providing, Larkin found herself surrounded by people, most of them strangers, and it wasn't sending her into a panic. She was open and talking, telling them her experiences, about Sarah's experiences, and even about Anahita, and she was holding herself together. Until this moment, in fact, she hadn't even thought about potential threats or felt her body freaking out. She was simply enjoying herself, and the freedom of that felt delicious.

She made her way to the edge of the festivities, where she

took a moment to watch the last of the sun shine through the trees and set the stone monuments scattered around the meadow aglow in the spring evening. Tears stung her throat as she thought over the last months.

"You would've loved today, Sarah," she whispered out loud like she used to do when she'd talk to her friend's urn. "It's so peaceful here."

A hand touched her back, and she turned to find Zach there, his eyes warm. "There you are. I was looking for you."

"I was talking to Sarah."

His face took on the sad yet joyful expression she'd seen often when they talked about his sister. "Did you know Sarah used to wrap a cloth around her chest and dress up in my clothes so she could be like Emily Wilson?"

Larkin laughed and felt the knot of sadness in her chest loosen a little more. "No, she never told me that."

"Yeah, and she'd drag me through the neighborhood, duck-ing behind bushes and garbage cans as we snuck up on enemy camps. She cut an old broomstick in half to be our muskets."

Larkin laughed and thought about how she'd forced Kaia and Jenna into similar pretend play. "I always knew Sarah was my soul sister."

Though he dropped his hand, Zach remained so close she could feel the warmth of his body. "Today was pretty great, wasn't it?"

She smiled. "Yeah, we did good. I really like the Ellerys, don't you?" They talked for a while about the reception and all the people who were there. Then, remembering something she'd been meaning to ask him, Larkin said, "I can't believe this hasn't already come up, but did Emily ever have more children, besides the three orphans?"

He shook his head. "No, she never did."

Larkin thought about this. "So, since your family is in California, where her daughter moved, which prompted her own move there, does that mean you and Sarah are descended from the little girl, Nellie?"

Zach smiled incredulously. "I thought you knew. No, we're descended from Gabriel."

"You're part black?" she blurted without thinking.

Zach was still laughing. "Yes, very much so."

Larkin smiled. "Gabriel was my favorite," she admitted. "I love how he protected the other kids."

"Yeah, my grandmother said he grew up and became a cattle rancher. Married another former slave and raised six kids."

"A cattle rancher, like Willie's brother." Larkin knew this must have made Emily very happy.

"It was Sarah's backup plan if the Army didn't work out."

Larkin had to look at him closely to see if he was joking and, upon seeing that he wasn't, shook her head and laughed. Sarah had been vegetarian. Raising cattle would have been a stretch.

A burst of laughter from the tent reminded Larkin they should be getting back. She had one more question first. "Do you know anything more about Emily's life, other than what was written by her granddaughter at the end of the diary? Did she keep having nightmares about the war?"

Zach understood what she was asking. "I don't think it's something people back then really talked about, so we can't say for sure. Grandma said that she believed Emily was happy with her husband and family. She died sitting in a rocking chair on her front porch at the age of eighty-six. That sounds like a peaceful way to go, if you ask me."

Larkin closed her eyes to imagine the scene and felt a longing stir in her chest. That would be a peaceful way to go, indeed. She imagined herself on a front porch someday, hopefully a long time from now, rocking while she listened to the birds sing and watched the flowers sway in the breeze. From the yard beyond, she could hear the laughter of her grandchildren playing, and she felt a deep certainty that she'd had a good life.

She opened her eyes and was surprised to realize her cheeks were wet with tears. Something had shifted inside her. She'd used to believe happiness could only be found in a military career. Now she hoped it might be found on her own front porch.

"Thanks for helping me with all this, Zach," she said, wishing he lived closer to her.

He was looking down at her, and in his expression was a spark of something that started her heart racing. "It's me who should be thanking you."

Larkin found that she couldn't speak. As she looked at him, Zach placed a warm palm on her cheek, and his eyes dropped to her lips. "I want to see you again, Larkin. Now that this is all over, I want to see what this thing is I feel between us."

Larkin's breath hitched. All she could do was nod. As Zach's lips lowered toward her own, she closed her eyes and gave in to the sensation of his kiss. Heat. Hunger. And, strangely, home. With him, even across the country here in Tennessee, with him she was home.

When the kiss ended, Larkin squeezed his hand and said, "Give me a minute, okay? I'll meet you back inside."

He gave her another kiss and then said, "I look forward to doing more of that later." He turned and disappeared inside the tent.

Though she'd been intending to have one last quiet moment to herself, a movement in the corner of her eye caught Larkin's attention, and she turned just in time to see the female Civil War reenactor from earlier disappear around the side of the tent. Making a quick decision, Larkin followed.

As she rounded the tent to the south side, she saw that night was falling fast. The park was full of shadows. Across the field she could see the cannons pointing toward the woods of Dill Branch. Somewhere along there, Emily had spent the night before battle lying in the mud and listening to the sounds of the dying between the shrieks and booms of the gunboats on the river. Larkin shook her head, knowing how terrifying that must have been.

She looked for the reenactor but couldn't find her anywhere. As she was about to give up and go back inside, she spotted her walking toward Dill Branch.

Larkin started to go after her. She wanted to talk to her, learn who she was and what she knew about the battle that took place here.

But then Larkin saw something that stopped her in her tracks. Standing in the woods, just inside the tree line, were two other figures. Both wore the blue uniforms of the Union Army, and both carried haversacks and canteens like the woman did.

As Larkin watched, they turned toward the woods, linked their arms together with the woman, and started walking. Before they'd gone two steps, though, they disappeared.

Larkin blinked. Surely, she hadn't just seen that. The three had not disappeared behind the trees or into the shadows. They'd simply disappeared. There one moment, gone the next.

Before she could decide what to do, banjo music echoed across the field from the woods. The sound of men laughing drifted after it.

"You hear it too, do you?"

Larkin jumped when she heard the voice, but then laughed when she saw it was Mr. Northcott, the park superintendent to whom she'd presented the diary earlier.

He nodded toward Dill Branch. "Locals around these parts hear them all the time. Ghosts of the men playing poker in camp and singing songs. Some have even seen them."

Larkin looked to where the three soldiers she'd seen had disappeared. "Yes, I can believe that."

Northcott wished her a good night and went on his way. Larkin wandered over to the woods, hoping the woman she'd seen had been who she now believed her to be.

"Emily Wilson," she said aloud, feeling silly. "Are you here?"

There was no reply, though Larkin did not expect one. "Willie? Ben?" she asked this time.

Still no reply.

Larkin pressed her lips together and swallowed the lump she'd been carrying in her throat all day. As it finally released, she felt a sense of peace flow over her. "Thank you," she whispered to the woods. "Thank you so much." And then she turned and walked away.

As she went, the sound of warm laughter came from the woods again, this time with two distinctly female voices blended in.

Larkin smiled and kept walking. She had her own party to return to, her own life to get started.

No matter what the future held in store for her, she was no longer afraid of it. If Emily could experience what she'd lived through and still end up happy, Larkin could do the same.

Hope tasted so sweet.

A Note from the Author

I do not have a military background, nor am I an expert on the Civil War, so I must beg your forgiveness for any mistakes I have made in the telling of this story. The story found me when I first stumbled across mention—in an online search for "strong women in history"—of women who fought in the Civil War. Results came up for a number of women including Sarah Emma Edmonds (a.k.a. Private Franklin Thompson), who appears in this story, and Jennie Hodgers (a.k.a. Private Albert D.J. Cashier), who does not, although her story is fascinating and I urge you to look her up. I learned for the first time that women did not only tend home fires during the Civil War as I was taught in school, but several hundred of them fought in battle right alongside the men so successfully that many of them never were discovered.

The more I learned about these women and how history twisted their contributions into something frivolous or shameful, the angrier I became and the more I knew I had to write about them. And so, Emily Wilson, a.k.a. Jesse Wilson, was born.

Knowing that the best person to process Emily's military story would be a present-day female military member, I launched into research on women in the military today. Again, I was surprised and angered by the realization that women are still battling sexist beliefs and practices that dismiss their contributions as unimportant, ancillary, or even shameful. I was even more horrified to realize that I had grown up believing that women in the military did not perform the same duties as the men, that they were protected from serious harm and more in support roles.

Let me now beg forgiveness from all women who have ever served. I was wrong. I was ignorant. Sure, until 2013 when the U.S. Department of Defense lifted the ban on women in combat, women were "officially" kept from serving in the same capacity as men. But throughout history, numerous women stood on the battlefield being shot at and killed, whether they were *officially* there or not. Women served on the front lines in all our wars—as nurses or spies, or in some other role—and were in the same danger as the men from enemy fire and bombs.

Many nurses refused to leave when ordered to because injured soldiers needed their help. But women weren't only there as nurses. They volunteered for service in women's auxiliaries and proudly served their country, only to face intense discrimination, sexual harassment, and shaming from the country as whole as a result of rumors that they were nothing more than "clean" girls there to meet the soldiers' needs. This book is my attempt at righting the record and spreading the word that women in the military were and are badass. They are strong, resilient, equally as capable as men. To all women who have served, you are my heroes, and I struggle to find adequate words to convey the depth of my gratitude and reverence for you. All I have is *thank you*. From the bottom of my heart, thank you.

Many military service members and veterans are, like Larkin and Emily, suffering from the traumas they experienced while in the service. Each person's story is different. Each trauma is different. Each path to healing is different. We civilians owe our sisters and brothers who served our support, compassion, patience, and respect.

As of this writing (December 2018), there are 1,067,917 active duty enlisted personnel in the American military. Of those, 16.30 percent are female. If you count officers, enlisted and cadets/ midshipmen, the total serving is 1,310,731, with 16.70 percent women (source: www.dmdc.osd.mil/appj/dwp/dwp_reports .jsp). Women are more than twice as likely as men to develop PTSD (post-traumatic stress disorder) at a rate of 10 percent for women and 4 percent for men. Reasons for this include the fact that women are more likely to experience sexual assault, which is more likely to cause PTSD than many other events, and because women are more likely to blame themselves for trauma experiences than men [source: www.ptsd.va.gov/public/PTSD -overview/women/women-trauma-and-ptsd.asp]. Among female veterans who have served in Iraq and Afghanistan, 20 percent have been diagnosed with PTSD. The rate of PTSD among female Vietnam veterans is 27 percent.

Although military sexual trauma (MST) is the cause of many female veteran's PTSD symptoms, I chose not to address the issue in this book, primarily because it is such a huge problem that it warrants a book of its own. I also noticed as I was researching for this story that many people make the assumption that MST is the only trauma women experience while in military service, but that is simply not the case. Women were in combat long before they were officially allowed to do so, and they have the lasting trauma from it, just like the men with whom they served.

Now, let's discuss suicide. We've all seen the posters saying that there are 22 veteran suicides per day. Even one is too many. Veterans have a suicide rate 50 percent higher than those who did not serve in the military, and their suicides are most likely to occur in the first three years of returning home to civilian life. The suicide rate for female veterans in 2014 was 19 per 100,000. From 2001 through 2014, the suicide rate among female veterans increased to a greater degree (62.4 percent) than the suicide rate among male veterans (29.7 percent) (source: www.mentalhealth .va.gov/suicide_prevention/Suicide-Prevention-Data.asp). I don't know the answers, and I'm certain there are professionals working to reduce these numbers. Still, another hand reaching out to help cannot hurt. Let's all reach out to our veterans.

Our female veterans deserve the respect of being recognized by their country and honored for their service, the same as men. Did you know that female veterans typically don't self-identify as veterans? They don't. Why would they when civilians and sometimes even male veterans completely push them to the background? Let's change that. When you meet a woman veteran or actively serving female military member, please, take a moment to really listen to her and know that her sacrifices and experiences are equally as valid as those of the men who serve. And please, whatever you do, when you see a woman wearing military logos or driving around with a veteran bumper sticker, do not, in any instance, assume it was her husband who served and not her. Thank *her* for her service.

See her. Hear her. Thank her.

More about the Real Women Featured in This Story

Source: *They Fought Like Demons: Women Soldiers in the Civil War* by DeAnne Blanton and Lauren M. Cook. Published in 2002 by Louisiana State University Press, Baton Rouge.

Sarah Emma Edmonds, a.k.a. Pvt. Franklin Thompson: Edmonds took on a male identity prior to the war and supported herself as a Bible salesman and publisher's agent. Although Canadian, she enlisted when the war broke out as a way to support her adopted country in its time of need. She served in the Flint Union Greys, Company F of the 2nd Michigan Infantry, and first worked in hospital duty in the Washington, DC, area and was on the field tending soldiers at the First Battle of Bull Run (Manassas). She went on to fight in other battles as well as perform military duties as a mail carrier and orderly for General Poe, as well as a spy. Edmonds served, undiscovered as a woman, for two years and then decided to desert when she contracted malaria and was afraid medical care would reveal her secret. She went on to serve, as a woman, with the United States Christian Commission until the end of the war. In 1864, she published her memoir of her war experiences, *Nurse and Spy in the Union Army*, which while largely true, was "not strictly a factual account," she later admitted.

V. A. White: White left her home after having a daughter out of wedlock and made her way to Nashville where she became a prostitute at 154 College Street, one of the fancier bordellos in the city. She was successful at her trade and managed to save a good amount of money. After four months, she tired of that life and began to study how to escape it. She bought herself a Union Army uniform, cut her hair, and was sworn into the 1st Michigan Regiment Mechanics, Company D. She served with her regiment until it was mustered out of service in Au Sable, Michigan. She had managed to hold on to her significant savings from her bordello days, and with the money, she bought a home on the shore of Lake Huron where she lived free and independent for the rest of her life.

Loreta Janeta Velazquez, a.k.a. Lieutenant Harry T. Buford/Alice Williams/Mrs. DeCaulp: Much of what we know about Velazquez comes from her own memoir, *The Woman in Battle*, published in 1876. Raised in a wealthy family in Cuba and New Orleans, Velazquez eagerly joined the Confederate cause for the adventure. Wearing custom-made wire contraptions to flatten and thicken her feminine figure, she had her hair cut in the fashion of the day and donned men's attire. Occasionally, she donned a false mustache. Velazquez claimed to have raised her own troop of soldiers and, with them, joined the fighting. After three months she left her battalion to seek work as an independent soldier and later claimed she'd fought at the First Battle of Bull Run, Ball's Bluff, Fort Donelson, and Shiloh. Her gender was discovered twice, but she persistently reenlisted and later became a spy under the name Alice Williams, working as a double agent for the Confederate Secret Service. Although not mentioned in her memoirs, it is suspected that Velazquez, under her Williams identity, plotted to assassinate President Lincoln. After the war, she lived in New York, toured Europe, then lived for a time in Venezuela, California, Utah, and Texas, and finally in Rio de Janeiro, Brazil, where she disappeared from public record. Although many of her claims are corroborated, there are glaring historical inconsistencies. Many of the aspects of her personality and story were offensive to Victorian sensibilities, and she was widely condemned.

Maria Lewis, a.k.a. George Harris: Lewis's story is the one with which I took the most liberties. She likely did not serve as early in the war as I have included her here, and likely did not serve time in a Confederate prison in Alabama where I have her encountering Emily. In reality, not much is known about Lewis other than that she was an African American woman who passed for a white man and was serving in the 8th New York Cavalry when the war ended. Near the end of the war, she was a member of an honor guard who presented the War Department with seventeen captured Confederate battle flags.

There are hundreds of other women with fascinating experiences who served in the Civil War, but I could not fit them into this story. To learn about them, I urge you to read *They Fought Like Demons: Women Soldiers in the Civil War* by DeAnne Blanton and Lauren M. Cook.

Others of Note

The 9th Indiana Infantry: All movements, camps, and battles of the 9th Indiana as portrayed in this story are accurate. All of the privates of the 9th Indiana are fictional in this story with the exception of Ambrose Bierce. The officers, however, were the names of the men who actually served.

Reading Group Guide

1. A major theme of the story explores the female soldier's experience. Did any of these women's experiences surprise you? If you have military experience, what are some challenges, prejudices, abuses, etc. that you experienced as a female military member or witnessed by other women in the military?

2. Emily enlisted so she could be with her brother as well as for the adventure. Willie enlisted as a means of financial support. Neither were sexually or romantically motivated, yet women discovered in Union or Confederate ranks were usually accused of such. Why do you think this was? Has this changed in society and/or the military today?

3. Emily lived in a state that declared it illegal for black people to live, work, or even visit. (Article 13 of Indiana's 1851 Constitution: "No negro or mulatto shall come into or settle in the State, after the adoption of this Constitution.") Do you think this helped or hindered her understanding of slavery and the growth of her abolitionist beliefs? Do you see any correlation

between this lack of exposure to people of a different race and how we still experience racism today?

4. Opening all military jobs to women in recent years has started the debate on whether women should be included in any future drafts/conscriptions. What do you think?

5. The epigraph at the beginning of the book reads "Home isn't where our house is, but wherever we are understood." Emily's home was in Indiana, yet it stopped being the place where people truly knew her. Larkin grew up in Seattle but chose to go home to her grandmother's house in Woodinville because that's where she'd feel best loved. What does *home* mean to you? Where is your "home"? Why?

6. Through most of the story, Emily's family is made up of her brother and Willie. For Larkin, it is her grandmother and cousins. Both women have other family members, but they feel emotionally disconnected from them. Who do you consider your true family, no matter if they are actual family? What is it about these people that you love so much?

7. There are people still today who don't believe the Civil War was about slavery. What do you think, and why?

8. Were you surprised to learn that so many women disguised themselves as men to fight in the Civil War? Had you heard about any before reading this book? Did you look up any online while reading? Share what you know or learned with the group.

9. Was it a surprise to you to learn that black men were not allowed to join the Union army until 1863? That they were segregated from white soldiers and led exclusively by white officers? That they were not paid the same wages as white soldiers until June 1864? That, if caught by Confederate forces, they were usually brutally killed and never taken prisoner? Do you think the war might have ended sooner if any of these facts were different?

10. PTSD, while certainly discussed in relation to veterans, can also arise in people who have never served in the military. Even children can suffer from PTSD. Some known causes are sexual, physical, or emotional abuse; a natural disaster; a car accident; a long-term illness; etc. Do you have personal experience with PTSD (yourself or a loved one) that you can share with the group?

11. Did the information in the story about the *bacha posh* of Afghanistan surprise you? Are there any similar practices in your culture where a female takes on the appearance and social expectations of a male? Why is the practice accepted in some cultures and not in others? Is it different if the decision is that of the child rather than the parents?

12. Emily's diary directly influenced Sarah's decision to join the military. Imagine one of your ancestors left a diary detailing his or her experiences during an interesting time in history. What would you do with that information? Share with the group what you already know about your ancestor and the time he or she lived. How might learning more about this ancestor's experiences through a diary affect you?

13. After Emily's story ends, her granddaughter makes an entry in her diary that gives some clues to what happened to Emily and the children. What do you think their lives were like living on the prairie? What, especially, do you think life was like for Gabriel as a cattle rancher when there were likely very few others who looked like him?

14. Do you now think differently about women serving in the military? What are some actions you can take to support female veterans and show your appreciation for their service?

A Conversation with the Author

The main characters in _Today We Go Home_ served in the military. Did you ever serve?

As a kid, I didn't think anyone in my family had ever served in the military, because it was never discussed. Only later did I learn that my father served in the National Guard. I grew up thinking that only boys served in the military, so it never crossed my mind as an option for me. But, even if I had wanted to serve, I would not have qualified, since I am totally blind in my left eye.

What inspired the story? How did you discover that women served in battle in the Civil War?

As I was searching for new story ideas, I did an online search for _strong women in history_ and got a result of several names, three of which were women who disguised themselves as men to fight in the Civil War. This was the first time I had ever heard that any women had been in battle during that war, and I was fascinated to read these women's stories. This led to books, articles, and anything else I could find on the subject, and it wasn't long before I knew I had to write about these brave women. One thing that really frustrated me in my research was learning that Victorian sensibilities twisted these women's service into something somehow shameful, and I knew I had to set the record straight. Also, right about the time I was discovering this history, I was following with great interest the political and social discussions about the changing policies regarding women in today's militaries, and I thought it would be interesting to see how a present-day female soldier might be impacted by learning about her Civil War sisters in arms and how their experiences were similar or dissimilar to her own.

What research did you do to bring this novel to life? Did you visit any Civil War sites?

Coming from a place of very little knowledge about the military, I had a steep learning curve. I read dozens of books about today's military, especially women in the military. I also read dozens of books about the Civil War and about a handful of books (all I could find) on women who fought in those battles. Once I knew Larkin would have served in Afghanistan and befriended an Afghan girl, I also read a number of books on women in Afghanistan. Clearly, I did a lot of reading! Oh, and I mustn't forget all the videos and documentaries I watched on Netflix and YouTube on various subjects having to do with the Civil War, the war in Afghanistan, and the U.S. military.

Beyond that, my family and I took a weeklong trip to Tennessee, where we spent a day walking in the steps of my characters on the Shiloh Battlefield, as well as visiting other Civil War and antebellum sites around Nashville. I visited the Tennessee State Capitol building on the day before Thanksgiving (not smart planning on my part) to discover that the information desk was not staffed. Fortunately, the state troopers on duty were incredibly knowledgeable about the history of the building and were very helpful in answering my questions. Our day in Nashville also included a visit to the Tennessee State Museum and hours of wandering the streets with me trying to imagine it as it was in 1862.

As for other research, I live in Woodinville, Washington, so the present-day setting did not pose too many challenges.

Larkin's PTSD did, however, send me to more reading (books, articles, websites…). I was very lucky to find several people, including veterans, mentioned in the acknowledgments who were so generous with their time and knowledge and who answered all my random questions. I owe a lot to each of those individuals.

How long did it take you to write *Today We Go Home*?

It is sometimes difficult to quantify how long it takes to write a book because I spend so much time researching a vague plot or character idea before I ever put words to paper. I am also a plotter, which means the bulk of my research and story plotting is done before I ever type *Chapter One*. In general, I developed the idea for the story while concurrently doing research on the topics and themes for about one year. Writing the first draft took me four months, followed by roughly seven months of revisions and edits (with some breaks for holidays and travel). All together, that adds up to about two years.

How did you choose the settings: Woodinville, Washington; Stampers Creek, Indiana; and the movements of the 9th Indiana Infantry?

For me, setting is very important, and I spend a lot of time thinking about how the setting impacts the characters. Because this book was so research-heavy for me, I decided to set the present-day story in the town where I live: Woodinville, Washington. As for Stampers Creek, Indiana, I found the tiny town (which really isn't a town anymore) on my family tree many generations back, and I wanted to learn more about it. I make a point to follow my curiosity, and it always leads to fascinating discoveries. Because Emily came from Indiana, I looked up Indiana regiments and found that the 9th Indiana Infantry was the first regiment to leave for battle and they were present at the Battle of Shiloh, which clinched the deal for me.

Are there any other Civil War women you wish you could have fit into this story?

Oh boy, are there! Hundreds of them. First, there's Jennie Hodgers, who lived most of her life, even after the war, as Albert D. J. Cashier. She served three years in the 95th Illinois and was never discovered to be a woman until near the end of her long life while living in an old soldier's home. She was buried with full military honors, as a man.

And then there's the unnamed woman with the 20th Army Corps who fought in the Battle of Stones River while five months pregnant who was only discovered when she gave birth in her tent four months later. Similarly, a corporal in a New Jersey regiment who had served in at least three significant battles became severely ill while on picket duty. After being carried by his officers to a nearby farmhouse, he gave birth to a baby boy. I also mustn't forget the unidentified woman in the 29th Connecticut Infantry who gave birth in the trenches during the siege of Petersburg.

Florena Budwin enlisted with her husband, and both were captured and sent to the gruesome Andersonville Prison, where her husband was killed by a guard. Revealing her true gender would have secured her release, but she kept her secret. When Union forces were advancing into Georgia, Confederate authorities moved some prisoners to Florence, South Carolina, Budwin among them. She kept her secret for a year until she fell gravely ill and the prison doctor discovered she was a woman. Although she was moved to a private room and given care, she died of pneumonia one month before all sick prisoners at Florence were paroled and sent north.

The story of a woman known only as Charlie really sets my imagination on fire. In May 1863, the New Orleans *Daily Picayune* reported that Charlie followed the man she loved into the 14th Iowa Infantry (although the newspaper may have recorded her regiment incorrectly). When she was discovered to be a woman and she realized she would be sent away from her lover, she took his revolver and shot herself in the heart on the parade ground.

Recommended Reading

Women in the Civil War

Blanton, DeAnne, and Lauren M. Cook. *They Fought Like Demons: Women Soldiers in the Civil War*. Baton Rouge, LA: LSU Press, 2002.

Grant De Paw, Linda. *Battle Cries and Lullabies: Women in War from Prehistory to the Present* Norman, OK: University of Oklahoma Press, 1998.

Tsui, Bonnie. *She Went to the Field: Women Soldiers of the Civil War*. Guilford, CT: Globe Pequot, 2003.

Women in Military Service Today

Biank, Tanya. *Undaunted: The Real Story of America's Servicewomen in Today's Military*. New York, New American Library, 2013.

Crow, Tracy, and Jerri Bell, eds. *It's My Country Too: Women's Military Stories from the American Revolution to Afghanistan*. Lincoln, NE: Potomac Books, 2017.

Holmstedt, Kirsten. *The Girls Come Marching Home: Stories of Women Warriors Returning from the War in Iraq*. Mechanicsburg, PA: Stackpole Books, 2009.

Jenning Hegar, Mary. *Shoot Like a Girl: One Woman's Dramatic Fight in Afghanistan and on the Home Front.* New York: Berkley, 2017.

Thorpe, Helen. *Soldier Girls: The Battles of Three Women at Home and at War.* New York: Scribner, 2014.

Tzemach Lemmon, Gayle. *Ashley's War: The Untold Story of a Team of Women Soldiers on the Special Ops Battlefield.* New York: Harper, 2015.

PTSD

Bonenberger, Adrian. *Afghan Post: One Soldier's Correspondence from American's Forgotten War.* Philadelphia: The Head & the Hand Press, 2014.

Finkel, David. *Thank You for Your Service.* New York: Sarah Crichton Books, 2013.

Williams, Kayla. *Plenty of Time When We Get Home: Love and Recovery in the Aftermath of War.* New York: W. W. Norton, 2014.

Afghanistan

Elliott, Marianne. *Zen Under Fire: How I Found Peace in the Midst of War.* Naperville, IL: Sourcebooks, 2012.

Kargar, Zarghuna. *Dear Zari: The Secret Lives of the Women in Afghanistan.* Naperville, IL: Sourcebooks, 2012.

Kelsey, Peggy. *Gathering Strength: Conversations with Afghan Women.* Plano, TX: Pomegranate Grove Press, 2012.

Nordberg, Jenny. *The Underground Girls of Kabul: In Search of a Hidden Resistance in Afghanistan.* New York: Crown, 2014. (This book discusses *bacha posh*.)

Books Mentioned in the Story

Ballou, Maturin Murray. *Fanny Campbell: The Female Pirate Captain: A Tale of the Revolution.* North Charleston, SC: CreateSpace/Amazon, 2017. (Originally published in 1844.)

Beecher Stowe, Harriet. *Uncle Tom's Cabin.* Mineola, NY: Dover Publications, 2005. (Originally published in 1852.)

Bierce, Ambrose. *What I Saw at Shiloh.* North Charleston, SC: CreateSpace/Amazon, 2017. (Originally published in 1881.)

Edmonds, S. Emma E. *Nurse and Spy in the Union Army.* Charleston, SC: CreateSpace/Amazon, 2015. (Originally published in 1865.)

Resources

If you are a veteran in crisis or you know a veteran in crisis, please call the Veterans Crisis Line for confidential support twenty-four hours a day, seven days a week, 365 days a year: 800-273-8255 and press 1. Chat online at VeteransCrisisLine.net /Chat, or text 838255.

U.S. Department of Veteran Affairs Suicide Prevention:
mentalhealth.va.gov/suicide_prevention

Vet Centers for mental health counseling:
vetcenter.va.gov

Vet Center call number:
1-877-WARVETS (1-877-927-8387)

National Suicide Prevention Lifeline:
1-800-273-TALK (8255)

National Center for PTSD:
ptsd.va.gov

PTSD & CPTSD Global Peer Support Community:
myptsd.com

Military One Source:
militaryonesource.mil

Acknowledgments

Although mostly a solitary endeavor, the commercial success of a book absolutely depends upon the readers, booksellers, librarians, bloggers, reviewers, women's groups, and book clubs who read it and encourage others to do the same. I am so grateful for each and every one of you who read and recommended my first book. Thank you for making my dreams come true. I hope you enjoy this book, too!

To Anna Michels, my editor at Sourcebooks, thank you for all the hours you put in reading and editing my work. My story is so much stronger because of you. To everyone at Sourcebooks—the editorial, production, marketing, and sales teams—thank you for all that you do in support of my books and me. You are a dream to work with. Thank you to Nicole Hower for the gorgeous cover.

To my agent, Beth Miller, for always being just an email or phone call away. Your steady support, advice, and work on behalf of my books has made all the difference. Thank you.

To Maja, Kate, Natalie, Jessica, and everyone in the Foreign Rights Department at Writers House, thank you for consistently championing my books. I didn't even know to dream of foreign sales with my debut novel, and you've thrilled me with each and every one. To Kathryn Stuart and others in the Rights Department, thank you!

I have so many people to thank who helped me as I wrote *Today We Go Home*. For starters, while on a flight from Orlando to Seattle during the early stages of this book, I serendipitously met Renee Moore, who offered to introduce me to two veteran friends of hers, Paula and Sara. She then invited all three of us to her home, where I was able to learn a lot about these women's experiences in the military. Thank you, Renee!

When I first met MA2 Paula Ellison (USN, Retired), I already had a good idea that my character would have served as Army military police, and Paula was able to share with me how that job looks in the Navy, where the officers are called masters-at-arms. As I listened to Paula talk, years after she left the service, I was struck by the depth of love she felt for the service members whom she protected. To me, it seemed she was still struggling to understand why in the civilian world people don't support each other as they should. Thank you, Paula, for sharing your experiences with me, and even more, thank you for your service.

When Sgt. Sara Rowland Bernardy (USA, Retired) arrived for our discussion, I could tell immediately that she was nervous about talking about her experiences. She served in Army communications and was with the first wave of U.S. forces into Iraq. Sara really brought home for me what it is like to be female in the military, but even more, what it is like for service members to return from deployment to a country that doesn't seem to care. In this story, I borrowed Sara's experience with a stranger who, seeing her Army bumper sticker, thanked her non-military husband for his service and completely ignored Sara. Thank you, Sara, for trusting me with your experiences. I know it wasn't easy. More importantly, thank you for your service.

While reading dozens of books, I read one that featured Cpt. Bergan Flannigan (USA, Retired). I strongly encourage you to read *Undaunted: The Real Story of America's Servicewomen in Today's*

Military by Tanya Biank to learn more about these servicewomen, especially Bergan, who lost her right leg to an IED while serving as an Army MP officer in Afghanistan. I reached out to Bergan on Facebook, and she generously agreed to answer my questions and help me figure out Larkin's timeline. Bergan, thank you for responding to my message and helping me with my story. And thank you for all you sacrificed in service to our country.

Eric Larson was the first former military member I met with when I started thinking about writing this book. He helped me to understand military structure and terminology and gave me a sense of what a deployment is really like. Because he's my sister-in-law's brother, I was also able to witness the strain put on the family at home. Thank you, Eric, for being so open with me in sharing your experiences, and thank you for your service.

To all servicemen and servicewomen, thank you for doing what 98 percent of our country does not. You stepped up and said "Send me" while the rest of us waited at home, full of opinions about what you were doing over there. Your strength, dedication, loyalty, sacrifice, and example have directly influenced the writing of this book, and if I could individually thank each and every one of you, I would. Thank you!

To Jessica Slagg, LICSW, thank you for patiently answering all my questions about PTSD and treatment. Thank you, too, for the documents and resources you sent my way, all of which helped immensely.

There are so many people who have helped me brainstorm this story or who suggested a resource or contact, and I wish I could thank each of you here. But, unfortunately, that would take several more pages. You know who you are. Thank you so much. Still, I must name a few of you. Thank you, Anna Richland, for answering my military questions and for the extremely valuable beta read (and thank you for your service!). Thank you, Fatima Benghaly, for giving me feedback on a particular passage. Thank you, Susanna Kearsley, for sitting in the conference bar with me and helping me brainstorm this story. I hope to write as well as you someday. Thank you to the friends who sent me notes of encouragement throughout the process, including Carla Crujido, Patty Ward, Rosann Ferris, Stephanie Christenson, Pat White, Carolynn Estes, Elizabeth Boyle, and members of Women's Fiction Writers Association. Your unwavering support keeps me going. Thank you!

To the women working the front desk of the Hampton Inn in Counce, Tennessee, thank you for sharing your ghost stories with me. As you can see, a few made it into the book. I'll never forget the photo you showed me of the ghost with an eye patch!

Thank you to Mr. Larry DeBerry of the Shiloh Museum for sharing your passion for history with me as you pointed out artifacts and told stories and then even went so far as to send me away with a folder of articles and brochures. This impromptu stop was the best decision ever!

Thank you to the Shiloh National Military Park and the Corinth Civil War Interpretive Center for all the valuable information on your websites and in your parks. I hope to return someday for another visit. Thank you to park guide Timothy L. Arnold for providing me with information on where Shiloh prisoners were sent after being marched to Corinth, Mississippi.

I must not forget the many Woodinville Neighbors Facebook group members who answered my random questions about the Tolt Pipeline Trail. Thank you!

Thank you to Linda and Rich Beck for translating my German epigraph into English. And for doing it the first week back to teaching in a new school year. *Danke schön!*

Finally, and most importantly, thank you to my husband, Chad, and our two boys. You three are my rock. Your unwavering support for all I do means so much. Thank you for letting me drag you through battlefields and museums, and for always being willing to discuss ideas with me. My greatest joy is being yours. I put a couple Easter eggs in this story for each of you!

About the Author

Photo by Chad Estes

Kelli Estes is the author of the *USA Today* bestselling novel *The Girl Who Wrote in Silk*, which has been translated into multiple languages and is the recipient of the PNWA Nancy Pearl Book Award and the WFWA Star Award, Outstanding Debut category. She lives in Woodinville, Washington, with her husband and two sons. Find Kelli on Facebook, Instagram, or at kelliestes.com.